The Billionaire Banker Series Box Set 1-3

The Billionaire Banker Series Box Set 1-3

The Amazon Bestselling Box set

The Billionaire Banker Series,
Including, *Owned, Forty 2 Days,* and *Besotted*

Georgia Le Carre

Published by Georgia Le Carre

All characters in this publication are fictitious, any resemblance to real persons, living or dead, is purely coincidental.

ISBN: 1910575011
ISBN: 9781910575017

Editor: http://www.loriheaford.com/
Proofreader: http://nicolarhead.wix.com/proofreadingservices

You can discover more information about Georgia Le Carre and future releases here.
https://www.facebook.com/georgia.lecarre
https://twitter.com/georgiaLeCarre
http://www.goodreads.com/GeorgiaLeCarre

Table of Contents

The Billionaire Banker Series

Owned

He is seized by an unthinking irresistible call to hunt. To possess. To *own* her...

When Lana Bloom learns the devastating news that her mother is dying, she is faced with a terrible dilemma. The one thing that can save her is the one thing she does not have.
For young and Innocent Lana, The unthinkable is her only choice.

When she walks through the door of that exclusive restaurant she has no idea of the seismic shift her life is about to take, for the highest bidder will not be the rich man she has accompanied.

Fate drops her at the feet of the deeply mysterious and dazzlingly gorgeous American banker, Blake Law Barrington. Throbbing with raw masculinity and arrogance, this is a man who owns all that he pursues.

And now he wants her.

Lana cannot deny she is both intrigued and intoxicated by the world Blake inhabits and the smoldering passion he stirs in her body, but she is also fearful for this man is addictive and right now she is very vulnerable. She knows she should focus only on the arrangement, but how can she?

When he has opened a door that cannot be closed...

Forty 2 Days

Beyond the seductive power of immense wealth lies...Dark Secrets...

Devastatingly handsome billionaire, Blake Law Barrington was Lana Blooms first and only love. From the moment they touched his power was overwhelming. Their arrangement quickly developed into a passionate romance that captivated her heart and took her on an incredible sexual journey she never wanted to end. The future together looked bright until Lana made a terrible mistake. So, she did the only thing she could...she ran. Away from her incredible life, away from the man of her dreams, but she should have known a man such as Blake Law Barrington was impossible to escape. Now, he's back in her life and determined that she should taste the bitterness of his pain. Shocked at how rough the sex has become and humiliated that she is actually participating so willingly in her punishment, she despairs if she will ever feel the warmth of his touch—the solidity of his trust again? And even if she can win his trust, loyalties are yet to be decided, and secrets to be revealed—secrets that will test them both to their limits. Will Lana be able to tear down the walls that surround Blake's heart, and break him free of the brutal power of immense wealth? Can Blake hold on to Lana's heart when she discovers the enormity of the dark secrets that inhabit the Barrington family? Lana has always believed that love conquers all. She is about to test that belief…

Besotted

My heart was in a coffin, safe, dark, motionless…
Until I found you in a secret place, among the shadows of my soul. You saved me.
Blake is now the new head of the Barrington dynasty. 'Forget the past. You are safe now,' he whispers. But I can't feel safe.
How can I? I fear for him. The secrets are many. the road he travels is dark and treacherous, and I still need answers to many burning questions. Why has he still not dealt with Victoria, the enemy that still remains too close for my comfort. What will happen if Marcus re-enters our lives? Will we ever truly be free from the tentacles of this ancient and dangerous family?

GEORGIA LE CARRE
OWNED
He is seized by an irresistable call to hunt. To possess. To own Her...
The Billionaire Banker Series Book # 1

Owned

Book One

Dedicated to all who have love and passion in their lives, and
to those who are still searching…

You aren't wealthy until you have
something money can't buy.
—Garth Brooks

One

Blake Law Barrington

I drop a cube of sugar into the creamy face of my espresso, stir it, and glance at my platinum Greubel Forsey Tourbillion, acquired at Christie's Important Watches auction last autumn for a cool half a million dollars.

Eight minutes past eight.

I have a party to go to tonight, but I'm giving it a miss. It's been a long day, I am tired, I have to be in New York early tomorrow morning, and it will be one of those incomprehensibly dreary affairs. I take a sip—superb coffee—and return the tiny cup to its white rim.

Summoning a waiter for the check, I sense the activity level in the room take a sudden hike. Automatically, I lift my eyes to where all the other eyes, mostly male and devouring, have veered to. Of course. A girl. In a cheap, orange dress and lap dancer's six-inch high plastic platforms.

You're looking for love in all the wrong places, honey.

A waiter in a burgundy waistcoat bearing the bill has silently materialized at my side. Not taking my eyes off the girl—despite the impossible shoes she has a good walk, sexy—I order myself a whiskey. The waiter slinks away after a right-away-sir nod, and I lean back into the plush chair to watch the show.

It is one of those swanky restaurants where there are transparent black voile curtains hung between the tables and discreet fans to tease and agitate the gauzy material. Three curtains away she stands, minus the shoes, perhaps five feet five or six inches tall. She has the same body type as Lady Gaga, girlishly narrow with fine delicate limbs. Her skin is the color of thick cream. Beautiful mouth. My eyes travel from the waist-length curtain of jet-black hair to the swelling curve of her breasts and hips, and down her shapely legs.

Very nice, but…

At twenty-nine, I am already jaded. Though I watch her with the same speculation of all the other men in the room she is a toy that no longer holds any real excitement for me. I do not need to meet her to *know* her. I have had hundreds like her—hot, greedy pussies and cold, cold hearts. It is always the same. Each one hiding talons of steely ambition that hook into my flesh minutes after they rise like resurrected phoenixes from a night in my bed. Safe to say I have realized the error of my ways.

Still….

Something about her *has* aroused my attention.

She comes further into the room and even the billowing layers of curtains cannot conceal her great beauty or youth. Certainly she is far too young for her dining companion who has just barged in with all the grace of a retired rugby player. I recognize his swollen head instantly. Rupert Lothian. An over-privileged, nerve gratingly colossal ass. He is one of the bank's high profile private customers. The bank never does business with anyone they do not check out first and his report was sickening.

Curious. What could someone so fresh-faced and beautiful be doing with one so noted for ugly games? And they are ugly games that Lothian plays.

I watch three waiters head off towards them and the fluid, elegantly choreographed dance they perform to seat and hand them their menus. Now I have her only in profile. She has put the menu on the table and is sitting ramrod-straight with her hands tightly clasped in her lap. She crosses and uncrosses her legs nervously.

Unbidden, an image pops into my head. It is as alive and wicked as only an image can be. Those long, fine legs entangled in silky sheets. I stare helplessly as she pulls away the sheets, turns that fabulous mouth into a red O, and deliberately opens her legs to expose her sex to me. I see it clearly. A juicy, swollen fruit that my tongue wants to explore! I sit forward abruptly.

Fuck.

I thought I had passed the season of fantasizing about having sex with strangers. I reach for my whiskey and shoot it. From the corner of my eyes I see a waiter discreetly whisper something to Lothian. He rises with all the pomposity he can muster and leaves with the waiter.

I transfer my attention to the girl again. She has collapsed backwards into the chair. Her shoulders sag and her relief is obvious. She stares moodily at the tablecloth, fiddles with her purse and frowns. Then, she seems to visibly force herself away from whatever thoughts troubled her, and lets her glance wander idly around the room until her truly spectacular eyes—I have never seen anything like them before—collide with my unwavering stare. And through the gently shifting black gauze my breath is suddenly punched out of my body, and I am seized by an unthinking, irresistible call to hunt. To possess.

To *own* her.

Two

Lana Bloom

It can have been only seconds, but it seems like ages that I am held locked and hypnotized by the stranger's insolent eyes. When I recall it later I will remember how startlingly white his shirt had been against his tanned throat, and swear that even the air between us had shimmered. Strange too how all the background sounds of cutlery, voices and laughter had faded into nothing. It was as if I had wandered into a strange and compelling universe where there was no one else but me and that devilishly handsome man.

But in this universe I am prey.

The powerful spell is broken when he raises his glass in an ironic salute. Hurriedly, I tear my gaze away, but my thin façade of poise is completely shattered. Hot blood is rushing up into my neck and cheeks; and my heart is racing like a mad thing.

What the hell just happened?

I can still feel his gaze like a burning tingle on my skin. To hide, I bend my head and let my hair fall forward. But the desire to dare another look is so immense it shocks me. I have never experienced such an instant and physical attraction before.

With broad shoulders, a deep tan, smoldering eyes, a strong jaw, and straight-out-of-bed, vogue-cool, catwalk hair that flops onto his forehead, he looks like one of those totally hot and brooding Abercrombie and Fitch models, only more savage and fierce.

Devastatingly more.

But I am not here to flirt with drop dead gorgeous strangers, or to find a man for myself. I press my fingers against my flaming cheeks, and force myself to calm down. All my concentration must go into getting Rupert to agree to my proposal. He is my last hope.

My only hope.

Nothing could ever be more important than my reason for being there with such a man as him. I look miserably towards the tall doors where he has gone. This cold, pillared place of opulence is where rich people come to eat. A waiter wearing white gloves comes through the doors bearing a covered tray. I feel out of my depth. The orange dress is itchy and prickly and I long to scratch several places on my body. Then there are the butterflies flapping dementedly inside my stomach.

Don't ruin this, I tell myself angrily. You've come this far. Nervously, to regain my composure, I press my lips together and firmly push the sarcastically curving mouth out of my mind. I must concentrate on the horrible task ahead. But those insolent eyes, they will not go. So I bring to mind my mother's thin, sad face, and suddenly the stranger's eyes are magically gone. I straighten my back. Prepare myself.

I will not fail.

Rupert, having met whomever he had gone to meet, is weaving his way back to me and when our eyes touch I flash him a brilliant smile. I will not fail. He smiles back triumphantly, and coming around to my side drops me a quick kiss, before slumping heavily into his seat. I have to stop myself from reaching up to wipe my mouth.

I stare at him. He seems transformed. Expansive, almost jolly.

'That's one deal that came in the nick of time. As if the heavens have decided that I deserve you.' The way he says it almost makes me flinch with horror.

'Lucky me,' I say softly, flirtatiously, surprising myself. I tell myself I am playing a part. One that I can vanish into and emerge from unscathed, but I know it is not true. There will be repercussions and consequences.

He smiles nastily. He knows I do not fancy him, but that is part of the thrill. Taking what does not want to be taken.

'Well then,' he says. 'Don't be coy, let's hear it. How much are you going to cost me?'

I take a deep breath. A bull this large can only be taken by the horns. 'Fifty thousand pounds.'

His dirty blond eyebrows shoot upwards, but his voice is mild. 'Not exactly cheap.' His lips thin. 'What do I get for my money?'

We are both startled out of our conversation by a deep, curt voice.

'Rupert.'

'Mr. Barrington,' Rupert gasps, and literally flies to his feet. 'What an unexpected pleasure,' he croons obsequiously. I drop my head with searing shame. It is the stranger. He has heard me sell myself.

'I don't believe I've had the pleasure of your companion's acquaintance,' he says. His voice is an intriguing combination of velvet and husk.

'Blake Law Barrington, Lana Bloom, Lana Bloom, Blake Law Barrington.'

I look up then, a long way up—he is definitely over six feet, maybe six two or three—to meet his stormy-gray stare. I search them for disgust, but they are carefully veiled, impenetrable pits of mystery. Perhaps, he has not heard me sell myself, after all. I begin to tremble. My body knows something I do not. He is dangerous to me in a way I cannot yet conceive.

'Hello, Lana.'

'Hi,' I reply. My voice sounds tiny. Like a child that has been told to greet an adult.

He puts his hand out, and after a perceptible hesitation, I put mine into it. His hand is large and warm, and his clasp firm and safe, but I snatch mine away as if burnt. He breaks his gaze briefly to glance at Rupert.

'There is a party tonight at Lord Jakie's,' he says before those darkly fringed eyes return to me again. Inscrutable as ever. 'Would you like to come as my guests?' It is as if he is addressing only me. It sends delicious shivers up and down my spine. Confused, by the unfamiliar sensations I tear my eyes away from him and look at Rupert.

Rupert's eyebrows are almost in his hairline. 'Lord Jakie?' he repeats. There is unconcealed delight in his face. He seems a man who has found a bottle of rare wine in his own humble cellar. 'That's terribly kind of you, Mr. Barrington. Terribly kind. Of course, we'd love to,' he accepts for both of us.

'Good. I'll leave your names at the door. See you there.' He nods at me and I register the impression that he is obsessively clean and controlled. There is no mess in this man's life. A place for everything and everything in its place. Then he is gone.

Rupert and I watch him walk away. He has the stride of a supremely confident man. Rupert turns to face me again; his face is mean and at odds to his words. 'Well, well,' he drawls, 'You must be my lucky charm.'

'Why?'

'First, I get the deal I've been after for the last year and a half, then the great man not only deigns to speak to me, but invites me to a party thrown by the crème de la crème of high society.'

'Who is he?'

'He, my dear, is the next generation of arguably the richest family in the world.'

'*The* Barringtons?' I whisper, shocked.

'He even smells of old money and establishment, doesn't he?' Rupert says, and neighs loudly at his own joke. Rupert himself smells like grated lemon peel. The citrusy scent reminds me of Fairy washing up liquid.

A waiter appears to ask what we would like to drink.

'We'll have your finest house champagne,' Rupert booms. He winks at me. 'We're celebrating.'

A bottle and ice bucket arrive with flourish. The only time I have drunk champagne is when Billie and I dressed up to the nines and presented ourselves as bride and bridesmaid to be, at the Ritz. We pretended I was about to drop forty thousand pounds into their coffers by cutting my wedding cake there. We quaffed half a bottle of champagne and a whole tray of canapés while being shown around the different function rooms. Afterwards, Billie thanked them nicely and said we would be in touch. How we had laughed on the bus journey back.

I watch as the waiter expertly extracts the cork with a quiet hiss. Another waiter in a black jacket reels off the specials for the night and asks us if we are ready to order.

Rupert looks at me. 'The beef on the bone here is very good.'

I smile weakly. 'I guess I'll just have whatever you're having.'

'I'm actually having steak tartare.'

'Then I'll have the same.'

He looks at the waiter. 'A dozen oysters to start then steak tartare and side orders of vegetables and mashed potatoes.'

'I'm not really hungry. No starter for me,' I say quickly.

When the waiter is gone, he raises his glass. 'To us.'

'To us,' I repeat softly. The words stick in my throat.

I take a small sip and taste nothing, so I put the glass on the table and look at my hands blankly. I have to find something interesting to say.

'You have very beautiful skin,' he says softly. 'It was the first thing I noticed about you. Does it... mark very easily?'

'Yes,' I admit warily.

'I knew it,' he boasts with a sniff. 'I am a connoisseur of skin. I love the taste and the touch of skin. I can already imagine the taste of yours. A skin of wine.' He eyes me greedily over the rim of his glass.

I have been trying my best not to look at the dandruff flakes that liberally dust the shoulders of his pin-striped suit, but with that last remark he has tossed his head and a flurry of motes have floated off his head and fallen onto the pristine tablecloth. My eyes have helplessly followed their progress. I look up to find him looking at me speculatively.

'What will I be getting for my money?' His voice is suddenly cold and hard.

I blink. It is all wrong. I shouldn't be here. In this dress, or shoes, sitting in front of this obscene piece of filth hiding behind his handmade shirt, gold cufflinks and plummy, upper class accent. This man degrades and offends me simply by looking at me.

I wish myself somewhere else, but I am here. All my credit cards are maxed out. Two banks have impolitely turned me down and there is nothing else to do, but be here in this dress and these slutty shoes...

My stomach in knots, I smile in what I hope is a seductive way. 'What would you like for your money?'

'Forget what I would like for the moment. What are you selling?' His eyes are spiteful in a way I cannot understand.

'Me, I guess.'

That makes him snort with cruel laughter. 'You are an extraordinarily beautiful girl, but to be honest I can get five first class supermodels right off the runway for that asking price. What makes you think you're worth that kind of money?'

I take a deep breath. Here goes. 'I'm a virgin.'

He stops laughing. A suspicious speculative look enters his pale blue eyes. 'How old are you?'

'Twenty.' Well, I will be in two months' time.

He frowns. 'And you say you're still a virgin?'

'Yes.'

'Saving yourself up for someone special, were you?' His tone is annoying.

'Does it matter?' My nails bite into my clenched fists.

His eyes glitter. 'No, I suppose not.' He pauses. 'How do I know you're not lying?'

I swallow hard. The taste of my humiliation is bitter. 'I'll undergo any medical tests you require me to.'

He laughs. 'No need. No need,' he dismisses genially. 'Blood on the sheets will be enough for me.'

The way he says blood makes my blood run cold.

'Are all orifices up for sale?'

Oh! the brutality of the man. Something dies inside me, but I keep the image of my mother in my mind, and my voice is clear and strong. 'Yes.'

'So all that is left is to renegotiate the price?'

I have to stop myself from recoiling. I know now that I have committed two out of the nine sorts of behaviors my mother has warned me are considered contemptible and base. I have expected generosity from a miser and I have revealed my need to my enemy. 'The price is not negotiable.'

His gaze sweeps meaningfully to my champagne glass. 'Shall we give this party a go first and bargain later, when you are in a...better mood?'

I understand his thinking. He thinks he can drive the price down when I am drunk. 'The price is not negotiable,' I say firmly. 'And will have to be paid up front.'

He smiles smarmily. 'I'm sure we'll come to some agreement that we will both be happy with.'

I frown. I have been naïve. My plan is sketchy and has no provisions for a sharp punter or price negotiations. I heard through the office grapevine where I worked as temporary secretary that my boss was one of those men who are prepared to pay ten thousand pounds a pop for his pleasure and often, but I had never imagined he would reduce me to bargaining.

While Rupert stuffs himself with cheese and biscuits I excuse myself and go to the Ladies. There is another woman standing at the mirror. She glances at me with a mixture of surprise and disgust. I wait until she leaves, then I call my mother.

'Hi, Mum.'

'Where are you, Lana?'

'I'm still at the restaurant.'

'What time will you be coming home?'

'I'll be late. I've been invited to a party.'

'A party,' my mother repeats worriedly. 'Where?'

'I don't know the address. Somewhere in London.'

'How will you get home?' A wire of panic has crept into her voice.

I sigh gently. I have almost never left my mother alone at night; consequently she is now a bundle of jittery nerves. 'I have a ride, Mum. Just don't wait up for me, OK?'

'All right. Be careful, won't you?'

'Nothing is going to happen to me.'

'Yes, yes,' she says, but she sounds distracted and unhappy.

'How are you feeling, Mum?'

'Good.'

'Goodnight, then. I'll see you in the morning.'

'Lana?'

'Yeah.'

'I love you very much.'

'Me too, Mum. Me too.'

I flip my phone shut with a snap. I no longer feel cheap or obscene, but strong and sure. There is nothing Rupert can do that can degrade me. I will have that money no matter what.

I look at myself in the mirror. No need for lipstick as I have hardly eaten—just watching Rupert gurgle down the oysters made me feel quite sick, and how was I to know steak tartare was ground raw meat. For a moment I think again of that sinfully sophisticated man, his eyes edged with experience and mystery, his lips twisted with sensuality, and I am suddenly overcome by a strong desire to press my body against his hard length. But he is gone and I am here.

I return my phone to my purse and go out to meet my fate.

Three

'Shall we go?' Rupert asks, and before I can agree, he imperiously clicks his fingers for the bill. Outside, Rupert hails a black cab. It is such a warm evening that I carry my coat in my hands. Rupert gives the address to the cab driver and we climb in. My dress rides up my thighs, and when I try to pull it back down, Rupert puts his meaty, white hand over mine and in a firm voice orders, 'Leave it.'

Embarrassed, I look into the rearview mirror. The taxi driver is observing us. Wordlessly, I drape my coat over my exposed thighs and knees and turning my face away from Rupert, stare out. Damn him. As I gaze unseeingly out I feel his hand slide under my coat and settle on my thighs. Biting my lip I try to ignore the hand, but it is steadily slithering upwards. When it is almost at my crotch I catch the offending hand in a firm grip. I turn to him and look him in the eye.

'We don't have a deal yet.'

'True,' he says in a mild and reasonable way, and retracts his hand, but the smile on his face is taunting and smug. He has already figured out that I need the money desperately and my body is my last option.

The rest of the journey passes in silence while my stomach churns. I am so nervous I actually worry I will lose the few vegetables I did eat on the floor of the cab. Fortunately, the taxi turns into Bishop's Avenue and we come to a stop outside a large, white, three-story Regency house. There are fancy cars parked bumper to bumper along the length of the street.

Rupert pays the cab driver and we walk up a short flight of steps to a set of black doors. Rupert rings the bell and through the tall windows I get a glimpse of the kind of people that I have only seen in magazines: immaculately dressed and dripping in jewelry. I look down upon my cheap orange dress in dismay. I try to pull at the hem, but my efforts at modesty are counter-productive, as more of my cleavage falls into view.

'Don't worry,' Rupert lies cheerfully. 'You'll do.'

A round man in an old-fashioned butler's uniform opens the door. His manner suggests disdain. He can tell instantly we do not belong. Rupert haughtily informs him that we are guests of Blake Barrington. The man's eyes register recognition and a glimmer of a smile surfaces. He nods politely and stands aside to allow us in. I fill my lungs with as much oxygen as I can and enter the grand hallway. Inside I stifle a gasp at my splendid surroundings.

From outside it had not appeared so large and spacious. Now I understand what Rupert meant by the smell of old money. I have never been anywhere so beautiful. The walls are covered with museum quality paintings. I gaze up with awe at the cherubs and Madonna-like women looking down at me. They are so beautiful that I want a closer look, but Rupert is guiding me firmly by the elbow towards a sort of anteroom where a young woman takes my coat in exchange for a ticket.

From two open doorways live classical music and voices emanate. A waiter carrying a tray of champagne stops in front of us. I hardly drunk at the restaurant in an effort to remain sober and level-headed, but now I know I must be drunk or I will never be able to go through my deal with the devil. A pasty white devil with dandruff.

I take a glass, and with a restraining hand on the surprised waiter's arm, drain the tall flute. The bubbles hit me at the back of my throat and make my eyes water. I return the empty glass to the tray and snag another two.

'Thanks,' I say breathlessly, and the waiter, a young Mediterranean type, allows his dark, restless eyes to wander down to my chest.

Rupert watches me with feral, excited eyes. He wants me drunk. He has plans for me. By the small of my back he guides me into one of the rooms.

Surreptitiously, I note the other women's clothes. Classy, understated and expensive, very expensive.

I feel many pairs of eyes on me and it is impossible not to be aware that I stand out like a sore thumb. I turn resolutely away from their openly condescending gazes and look towards the string quartet only to find their eyes on me too. Damn that Barrington guy for inviting us here. Defiantly, I suck my champagne glass dry. Another waiter passes and I pull another glass from the tray.

'Go easy,' Rupert warns.

I turn towards him with a bright smile. 'I thought you wanted me drunk and pliable.'

He takes my elbow and leads me deeper into the room close to a large palm plant. With his back to the party he says, 'I don't like fucking inert bodies.'

My eyes widen. Still the champagne must have already gone to my head for I feel inordinately courageous. I'm ready to talk terms with him. 'Right, you don't want inert bodies. What do you want, Rupert?'

From the camel's lips came cold breath. 'Have you read *Fifty Shades Of Grey*?'

Almost all the other girls at the agency have read the book and I have been present while they have raved about it, but I have been confused by its popularity. Did women really have a secret desire to be *owned* by a powerful man? Could it be love when a man wants to tie you up and flog you raw? When I mentioned it to my mother, she smiled and astutely remarked, 'The Western woman sneered at the woman in the purdah and now she dons a dog collar and worships at the same altar.'

I look into Rupert's pale eyes. 'No, but isn't it about a sick man who abuses his lover?'

'Perhaps it is not a sickness, but a matter of taste.'

'Is that what you want from me?'

'Not quite. What I really like is taking a woman by force. A dangerous activity likely to end me behind bars, so I am willing to settle for consensual rape. You will meet me in parks and alleyways, or I will pick you up in my car from a street corner and you will pretend to resist while I overpower you and rape you. There will be a bit of pain and sometimes it will involve a little bleeding, but I will never mark your face or leave any permanent scars. And when I am finished I will leave you in the gutter to make your own way back. Would that be acceptable to you?'

Shocked to my core, I hear my own voice as if from far away ask, 'How many times would you expect this…service from me?'

'Let's say five times?' Rupert's face freezes into a cold, calculating mask. A businessman to the end. Ten thousand must be the going price.

I feel as if I am a stick-figured bird precariously perched on a thin wire. Can I really agree to let someone rape me? Even with all the champagne sloshing inside me I find I am unable to speak. I nod.

'Perhaps I should let you lick the brim to taste the poison,' he murmurs, and moves closer to me. Instinctively, I take a step back on my tall shoes, and if not for the solid wall against my back, I would have fallen. With the trailing fronds of a palm tree and his big body hiding me from the party his hand comes up to pinch my right nipple. So hard I gasp in shock and pain.

He takes that opportunity to crash down on my parted mouth, bumps his teeth against my lips, and pokes a pointy, muscular tongue into my mouth. His tongue tastes coppery and bitter.

Copious amounts of saliva pour into my horrified mouth making me want to gag. The oysters I have not eaten but watched him eat flash into my mind. His tongue feels slimy and dirty. It makes me want to brush my teeth, rinse, spit, and rinse again with the extra-strong mouthwash that my father used to have in the bathroom cabinet. I truly, truly need to go somewhere and be sick, but pinned tightly to the wall by his strong ox-like body I am totally unable to move.

I feel his hand force itself between my thighs and slide up quickly. His rough, sausage-like fingers are already grasping the rim of my knickers and pushing the material aside. And there is not a single thing I can do about it. Helpless tears gather at the backs of my eyes and begin to roll down my face.

Suddenly he removes his smelly mouth and looks down at me. My face, I am certain, must be white with horror and I am gasping for breath. My distress seems to please him and my suffering appears to have brought him pleasure. Without knowing it I am playing the part perfectly. If I had enjoyed it, it would have spoilt it for him.

He brings up a hand and touches my face. 'For most part the symptoms of excitement and fear are so similar most men cannot tell the difference. I can,' he whispers close to my ear, the thick fingers of his other hand moving into the folds of my flesh. 'I am going to finger-fuck you amongst all these high and mighty people and none of them will ever know.'

At that moment I am filled with an unspeakable loathing for him. My brain scrambles for escape. 'Don't you care,' I whisper back, 'what these people will think of us? Of you? I thought you were pleased to be in the company of the crème de la crème of society.'

His laugh is harsh and sudden. 'Did you see anybody come to greet me or talk to me? I am as invisible as you are, probably more so. Nobody is looking at us, because nobody cares about us. We are the outsiders.'

Desperately, I push the palms of my hands against his chest. The nausea is already almost in my throat. I must be sick. 'I need the toilet,' I gasp.

He hesitates for a second and then he smiles. It is the smile of a man who is too pleased with himself. 'It's not very posh to say toilet. This lot call it the loo. Go on, then,' he says, and steps aside.

The first thing my shocked, ashamed eyes meet is Blake. There is a blonde in a long red dress wrapped around him, but he is staring at me with an expression on his face I cannot fathom. His eyes are blazing.

For a moment I stare back. Then I snap my mouth shut, tear my eyes from his, and pushing myself away from the wall take a step forward. My knees feel shaky and I am terrified I will fall, but I do not. I just need to get away. Away from the scene of my humiliation. I sense heads turning to watch me, disgusted expressions and haughty whispers. I stumble away towards the doors hardly able to control the rising nausea.

I don't dare open my mouth to ask anyone where the loos are, but I spot two young women disappearing down a corridor and I stagger after them. They lead me to a cloakroom and I rudely push past them, ignoring their offended cries of 'Hey'. I run into one of two cubicles and falling to my knees violently throw up the bits of vegetables I have eaten and almost all the champagne. One of the girls asks if I am all right and I choke out, 'Fine'.

I hear them go into the other cubicle and lock the door.

I sit back on my heels and the hot tears come. I cover my mouth to muffle any stray sounds. I have made a complete fool of myself. What do I do now? What can I do? Numbly I hear the girls in the next cubicle giggling about what all girls giggle and chat about—men. Then my ears pick up the sounds of them snorting lines of cocaine. When they leave I flush the toilet and open the door.

Miserably, I walk towards the very large ornate, gilded mirror stretched across the wall. The other toilet seems to be in use and a thin woman with immaculate hair is perched on one of the gold and cream chairs waiting her turn. There is an air of superior calm about her. Her eyes meet mine briefly but curiously, before she enters the cubicle that I have vacated.

I stare at myself in the mirror. My face is deathly pale and the cheap mascara I purchased from the market is smudged and running; my lips look as if I have smacked my mouth on a wall, and my eyes are red and puffy from crying. *This is what Blake Barrington saw.* I look like I feel. Soiled.

The woman in the other cubicle comes out. She looks identical to the woman who had perched on the chair before. With a quick, surprised glance at me, she goes to stand at the other end of the mirror. She pats her immaculate hair, brushes away imaginary specks of dust from her soft pink dress suit and leaves.

I turn on the tap and rinse my mouth with plenty of water. Scooping water in my palms I wash my face with hand soap and scrub it dry with a paper towel. Without my make-up I feel defenseless and naked. But I'm not going to try and put lipstick on these swollen lips.

I hunker down and weigh my situation.

There is a sick pervert out there who wants to rape me and leave me torn and bleeding in alleyways. Five times. *I could walk away. Say fuck you.* Actually, no I can't. It is so much money. And he knows it. I *need* that money. I consider taking the money and not delivering. What could he do? It's not like he could go to the police or I would be running a refund desk. Then I remember his eyes. How cold and dangerous. No. Anyway, I have always said, I'd rather be the one who bought the Brooklyn Bridge than the one who sold it.

Again my thoughts turn to the Barrington man. Why is he still in my mind? Probably the way he looks at me. No one. Absolutely no one has looked at me like that.

I indulge in a moment of fantasy. Perhaps he really wants me. He is filthy rich so he will simply give me the money I need. Gallantly, he will then fall in love with me and we will marry. As I am standing inside my dreams another woman opens the door and enters. It is the blonde in the red dress. She is tall and severely beautiful with an aristocratic nose and bottle-green eyes. She has the same superior air of all the people at this party. The same air that Blake Barrington has claimed for himself.

I cannot help but watch her through the mirror. Our eyes meet for a second, then hers slide away, but in that second there is pure speculation. Everybody knows I do not belong.

I look at my reflection. Who am I kidding? Blake Barrington is the biggest cheese on the board. Simply the way Rupert behaved in his presence told me that. He was probably looking at me because I am dressed like a hooker and he thinks I am one. The only real thing I have is my mother. And there is nothing I will not do for her. I think of my father. How easily he had walked away when we had needed him most. How weak his love for us had been. Mine is different. I will not walk away even if I have to walk upon a path of thorns. Bleed in alleyways I will. And that will be the test of my love.

I will not let myself be distracted by anything. I will survive any sexual humiliation Rupert can dish out. Five encounters? My champagne-addled brain scoffs, that's fucking nothing. The beautiful blonde has turned away from the mirror and entered one of the cubicles.

Blake Barrington is welcome to her.

I straighten my spine. I can do this, I tell my reflection. I love you, Mum, better than Dad did, much, much better. I practice the smile I will bestow on Rupert in the mirror, and despite the revulsion in my belly I tell myself that when I am old and wrinkled I will be glad I made this sacrifice. The price will always be worth it. Then there is nothing left to do in that opulent loo, but to walk out of it, and face my decision, and the lengths I will go to for my mother.

I open the door and my heart drops.

Blake Barrington is lounging casually against the wall of the corridor.

Four

He straightens when he sees me. He looks annoyed. Perhaps, he is pissed off that he invited Rupert and me to his mate's fine party, and we've showed him up and behaved in a disgusting manner. But, quite frankly, I didn't ask to be invited. The very last thing I need is another confrontation. I have quite enough on my plate. I consider ignoring him and walking right past but he raises a detaining finger. I look defiantly up at him. Thank God, for my shoes. They lift my eyes to the level of his straight, stern mouth.

His eyes scan my face, now devoid of all make-up. 'Are you all right?'

Up this close his skin is sun kissed and his voice pure velvet. I fold my arms around my body and resist the instinct to take a step back, such is the immensity of animal power he exudes. It is magnetic and irresistible. It's trite I know but he reminds me of a caged panther. Prowling and ready to pounce, full of suppressed restless energy. Muscular, strong.

I raise my chin, meet him square in the eye, and in my best secretarial voice, say, 'Yes, I'm fine. Thank you.'

'I need to talk to you.'

Oh God, he is going to lecture me. 'So talk.'

'Privately—through here, please.' He gestures with his hand, and is careful not to touch me. The corridor leads to a door. He goes ahead of me and holds it open. I hesitate for a moment, then think, fuck it, I'm not scared of you, and walk through. The room appears to be some sort of library with walls full of shelves filled with leather-bound books. It smells of wood polish and tobacco. I hear him close the door and turn around to face him.

He is leaning against the door and simply watching me.

'Well?' I prompt.

'Are you over eighteen?'

'Yes.'

'Are you sure?'

'Of course I am,' I snap. 'Not that it is any of your business.'

'What will Lothian get for his money?'

So he *did* hear. Oh the shame. If the ground could have opened up and swallowed me... Fortunately, a fine anger comes to my rescue. How dare he? The audacity. Overbearing, arrogant bastard. With all the hauteur I can manage under the circumstances, I grate, 'That's private if you don't mind, and if that was all...'

'It's not idle curiosity. I'm quite happy to double the sum if it's what I think it is.'

I stare at him blankly. I can understand why someone like Rupert would have to pay, but Blake Law Barrington? He could have anyone he wants. Then it occurs to me that, perhaps, he is just toying with me. Perhaps it is a thing all rich men do.

My pride comes to the fore. I will not be humiliated twice in one night. 'Whatever I have offered is for Rupert and Rupert only. Now please get away from that door and the hell away from me.' My voice has risen in anger.

His eyes spark. 'Do you know your eyes are like the blue of struck matches when you are angry.' Then more softly, 'Why would anyone, let alone a stunner like you, get involved with someone who, if the most impeccable sources are to be trusted, is an absolute brute? He beat one woman so badly he broke her jaw, and blinded her in one eye.'

I have drunk too much champagne. The whole situation has become impossible for me to deal with in my present condition. I have ventured where I should never have gone. I feel the sting of defeat in mybones. 'What do you want from me?'

He leaves the door and walks towards me: again that sensation that he is a predatory animal. 'Well for a start...' He reaches me and suddenly jerks me towards him. I fall forward and am pitched against the unyielding hardness of his body. My palms come into contact with the smooth material of his jacket. Shocked, I am filled with the scent that Rupert called old money and establishment. Difficult to define, but it reminds me of rosemary, not because of its smell, but because it is so clear and distinct. Nothing wishy-washy about it.

Everything takes on an unreal appearance. The fabulously wealthy interior. The man outside that door that wants to rape me for money. The frighteningly remote man in front of me that brings into my body sensations I have never experienced before. A pulse at the base of his throat is throbbing. I watch it curiously. I have never seen it in a man before.

And then an arm comes around me, a fistful of hair close to my nape is grasped and tugged so my confused face is tilted up towards him. 'This,' he says and his mouth swoops down to possess mine. His breath smells like brandy or whiskey. Wicked, anyway.

Twice today I have had to endure a stranger's uninvited and unwelcome lips, but my reaction to this overbearing man is shocking and immediate.

His mouth drives me wild in a way that I could never have imagined. Heat ripples through me, and the reasoning, reliable part of my brain, that part that has never failed me before, stops responding. Stops functioning. My arms snake up to twine around his neck and tangle in the thick hair. I thrill in his possessive hold.

He circles my tongue, sucks it deep into his mouth and kisses me with such ferocity that some slumbering beast inside answers his animal call. A dangerous excitement kicks hard in the pit of my belly. No man has ever done this to me in this way before. I cling to him. Like a blind animal that moves only with instinct I push my body into his. There is only the need to find more of such addictive heat. What I find is the thick hardness of his desire for me. It presses aggressively against the softness of my stomach and excites me beyond all reason.

A pleasure that is at once sweet and piercing courses through my body. This rock-hard erection is mine. I caused it. Heat pools between my legs. And suddenly I am wet with wanting and filled with an irresistible desire to have that hard meat inside me, as deep as it will go…

I totally forget where I am.

It is Rupert's cold, hard voice that drags me back into that room. We had both not heard him enter. 'I'm afraid she's rather spoken for,' he drawls, but there is so much suppressed anger that his voice is like a blast of icy air.

I snatch my mouth away from Blake's. He is positioned between Rupert and me so his wide chest hides me from Rupert's condemnation and my eyes, cloudy with confusion and desire, are still caught in his gaze. For a few seconds more he does not release me, but simply stares into my eyes with something approaching surprise. Then his eyes turn into hard granite chips and his body stiffens even as his hands tighten and curve protectively around my waist. Slowly he turns to face Rupert.

'But still unpaid for, I believe?' he says, and looks down with a smile at my flushed, troubled face. I have two very quick impressions. He is a brilliant actor and he is a cold man. A shockingly cold and unemotional being.

Rupert directs his astonished, vicious eyes at me. 'You offered yourself to him too?'

I stare mutely at Rupert while his gaze moves derisively, hatefully over me. I feel myself cringe horribly, but I try not to show it.

'Does he know how much you charge?'

One sculptured eyebrow rises gently. 'Do you doubt I will be able to afford her?'

Rupert shrivels the way a leech that has had salt thrown on it does. 'This is why you invited me here, isn't it?'

'Yes.'

'What a joke!' he taunts, but his jibe lacks any real bite. 'The great Barrington can't find his own whore. He has to steal mine.'

'I didn't steal her,' Blake notes reasonably. 'I just offered to pay more.'

Rupert's eyes bulge, bug-like. 'She's just a cheap bloody tart. I've just finger-fucked her out there,' he lies maliciously, jerking his dandruff-laden head in the direction of the door.

I feel Blake's hand tighten around my waist. 'Consider it an unearned freebie, then,' he says quietly, but there is warning in the calm words. A warning that is not lost on Rupert. The air becomes tight with tension. I look from one man to the other. It is like watching two lions fighting for supremacy. But my body knows which lion it wants to win this fight.

Rupert shrugs. He knows he'd be a fool to go against a Barrington. He has much to lose. 'If you think I'm going to fight over her you're mistaken. Have her.'

He turns on his heel and leaves.

Blake lets go of me and I realize I am trembling. I lean against the desk, hating myself, but unable to stop—nothing is more important than the money—I ask, 'Did you…did you mean it about the money?'

'Yes.'

A sob of relief escapes my throat. I cover my mouth with both hands. 'Thank you.'

He looks at me with narrowed eyes, as if surprised by the intensity of my reaction, but he does not offer any comment. 'Did you have a coat?'

I nod, unable to speak.

'Give me the ticket. I'll get it.'

I rummage through the purse hanging by my hips, my hands unsteady, and shake my head glumly. For the life of me I cannot remember what I have done with it. 'I've lost it. I think it might have fallen out in the…' I am about to say loo when I decide I am not like them and I won't pretend to be something I am not…'Ladies room.'

'Let's go. I'll buy you another.'

'I can't leave without it. It's not mine,' I whisper.

He sighs. 'It's all right. I'll get it. Is the coat… er…orange?'

I look at him carefully—there is an insult there, somewhere—but his face is blank. 'Yes.'

'Wait here. Don't go anywhere.'

I stand in the middle of the room feeling light-headed. I've got the money and I don't have to get raped for it. My hands find their way to my mouth. That kiss. The way it made me feel. Just thinking about it makes me long for the feel of his solid body melded into mine.

The door opens, and oh shit—Rupert walks in.

'You look frightened. Why? I don't wish you harm. In fact, I realize now that I am actually very interested in your offer. If I seemed unappreciative before please forgive me.'

'There is,' I say, shaking my head and taking a step backwards, 'nothing to forgive.'

'Is he really paying double?'

'I don't need more than what I asked you for.'

'Then why go to him? He is no different from me. He will drop you like a bad mortgage when he is finished with you too.'

I nod. 'Of course he will, but like you said, I came with a price. You wanted to bargain and he was willing to pay it.' If only I can keep him talking until Blake returns.

'So am I, now.'

'Besides, you want fifty shades of gray and he just wants a woman.'

'Perhaps I've changed my mind. Perhaps I just want a woman too.'

He comes closer.

'Blake has gone to get my coat. He'll be back any time.'

'Not without this he won't.' He holds out my ticket.

He puts out a hand suddenly. I try to move back, but he grabs me by the arm, his grip vice-like, his fingers digging painfully into my flesh. He hauls me closer.

'You're hurting me.'

'You'll be surprised how much pain the human body can take.'

'What do you want, Rupert?'

'I feel aggrieved. Something I wanted and was promised to me has been stolen by another. I was given a taste of something, which I very much liked. You resist beautifully, Lana. Perhaps, you will do both of us. I will pay you too.'

I blink. I can't believe what I am hearing. If it wasn't so humiliating, it would be surreal. The surroundings I am in, the obviously powerful men who are suddenly apparently willing to pay huge sums to have sex with me.

'I wouldn't do that to Blake.'

'He'll never know and even if he does, he won't care. It's not like he wants to marry you. You're just a fuck, Lana,' he pronounces dismissively.

The door opens and Blake stands at the threshold with my orange coat folded over his arm. His face is like a closed steel door. He comes into the room and Rupert lets go of my arm and I immediately move away from him, rubbing my stinging flesh. Already there are red marks on it. Blake eyes them silently, then helps me into my coat.

'Ready?' he asks.

I nod.

He turns towards Rupert and socks him hard on the chin. So hard the ex-rugby player falls to the floor with a grunt.

'She may be a cheap slut, but I'm paying what you baulked at, so she is my cheap slut now. You'd do well to remember that,' Blake throws casually over his shoulder.

Rupert clutches his busted, bleeding lip and shows his fury to the only person he dares to. 'You're fired, Bloom,' he shouts impotently.

Blake takes my arm and leads me out of that place. There is not a single person at that party that does not turn to watch us leave.

Five

Blake's monster of a car, a gleaming sable-gray Aston Martin is parked beside a lamppost. It is one of those old-fashioned wrought-iron ones with a fluted surface. I stand on the curb and loop my hand around its rough, cold metal.

'Get in,' he says.

'What if I'm sick in your car?'

'My secretary will have it valeted.'

I unhook myself from the metal post. Is life really this easy? With these shoes and the drink in me it is impossible to get into the low-swung seat elegantly. Blake's eyes are on my legs. He is going to be seeing a lot more soon, so I swing the last one in and shut the door.

The interior of his car is plush and luxurious. It even smells expensive. I have never been in such a car. The sound system is excellent and superb music fills the car.

'What is this music called?'

'Handel's *Messiah,*' he says, and switches it off. He turns to me. In the light of the streetlamp he looked harsh and distant. In the softly lit darkness of his car there is still no softening to his face. Again the thought, a cold, cold man.

'I have to be in New York tomorrow, but my secretary will call you and make all the necessary arrangements.'

I nod gratefully and look away. It is as if I am in a dream.

'Where do you live?'

'Kilburn.'

'Got a postcode?' He sounds very American then.

I give it to him and he sets his GPS system.

We drive in silence, until I can bear it no more. 'Don't you want to know how much?'

'Yeah, tell me.'

I tell him and his eyes leave the road briefly to look at me. 'What made you think Rupert was the man for the part?'

I shrug in the dark. 'I don't know. I heard a rumor that his secretary was sometimes tasked with stuffing envelopes with ten thousand pounds in cash and booking pricey hotel rooms for him.'

'I see,' he says quietly.

We come to a red light.

'Why me?' I ask.

His fingers tap at the steering wheel. Long, strong fingers. I stare at them and think of the way they moved on my body. He turns to me. His eyes are edgy and dangerous, full of promise. 'Do you want it flowery or straight.'

I bite my lip. 'Straight.'

'I wanted to fuck you senseless from the moment our eyes met.'

'And the flowery version?'

'Now I think about it, there is no flowery version. It is what it is.'

I turn to look at his profile. It is very stern and still. Have I jumped from the frying pan into the fire? Are all rich people secretly deviant in their sexual desires? 'Does fucking me senseless involve any weird or kinky stuff?'

He glances at me. Again that expression that is beyond my comprehension. 'No, but I want to be able to use you as often as I please in whatever manner I desire for as long as I choose.'

'Oh!' How strange, but his insulting words unleashes a lightning thrill of sexual excitement in my body. 'I…How long were you thinking?'

'I'll decide tomorrow. But I imagine one month should do it.'

'Do it?'

'Get me bored.'

'And you are willing to pay a hundred thousand pounds for that?'

His lips twist into a wry smile. 'When I made my offer I didn't realize you had valued yourself quite that highly, but I'm not displeased that you did. Despite all protestations to the contrary, nobody really wants a bargain. They settle for it because they can't afford better.' He glances at me. 'Cheap usually means get your guard up, you are being offered something undesirable.'

I think of my mother trawling the supermarket aisles looking for stuff that has been discounted because it is reaching the end of its sell by date. 'I will require the money up front. So, how will we do this?'

'My lawyer will draw up the appropriate contract for you to sign. Once you have done so the money will be in your account within minutes.'

'What sort of a contract?'

'A non-disclosure agreement.'

I nod. 'I suppose rich people have to protect themselves.'

'Yes,' he replies shortly.

An awkward silence follows. He seems preoccupied with his own thoughts. I turn my head—it has begun to throb—and look out of the window. He is a fast driver and we are already on Edgware Road.

'I'll send someone around tomorrow at noon to take you to your workplace so you can collect your personal belongings.'

'It's OK, I can go on my own.'

'I'd feel happier if you were accompanied. Indulge me.'

I think for a moment. I don't exactly relish the prospect of accidentally bumping into Rupert either. 'Well, I only have an old pair of trainers there. I won't bother to pick them up.'

'As you wish.'

We arrive at the block of council flats where I live and he looks around him in surprise as if he has never been to such a poor area before.

'You live here?' He cannot hide his distaste. I guess to him it must be a horrible housing estate, what he would probably consider the underbelly of the city.

'Yes,' I say simply.

He stops the car outside a two-story block of flats. 'Which one is yours?'

I point to the last flat on the first floor, and say, 'That's me.'

He doesn't switch off the engine but turns to me. 'Give me your phone.'

I hand it to him.

He punches in some numbers and waits. When his phone rings, he ends the call. 'I've got your number and you've got mine,' he says and hands my phone back to me.

'Thank you.'

'Take a couple of aspirins and go to bed. Keep yourself free tomorrow. The entire day.'

'OK.'

'I'll be in touch tomorrow evening.'

Instead of driving off he sits in his car and watches me totter and wobble in my ridiculously high shoes over to the cemented verge, gain the cracked concrete concourse, and go up an outer staircase while holding onto the metal railings. At the entrance to my home I turn back and flick my wrist to indicate that I am safely home and that he need wait no more. He doesn't respond. Simply sits there. Watching me.

'Fine. Whatever,' I huff to myself. Sitting on the front step, I take off my shoes. With them in my hand I put my key in the door and turn it.

It is only after I close my front door and hear the powerful engine take off that I realize neither man has wanted to know why I need the money. The flat is lit only by the lights from the streetlamps. I walk barefoot into the kitchen and fumble around in the darkness. Finally, I find a tab of paracetamols, punch two out and sit with a glass of water at the kitchen table in a stunned daze. What a night it has been. I set out with an absurd idea and…

'I've done it,' I whisper to the familiar shadows, and grin.

I think of the stone-like biceps and the hard slab of his stomach that my hands and body encountered and I touch my mouth. I can still feel his lips, his hands. I remember how I lost control and totally forgot myself. And the unfamiliar too damn good sensation he caused in my body, between my legs. Is it too dreamlike to be true?

This cannot be just my life.

Don't be too happy yet. He could still change his mind.

I swallow the paracetamols and avoiding all the creaky areas on the stairs tiptoe upstairs. The light is off in my mother's room, so I quietly open the door to look in on her sleeping form. But my mother is sitting on a chair by the window. She must have seen me come in.

'What are you doing?' I ask.

'I heard you come in,' she says softly.

'Could you not sleep?'

'No. I start my chemo next week. Just enjoying the feeling of well-being I guess.'

I cross the room and kneel beside my mother. She is not wearing a scarf, and her bald head glints in the moonlight. It makes me sad. 'I've got good news for you, Mum. Remember that clinic in America that I was telling you about.'

She frowns. She is only fifty but the worry and pain make her appear haggard. 'The one we can't afford.'

'Well, it's not a hundred percent yet, but I think I've managed to raise the money.'

'How? How did you do that?' My mother's voice is suspicious and frightened.

'I met a guy. A rich guy who just wants to help.'

'A rich man who wants to help?' Her tone is frankly disbelieving.

'Mum, please don't be like that. It's not anything like you are thinking.'

'Oh no? What is it like then?'

'He's just a nice guy who likes me.'

'I wasn't born yesterday, girl.' My mother's skeletal fingers grip my hands. 'You haven't done anything you'll regret, have you?'

'I promise I haven't. I just drank too much champagne,' I put my fingertips to my temples, 'and my head's pounding. I promise, I'll tell you everything tomorrow when I've had some sleep.'

The last time I remember lying to my mother was when I was nine and I had pretended I had brushed my teeth. Guilty and terrified of being discovered I had raced up the stairs to wet my toothbrush.

My mother's hands move up my arm urgently. She touches the tips of her fingers on the dark bruises on my arm, while her worried eyes burn into mine. 'Where did these come from?'

'That's not him,' I explain nervously.

'The road to hell is paved with good intentions,' she warns darkly.

'I promise, I'll tell you everything tomorrow, but it's not what you think.' Really it is worse, a little voice says. 'All will be well, you wait and see,' I say brightly and smile.

My mother does not return my smile. Instead she gazes at me sadly.

'Goodnight, Mum. I really love you.'

'I love you too.'

I stumble down the short corridor to my room, and making it to the edge of my bed, drop the shoes clutched in my hands. Then, like a tree that has been felled I fall onto the top of my bed and am almost instantly inside a deep, dreamless sleep.

Six

The muted but insistent ringing of my mobile phone jars me awake. For a moment I lay crumpled and confused on my bed. My head is banging furiously. Then I pat the duvet around me, locate my purse and pulling my phone out squint at the number. It is the agency.

I sit up, clear my throat, and say, 'Yes?'

'Hello, Lana. It's Jane here.'

'Hi, Jane.'

'Well, we've received a disturbing and very serious accusation from your current employer. They have also requested a replacement to finish the booking. So please do not go into work today. Mrs. Lipman would also like to see you to sort out this situation. Can you come in later today?'

I remember Blake telling me to keep the day free. 'Not today but tomorrow.'

'Oh.' There is a surprised pause. 'All right. What about ten thirty tomorrow?'

'OK, see you then.'

I gently ease my head back on my pillow. Listening carefully I hear my mother moving around the flat, and sigh. I will have to go out soon and face my mother and tell fresh new lies, but I feel so tired I fall back to sleep.

Again it is the phone that wakes me. I lift it up to my face. It is a number I do not recognize.

'Hello,' I croak.

'Miss Bloom?' a woman's voice enquires. Her voice is extremely efficient and professional. And wide awake.

'Yes.'

'Laura Arnold, Mr. Barrington's personal assistant, here. Is this a good time for you to talk?'

'Yes. Yes, of course.' I jerk upright and take a gulp of water from a bottle by my bedside.

'Mr. Barrington has asked me to make some appointments for you today. May I run through them with you now?'

'What kind of appointments?'

'Tom Edwards, Mr. Barrington's driver, will be around your flat at ten forty-five. Your first stop will be your doctor where you have an appointment to see the nurse.'

'How do you know who my doctor is?'

There is a pause. It is pregnant with possibilities, perhaps even explanations.

'It doesn't matter,' I say quickly.

As if she has not been interrupted, the woman continues, 'She will discuss various contraceptive options with you if you are not already on some form of birth control. Next, you have a meeting with Mr. Barrington's lawyer. Once you have concluded your business there, you will be dropped off at our publicist, Fleur Jan's office. Ms. Jan will take you shopping and then on to your appointment with the hairdresser. After that Tom has instructions to take you to a beauty salon where you are booked for a full body wax, manicure and pedicure. Please bear in mind that Mr. Barrington does not like garish colors. He prefers light colors, but likes French manicures best.

'When you are done at the salon, Tom will take you to the apartment in St John's Wood and show you around. Please do settle in. The fridge and cupboards will be fully stocked, but should you require, I can also arrange for a meal of your choice to be delivered to you from one of the local restaurants. It would be advisable to eat lightly as Mr. Barrington gets into London late evening, and he wishes to take you out for supper about nine p.m. He tends to be very punctual so do be ready by eight thirty. Do you have any particular dietary needs or preferences?'

'No.'

'Food allergies?'

'No.'

'Good. Would you like me to order your dinner?'

'No, I'll make do.'

'Fine. Do you have a passport?'

'No.'

'You will need one.'

'Why?'

'Mr. Barrington travels often and I believe you will be required to accompany him on some of those trips.'

'Uh...I see.'

'I will make the necessary arrangements for you and contact you tomorrow.'

'Thank you.'

'Oh, and when you go to meet the solicitor please take some form of identification with you. Do you have any questions?'

'Er...No. I don't think so.'

'If you do come up with any question or requests call me on this number. I will be happy to assist.'

'OK. Thanks, Miss Arnold.'

'It's Mrs. Arnold, actually. Have a nice day, Miss Bloom.'

I let myself fall backwards and feel a surge of wild surge of joy inside me. I begin to grin. He has not changed his mind. It seems almost impossible to imagine but I have pulled it off. Raised the money.

Mother *will* go to America.

Still, I never expected such competence or thoroughness. This is more like a business takeover than the simple transaction I had envisaged. Naively, I had thought up the oldest scheme in the book, imagining visits to seedy hotels or an odd-smelling flat somewhere in London, probably Soho, but with brutal efficiency he was drawing up my reality to mirror his unemotional world where everything is black and white, and every effort must be made to stop any sort of gray in the form of confusion or disorder creeping in.

I glance at my alarm clock. I must have been more tired than I had realized. It is already nine thirty even though it is another gray day outside. I hold my tender head in my hands. A couple more paracetamols should do the trick.

I sit up, swallow them down and lying back on the bed close my eyes and remember last night. The details are fuzzy. Only the kiss remains crystal clear. I remember his eyes—how unaffected he was. If not for that pulse drumming madly in his throat I would have thought he had felt nothing. Eventually, I can no longer put off meeting my mother so I drag myself out of bed and pad to our shared bathroom. The tiles are sickly green and one or two are cracked, but everything is sparkling clean.

The orange dress is badly crumpled. I take it off and carefully hand wash it in the sink. After wringing it out, I hang it inside the bath, and get in it myself. I turn on the shower head, and hold the warm stream over my body.

When I come out, I feel like a new person. Quickly, I slip into clean underwear and dress in jeans and a white shirt. Then I comb my hair, tie it into a ponytail high on my head and with a last look in the mirror I brave the kitchen.

'Morning, Mum. How are you feeling today?' My voice is bright.

My mother smiles at me. 'Today is a good day.'

I smile back. Both of us look forward to the good days. The good days are what keep us going.

'Didn't you have to go to work today?'

'Nope. Got fired yesterday.'

My mother shoots me a surprised, worried glance. 'Sit down. I want a word with you.'

I sit and she puts a bowl in front of me. 'Is this man really giving us the money?'

'Unless he backs out,' I say and pour some cereal into the bowl.

'What's his name?'

'Blake,' I reply pouring milk.

My mother sighs. 'Are you purposely making this hard?'

'All right. His name is Blake Barrington.' Casually I sprinkle two spoons of sugar on my cereal.

'Barrington?' My mother's forehead creases into a frown. 'Why is that name familiar?'

I finish chewing before I answer. 'Because it's that famous banking family,' I mumble, and quickly spoon more cereal into my mouth.

My mother gasps and sits on the chair opposite me. There is something in her eyes I have never seen before. 'How long have you been seeing him?'

'I met him yesterday.' More cereal gets immediately shoved into my mouth. I want to end this conversation as soon as possible.

'You met him yesterday and he agreed to give you fifty thousand pounds.'

'Mmnnn.' I make a production of munching.

'Why?'

'Guess it must have been love at first sight.'

My mother's eyes narrow dangerously. 'Is there something you are not telling me, young lady?'

'Nope. The rest are all gory details,' I dismiss cheerfully.

But mother is not put off. She is like a hound that has scented blood. 'How old is he?'

'I didn't ask, but he didn't look a day over thirty.'

'So he's not an old man?'

'Definitely not.'

'When do I get to meet him?'

I slip out of my chair with my empty bowl and go to the sink. 'Soon, Mum. Very soon,' I say, quickly rinsing the bowl and spoon.

My mother sits at the table as still as a statue. 'Does Jack know?'

'Jack?' I turn to face her. 'We're not boyfriend and girlfriend, you know.'

'I know, I know but…'

'But what?'

'Well, I always assumed you'd end up with him.'

'We don't feel that way about each other.'

She sighed. 'You just seem so right for each other. I always dreamed that he'd be my son-in-law.'

'Since when?'

'You could do a lot worse than him, Lana. He's tall and handsome and he'll be a doctor soon.'

'I'm not marrying Jack, Mum. He's like my brother.'

'The path of true love is not always smooth,' she insists stubbornly.

I go into my bedroom, put the orange coat on a hanger, pick up the orange shoes off the floor, and go out of the front door, saying, 'Popping over to Bill's.'

Seven

The door next to our home is open and I enter it without knocking or calling out. The air is full of the smell of bacon cooking. A big woman wearing a faded apron in the kitchen shouts out to me.

'Morning, Jane,' I greet and take the blue stairs two at a time. Billie has been my best friend since we were in primary school, and I have been taking these stairs all my life. I don't knock on Billie's bedroom door, but enter and shut it behind me.

Billie's room has exactly the same view and dimensions as mine but it has been done up in myriad colors and is perpetually messy. When it is clean, it reminds me of a piece of modern art. I hang the orange coat on a hook behind the door, open a cupboard, put the shoes inside and close it. Then, I carefully sidestep over a mess of clothes and a pizza takeaway box to sit at the edge of the single bed.

Billie has her head buried under a pillow. She was born nondescript with pale eyes and mousy brown hair and given the equally nondescript name

Jane, but when she was eleven years old she reinvented herself. She turned up in school one day, her hair bleached white and turned into an Afro.

'Why have you done *that* to your hair?' the bad, white boys taunted.

'Because I *like* it,' she said so coolly and with such confidence that their opinion no longer mattered. She became a law unto herself and changed her name to Billie knowing that it would be shortened to Bill. Then she found a tattooist in Kilburn High Street, who agreed to tattoo a spider on her left shoulder.

'Wouldn't a butterfly have been better? Spiders are so creepy,' her mother worried. But more and more spiders crawled onto her back, down her thin left arm, and eventually a few small but intrepid ones began to climb up her neck. Now Bill Black has given up the Afro, but her hair is still dead white and her lips perpetually crimson.

'Wake up, Bill,' I say.

Billie mutters something. It sounds very much like fuck off, but I know to be persistent.

'I've got something to tell you,' I say, and shake her shoulder firmly.

'What time is it?'

'Nearly ten.'

Billie extracts her crown of white hair from under the pillow. 'This better be good,' she grumbles and hangs her head off the side of the bed with her eyes still shut.

'Come on, Bill. I've only got thirty minutes.'

'Pass me a fag,' she mumbles, and makes a silent snarl with her lips. I take a cigarette out of a box I find by the bedside, light it and put it into the curve of her snarl. She inhales lustily.

I stay silent until Billie has sat up, propped up some pillows behind her, and is leaning back against them. 'OK,' she says, 'did you do it?'

I nod.

Billie's eyes pop open. 'Whoa.... You did....? And you got the money?'

I grin.

Billie almost chokes on her cigarette. 'I don't believe it! The fat bastard agreed to cough up fifty grand?'

'Actually, it wasn't him.'

Billie holds a palm up. 'Back up, back up. What?'

'OK, I did ask him, but he turned out to be a total perv; you won't believe what his idea of a good time is. Fortunately, someone else cut in and offered double what I had asked him.'

'Bloody hell!' screams Billie.

'Keep your voice down,' I whisper. 'Your mother's in the kitchen.'

'Double, as in a hundred thousand pounds?'

I nod a lot.

'So who is this guy then?'

'Have you heard of the Barringtons?'

'Who?'

I walk to the laptop sitting on Billie's messy desk and, flip it open. When the familiar Google emblem pops up on the screen I type in Blake Barrington.

As the page starts to load I carry the laptop over and hold it out to Billie. Billie grinds out her cigarette in an overflowing ashtray and takes it wordlessly.

She whistles low and long and looks up at me with shining eyes. 'Oh! Mr. Bombastic, call me fantastic. I thought all the best-looking males were gay?'

I blush. 'Pick the Wikipedia entry,' I advise.

Billie hits the Wikipedia link and proceeds to read aloud from the screen.

'The Barrington banking dynasty, also referred to as the House of Barrington is one of the world's oldest existing banking dynasties with a history spanning over four hundred years. The family is descended from Lord John James Barrington.

'Unlike the courtiers of earlier centuries, who financed and managed European noble houses, but often lost their wealth through violence or expropriation, the new international bank created by the Barringtons was impervious to local attacks.

'Their strategy for success was to keep control of their banks in family hands through carefully arranged marriages to first or second cousins. Similar to royal intermarriages, it allowed them to maintain full secrecy about the size of their fortunes. By the late nineteenth century, however, almost all of the Barringtons had started to marry outside the family into other great, old families.

'The family is renowned for its vast art collections, palaces, wine properties, yacht racing, luxury hotels, grand houses, as well as for its philanthropy.

By the end of the century, the family was unparalleled in wealth and luxury even by the richest royal families.

'The Barringtons are elusive. There is no book about them that is both revealing and accurate. Libraries of nonsense have been written about them. An author who planned to write a book entitled *Lies About The Barringtons* abandoned it, saying, "It was relatively easy to spot the lies, but proved impossible to find the truth."

Billie pauses and lets her eyes skim down the screen. 'Well, the rest seems to be stuff about their international investment banking activities, the mergers they have been involved in, and is as interesting as a man in a wet T-shirt. Yup, and more shite here about them being one of the oldest institutions operating in the London Money Market.'

Billie yawns hugely.

'It just goes on and on about their...hedging services...worldwide assets...Boring, boring...Holding companies...Swiss registered. Boring, boring, primarily a financial entity but...largest shareholders in the DeBeers...a virtual monopoly of quick silver mines. Ah! Here is something a little more meaty. In 2008 the group had one hundred billion in assets! God! Can you imagine having that kind of money? No wonder the great, great grandson is spending it like water.

'Oh look. Some pictures. Wow! Get an eyeful of how the rich live.'

She turns the laptop around so I can look at the images as she scrolls down.

'Just some of their chateaus, palaces, castles, garden-mansions and city houses. Wow! Look at this one in St James' Park.'

There is silence for a while as we gaze in wonder at the photos.

'Do you think you will get to visit any of these places?'

'Definitely not. I have to sign a confidentiality agreement.'

'Still, it's an unbelievably exciting prospect, isn't it? Just don't fall for him.'

'I won't,' I say confidently.

'Let's skip back to Google and go to about... page three...and see what the conspiracy theories have to say about this august family. Oh dear... blood-sucking crew.

"If my sons did not want war, there would be none." His grandmother said that. Very nice."

Billie shuts the laptop. 'OK, quite enough of this. Let's not spoil a good thing. Let's celebrate your total brilliance, instead.'

I open my mouth to protest. I know exactly what Billie means by celebrate.

'Aaa-aaa...Don't say another word,' she says, reaching under the bed to pull out a bottle of vodka. She opens the drawer of her tiny bedside table and rummages around until she finds two dirty shot glasses. She puts the two glasses on her bedside table, which is marked with leftover circles from other vodka full glasses. These glasses will make new moons that overlap the other moons.

She fills them to the brim and holds one out to me.

I laugh. 'So early in the morning?'

'Are you kidding? This is an un-fucking-believable turnaround. You go out of here in borrowed plumes to snare a fat bastard and you come back with not just the most eligible bachelor on either side of the Atlantic, but the son of the richest family on earth. You've pulled off the deal of the century, girl. We have to celebrate,' she says firmly.

'I haven't pulled him, Bill. He wants to have sex with me in exchange for money.'

'So? Would you rather be having sex with the hunk or the perv?'

I say nothing.

'Look, I know you are into that deluded saving yourself for the special guy nonsense, but honestly, love, you really are getting too old to be playing virgin. Every puss needs a good pair of boots otherwise it shrivels up and dies.'

I smile. 'You don't have one.'

'Ah, but I have Mr. Rabbit. Nothing dies while he is around.' She opens the second drawer of her bedside cabinet to expose her huge and colorful dildo.

I gasp. 'With your mum in the next room?'

She shrugs. 'I use it when she's at the supermarket.'

I take the proffered glass, still shaking my head at her total lack of inhibitions. We clink glasses.

'Here's to…' Billie grins wickedly. 'Hot sex with anyone.'

We down the vodka and Billie thumps her chest. So early in the morning the alcohol has an immediate effect on me. Heat spreads quickly through my veins and makes me feel light-headed. The future seems exciting suddenly.

Billie's mother yells, 'Breakfast is ready,' from downstairs.

Billie lets her head hit the pillow behind her in disgust. 'God, she does my head in. If only she wouldn't do that. Every fucking morning she goes on about breakfast. You'd have thought after nineteen years she'd know I don't eat that shit.' She twists her body and reaches out to the little cupboard under the drawers of her bedside cabinet and takes out a jar of strawberry jam and a spoon. She unscrews the lid and feeds herself a spoonful of jam.

I open my mouth.

'Don't say it,' Billie warns.

'I won't, but really, Billie, your mum's right. How can you eat jam for breakfast?'

'For the one thousandth time because it's *delicious.*' She spoons another mouthful in, and commands, 'Now, tell me every inappropriate thing that happened last night. Don't leave a single thing out.'

I tell her everything except for the kiss, which I myself cannot quite make sense of yet and cannot bring myself to talk about. Billie's eyes alight on the orange coat and she smiles smugly. 'I told you the dress and coat were lucky. This is what you wanted, right?'

'Yeah, it's what I wanted. More than anything else in the world. You're still OK to travel with my mum, aren't you?'

'Of course. I love her too, you know.'

'Thanks, Bill.' My voice breaks.

'Don't thank me. I'm going on an all expenses paid trip to America! Yee…haa…'

'I don't know what I'd do without you and Jack.'

'Talking about Jack, what and when are you going to tell him?'

I sigh. 'Everything, this weekend.'

'He won't be happy.'

'I know, but he'll understand. I've got no choice, Bill.'

'I know, babe.'

'Bill, thanks again for agreeing to accompany my mum. I really don't know what I'd do without you.'

'There's a big, black car parked outside,' Jane hollers.

Billie leap-frogs to the end of her bed and, standing on her bed with her palms resting on the windowsill, cranes her neck to look out into the street below. 'Jesus, Lana, that's a Bentley with a driver in a peaked cap.'

I look at the clock face. 'That'll be my ride. Got to go. Call you later.'

Billie sits on the windowsill, exhales and, through the smoke says, 'Say hello to banker boy for me, won't you?'

I run down the stairs and find Jane standing at the bottom of them. Her round, red face looks quite animated. 'Is that car here for you?'

'Looks like it,' I say as I disappear into my own home. I pick up my rucksack, make sure my ID is in it, kiss mum goodbye, and run out towards the waiting Bentley.

Eight

The driver is standing outside the car by the time I get to it. He touches his cap. 'Miss Lana Bloom?'

I nod breathlessly.

'Good morning. Tom Edwards,' he says, by way of introduction and opens the back door for me. I sink into the fragrant, immaculately pale interior and he shuts the door after me. Along the building I see the heads of all my neighbors poking out of their windows.

I lean back. The leather under my palm is soft and cool. Tom gets into the front and looks at me in the rearview mirror. He has soft brown eyes that crinkle in the corners. He takes a white envelope from the passenger seat and twists around to hand it to me. 'Our first stop is the doctor. This is for him.'

'Thanks,' I say, taking the letter. It has my doctor's name written in blue ink and is unsealed. The glass that separates us closes and the engine hums into life. I open the letter and read it. It is a request for my medical records.

My mobile lights up.

'Hey,' says Jack. His voice is bright and full of life.

'Hey,' I reply matching his brightness.

'What's wrong?'

'Nothing. Why?'

'Come on…I know you better than that. Spit it out, Lana.'

'OK, but not on the phone. Are you coming down this weekend to see your mother?'

'Yeah.'

'Well, I'll tell you then.'

'No, you won't. I'll come by my mum's for dinner. You can tell me then.'

'I've got a date.'

There is a silence. 'Really? That's great. Anyone I know?'

'You don't know him, but you might have heard of him.'

'Well?'

'Blake Law Barrington.'

'*The* Blake Barrington?'

'Yeah.'

'You've got a date with a Barrington? How? What are you not telling me, Lana?' He sounds worried.

'It's not really a date, but I can't tell you on the phone.'

'You're not doing anything stupid, are you?' he asks apprehensively.

'No, Jack. I'm not. I'm doing the only thing I can do.'

'It's something to do with your mum, isn't it?'

'Yeah.'

'Oh! Shit, Lana. You didn't.'

'I did.'

'You're better than this.'

'Jack, my mum's dying. She's stage four. She doesn't have months to live. The doctors have given her weeks.'

'Oh, Lana. Can't we borrow the money?'

My laugh is bitter. 'Who can I ask, Jack? Jerry? And if I ask Jerry what will I need to do for the money?'

'What do you need to do for the money now?'

'What I am doing won't land me in prison. It's just sex, Jack.'

Jack goes silent.

'It won't be for long.'

'How long?'

'It's for a month.'

'That long?'

'It's a lot of money, Jack.'

'Don't give the shit a day more than a month.'

'I won't. I've got to go, but I will see you during the weekend. And thanks for caring about me.'

'It's just a bad habit.'

'Jack?'

'Yeah.'

'I miss you, you know.'

'Just be safe, Lana.'

'Bye, Jack.'

'Bye, Lana,' he says and there is so much sadness in his voice that I want to call him back and reassure him that it isn't so bad. I am not selling my soul, only my body.

In the doctor's surgery I pass over the envelope and am ushered into a room with the nurse who asks and performs the necessary blood tests with brisk efficiency. Afterwards, she discusses several options and recommends Microgynon.

'Take it from today. Since your last period ended two days ago you should be protected immediately, but just to be safe use a condom for the next seven days,' she advises. Twenty minutes after I entered that small blue and white room I have a prescription for three months' supply of contraceptive pills.

The receptionist has an envelope for me. It is addressed to Mr. Jay Benby. This letter is sealed.

I thank her and go outside. Tom jumps out of the car and opens the door for me before going around the back of the car and getting into the driver's seat.

'If you give me the prescription, I'll pick it up for you while you are at the solicitors.'

For some strange reason I feel the heat rush up my throat.

'I have daughters your age,' he says kindly, and I lean forward and hand him the prescription. 'Thanks, Mr. Edwards.'

'No worries. And call me Tom.'

'Er...How long have you been working for Mr. Barrington?'

'Going on seven years now.'

'Is he...Is he a fair man?'

Tom meets my eyes in the mirror. 'He's as straight as a die,' he says, and by his tone I realize that he will volunteer no more than that. I turn my head and watch the people on the street.

The solicitor's offices are in an old building in the West End. I am surprised to note that it is not the slick place I expected. The hushed air of importance, mingled with an impression that nothing much ever happens here, makes it feel more like a library. A receptionist shows me into Mr. Jay Benby's room.

The room smells faintly of air-freshener. The carpet is green, his table is an old antique inlaid with green leather, and the old-fashioned, mahogany bookshelves are filled with thick volumes of law books. Behind Mr. Benby there is a dark, rather grim painting of a countryside landscape in a gilded frame. The painting is so old that the sky is yellow in some parts and brown in others.

Mr. Benby rises from the depths of a deeply padded black leather chair. His grip is very firm and his smile serves as a polite welcome. He is wearing a dark, three-piece suit and a red, silk tie. And his hair—what little is left of it—has been carefully slicked back.

He waves his hand towards one of the chairs in front of his desk and I see that he is wearing a ring with a large, opaque, blue stone on his little finger. It strikes me as incongruous. I remember a story my mother once told me.

He was rich and wore a turquoise ring from Nishapur on his little finger.

Everything else about Mr. Benby and his office says, *Trust me. I'm good for it.* The opaque ring alone screams, *I'm a liar.*

After exchanging brief pleasantries he pushes a stapled, thin bunch of papers towards me. 'Here is your contract.'

I look at it. *Consensual Sexual Acts and Confidentiality Agreement.*

'You are within your rights to take it home, read it yourself and if you prefer, get your own lawyer to look at it, but no amendments can be made to it.'

I bite my lip and eye the contract. 'Can you show me where it says I will receive the hundred thousand pounds?'

He appears surprised. 'Of course.'

His kind obviously don't talk about money openly. They just bill you. He turns the contract to its second page and puts a clean, blunt finger to the clause that I was asking for. And I see that it clearly states that I will be paid the sum as soon as I sign the contract. I look up at Benby. 'Do you have a pen?'

His eyebrows rise. 'Don't you want to read it first?'

I shake my head.

He looks at me disapprovingly. 'This agreement has been drawn up so there is never any…

misunderstanding. You must be fully aware of the gravity and nature of the contract you are about to sign and agree to abide by its conditions. There are some clauses in there that are of utmost importance.'

'Like what?'

'The most important being the confidentiality understanding. This clause means that you will never be able to write a book, sell your story, or reveal any personal details about Mr. Barrington or his family. There is no information, even outside of sexual activities, that may be revealed to anyone. Not even friends or family. You can never bring a guest to the apartment you will share with Mr. Barrington. This clause applies to family, friends and acquaintances. In the event that they reveal anything, you will be held liable.'

He stops and flips the pages of the contract.

'Please pay particular attention to this section,' he says stabbing a stubby finger on the paper. 'It expressly prohibits any form of recording device while in the company of Mr. Barrington.'

I nod.

He clears his throat. 'And you must practice some form of birth control. In the event that you get pregnant you must terminate the pregnancy immediately.'

I stare at him. What kind of people are these?

Undaunted by my astonished face the lawyer carries on talking, 'You must understand that this contract is binding. At the dissolution of your relationship you will not receive anything more than is already stipulated in this contract. Other than the agreed sum you will not seek further financial gain, notoriety or advancement in any form as the result of this relationship. Breach of contract or failure by yourself will result in immediate termination of the agreement, and in the case of breach, the offended party may seek all remedies available at law or in equity. This section shall survive termination of this agreement and remain in effect for the rest of your life.'

'Fine.'

'One more thing. Mr. Barrington wanted me to emphasize that the contract will be for three months.'

'I thought it was going to be for one month?'

The lawyer's face does not change. 'Your services will be required for the period of three months.'

I press my lips together. I was very drunk last night, but I am sure he said one month. 'Can I speak to him?'

'Of course.' He picks up the phone and speed dials his client's number. 'Mr. Barrington, Miss Bloom would like to have a word about the length of the contract.' He pauses to listen to something Blake says. 'Yes, she has.' Then he passes the phone to me and quietly leaves the room. I wait until he closes the door before I speak. I am dismayed to hear my voice sound uncertain and timid.

'Hello, Blake.'

'Hello, Lana.' His voice is different than I remembered. Colder: he seems a total stranger.

I swallow. 'About the duration of the contract. The lawyer says…' I begin.

'Sorry, Lana, but that is not negotiable,' he says, not sounding sorry at all.

'Oh.'

'Was there anything else you wanted?'

'Er…No.'

'Well, have a good day then, and I will see you tonight.'

There is a click and the line goes dead. I replace the phone slowly. It dawns on me then that Scott Fitzgerald was right—the rich are different. They are unashamed by their ruthlessness. The lawyer, who must have been watching an extension light, walks into the room.

'All sorted out?'

'Yes. Where do I sign?'

'You do realize that you will have to read it at some point as there are other clauses than the ones we have discussed in there that you must adhere to.'

'Yes.'

'Do you acknowledge that you have received, read and understood the terms and conditions outlined, and agree to abide by the said terms?'

'Yes.'

'All right,' he drawls and looks at me expectantly. And I realize he has opened the contract up at the last page.

'Sign here.'

I sign. My hands are dead steady.

'And date it here.'

I date it.

He opens another contract. 'Sign and date again, please.'

When I raise my head he is watching me steadily. He smiles coldly. It occurs to me that he believes his dealings with me to be beneath him. I am expensive trash. He has thoughts about me that are supremely unflattering.

'Well, that's that, then. Here is your copy.'

He presses a buzzer that brings his secretary. 'Helen here will take your bank details and tell you everything else you need to know.' He half stands and holds his hand out. 'Thank you, Miss Bloom. Please do not hesitate to call me if you have any further queries.'

In the back seat of the Bentley, I find a Boots bag and inside it my prescription. I ask Tom to stop at a cash machine. I pop my debit card into the hole in the wall and can hardly believe it. One hundred thousand and thirty-two pounds, seventy pence. By heaven!

Nine

'Hi, I'm Fleur Jan,' the publicist says, coming forward, her hand held out to me.

'Hi,' I greet with a smile.

Fleur's eyes are very large, a much deeper blue than mine, and are enhanced by false eyelashes that she bats with great effect. Her hair is cut very short around her lovely face. Dressed in a brown pencil skirt and a pink top she is effortlessly chic.

'What we will be doing today has nothing to do with publicity for the company, but Mr. Barrington knows how much I love shopping so he asked if I wouldn't mind going shopping with you. Of course I said yes,' she explains with a twinkle in her eyes.

'Cool,' I say, some of Fleur's enthusiasm already rubbing off on me. Fleur is a good change after the drawling Mr. Benby.

'Mr Barrington mentioned formal attire, beachwear and a pair of new trainers.'

I nod. Wow, he remembered the trainers. The man is thorough, I will give him that.

'Do you want a coffee or tea or shall we hit the road?'

'Hit the road.'

We walk together to the lift. Fleur calls it and turns to me. 'Do you have any specific shops or do you want to leave it to me?'

'You decide everything.'

And that turns out to be an excellent decision as Fleur proves to be an expert shopping companion. She knows exactly where to go to get what.

Our first stop is Selfridges. Fleur guides me towards a cosmetics counter.

'This girl is a genius. She can make a chimp look sexy, so listen carefully to her advice,' she says about a sweet-looking lady standing behind the counter called Aisha.

I am popped on a high stool, given a hand mirror and taught how to make the best of my make-up.

'Have you ever tried wearing waterproof mascara?' Fleur asks smoothly. Her face is innocent, but it is clear that Blake has mentioned something about my smudged mascara.

Together the three of us choose two lipsticks, some sparkly eyeliner, cream blusher and waterproof mascara.

'Now to the perfume department,' directs Fleur. 'Something terribly exotic to go with your dark hair and gorgeous eyes.'

Afterwards, Tom drops us off at the front entrance of Harrods. I have never been inside before, but Fleur seems to know her way around, and we quickly make for the first floor where we pick up what Fleur calls the basics: a white blouse and plain black trousers. We walk out of the side entrance of Harrods on the east side and enter Rigby and Peller. Fleur has made me an appointment for a fitting. The woman who calls me into the changing room is middle-aged with large strong hands.

'Most women are walking around in the wrong bra size,' she says, and makes me bend over while she fits me with a bra. It turns out so am I. I am not a 34A but a 32B. When I have chosen the designs I want Fleur flashes her company credit card.

'Now let's go get the good stuff,' she says, batting her eyelashes.

'How much are you allowed to spend on me?' I ask curiously.

'Actually,' she says, 'Mr. Barrington didn't see fit to set a limit.' She winks conspiratorially. 'So we make hay while the sun shines.'

We walk around the back of Harrods and down Old Brompton Road. Fleur is a mine of information. She knows everything about fashion, what's so in, what's so out, what's in if you are not really in, what gets the best second-hand prices when you want to flog it.

She suggests a beautiful red and silver handbag in Gucci. 'To die for,' she says.

'It is a limited edition. Pure crocodile skin,' explains the snooty-faced sales assistant helpfully.

'OK,' I agree, bewildered by the price tag. I stand by the counter while Fleur pays and wonder what sort of reception I would have received if I had come here alone.

'Let's go,' Fleur sings merrily.

Then I am being led into Chanel. All my life I have dreamed of owning a Chanel bag. Once someone gave me a fake Chanel bag for Christmas and I waited until a reasonable time had passed before giving it away to a charity shop. If I can't afford the real thing I don't want to pretend.

Fleur is clever. It is as if she understands; here her suggestions are unnecessary. All she says is, 'Choose.' I feel I am in Aladdin's cave. It is impossible to choose, but in the end I pick the classic black with the leather interlaced gold chain strap. When Fleur goes to the counter she says, 'And we'll have that pink one too.'

'That's nearly seven thousand pounds!'

'Yes, but we have no limit. Besides, every girl needs a pink handbag. What else can you carry when you want to dress in white?' Fleur argues reasonably. She phones Tom to come and pick up the packages.

Almost in a daze, I am led into and out of a string of designer boutiques. Most of the shop assistants seem to recognize and head for Fleur immediately.

'Cupboard love,' Fleur dismisses, as they flutter around her with accommodating smiles. 'I am often here helping the wives of our high profile Middle Eastern clients spend their money.'

Fleur seems very sure of exactly what will look good on me. We buy a cream and gold suit, a red cocktail dress; a backless, sequined, black evening gown, and a sleeveless signature dress from Pucci, and of course shoes to match. Fleur decides that I will need a black pair of court shoes for the trousers, dainty diamond-studded stilettos, two tone sandals, tall brown boots, and multi-colored, ultra fashionable platforms.

'Right, we are almost running out of time, but first a quick trip to Versace. Versace can be too gaudy and whorish, but this season they have something that I think will suit you perfectly.'

That something turns out to be an electric blue silk shirt that is almost the same color as my eyes and skin-tight black leather trousers.

'Exactly as I thought—fantastic,' she says, pleased with herself. She looks at her wristwatch. 'Perfect timing. Let's have some tea.'

Once again Tom comes to collect the packages, and we find ourselves a table in a French patisserie full of women. We order cream tea. I bite into a buttered cream and jam filled scone ravenously.

'It is wonderful that you can eat so much and still be so slim. I have to be careful,' Fleur says, sipping lemon tea and breaking off small crumbs of her croissant.

'Missed lunch,' I say, swallowing.

Once I catch Fleur looking at me with an unreadable expression.

'Do you have to do this often for Blake?' I ask.

'To be perfectly honest, I have never done this before or heard of Mr. Barrington asking anyone else to do something similar, and though I was flattered to be asked, I was also dreading it. I thought you would be a brash gold-digger, but you are an unassuming breath of fresh air. It has been a delight to take you around.'

After tea, Fleur and me climb into the Bentley and Tom takes us to a hairdressing salon that belongs to one of the top hairstylists in the country. We walk into the perfumed space and a young girl with bright red hair comes to greet and lead us into a private area. Two glasses of champagne arrive on a tray.

'Go ahead,' Fleur encourages. 'You'll be grateful for it when you are at your next appointment.'

'Why? What's next?'

Fleur smiles cheekily. 'Full body wax.'

My jaw drops when the celebrity stylist himself appears. He noisily air-kisses Fleur on both cheeks and does the same with me. Then he stands back to look at me thoughtfully. Tipping his head slightly to the side he reaches for my hair.

'Oh,' he exclaims, rubbing it between his fingers. 'Virgin hair. You have never bleached or permed it, have you?'

I shake my head.

'It is a sin to cut such hair. Come, come,' he says leading me to a single chair in front of a mirror and waiting while I sit. 'We will leave the length, but we will do something wonderful for this heart-shaped face. We will give it a fringe.'

He picks up his comb and scissors. When he is finished I can hardly believe what a difference a fringe has made. My eyes are suddenly enormous and my little chin now looks delicate and cat-like.

'Beautiful,' declares the stylist flamboyantly.

'Very beautiful, indeed,' agrees a smiling Fleur.

While Fleur is paying, I stare at myself in the mirror. It is truly amazing how much a fringe can change one's face. I look so different I almost don't recognize myself.

'This is where I say goodbye,' Fleur says from behind me. I turn around to face her. 'Tom will take you to the beauty salon where you have your last appointment. That over with, he will take you to the apartment where you will soak in a lovely bath and then you will dress in your new clothes. I believe you have a hot date at nine.'

'Thank you, Fleur.'

'The pleasure was all mine.'

'I don't know if we will ever meet again, but I'll never forget you.'

'Nor I you,' she says, and bending forward plants a light kiss on my cheek.

My next stop is in High Street Kensington. In an all-white salon an olive-skinned, middle-aged, barrel-like woman in a white trouser uniform with a clipboard, smiles and introduces herself as Rosa Rehon. Rosa is Spanish and has retained her thick accent despite having been in England for fifteen years. She shows me into a small room with a beautician's bed.

'Ever had a full body wax before?'

'No.'

'No problem. We use three different waxes here. For the longer hair, the medium length, and for the pesky short ones.'

The waxes are heating in three pots. Each one is a different color.

'Shall we do waist down first?'

'Will this hurt a lot?'

'Well, it depends on your pain threshold. Some people fall asleep while I am waxing them.'

'Really?'

Her pearly whites flash. 'Really. Pop on board. We will start with the legs.'

I reluctantly climb on the bed that has been lined with paper, and lie down.

Rosa paints a thin layer of warm wax on my calf and lays a strip of cloth on the wax. 'Ready?' she asks.

I nod and she rips.

'Ow,' I cry.

'The first one always hurts. The next one will be better,' she says.

She paints another layer of wax and, stretching my skin, rips it off.

'Ow,' I cry again.

'It gets better after a while,' she consoles unconvincingly, and launches into a monologue about how she and her husband have jam sandwiches every night while they are watching TV. 'Sometimes, on weekends we will turn to each other and say, "Shall we have another?" and we do,' she enlightens.

Despite a penchant for innocuous jam sandwiches, Rosa turns out to be a hair Nazi. She will not tolerate even the smallest hair anywhere. A painful hour later, I am red and hot and stinging all over. I have been asked to assume embarrassing positions so any stray hairs around what Rosa calls the bum hole can be ripped off.

'Why would anyone want to do that?' I ask.

'It looks prettier this way,' Rosa says, as she rips another offending hair out.

My reply is another cry of pain.

When it is all over Rosa squints at my face. 'I can do your eyebrows for free,' she offers. 'Eyebrows don't hurt at all.'

'Yes, I know. Some of your customers fall asleep.'

Again a flash of strong teeth. 'Well, shall I? I can make them look very beautiful.'

'OK.'

The Rehons have a son in art school apparently, and Rosa fills me in about him while she works on my eyebrows. When she is finished she applies aloe vera gel before bringing a round mirror and giving it to me. The skin looks red and a little swollen but Rosa is right—my eyebrows actually arch and frame my eyes rather fetchingly.

After that torture the manicure and pedicure are a pleasure. I watch the orange nail varnish that Billie so painstakingly painted onto my fingers and toes yesterday get wiped away. On the drive to the apartment I examine my French manicure and have to admit it is very pretty.

The car comes to a stop at a tall white building with a glass-fronted entrance.

'Here we are,' says Tom, switching off the engine.

Ten

The reception is plush with deep, cream carpets and chandeliers in every hallway. There is an Indian guard slumped behind a desk reading a newspaper in a foreign language who immediately straightens and stands to attention. Tom introduces me.

'Lana, this is Mr. Nair.'

Tom turns to Mr. Nair. 'This is Miss Bloom. She will be living in the penthouse for the next three months. Please ensure that she will be well taken care of.'

Mr. Nair smiles broadly. 'Certainly. That will be my number one priority,' he says in a strong Indian accent while shaking his head like one of those nodding dogs in the backs of people's cars. He turns to look at me. 'I am very pleased to meet you, Miss Bloom. Anything at all that you need, please do not hesitate to ask.'

We shake hands, then Tom accompanies me into the lift. He inserts a card key into a slot and hits the top floor button. I lean against the shiny cold brass handrail while the lift silently races upwards. When the lift doors whoosh open, he allows me to exit first, and then precedes me into the corridor. The corridor is thickly carpeted and tastefully wallpapered in beige and silver.

'There is only one other apartment on this floor,' Tom explains and opens the door. He deposits the shopping bags on the floor by the doorway. 'I will go and get the rest of your shopping and then I will show you how everything works.'

I close the door behind him and lean against it.

Wow! Just wow!

A long corridor with richly enameled walls seems to lead to a light-filled room. As if in slow motion I let my fingers trail on the cool, enameled surface as I walk down the deep white runner carpet towards the glorious light. With the evening sun pouring in, I stand at the doorway to what is the living room, and look at my surroundings in wonder. At the imposingly high ceilings, the amazing glass walls that lead to a wide balcony laid out with a table, chairs and potted topiary. At the mirrored wall that reflected the elegant silver patterned pale lilac wallpaper, the rich furnishings, and the deep-pile, white carpet.

It is so massive, so hugely extravagant and luxurious it is as if I have walked into a page of a glossy magazine. I turn when I hear the door opening.

Tom puts the rest of my shopping on the floor and walks towards me. 'Beautiful, isn't it?'

'Yes, very.'

He takes me around the spacious four-bedroom apartment and shows me how everything works. Which buttons on the remote cause the curtains to open and close and which one makes a gorgeous painting rise onto the wall to expose a TV screen. There are buttons for the shutters, buttons for working the wine cooler, buttons for the lights, the media room, and for the coffee machine. I nod and make sounds to indicate I have understood, but it hardly registers. The opulence overkill has numbed me.

'Any problems, just call the caretaker. The number is over there,' he says finally, indicating a card that has been placed on a side table near the front door.

'Thank you.'

'Be back for you at eight thirty. Mr. Barrington hates people to be late.'

'Don't worry, Tom, you won't have to hang around waiting for me. I'll be ready.'

I close the door, find my mobile, hit home, and wait for my mother's soft voice to answer.

'Hi, Mum,' I say brightly.

'Where are you?'

'I'm at Blake's apartment.'

'Oh! When are you coming home?'

I swallow. This will be the first time I will not return to my own bed. I know it will be difficult for my mother. 'Not tonight, Mum. I won't be home tonight, but I'll be there first thing in the morning.'

First she goes silent. Then she expels a soft sigh. 'All right, Lana. I will see you tomorrow. Be safe, daughter of mine.'

'See you tomorrow, mum.'

I walk down the enameled corridor and go into the main bedroom. It is very large with a huge bed. The décor is deep blue and silver. I kick off my shoes and walk barefoot on the luxurious carpet towards the bathroom. The bathroom is a green marble and gold fittings affair. There is a Jacuzzi bath and a large shower cubicle. By the washbasin, lush toiletries still in their packages, have been laid out for my use. I unwrap a pale green oval of soap and wash my hands.

Afterwards, I open cabinets and find them all empty. I go back into the bedroom and walk through to the walnut dressing rooms. The built-in wardrobes are all as bare as the bathroom cabinets.

So he does not live here.

This is a place purely for sex.

I walk out of the bedroom and head for the kitchen. It has been done up in sunny yellow with glossy black granite worktops and surfaces. There is an island in the middle and stools around it. When I was young I dreamed of such a kitchen. I perch on one of the tall stools, swivel around a few times, and hop off. I venture to a cupboard and open it. It is full of stuff—expensive stuff that is never found in my poor mother's cupboards. Tins of biscuits from Fortnum and Masons, Jellies from Harrods, French chocolates with fancy names. I take a few down and admire the exquisite packaging.

Then I shut the cupboard and turn towards the fridge. More exotic stuff: truffles, hand-made blue cheeses, gooseberries, cuts of dried meats, wild smoked salmon, a dressed lobster, caviar… The vegetable drawer is packed with organic produce. Even the eggs have blue shells. There are two bottles of champagne lying on their sides. I take one out and look at the label. Dom Perignon.

'Hmnnn…' I say into the silence.

Carefully, I peel back the foil and the wire that holds down the cork. Holding the bottle between my thighs I twist the cork as I have seen the waiter do, but it takes many tries, and when it finally pops out, I have shaken the bottle so much, it sprays everywhere.

I clean up with some paper napkins, and finding a glass in one of the cabinets pour myself a drink. Carrying the glass I go back into the living room, slide back the doors, and step outside. I stand there for a long while looking at the wonderful view of the park and surrounding area, but I can feel no joy in my heart. My thoughts are with my mother. Eventually I close my eyes and pray that all will be well.

I raise my glass to the sky. 'Oh, Mum,' I whisper, 'be well again.' Then I bring the glass to my lips and drink to my mother's health.

There is not enough time to try the Jacuzzi bathtub, so I have a shower. The showerhead is wonderfully powerful unlike the weak one I am used to. The shower invigorates me and I go through my shopping bags with some measure of excitement. The bruises from the night before mean that I am only able to wear the Versace silk shirt. I pull on the tight leather trousers that end at my ankles and slip on the strappy stilettos.

Then I do my eyes the way Aisha taught me to and paint my lips soft pink. I am so nervous my hands tremble slightly. Dressed, I go back into the living room and pour myself another glass of champagne.

At eight thirty sharp the bell rings.

Tom comes in with a large, flat cardboard box, which he carefully places on the side table. 'I was asked to drop this off for Mr. Barrington. You look beautiful, Miss Bloom,' he compliments awkwardly.

'Thank you, but will you call me Lana, Tom?' The champagne has made me feel light-headed and I smile at him mistily.

'Of course, Lana,' he says smiling.

The reception desk is no longer manned by Mr. Nair. A small, white man with beady, suspicious eyes is introduced as Mr. Burrows. He smiles politely, but distantly. This was a man who did not want to get involved with any of the occupants of the building.

After that Tom drives me to a private club in Sloane Square called Madame Yula.

Eleven

Blake cuts a dashing if remote figure at the bar. He is wearing an oyster gray lounge suit and a black shirt, and is even more disturbingly attractive than I remember. He stands when he sees me and I stop, frozen by his eyes. Neither of us moves. It is as if we are again in a world of our own. Just his smoldering eyes and my strong desire for more from him—what exactly I do not quite know. Then he breaks the spell by moving towards me.

'You look edible,' he purrs, his eyes lingering on the curve of my hips.

I blush and touch my bangs.

'I like the hair, too,' he murmurs.

'Thanks.' My voice sounds nervous and shaky.

He reaches a hand out to touch me and instinctively I pull away. I had not meant to, but my body has its own reactions to him.

He drops his hand and eyes me coldly. 'Look,' he says. 'We can make it a totally sex thing or we can dress it up a little and it will look pretty in the corner. It's up to you. It's all the same to me.'

Pretty in the corner. Strange turn of phrase. I study him from beneath my eyelashes. 'Dress it up a little,' I say.

'Good. Can I get you something to drink? A glass of champagne? You're partial to it, if I remember correctly,' he says, and leads me to the bar.

I look around the bar. It is decorated in dark wood and deep red curtains. It actually looks like an old-fashioned French brothel. 'I've already had two glasses.'

His eyebrows rise. 'You found the alcohol.'

'It found me. I opened the fridge and there it was begging me to drink it.'

His eyes twinkle. 'Yes, alcohol has a habit of doing that.'

'I'm hungry, though.'

'Let's get some food into you then.'

We are shown into a private booth. The sommelier arrives and I listen to Blake order a bottle of wine that I have never heard of, and realize that the poor and the middle classes have been conned into believing that Chablis, Chateauneuf-du-Pape, Pouilly Fume, and Sancerre are superior wines for the discerning, but the truly rich are imbibing a totally different class of drink.

He picks up the menu and my eyes are drawn to his wrists. They are so utterly masculine they make my stomach tighten.

'How was your day?' he asks.

'I don't want to sound ungrateful, because I really am *very* grateful, but why did you buy me so much stuff?'

He leans back in his chair. 'Did you have a doll when you were young?'

'Yes.'

'Did you make little clothes for her?'

'Yes.'

'Did it give you pleasure?'

'Yes.'

'Why?'

'I don't know. It was my doll and I wanted it to look good.'

'That is how I feel about you. You are my doll. I like the idea of dressing you the way I see fit. I want you to look good. Besides, I like that every stitch on your body has been paid for by me.'

I feel a frisson of electricity run up my spine. 'I'm not a doll.'

'To me you are. A living, breathing doll.'

'What happens in three months' time?'

'Did you eventually get bored with your doll and stop playing with her?'

'Yes.' My voice is soft. I know where this conversation is going.

'So will I and when I do I will put you aside as you did your doll.'

'Well, that's clear enough.'

'Good.' His face is expressionless. 'What would you like to eat?'

I look at the menu. There is fish and chicken. I hope he will order one of those. But there is also foie gras, which I'd rather die than eat. The waiter appears at Blake's side. 'Are you ready to order, monsieur?'

Blake looks at me enquiringly.

'I'm just going to have whatever you're having,' I say breezily.

'Mussels in white wine to start followed by the herb crusted lamb cutlets.'

'Pommes sables or pommes soufflé?' the waiter enquires.

I look blankly at Blake.

'Try the potato soufflé,' he says. 'You might like it.'

'OK, potato soufflé,' I agree. When the waiter is gone, I take a sip of wine. It must have been good, but I am so nervous I register it only as a cold liquid. 'So,' I begin, 'You are a banker.'

'And you have been on Google.'

'Wikipedia actually. I was curious. All my life I imagined bankers were thieves utilizing fractional reserve banking to create money out of nothing, and then they take your house and car and business when you can't keep up the repayments.'

'Ah, this is like all bankers are thieves, all lawyers are liars, and all women are whores.'

'I'd rather be a whore than a banker.'

'That's handy then. I'd rather be a banker who buys a whore.'

'Why do you need to buy a woman, anyway? With that flashy car of yours, they must be leaving their phone number by the droves on your windscreen wipers.'

'You were an impulse buy.' His eyes crinkle at the corners. I amuse him.

I look at his perfectly cut suit, his beautifully manicured hands, and the Swiss precision watch glinting on his wrist. 'There is nothing impulsive about you.' My eyes take in that delectable lock of hair that falls over his forehead. 'Other than your hair.'

He laughs out loud. I look at him. The man has lovely teeth.

'This might turn out to be a lot more interesting than I thought,' he says.

The mussels arrive in tiny, covered black pots. When Blake opens his I follow suit. The smell is maddeningly good, but I wait until Blake reaches for his utensils before I copy him.

'Bon appétit,' he says.

'Bon appétit,' I repeat.

The mussels are meltingly soft in my mouth.

'Good?' asks Blake.

'Very.'

But the portion is so small it is quickly gone. 'I don't understand something,' I say, daintily dabbing the corners of my mouth. 'How come the paparazzi never follow you around like they do other celebrities and eligible bachelors to expose all your escapades and wrongdoings?'

'For the same reason my family and the other great families are not on the Forbes richest list. We don't like publicity. Unless it is sanctified by us you won't see it in the papers.'

'Are you trying to tell me your family has that much power?'

'I'm not trying to, I'm telling you. It's easy when you control the media.'

'Your family controls the media?'

'The great, old families do. It is in our interest to work as a group.' His eyes glitter in the soft light. Suddenly his lips twitch. He leans back and flashes a smile. 'But enough about me. Tell me about yourself.'

'What do you want to know?'

'Other than the fact that you live on a council estate and don't earn enough, I know nothing at all about you.'

'That's not strictly true. You know I am AIDS free, don't have any sexually transmitted diseases, own a clean bill of health, am on contraceptives as of today, and have had a full body wax.'

His smile becomes a wolfish grin. 'How was the waxing session? Not too painful, I hope.'

'Not at all. You should try it sometime.'

He laughs outright. 'The day you pay me to have sex with you, I will.'

I don't smile back.

The lamb arrives. I look at my plate. Blood has eddied under the meat. I cannot eat that. I sigh inwardly. It will be vegetables and potato again.

'Where do you get your unusual coloring from?'

'My grandmother on my mother's side was Iranian. The hair is from her and the blue eyes are from my father's side of the family.'

He lets his eyes wander around my face, lingering on my mouth. 'Have you been to Iran before?'

'I went once as a child, but it is my dream to take my mother back there.'

'It's dangerous there now.'

'For you maybe, but not for me or Mum it isn't.'

'Still, don't you think you should wait until all this talk of war is over?'

'There will be war. It is better to go now, before Iran becomes another Iraq or Libya.'

'What was it like when you were there?'

'When I went it was a wonderful place. We stayed in the desert. It was very beautiful. At night there was pure silence. And the sand dunes sing.'

'You can go to Saudi Arabia for sand dunes.'

'You don't understand. Isfahan is in our blood. I remember when my mother was leaving she climbed to the top of the steps of the plane, then she turned around and did this.' I open my arms out as if to gather something in the air and bring my arms back towards my face and kiss the tips of my fingers. 'I asked her what she was doing and she said she was kissing the air of her motherland goodbye. I remember thinking even then that I must bring her back to that beloved land of hers.'

'I've never been to Iran.'

'Of course you haven't. Iran doesn't have a central bank. My mother says it is why the world wants to wage war with it.'

'Does she also believe Elvis is still alive?'

My eyes flash and I glare at him. 'We can dress this arrangement up and play it any way you want to, but don't you dare criticize my mother. Even the dirt at the bottom of her shoes is better than you,' I cry passionately.

He gazes at my flushed cheeks and glittering eyes without anger, almost speculatively. 'You brought her up,' he says softly.

My anger subsides as suddenly as it came. 'Yes, I did,' I agree flatly, and must have looked as lost and as naïve as I felt for he reaches out to cover my hand with his. I pull mine away.

He takes his hand back to his end of the table and looks at me coldly. 'OK, have it your way,' he says, and looks for the waiter.

A waiter appears almost immediately.

The waiter looks at my plate. 'Was everything all right, mademoiselle?'

'It was fine. Just not hungry.'

'Perhaps you have left some space for dessert?' he suggests with a tilted head.

I shake my head and the waiter looks at Blake. 'Monsieur?'

'Just the check.'

'Of course,' the waiter says with a nod, and raises his eyebrow to another waiter hovering by a pillar. The man comes and begins clearing away the plates.

The bill is presented discreetly in a black wallet and Blake drops his card into it. When his card comes back, Blake says, 'Shall we?'

He stands and, with his hand on the small of my back, leads me out.

Twelve

The drive is completed in tense silence. When we get into the softly lit apartment, Blake tosses his card key on the side table and turns to me. 'Money's in the bank?'

I nod.

'We're good?'

I nod again.

'I gave you what you need; now you will give me what I need.'

I nod, ashamed by my own rudeness. It was a deal and he did keep his side of it.

'I'll pour us a drink. Change into those and meet me in the bedroom,' Blake says, gesturing towards the flat box that Tom brought in and put on the side table earlier. Then he turns his back on me and walks down that beautiful corridor into the living room.

I take the box and turning into the first door in the corridor, make my way into the main bedroom. Someone has come in and turned on the bedside lights, and turned down the bed. I go into the bathroom and close the door. Inside the box are wisps of lace and silk. I take them out.

A little dress in some transparent white material, an all lace bra, a thong, suspenders and silk stockings and a pair of platform shoes very similar to the ones I was wearing the night we met. Except for the fine baby blue ribbons on the suspenders, everything is in pure white. I glance at the size on the bra.

Of course. 32B.

I slip out of my clothes and get into the bra and suspenders. Then I carefully pull on the stockings. I have never worn suspenders before and the little hooks are fiddly and take me a long time. I hear a noise in the bedroom. Blake has already come in. Nervously, I pull on the lacey white knickers and look at myself in the mirror. I can hardly believe it is me. I rinse with mouthwash, take a deep breath and, opening the door go into the bedroom.

And just stand there staring, my heart crashing against my ribcage.

Good God! He is lying shirtless on the bed, propped against pillows, all sexy and toned and... and bristling with animal magnetism. There is not an ounce of fat on that sleek body. This is definitely not a man who imbibes Hobnobs. His legs are crossed at his ankles and his eyes are hooded. There is no expression in his face and no way of knowing what he is thinking. There is also something very bad and exciting about being in that lush bedroom with a cold, cold banker who has paid for you.

'Come closer,' he invites.

Clubland chart music is playing in the background. 'Give Me a Reason' by Pink and Nate Ruess comes on. Pink is singing, *Right from the start you were a thief. You stole my heart. And I your willing victim.*

I walk slowly into the middle of the room: my stomach is in knots: my mouth is dry: my eyes are saucers.

When I am two feet away from the bed, he says, 'Stop.'

I stop.

'Strip. Slowly.'

I freeze with shock.

He laughs. The sound is soft but carries some hint of cruelty. He is the cat playing with a mouse. From his position of dominance and control he says, 'I won't say relax, I'm not going to eat you, because I am.'

I straighten my back and step out of my platforms.

'No,' he commands. 'Not the shoes. Keep those on.'

Silently I step back into them. I can hear the blood pounding in my ears. No man has seen me nude. I untie the ribbon in front of the diaphanous dress and shrug. It slips off me, whispering and sighing.

For a moment I stand in my lacy underwear, suspenders and stockings.

Pink and Nate are belting out, *Just give me a reason. Just a little bit's enough.*

For a second I think of Billie saying every puss needs a good pair of boots, and I tell myself, sure, why not? It is just sex. I twist my hands behind my back and take my bra off. Let it dangle at the tip of one finger before I let it drop.

I see his chest rise with an indrawn breath, and I slip the fingers of both hands into the bit of lace and string and ease it slowly down my legs. I come up slowly resisting the urge to cover myself with my hands.

'You have a very, very beautiful body, Lana Bloom,' the man on the bed says. His voice is thick with lust.

We're not broken, just bent. And we can learn to love again.

I face his gaze again. His eyes are eating me alive. I have never seen hunger like that.

'Turn around.'

I turn around.

You're pouring a drink. No, nothing is as bad as it seems.

'Now spread your legs.'

We'll come clean. We're not broken, just bent.

I step outwards.

'More.'

I oblige. My calf muscles strain to hold the position in the high shoes.

'Bend forward.'

I bend.

'Touch the floor.'

I spread my fingers, lay them on the floor, and hear his gasp. For some long seconds I am bent forward, my legs spread far apart, and my ass high in the air. His eyes are a hot tingle on my exposed skin. The pose is blatantly demeaning. I should feel degraded and humiliated. Instead there is an unfamiliar heat between my legs. And my belly is clenched with feral excitement.

'Come here.'

I drop to my knees and crouching low, turn around. He is sitting on the edge of the bed. I stand and go to him. His strong hands span my waist and before I know it I am travelling in the air. I land on the bed with a slight bounce and a shocked gasp. On my back I watch him with widened eyes. His eyes are black and impenetrable. His body hard and big, the muscles rippling.

'I own you,' he says possessively. 'You're mine to do with as I please.' Then he pins me on the bed and I watch with even wider eyes as he takes off his trousers and steps out of his boxers, a truly magnificent creature.

I stare at his cock with fascination. It is thicker than my wrist and huge. Will it fit inside me? He picks up a condom by the bedside, tears it open, and puts it on. Then he bends over me, opens my legs and stares at my opened, freshly waxed pussy. I feel my body tremble with anticipation.

'What a beauty you are.' He runs his fingers along the slit of flesh. It opens out further. 'Like the petals of a pink flower,' he purrs.

I flush with excitement.

'Soaking wet.' He takes his fingers out and puts them in his mouth. 'And as I expected: sweet.'

My heart is hammering in my chest.

'You want this too,' he says so softly I have to strain to hear him. 'As much as me.' And I realize that he is right: I do. I want him as much as he wants me. I want from him what I have never wanted from any other man. I want him inside me, stretching me, possessing me.

I stare transfixed at his angrily throbbing, erect dick. I want all of that inside me. My hands come up and touch it. Rock hard but silky.

That small and tentative response from me drives him over the edge. 'Sorry,' he grates suddenly. 'I just can't do foreplay this time.'

He put his hands on either side of me and plunges into me. The shock of his sudden entry makes me cry out in pain. He hurt me. A lot.

He freezes. The ferocious lust is wiped away from his eyes. 'Fuck,' he swears, and pulls out of me.

I cannot help it. Tears well up in my eyes and escape down the sides of my temples. Ashamed to the core, I close my eyes.

'Why didn't you tell me?'

'You didn't ask,' I sniff, feeling incredibly stupid.

His hard length shifts and he sits facing away from me. 'It will be better next time,' he says, and without touching me or attempting to comfort me, stands and begins to dress. Rejected and defeated, I watch his strong V-shaped back, the beautifully proportioned buttocks, and the columns of his muscular legs as he shrugs into his shirt. He buttons it as he walks to the door.

He cannot wait to get away from me.

It is obvious that I am a great disappointment to him. I should have asked Billie for some lessons on how to pleasure a man. Instead I have lain there like a pillow and then worse still, I screamed when he entered me. I cover my cheeks with my hands. Oh, the shame of it. And this was what I saved up for. A fine mistress I was going to make. I hear the door close and I am all alone in that stupendous apartment.

Blake Law Barrington

I punch the button on the elevator and curse audibly. I am in a state of shock. It is unbelievable, but I never suspected that air of untouched innocence was not cultivated. I pull my hand down my cheek to my chin. I should never have been so rough. I treated her like a common prostitute.

Strange how badly I want to go back into that darkened bedroom and to kiss that trembling mouth. How much I want to wipe away those tears, take her in my arms and hold her until she falls asleep. But a larger part of me hates the way I feel. The sick pull she has on me irritates and angers me.

It is unnatural. I have been with hundreds of women, some as beautiful, and others sexually accomplished, but none of them have done this to me. I don't want to *feel* for her. I am glad I have left her body. Away from her essence I can think rationally.

Still I shouldn't have done what I did.

I got carried away and lost myself in what seems to be a growing and undeniable need to possess her completely. I don't exactly understand why, but whenever I am near her, I lose all my carefully cultivated 'cool'. All I want to do is drag her by the hair to my bed and fuck her until she is so sore she is screaming for me to stop. What I want is to have total control of her body. And why shouldn't I? I have paid for the privilege. The urge is strong now, I tell myself, but it will lessen with every single coupling.

She will never be more than a three-month itch.

A bottle-blonde is walking down the corridor towards the lift. The occupant of the other penthouse is an Arab sheik. I glance at her. She is wearing a tube top and white leggings. Her boobs are obviously fake, but she is beautiful in a hard sort of way. The way a mistress should be.

I think of Lana again. The way the helpless tears escaped. I had not expected that. I can't understand it. Why would a virgin be propositioning someone like Lothian for money? For the first time I wonder why she had wanted the money.

The lift arrives and I stand back to allow the woman to enter first. She has a good arse. She turns around in the lift and our eyes touch. We neither smile, but her mouth twists. The air becomes thick with her unspoken invitation.

I let my eyes travel down her body and convince myself Lana is not special. Even this one will do too. Nothing has changed.

I will marry Victoria. I take my phone out of my pocket and leave a text for my secretary:

Red roses—Lana.

White roses—Victoria.

Thirteen

Lana Bloom

'I'm baking a cake,' my mother says.

'You are?' There is a brightness in my voice. My mother only bakes when she is feeling good.

'Lemon, your favorite.'

'Oh good.'

'What time are you coming home?'

'I'm leaving now, actually.'

'Good. I want you to take a quarter over to Jack's mum.'

'OK. See you in twenty minutes,' I say and after putting a jar of blackberry jam, two tins of biscuits, and a box of fancy chocolates into my bag, leave the apartment. I take the bus to Kilburn.

As I am running up the steps I meet Jerry's sister who calls out, 'Heard you snagged yourself a rich boyfriend.'

'Not quite,' I reply, and before I can be bullied into a confessional conversation step aside, saying, 'Sorry, Ann, but got to rush.' I run past her taking the shallow steps two at a time. Already the curtain twitchers have spread the story.

I turn my key in our blue door and am greeted by the fragrant smell of my mother's baking. It is instantly familiar and dear. This is my home. My mother is at the kitchen sink washing dishes.

'Hey, I can do that for you.'

'No, I'm finished,' she says, turning the tap shut and snapping off her rubber gloves. She faces me, but her eyes, assessing, careful, and worried, change when she sees me.

'Oh my God!' she cries. 'Your hair. I can't believe how beautiful you look.'

I smile at her. 'I missed you yesterday.'

'Have you had breakfast?'

'Yeah. I brought some stuff for you.' I reach into my knapsack, bring out the tins of biscuits and chocolates and put them on my mother's small kitchen table.

My mother comes forward, but she does not touch the food. Instead she looks at me. 'Did you steal this?' Her voice is no more than a whisper.

'Mum!' I cry, shocked. 'What are you saying? Blake's secretary bought all this for me and I brought some back for you.'

She sinks weakly into a chair. 'Sorry. Sorry, Lana. Of course, you would never steal. I've just been so worried about you. Everything is so different. I don't know what to think anymore.'

The oven pings and she stands, but I push her down gently.

'I'll get it,' I say, and donning the oven gloves, take the cake out. It smells divine and is nicely risen. I close the oven door, put the cake on the metal rack and lean against the sink. 'Shall I put the kettle on? We need to talk.'

Mum nods and I set about making the tea. While the tea is boiling I lay cups and saucers. Everyone else in the estate drinks from mugs except my mother, who always uses a cup and saucer. I pour the boiling water into the teapot and carry it to the table. When the tea has brewed I pour it out into two cups. Then I open a tin of biscuits from Fortnum and Masons and hold it out to my mum. My mother's thin, pale fingers hesitantly take one. She bites into it and chews.

'Nice?' I ask.

My mother nods slowly.

'You're going to America on Wednesday, Mum.'

My mother puts the biscuit down beside the saucer. She links her hands tightly on the table and faces me. 'I'm going nowhere until I know exactly what is going on. Exactly how you are getting all this money? And what you are doing for it?'

'I explained last night. The man I am seeing has given it to us.'

'Who is this man who has fifty thousand pounds to spare?'

'Mum, he's a millionaire many times over. He gave me double what I asked.'

She stares at me aghast. 'You asked him for money? I didn't bring you up to ask strange men for money.'

'Yeah, I asked him and so what? I didn't force him or steal it.'

'Well, I don't want it. I'd rather shrivel up and die than use this dirty money.'

I stare at my mother in shock. Her face is set in the stubborn lines that I know mean that her mind is made up. It cannot be changed. I swallow the lump in my throat and stand suddenly. 'You'd make me an orphan for your stupid pride,' I accuse.

My mother blinks suddenly, the wind taken out of her sails.

'Are you going to sit there and tell me that if I was dying and had a few weeks left to live you wouldn't have asked a filthy rich stranger for a bit of money?'

My mother says nothing.

'High and mighty ideals and principles are all right when you are not utterly, utterly desperate, Mum.'

'You didn't just ask him, did you? Tell the truth. You prostituted yourself.'

'Assuming that I did. And I didn't.' I say a little prayer for my lie. 'Wouldn't you have done the same for me?'

My mother begins to cry softly. 'You don't understand. You will, one day, when you have your own child. I am not important.' She beats her chest with both her hands. 'This is just worm food. I won't have you sully yourself for this destroyed body. You are young. You have your whole life ahead of you and I am going to die, anyway.'

'No, you're not,' I whisper fiercely.

'But I am. And it's time you accepted that.'

'Remember when Daddy left and I swore to take care of you?'

My mother's eyes become bleak. 'Yes.'

'Would you have me break my promise?'

'I'm going for another bout of chemo on Monday.'

'What for, Mum? What for? That stuff is so dangerous it'll probably kill you before the cancer does.'

Her lips move wordlessly. Then she covers her mouth with one hand. 'Sit down, Lana,' she whispers. 'Please.'

I shake my head. 'No, I won't. What's the point? In all the time I was trying to find a way to keep you alive I never thought that it would be you that would stand in my way.'

I turn away from her and begin to walk out of the house. I have sold myself for nothing. I reach the front door and I hear my mother shout from the kitchen, 'Do you like him?'

I turn around and she is standing there, so frail and breakable my heart hurts. Now I can be truthful. 'Yes.'

'I'll go.'

I walk towards her.

'I'm sorry,' she sobs.

I take her poor wasted body in my arms and the tears begin to flow. Neither of us say anything. Finally, when I can speak, I choke out. 'I love you, Mum. With all my heart. Please don't leave me. You're my mum. I'd do anything, anything for you.'

'I know, I know,' my mother soothes softly.

'Oh shit,' I say.

'What?'

I step away from my mother, put my hand into my pocket and bring out bits of blue shell. 'I brought you a blue egg.'

My mother tries, she really tries hard, but a giggle breaks through. For a few moments I can only stare at the rare spectacle of my mother stifling laughter. Then I too crack up.

'Take that jacket off and go wash your hand,' my mother finally says. 'I'll make us a fresh pot of tea and we'll have some of those nice biscuits you brought.'

'They *are* nice, aren't they?' I agree, slipping my soiled jacket off and walking towards the sink.

I am wiping my hands on a tea towel when my mother says, 'And you'll have to bring that nice man—Blake Barrington, did you say—over to dinner.'

'Uh, yeah…When you get back from your treatment.'

My mother stops and looks at me. 'I'm going to meet that young man before I get on the plane and I'll have no more said on the matter,' she says firmly.

While we are having our tea I tell her about the appointment I have made for a wig fitting in Selfridges.

Unconsciously she puts her right hand up to her scarf. 'Oh,' she says. 'Will that be very expensive?'

I grin. 'We're not paying for it.'

And my mother laughs. For the first time in many months, my mother throws back her head and laughs. 'That's good. That's very good,' and while she is laughing she begins to cry. When I go to hold her, she takes a deep, steadying breath and says, 'I know what you have done for me. You have used your body as a begging bowl.'

For a moment I am struck dumb by my mother's perceptiveness. Then my great, great love for her intervenes and I lie and lie and lie. 'You only say that because you have not met Blake yet. He is beautiful and strong and kind. It was love at first sight. When I told him about you, he gave double what he knew I needed.'

My mother sighs. 'I pray to God that I will be alive for your wedding.'

I feel the hollowness spread through my body. It doesn't matter, I tell myself fiercely. So what if my mother will be disappointed? All that counts is she will be cured. I will forget this one in time and marry someone else, another who will not consider me so lowly that I am only fit to be hidden away like a dirty little secret. Someone with a beautiful heart like Jack.

Yes, someone like Jack.

Fourteen

I leave my mother's house and going past Billie's door run two floors down to ring Jack's mother's doorbell. While I am waiting for her to open the door I look down the railing, and see Fat Mary browning herself into an uneven shade of lobster.

Fat Mary is a big woman who lives in the corner downstairs flat and sunbathes topless in her garden, even though it is overlooked, by all the other flats in the block. Every Friday night she makes her hair big, stuffs herself into a tight dress and high heels, and goes to the Irish nightclub on Kilburn high street to find herself a bloke to bring home. Like clockwork they slip out of her door, all sheepish before lunch on Saturday.

All the little boys on bicycles always call out, 'Hey, Mary, how's your mary?' Her fat face never alters as she shows them her middle finger.

Jack's mother's face appears at the kitchen window. 'Oh, hello, dear,' she says with a smile, before she comes to open the door. She has the same beautiful eyes fringed by thick sooty lashes as Jack.

'Hi, Fiona. Mum sent you some cake.'

'How lovely. How is she feeling today?'

'It's a good day today.'

'That's good. Would you like to come in, dear?'

'Nah, I've got to run.'

'Well, you run along, then.'

'See you later,' I say and turning begin to walk away.

'Lana?'

I turn around. 'Yeah?'

Fiona hesitates and I hitch my bag higher up my shoulder and take two steps towards her. 'What's the matter?'

'I…um…heard…you…ah…found yourself… a…boyfriend. A rich boyfriend,' she says anxiously.

I shift from one foot to the other. 'I just met him, Fiona. I wouldn't call him a boyfriend just yet. It might not work out.'

Fiona's timid face falls. It is obvious she has been hoping that the rumor going around is not true. Her voice is very tiny. 'You will be careful, won't you, my dear? I wouldn't say anything normally, but you've always been such an innocent thing. And I thought to myself, even if I come across as an interfering, old busybody, I've got to say something.'

She takes a deep breath. 'You know, I've always said you are the most beautiful girl on this estate, if not in all of Kilburn, and you should have become a model, but rich men are greedy. One is never ever enough for them.'

I put my rucksack on the concrete floor and leaning forward hug the woman. 'Thank you for caring, Fiona. I don't know how I would have coped all these years if not for Jack, Billie and you.'

Fiona hugs me tightly. 'Oh, child, you are like my own daughter to me. What you did for Jack; I've never thanked you.'

I untangle myself from Fiona. 'What I did for Jack? It is I who should thank Jack. He's taken care of me and fought my battles since the day I arrived.'

'He will never talk about it, but the year you arrived was the year his father died, and he became quite unmanageable and surly. He'd taken up with a gang who stole, carried knives and drank alcohol across the railroads. I was afraid for him, afraid that he would turn out like all the other boys on the estate—jobless drunks and drug addicts. But then your family moved in and suddenly he changed. He took over the job of being your older brother, and suddenly I got my caring, beautiful son back and thanks to you he's going to escape this terrible estate and become a doctor.' Tears filled her lovely eyes.

'If I was useful to him then I am glad, because I don't know what my life would have been like without him.'

Fiona smiles proudly at the thought of her good son.

'I've got to go, but I'll be around tomorrow with a box of biscuits like you've never tasted before.'

'Oooo.'

I laugh. 'More like oo la la...They're French.'

'Goodbye, dear girl.'

I wave, and run up the stairs. My phone rings and I stop to answer it. It is Mrs. Arnold calling to say she has booked an eight thirty table for Blake and me at The Fat Duck. She reminds me to be ready by 7.30p.m.

'Thanks,' I say. I end the call and think, 'I've been reduced to another appointment in his diary.'

Halfway up the second flight of stairs I hear Kensington Parish call out to me. I pop my head over the side railing and see that he is standing at his bedroom window at almost eye level to me.

'What's up, Kensington?'

'Hey, Lana,' he says. 'Do you think your man will let me have a ride in that car of his?'

'Unlikely,' I reply and carry on running up the stairs even though I hear him shout pleadingly, 'Oh! Come on, Lana. You haven't even asked. It's a 0-77. It's custom made, Lana. Come on... Lana?'

Billie's door is open and her mother is outside watering her hanging baskets.

'She's in her bedroom,' she says, by way of greeting.

'Thanks,' I reply, and run up the worn blue carpet. I knock once and enter. Billie is using up a can of hairspray on her hair. The room is choking with the stuff.

'Jesus, how can you bear to breathe this stuff?'

'Open the window if it bothers you.'

I open the window and take a deep breath before facing the synthetic smell in the room. Thankfully,

Billie has finished. Her white hair has now been sprayed into a stiff man's pompadour that will survive a hurricane. She looks at her reflection with satisfaction. Then she turns away from the mirror, switches off her small telly, and goes to sit on the bed. She pats the space next to her.

I sit next to her and put my bag down.

'Well, spit it out then. What was it like?'

'It was awful.'

'What? Sex with the loaded hunk was awful?'

'Can we talk about it in a minute? I need to talk to you about some important stuff first.'

'No problems.'

'You are still OK to travel to the States with my mum, aren't you?'

'Of course. Are you kidding me? I'd never get another chance like this. All paid.'

'Good. I'll sort the tickets out so you travel out on Wednesday. And Mum has an entire day to recover before her appointment on Friday. You don't have to babysit her the whole time. Go out sightseeing and do the touristy thing. You'll have to accompany her to the doctor, though.'

'Cool.'

'Oh! Before I forget. I brought something for you.' I dig into my bag and fetch the jar of blackberry jam.

Billie takes it from me. 'Posh jam? Wow, I've never had anything like this before.' She reaches over, opens a drawer and gets a spoon. She twists open the lid and dips her spoon into it. 'Wow, you get to have awful sex and I get to go to America and eat jam from Harrods. Brilliant. How long is your contract for, again?'

'Three months.'

'Are you sure you can't increase it?'

'Billie, don't be such a witch.'

She spoons more jam. 'Can we talk about your awful sex now?'

'He left as soon as he found out that I had never been with anyone.' I shake my head with the shameful memory. 'I was pathetic, Bill. I lay there like a lemon.'

'How do you mean? Didn't you have sex?'

'Sort of. As soon as he entered I sort of screamed in shock. It was so sudden and...well, painful, and he pulled out double quick.'

'What?'

I bite my lip. 'He just stopped and left.'

'What do you mean left?'

'He got dressed and left.'

'And said nothing?'

'He said, "It'll be better next time."'

'Fuck me. He didn't finish?'

'No,' I say uncertainly. 'Is that very bad?'

'Bad! He sounds totally fucked up. Nobody stops halfway for no good reason.' She chews her cheek and leans forward eagerly. 'Tell me what happened before he did the deed.'

I squirm. 'Well, he had me dress up in a white frock with white underwear and white stockings.'

'Oh. My. God,' Billie hoots and begins to cackle madly. 'He wanted a whore that he could pretend was a virgin, but when he found he had the real thing in his bed he freaked out and ran away. That is so funny.'

'It's not, actually.'

Billie sobers with impressive speed. 'Sorry, yeah it's not.'

'Bill, will you teach me some techniques?'

'I don't know what I can teach you. I don't do cock, remember?'

Then she looks at my distraught face and grins. 'OK, let's start with foreplay. Foreplay waist up has to be pretty similar, right?'

'OK,' I agree.

'The ear is wickedly horny. All kinds of things can happen when it is given a bit of attention. Run your finger along the rim like this.' She runs her finger along the rim of her own ear. 'Sometimes you can lick your finger first and afterwards gently blow on the wet rim. But the best effect can be achieved if you nibble your way gently all the way down to the lobe and then suddenly stick your tongue into his ear. If done properly that should drive him crazy.'

'Really?' I say doubtfully.

'You should practice on someone else. I'd let you practice on me, but I might start to really fancy you and that would be too weird.'

'Are you serious?'

'When you brush your teeth in the mornings do you ever look at yourself in the mirror? You're fucking stunning, Lana. If I met you in a club, yeah, I'd jump your bones. How about trying it out on Jack?'

'No, Jack is pissed off with me. He doesn't say it, but he thinks what I've done is no better than what a prostitute does.'

Billie looks sideways at me. 'I admire you for what you have done.'

'Oh well, he doesn't.'

'He's just mad because he's always had this older brother, dead protective complex about you. But the truth is we are all prostitutes. Some women will put out for an expensive dinner, another for a ring on her finger, or a better lifestyle. You did it to save your mother. That's a whole lot better than the rest of us, I'd say.'

'Thanks, Bill.'

'Oh, there is another thing you can do to banker boy. You can tie him up! You'd need a metal bed or a four-poster, of course. This bed here would be useless. I once tied Leticia to her bed and it was real good. I told her to strip naked then I blindfolded her and trussed her to the four corners of the bed. And while she was lying there full of anticipation, I calmly told her I was going out to the shops to get some chocolate, and that I was going to leave her bedroom door open. God, you should have seen the way she begged and then swore at me.'

She chuckles gleefully. 'Her mother had said she would be back in twenty minutes, you see. I stuffed her knickers in her mouth and went out. Made sure to close the front door with a bang too.'

My mouth drops open. 'That was some chance you took. What if her mother had come back and found her tied spread-eagled and naked on her bed?'

'Nah, I had met her mother going up the lift and she told me to tell Leticia that she was going to the hairdresser after the shops and would be at least an hour.'

'Was Leticia mad at you?'

'Mad at me. She was quivering like a school dinner pudding. I stuck the Yorkie bar up her fanny and ate it off her. She said it was the best orgasm she's ever had.'

I laugh. 'Oh, Billie. Somehow I don't think he's going to let me tie him to a bed.'

'You can still try the blindfold. It increases the sensation when you can't see. You could suggest a game. Put the egg timer on and he who climaxes first loses. When it's his turn, blindfold him and give him the best sucking he's ever had.'

'OK, maybe, I'll try that.'

'Let me know how it goes, won't you?' Billie says with a smile.

I look at my watch. 'I've got to pop into the employment agency so they can tear a strip off me for inappropriately offering myself to one of their clients, but before I go; you know the extra money Blake gave me? I've decided I want you to have half.'

Billie's eyes widen. It takes a moment for her to find her voice again. 'I'll take the free trip and I'll take the jam, but I'm not taking the money.'

'Remember when we were kids and we used to say if we won the lottery we'd share the money. Well...Isn't this like winning the lottery?'

Billie smiles at me. 'This isn't the lottery. Besides, what would I do with money?'

'You could go get your boobs done.'

'Very tempting, but…'

'No buts. Do you want me to turn into one of those people who are generous only when they don't believe they will ever have the money? Would you give me half if our positions were reversed?'

Billie thinks and grimaces. 'To be honest I don't know what I'd do. I think I'm just like everyone else, I want to go out, get wasted out of my mind and have fun, but you've always been different. You used to save up to buy violets when you were a child and take the bus to see paintings in the National Gallery. That was probably why I was drawn to you then, even though you wore boring clothes and read the book instead of waiting for the movie version.'

'While you painted the toenails of your gerbil bright red…'

'Hamster,' Billie corrects, and laughs.

'Whatever. I know you're on the dole and can't show that you have too much in the way of savings so I've opened an account in my name at the Abbey and here's the card. Use it as if it is yours.'

Fifteen

I am fastening my hoop earrings when I hear someone at the front door. Stomach churning, I stand away from the dressing table and look at my reflection. I am wearing my Pucci dress. The colors look good with my hair and I know I have never looked so fine, but my heart is in my mouth. I am so nervous my hands are clammy. I wipe them and rub lotion into them. Then I slip into my beautiful new Jimmy Choos and leave the bedroom.

I turn into the paneled corridor and hear him in the sitting room. He is looking down on the lighted view of London and has not heard my footfalls on the soft carpets. It is only when my reflection shows in the glass that he turns.

The crease of his pants leg looks very sharp and his shoes are beautifully polished. My eyes move upwards. He is wearing a navy suit and an open soft blue shirt. My gaze travels to his brown, strong throat towards the deliciously straight mouth and up to his eyes; dark and hooded and so full of secrets.

They are watching me intently. My breath catches. The flowers he sent are behind him.

'Thank you for the flowers. They are beautiful.'

'Come here,' he says and half sits on the table behind him. His voice is very soft. There is something in it I do not understand. I am nineteen and he is a man of the world. I go willingly to him. He catches me by my waist and pulls me to him until I am trapped between his thighs. I feel the heat that comes off his body.

'I'm sorry,' he says. 'I didn't know.'

I shake my head, embarrassed. 'You weren't to know. It's my fault. I should have warned you.'

'You look very beautiful tonight.'

I blush like an idiot.

He watches me blush, making me blush even more, then runs his finger along my lower lip. 'Are you for real?' he whispers.

I look at him without comprehension. He wants to tell me something. But what? I don't understand him at all. We are worlds apart. Maybe I shouldn't try to understand. This will all end in three months.

Without warning the expression in his eyes changes. His mouth twists. Something cold creeps into his eyes. 'We'd better go or we'll be late.'

Feeling the change I step away from him. Now I truly do not understand. Hot and cold. Perhaps it is a game. But he will not beat me. I can survive three months. I think of my mother and say. 'Yes, we don't want to be late.'

He offers me the crook of his arm. His voice comes out hostile and clipped. 'Shall we?'

I bite my lip. Now he is inexplicably angry with me. Nothing makes sense. Why is he angry with me? Confused, I thread my arm through his and we leave the apartment.

The Fat Duck is nestled in the middle of the English countryside, in a place called Bray. The women are all dressed to kill and the men are in dark suits. I have never been anywhere so glamorous, but it is bitter sweet: I have lied to my mother. I am with this man as his whore. And all of this will come to an end in three months' time. A young man with a French accent settles us into a waiting area and offers us delicate little bites of food and two glasses of champagne. Waiters nod and greet Blake by name as they pass. Apparently he is well known in this establishment.

'They are called amuse-bouches, mouth amusements,' Blake explains and watches as I nibble on the tiny offerings of mushroom and hazelnuts with basil oil and salmon mousse.

'Well?'

'I don't think I've ever tasted anything so delicious in all my life.'

The sommelier comes to help select the wine that will perfectly complement the food we intend to have, but Blake knows exactly what he wants.

'The 1996 Clos du Mesnil.'

The sommelier seems pleased with Blake's choice. The wine is brought and presented to Blake. When he nods, it is uncorked and a small amount is poured into a deep glass and given to Blake. He swirls it, sniffs it delicately, and pronounces it acceptable.

A fifth of my glass is filled. I raise it to my lips and taste it. What passed for wine until now seem like abrasive mixtures of grape juice and vinegar. With complicated scents that delicately tease and a distinctively smooth taste that slides down my throat, the wine is truly splendid.

I study the menu with fascination. It is no wonder that this restaurant is so famous. It has a uniquely original menu. There is even something called the mad hatter's tea party with mock turtle soup, a pocket watch and a toasted sandwich. Then there is snail porridge, crab biscuits and quail jelly, chicken served with vanilla mayonnaise, shaved fennel and red cabbage gazpacho with mustard ice cream, and something else I can't recognize served with oak moss and truffle oil.

Blake chooses roasted foie gras to start. I sigh inwardly. I am not eating force-fed goose liver.

The waiter looks at me. 'I won't bother with a starter, thank you.'

Blake orders the lamb with cucumber.

'I'll have the same,' I murmur.

The waiter moves away, and Blake looks at me strangely. His eyes are pitying. 'You can't read, can you?'

My head tilts back. 'Of course I can. I am a qualified secretary.'

'What was I supposed to think? Jay told me you signed the contract without reading it and this is the second time you've ordered the same as me and you hardly touched your food the last time. Why?'

I decide to be honest. 'I don't know which utensil to use to eat what.'

He is so surprised, he leans back in his seat, and regards me quietly. Not taking his eyes off me, he raises a hand slightly. Immediately, a waiter comes to his side. 'The lady would like to see the menu again, please. And hold the earlier order.'

'Of course, sir.'

Blake carries on watching me until the waiter returns with the menu.

'Would you like a moment with it?' he asks.

'No,' I say. 'I know what I want. I'd like the mock turtle soup to start and the poached salmon.'

When he is gone, Blake says, 'With utensils always start with the ones that are furthest out from the plate and work your way in. I will help you.'

'Thank you.'

'So what have you done today?'

'Well, I got taken off the books for er...inappropriate behavior so I went off in search of another temporary agency.'

He frowns. 'I don't want you to work for the duration of our contract.'

'Why?'

'Because I want you to be available to me day and night. I might want to have you at three in the morning or between meetings in the afternoon,' he explains brutally, and I feel the most surprising sexual thrill clench at my lower belly. I want to be available to this man day and night!

'It should be no problem for you.'

'What's that supposed to mean?'

'Don't you live on an estate where nobody works and everybody just scrounges off the state?'

I shake my head in wonder. 'Wow, that's one sweeping generalization you've just made there!'

'Why, is it not true?'

'While I was a child growing up my teachers and the governmental offices where my mother had to go for her weekly handouts, in subtle and unsubtle ways, tried to force into me the opinion you have just expressed. That we were parasites.'

I look him in the eye.

'But I always knew there was something inherently wrong about any train of thinking that could so conveniently dismiss all the unemployed and dependent population as parasites. And yet we did seem to be living off others. Then one day I learned the true nature of the parasite and it changed my life.'

He raises an eyebrow. Arrogant sod!

I smile. It does not reach my eyes. 'I learned that a successful parasite is one that is not recognized by its host, one that can make its host work for it without appearing as a burden. As such it must be the ruling class in every capitalist society that is the real parasite.'

'How is my kind a parasite to yours?' he scoffs.

I take a sip of the wonderful wine that he has paid for. 'How much tax did your family pay last year?'

He leans back and regards me without flinching. 'We paid what was legally due.'

Now it is my turn to scoff. 'Let me guess. Almost nothing.'

He shrugs. 'There is nothing wrong with legitimate tax avoidance schemes. I don't see how we are being parasitical, because we won't let the government take what is hard won and rightfully ours, and pass it onto the bone lazy masses who don't want to work and expect others to fund their lifestyles. In fact, I'll go so far as to say the system in this country is mad. Girls have babies when they are teenagers so the government will set them up in a flat and pay them a stipend for the rest of their lives. Crazy.'

I shake my head slowly. 'Do you really believe what you are saying?'

'Of course. Do you think teenage girls getting pregnant to secure a home for life is right?'

Our food arrives. It looks more like a work of art than food. I reach for the rounded spoon that has been placed furthest away and Blake nods.

He picks up his knife and fork. 'I'm kind of waiting for your reply.'

'No, I don't, but we are not talking about badly educated teenagers from troubled homes who think that getting pregnant is the best way out of grinding poverty for them. The teenage pregnancies are a result of a system that has marginalized and refused a good education to the poorest sections of society. They are not parasites. They are desperate people who have been trained to think that that is the best they can get out of life. But your lot....'

'We actually keep the country going, creating jobs—'

'Sure, in China and other Third World countries. Slave labor jobs. Besides, you're a banker. You don't create anything.'

He shifts in his chair. 'Hang on, let me get this right; my family is parasitical for not paying astronomical taxes, and your lot are not parasites even though you don't work a day in your lives and live entirely on government handouts.'

'Have you ever thought that people can be poor by design. When a child is born on the estate, he is already doomed to repeat his father's life. He will bear that same angry, helpless attitude of his father and never amount to much. In school he will be taught only to be a good worker. And if he has even a bone of rebellion in him he will refuse and become a scrounger. My mother was educated in a different country and she was from the middle class so she taught me middle class values. Work, earn money, pay your own way.'

'So why do you work only part-time?'

'I do that because my mother is often sick and I am her primary carer.'

'What's wrong with your mother?'

'Cancer.'

'Oh.'

'She *will* make it,' I say forcefully.

He nods slowly. 'Are you a Muslim?'

I sit back and watch Blake while our plates are cleared away. The hard planes of his face have been softened. There is a mad desire in me to reach out and stroke his face. 'No, my mother is a devout Christian. I am an agnostic. So far no God has impressed me as benign and truly interested in the welfare of humans.'

'Main course,' announces the waiter, and plates are lowered onto the table.

My salmon is encased in a tiny square parcel made of liquorice gel, and looks almost too beautiful to eat. I lift the fish knife and cut it open. Inside, the fish is perfectly cooked. I slip a tiny morsel pass my lips, and am surprised by how delicate and silky it is on my tongue.

'I have a very big favor to ask you.' I say.

He raises his eyebrows.

'It is very important to me.'

'Sure,' he says.

'You agreed without knowing what I am going to ask?'

'When people say I need a very big favor it's bound to be a small thing. It is when they ask for a small favor that I start worrying. So, what is it you want?'

'My mother has invited you around to dinner. It's just the once. You will have to pretend to be my boyfriend,' I say so quickly the words almost run into each other.

'What sort of thing will I have to do to convince her that I am your boyfriend?'

'Just the usual. Hold hands, a quick kiss. Nothing too heavy.'

He smiles cynically. 'I think I can manage that.'

'Thank you. I owe you one. Maybe one day you will need a favor and I can do something to help you.'

'I'll remember that,' he says, and falls silent. But the silence is not uncomfortable and we finish our main meal without further conversation.

He orders the macerated strawberries for dessert.

'I'll have the same,' I tell the waiter.

Blake grins. 'I thought you might go for the Like A Kid In A Sweetshop,' he says.

'I nearly did,' I admit. 'Do you know what's in it?'

'Just a selection, I guess. Want to change your mind?'

'No.'

The dessert is so delicious I wish my mother could try it. After the handmade chocolates, the bill arrives. I catch a glimpse of it. It is over four and a half thousand pounds. That is more than my mother spends on food for a whole year. It must be good to be so rich. I look at Blake in shock. He raises his eyes and returns my look. His eyes are sultry and slumberous.

And suddenly he seems devastatingly, impossibly handsome, but so aloof and unreachable that it is almost as if I have my nose pressed against a glass window and I am looking in at something I can never have.

Just like the poor match girl from Hans Christian Andersen's fairy tale who had to keep lighting her last matchsticks to see the fantastically beautiful sight in front of her.

When the matches run out she dies.

Sixteen

He opens the door of the apartment and waits for me to enter. I walk in and stand with my back to him, waiting. I hear the thick click of the door, then he is standing behind me. His breath is on my neck.

'Mmmm...You smell so good,' he whispers.

I lean my head back and find his chest. Rock solid it is.

I hear the sound of the zip and my dress is pooling around my shoes. He unhooks my bra and frees my breasts. In a smooth movement he has scooped me into his arms and is carrying me down the long corridor. There is something so caveman and primal about being carried to be ravished that I have to bury my head in his wide chest so he will not see how unbearably excited and flushed I am. I have been claimed. Now I will be taken and possessed.

He kicks open the bedroom door and lays me down on the bed.

Then he brings his mouth down on mine and kisses me ferociously. The feel and heat of his mouth is a shock to my system. Every coherent thought flees. From his mouth he transfers hunger into my very cells. Every fiber of my being wants him inside me again. He takes his mouth away and I come up heaving for air. They sound like desperate gasps. Sounds I have never heard myself make.

His tongue moves across my collarbone and I whimper. That small mewl of surrender seems to send him into overdrive.

He pushes his knee between my legs and forces them open. Licking the soft swell of my breast and circling his lips around one taut peak, he sucks it softly. I close my eyes and arch back. His large hand skims the soft flesh between my legs. The small bit of lace between us is no match for him. The sound of tearing is loud in my ears.

My eyes fly open and register his as smoldering and intently watching, my face, my mouth, my reactions. His roving fingers encounter thick juices and they make him growl. I stare at him, not understanding it to be the guttural rumble of possession and ownership.

My mouth opens in a silent O, but I do not look away when his fingers first one then two thrust into the wet crease. The thrusting is slow and languorous. Delicious. I raise my body to reach for his mouth. With a groan his hot hungry mouth swoops down to meet mine. As the kiss grows deeper I become lost in the foreign sensations inside me. The blood rushes through my veins and the action between my legs picks up pace, becomes more urgent.

Suddenly he takes his fingers out.

'Don't,' I breathe. My voice is ragged, an unfamiliar mess.

I run my fingers down his hard stomach towards the zip of his pants. My hands are trembling, useless things. He pushes them away gently, and does the job himself.

Naked he is magnificent. A god. Muscles rippling.

He positions himself over me and very slowly sinks his hard flesh into me. He is stretching me, filling me, in a slow, hot movement of pain and shock and…strangely, pleasure…as my sex struggles to accommodate the unfamiliar invasion. His eyes, glazed, the pupils so widely dilated with passion that they are nearly black, never leave me. Watching. Watching. The widening of my own eyes, the way my lips part, the shudders that come to shake my body.

It is sweet torture.

I arch with satisfaction and moan. My soft moans seems to incite him further and he increases the pace of his thrusts. He forces himself deeper and deeper inside me, filling me right to my core.

'Does it still hurt?' he asks.

This deep? Yes. Of course it does. 'No,' I gasp.

So he rocks inside me. Suddenly like a whip passion curls and races through my body, shocking me with its ferocity. It erupts in a strangled cry that surprises even him. He looks at me possessively, proudly, as if he has branded me. He is the owner of my lust. In his hands and mouth and body he holds my pleasure. He said he wanted to fuck me senseless and he does. His pace becomes punishingly hard and fast, but I love the pounding.

Something is billowing through me; it feels as though it could bring some kind of release. When it comes it is a riotous, glorious tidal wave that rips through me. I become one with him, one body, one mind, one soul. But he is still moving. Unfinished.

Then my name tears past his lips. Ah, the tidal wave is upon him.

I come back slowly. The lethargy is luxurious. I remain spread-eagled in my ecstasy. He gathers my tired limbs gently and shuts them. I look up at him dreamily.

He pulls a sheet over my naked skin, and then he leaves me. The door shuts with its thick click.

Seventeen

By the time I arrive at the Black Dog, it is heaving with lunchtime trade and Jack is already sitting at a table by a window nursing a pint. As always, the sight of him makes me feel warm inside. I long to run into his arms, he's been fighting my battles for me for as long as I can remember, but this time he can't help.

I make my way through the crowd, many of whom I know, towards him. His straight brown hair is still wet and has been slicked back carelessly. He looks so dear and near and yet so far away from me. He has always been a deeply mysterious person. Hardly anyone really knows him.

He looks up and sees me. He has the pained blue eyes of a tortured artist. He should have been one. He stands slowly, and, unsmiling, opens his arms to me. With a contented sigh, I go into that place where I have felt safest since I was a child. I breathe in the familiar smell of his soap, so clean, so honest. When I pull away, he looks at me carefully.

I can tell that he is in a bad mood. Perhaps he is even angry.

'Your hair…'

I smile. 'It'll grow back.'

'No, it's good like that.'

'Yeah?'

Yeah. You all right?'

'Yes.'

'Take a pew and I'll get you a drink. What d'you want?'

'Orange juice.'

He raises his eyebrows. 'And?'

I dimple at him. 'Vodka.'

He nods and makes his way to the bar. I watch him. He is tall and broad-shouldered and Julie Sugar is watching him eagerly. For as long as I can remember Julie has lusted after Jack. And now that he is studying medicine, her desire for him has grown to unmanageable proportions. She catches my eye and waves. I smile and wave back. Immediately, she begins to make her way towards me. I sigh inwardly. I like her, I really do, but I don't want to make small talk today. Besides, she is only coming to talk to me because Jack is here.

'Hey Lana?' she says. She is dressed from head to toe in shades of pink.

'Hi Julie.'

'So Jack's down?' She lays a palm down on the table and drums her fluorescent-pink, plastic nails on it.

'Mmnn.'

'Are you guys having lunch?'

'Probably.'

She looks lingeringly at the empty chair next to me, but I don't invite her to join us. I know Jack will be irritated and besides, I need to talk to Jack and explain.

Jack comes back and stands beside the table with my drink and two packets of salt and vinegar crisps—our favorite flavor.

'Hi, Jack,' Julie simpers up at him, fluttering her eyelashes like a black and white movie star.

Jack smiles tightly. 'Hi.'

'Lana was just telling me that you are about to have lunch. Mind if I join you?' She smiles invitingly.

'Not this time, Jules...We have private things to discuss.'

'Oh.'

'Sorry.'

'Maybe next time then,' she says, and, flashing a hurt smile, flounces off.

'Thanks,' I say, and take my drink off Jack.

Jack sits down and takes a sip of his pint. 'Well, then,' he probes. 'How's it going?'

'Great. No problems,' I say.

His eyes narrow on my face, flash down to my clenched hands, then focus on trying to read my eyes. 'Don't lie to me, Lana. I know you better than that.' His voice becomes hard. 'Has he hurt you?'

'No, course not.'

'Then what is it?' he prompts.

'I'm just confused, I guess. This is not how I thought my life would be.'

'Your life? It's only for a month, isn't it?'

I press my lips together. 'It was three months or no deal.'

Jack draws his breath sharply. 'I wish you hadn't done it, Lana. You never even told me.'

'I knew what you'd say. It was a spur of the moment decision.'

'But to sell yourself.' Jack looks openly angry.

'I'd do it all again, Jack.'

'Yeah, but this treatment you're paying for, it's not even properly recognized. I've looked up this Burzynski character on the net, and he seems well meaning enough, but it's not proper medicine, Lana. All his results are anecdotal. Some of his critics are even accusing him of selling hope.'

I lean forward. 'Do you really think after all these years that the FDA wouldn't have locked him up and thrown away the key if he was just selling hope? Hundreds perhaps thousands of people have been cured by him,' I insist passionately. 'Some people are even calling his method the greatest find of the century.'

'What kind of assurances have they given you?'

'None. In fact, they've already warned me that Mum's chances are slim at best. But even if she has only got a one percent chance of recovery, I'm going to take it. I've got nothing to lose. Everything else has failed. Maybe she'll be one of the lucky ones.'

Jack drops his eyes to the scratched wooden table. 'Remember that time when you were six years old, and I left you outside the newsagent to go in and get some sweets, and when I came out a pervert in a car was trying to persuade you to accept a lift?'

I nod. 'Of course. I remember it as if it was yesterday. Your face, as you came rushing out, and punched the guy through the window. He hit the gas pedal, swerved, nearly hit an oncoming car, and screeched up the road. How old were you then? Fiftteen?'

'Yeah. I couldn't believe my eyes. I leave you for one minute to buy some sweets, and you are almost snatched by a pedophile.'

'We didn't tell my mum, did we?'

'No, we didn't. You know what, Lana? It feels like I've just gone into the sweetshop for some sweets and I've come out and a pervert has driven off with you. It feels like I've failed you. I thought I was going to study medicine, get a good job, and be a proper brother to you and your mum. And now it turns out you're out there selling your body.'

'Please don't be angry with me, Jack. I can't bear it when you are.' My eyes well with tears and I blink them away.

His face softens. There is sadness in his voice when he speaks. 'I can't bear it when you cry. I'm not angry with you, Lana. I'm angry with myself for failing you.'

'You haven't failed me, Jack. I'm so proud of you. Of everyone we know, you're the only one who has made it out of this vortex of poverty and hopelessness. I'm not your responsibility. I'm a big girl now. I can take care of myself.'

Jack nods. 'I know. I just wanted better for you.'

'It's not so bad. It's just sex, Jack.'

'How's your mum, anyway?'

'She's bad, Jack. Real bad. The good days are less and less. You do see that I had to do this, don't you?'

'Maybe, but I don't like it, though.'

There is a lull in the conversation and I try to liven it up. 'Since we are openly discussing my sex life...are you gay?'

'What?'

'Are you gay?'

Jack laughs. 'That'll be a surprise to my girlfriend.'

I gasp. 'You have a girlfriend?'

'Mmnnn.'

'Since when?'

'About a week ago. I was always so focused on getting out of the estate I didn't allow myself to get distracted, but my goal is in sight now, and she's a great girl.'

'And just when were you going to tell me, Jack Irish?'

'Well, how could I with you springing your big news on me?'

'Tell me more about her.'

Before he can answer, my phone rings. It is Blake. 'Hi,' I say, looking at Jack.

'Are you at the apartment?'

'No.'

'Can you get there in thirty minutes?'

'I guess so.'

'See you in thirty minutes.'

'That was him?' Jack asks.

I nod. 'I've got to go. I'll take a rain check on lunch with you, but I'm buying and we're going somewhere nice.'

'With his money?'

I don't say anything. Of course it's his money. My credit cards were maxed out before him.

'Thanks, but no thanks. I understand why you're doing what you're doing, but I'll be damned if I'm going to help spend his money. As far as I'm concerned it's blood money—your blood. I'm not going to drink from it.'

I look at him helplessly. 'It's not that bad. Don't let it come between us, please,' I beg.

He reaches forward and grasps my hands in his. 'Nothing will come between us. I'll always be here for you and will be long after he is gone. No matter what happens, I want you to know I'm always here, a phone call away. You can always come to me.'

Tears spring into my eyes. 'What's the name of that girlfriend of yours?' I sniff.

'Alison.'

'She's lucky.'

He smiles. 'You must tell her.'

'When?'

'You'll see at Jerry's birthday party. I'm bringing her.'

I bite my lip. 'If I am allowed to be there, I would love to meet her.'

His eyes narrow dangerously. 'Are you some kind of sexual slave to him, Lana?'

I feel hot color run up my neck. 'No, but it's the arrangement—I have to be there whenever he wants me.'

Jack draws a sharp breath. 'That is just sick,' he fumes.

I cover my burning cheeks with my palms. 'Please, Jack, leave it.'

'You're such a fucking innocent. Does your mother know about this pact of abuse you have signed up for?'

'Of course she doesn't, but it's not abuse, Jack. It's not exactly a hardship to sleep with the man that *Hello*! magazine has called the most eligible bachelor in the world.'

'So what *does* your mother think?'

I close my eyes. 'She thinks I've got myself a rich boyfriend.'

'Jesus.'

I run a finger through the condensation on my glass. 'You know I don't believe in God. All my life I've thought it's a cruel God up there, if there is one at all, but you do, and your God is kind and forgiving. Will you pray to your god to save my mother?'

'I pray every day for your mum, Lana.'

Tears spill down my cheeks.

Sadly, he reaches out a hand and wipes them. 'Don't cry, little one. Maybe this treatment will work. Maybe she will get better.'

I smile through my tears. 'I don't know what I'd do without you, Jack. Sometimes when I am really sad I think of you studying in your dorm, and it makes me feel happy. "Dr Jack Irish, your next patient has arrived."'

Jack smiles, but it is a sad smile.

'I did what I had to do.'

He rests his forehead on his hand; his eyes are unexpectedly gentle. 'All right, Lana. We'll play it your way. Be safe and remember I'm here for you. Always. If ever it gets...strange or dangerous, call me immediately. I swear if he ever hurts you, I don't care if I end up in prison, I'm going to punch his lights out.'

I nod. 'I'll be all right. It's just sex,' I say and he winces.

'Please don't say that again, Lana. It hurts my ears.'

'I've not suddenly become Fat Mary, you know.'

'Perish the thought,' Jack says, the ghost of a smile flickering into his face.

'I have to go now.'

He stands. 'I'll pop by and see your mum later.'

'Thanks Jack. She'll like that. She likes you. Do you know she thought you and I would get together?'

He makes a face. 'Oh dear.'

I laugh. 'I know. Goodbye, Jack.'

I move forward, kiss him on his cheek and walk towards the entrance. As I cross it my phone flashes with an incoming text.

Wear nothing.

I look at the screen again. *Wear nothing*. And feel a stirring of excitement deep in my core.

Eighteen

In the bathroom mirror my eyes seem almost smoky. I undress quickly and pull on the bathrobe hanging behind the door. I still haven't got used to my hairless body. It seems too girlish, somehow, but I think I know why he wants it so. Everything in his life is neat and tidy. Not a pubic hair out of place.

When I hear him in the corridor I freeze.

Wear nothing.

I take the bathrobe off, slip into the bedroom and stand inside the door. He is already there dressed in dark gray trousers and white shirt. His tie is loosened and his shirtsleeves have been haphazardly folded up his muscular arms. His watch glints against his tan. He comes to me and leads me to the big black armchair by the large mirror. I see myself in the mirror. Nude.

Fully clothed he stands behind me.

'Porcelain skin and fuck me now, blue eyes. How beautiful you are,' he says, watching me through the mirror. His eyes are heavy-lidded and cloudy with desire.

He hooks his handmade leather shoe underneath my right foot and gently lifts it. The leather is cool and smooth and the laces rub erotically against the soft sole of my foot. His shoe deposits my foot on the padded seat of the big black chair.

The position has exposed my sex in the most indecent way. I don't recognize the woman in the mirror. She looks wanton and shameless. Now I know the real reason why I am bald. There is nothing to hide behind.

It is all so shameful it is exciting. I look away.

'I want you to see what I am doing to you.'

I meet his eyes in the mirror. He kisses my neck and I moan and try to turn towards him.

'No, watch.'

Throbbing with excitement I gaze at the mirror. I have willingly spread open my sex and allowed him access into my most intimate part. I feel his fully clothed body brush against me. Vaguely: buttons pressing into my back…soft wool against my buttocks and thighs.

'I love your skin. It is like the finest silk.'

Then his hand is moving towards my navel and sliding downwards without any resistance. All the while he is watching me watch myself.

His palm comes to press on my pubic bone and I watch the palm make circles. The circles become tighter and tighter until they are moving the flesh over my clit. Suddenly his index finger taps on the nub and I shiver with helpless wanting.

'Not yet,' he whispers. 'I will decide when you come.'

Then his fingers move quickly in a sweeping motion along my crack, gathering juice. There is more than enough there. The lubricated finger circles the swollen, throbbing bud. Watching him pleasure me is the most unexpectedly erotic thing I have experienced.

I draw a sharp breath and long for the feeling of being full. That feeling of having him inside me, but he does not give that to me. Instead he rubs around my sex, his fingers are cunningly methodical. The same movement again and again.

In minutes I feel the waves coming, but as I push eagerly towards them, towards release, his fingers stop, and even though I press my hips towards them, they stubbornly refuse to move, until the waves dissipate. I sag against him, frustrated, and he slowly pushes his finger into me.

'Wet, hot and tight,' he murmurs.

I look at his large hand; the thick, masculine wrist peppered with silky hair working me. Again that longing to be filled, not with one finger, but with the magnificently thick, long shaft inside his trousers. I have to bite my lip to stop myself from crying out, Fuck me.

'Kiss me,' he orders.

I twist my neck around and give him my mouth. His tongue enters it. I suck greedily. A finger becomes two and increases speed. Just as I am beginning to enjoy the rhythm the fingers are withdrawing, slipping and sliding around the lips. He takes his mouth away as his other hand leaves my waist and cupping my chin, holds it facing the mirror.

I stare at myself in shock. At his big hand moving and the glistening redness of my engorged sex—it is as if it is alive. A shameless greedy creature. And suddenly I am coming and…hard. Real hard. I open my mouth in a shout as my knees buckle and I feel myself losing balance. His hand tightens like a vice around my waist.

When it is over I lean my head back against his chest for a moment.

'Hold onto the chair,' he says, and bends me over. He puts a hand on my back at waist level and pushes down, so my hips are angled, my sex is more exposed. I hear his zip and the soft sound of his trousers dropping. Putting his palm on either side of my face he turns my head and makes me watch what he is doing to me.

'I want you to watch me fucking you.'

With wild eyes I look at the image our bodies make as he grabs me by the hips and his proud cock disappears inside me.

'Now, let me hear your cries. Purr for me, Lana,' he commands and rams ferociously into my willing, dripping wetness.

I cry out with the sensations: the fullness and the depths that he has gone into.

It is surprisingly painful, but such is my need to have him inside that I welcome the pain and push back against him, to take more of him. So he goes even deeper, until his thick shaft is buried all the way to the root. I grunt inelegantly. One hand falls on my back, pushing me into the armchair, while the other grasps my shoulder.

'Ah.'

Suddenly, the animal in him takes over. With bestial urgency he drives into me. Harder and faster. Grinding me against him. The solid armchair rocks with his thrusts. And at that moment I am utterly possessed by the man. His to do anything with.

As he slams into me I realize that the palm of his hand that is pressed against my pubic bone is bringing forth different sensations. The rubbing is causing me to crest again. It is explosive this time, it makes my body convulse uncontrollably and lasts, even past his last urgent thrusts and his own groan of release.

I feel his body slacken against mine. With both his arms around my waist he straightens me, and holds me close to him while he is still inside. I look at him in the mirror and find his eyes unreadable.

Wordlessly, he withdraws out of me and goes into the bathroom.

Without him in the mirror I seem alone and abandoned. On trembling legs I move to hide my nakedness inside the bathrobe.

Nineteen

I am so anxious about my mother meeting Blake that I forget to warn Blake of her wasted appearance. It is only when she opens the door in her best blue dress, a new blue scarf, and smiling through freshly applied lipstick that I realize what she must look like to a stranger. But when I look up at Blake he is smiling and suave. He hands my mother the bouquet of flowers he has brought for her and steps through the door into our home.

'Thank you for inviting me, Mrs. Bloom. It is a great pleasure to finally meet you.'

'Nice to meet you too, Mr. Barrington.'

'Please, you must call me Blake.'

'And you must call me Nys.'

'Nys? Ah...French.'

'Yes, not many people know that. My mother loved the sound of it.'

'I agree with her. A pretty name it is,' he charms.

'Come in, come in,' my mother invites.

Blake takes my hand. I am surprised at how casually he does it. As if he has done it many times before. My mother has decorated the table with fresh flowers and candles. The door to the small balcony is open and the sound of children swearing floats up. My mother quickly closes the door and puts on some music instead.

'Something smells very good,' Blake says.

Mother glows with pleasure. It is obvious she is taken with Blake. 'Oh, it's just chicken and rice. A Persian recipe.'

'With fruit?'

'Yes, pomegranates. How did you know?'

And so the night goes with my mother glowing and impressed and Blake urbane and genteel.

When the food appears it is delicious. Blake makes it a point to polish his plate. Occasionally, he looks with adoring eyes at me, and other times reaches for my hand, never too obvious, and so real it makes me freeze uncomfortably. Once he even reaches forward and lightly brushes his lips against mine. I blink with surprise and glance at my mother, but she is smiling happily at me. Another time he looks mockingly into my eyes as he strokes the inside of my wrist. I turn away in confusion. This Blake I cannot understand or deal with. This Blake is dangerous to my well-being.

This Blake I would want to keep beyond the three months stipulation.

For dessert mother serves a chocolate melt in the middle pudding. Again, Blake makes it a point to finish every last drop. When my mother offers him a strong, Middle Eastern coffee, he immediately accepts.

There is only one uncomfortable moment in the evening when my mother turns to Blake and asks, 'Have you ever done anything that you wish you could go back and undo? Something you regret?'

'No,' Blake says easily.

My mother turns to me. 'What about you, Lana?'

I look my mother in the eye. 'Absolutely not.'

We sit in the back of the Bentley with Tom driving.

'How is it you know so much about Persian history?'

'It was part of our school curriculum.'

'I don't remember learning anything like that in school.'

'That is because you were right in what you said yesterday. My education has been designed to make me a leader, and yours to turn you into an obedient worker. It is how a capitalist system works. No country can be successful without its workers.'

'But is it right?'

Blake turns away from me and stares out of the window.

For a while neither of us speak, then Blake turns towards me. 'You needed the money for her, didn't you?'

'To send her to America for treatment. She leaves tomorrow.'

'Where is she going?'

'The Burzynsky Research Center.'

'I have heard of Dr. Burzynsky. The FDA have taken him to court a few times and not been able to indict him. A good sign for your mother.' In the dark his eyes stare at me with an expression I cannot comprehend.

When we reach the apartment, he drops the key onto the side table. 'Want a nightcap?'

'OK.'

We go into the living room with its low lights. 'What will you have?'

'Baileys.'

I go to the long sofa and watch him pour me a drink, drop some ice cubes into it, and then pour himself a finger of Scotch. He stands over me and holds my drink out to me. I take it and he eases himself beside me.

'Would you like to go shopping with Fleur again tomorrow?'

'No.'

He turns to look at me. 'Why not?'

I shrug. 'I've still got things I haven't worn yet. Besides, I'd like to spend some time with my mum before she leaves in the evening.'

He nods. 'What kind of cancer?'

'It is in her lungs, liver, femur bone and pelvis.'

There is a flash of something in his eyes. He does not believe my mother will make it. He drops his eyes to his drink. He takes a sip, puts it down on the glass table.

'Come here,' he says.

I scoot closer, but he lifts me bodily by the waist while I squeal, and puts me so I am sitting astride him. My open pussy comes in contact with the bulge in his trousers. I stop laughing. I can feel myself becoming wet. I bend forward and run my tongue along his ear. When I reach his earlobe I take it between my teeth and nibble.

'Hey,' he says suddenly, and pulls me away from him.

I look at him surprised.

'Where did that come from?' he asks.

'My best friend Billie taught me the technique, but I probably did it wrong. Did I bite too hard or something?'

'Or something.' He rubs my plump lower lip absently. 'I can't believe an innocent like you still exists.' He lifts his eyes to mine. 'Here, let me show you a much more useful technique.'

And that night, he unzips his trousers and teaches me how to take his silky cock entwined by its two angry green veins and pleasure him with my mouth.

I awaken in the dark and know immediately that I am not alone. For the first time, he has stayed the night with me. I feel the heat from his body and listen to his deep, even breathing. Carefully, I ease my body away from his and as silently as possible grope across the surface of my bedside table. I find the remote control and switch on the bathroom light.

Light filters through the half closed door and dimly illuminates his face. I turn my head and for a long time simply watch him asleep on his side, facing me. The lines that hold his face so tightly during the day are relaxed and soft. Like this, he is heartbreakingly beautiful. I have an irrational desire to run my index finger along his stubby eyelashes. I don't. Instead, I slip out of bed and throwing a large T-shirt over my head, make for the light.

I close the door behind me, use the toilet and wait for its quiet whirling to end before I open the door. My trip to my side of the bed is interrupted by the sight of his wallet lying on his bedside cabinet. I stop and look at it. Once, when I was very young, I opened my father's wallet to look inside and was saddened by what I found inside. Two five pound notes, the coin purse bulging with small change, a petrol receipt, and no photographs of either my mother or me.

I had taken it to my nose and sniffed it. Many years after he left us, I would come across other men's wallets and wonder what they kept inside theirs. I find myself moving towards Blake's wallet. As my fingers connect with the expensive hide, a steely hand clamps down on mine. I gasp with shock and land on the bed beside him, my startled eyes flying to his face. His are alert and watching.

'What are you doing?'

'Nothing,' I say lamely, my face flaming.

'Ask if you need money.' His voice is cold and distant.

Only then it occurs to me what it must look like to him. I shake my head in horror. 'I wasn't trying to steal your money. I just wanted to see what was in it.'

For a moment he looks at me curiously, almost the way a dog will tilt its head when it is trying to figure out what you are trying to communicate to it. Then he takes the wallet and tosses it into my lap. 'So look.' His eyes move to my mouth as my teeth worry at my lower lip.

'What? With you watching?'

His eyebrows rise. 'Would that spoil the…er… experience?'

I swallow, sit up and open the wallet. It is slimmer than my father's, the leather wonderfully soft. And it smells new. There are no photographs behind the plastic of his wallet either, only the deep red card that it came with. I run my thumb along the stitching and down the credit card sleeves. There are only five cards in it, none of them from high street banks. One seems to be from Coutts, another is an American Express Black, and the other three I do not recognize. There is a wad of fifty-pound notes that have the look and feel of freshly-minted money. No small change at all in the purse section. I close it and return it to the bedside.

'Well?'

'You wouldn't understand.'

'Do you know that you're one strange girl?'

I look down at my bare feet and wriggle my toes. 'Have you never wanted to look in a woman's handbag?'

'Never.'

'Why not?'

He rubs his chin. 'Can't say the contents of a woman's handbag have ever held any interest for me. I was always more interested in the contents of their clothes.'

With a sigh, I get up to return to my side.

'Like now,' he says softly.

I look down on him, a half smile on my face, before I pull the T-shirt over my head and discard it on the floor.

His eyes begin to glitter, and instantly my body responds and yearns for him. The tug of anticipation is strong, but I don't go to him. I stand very still as the juices accumulate between my thighs.

'Come here,' he says finally, his voice at once husky and slumberous, and it is a relief to have that man's strong hands grasp me by my upper arms and press me into the mattress.

Twenty

I wake up early, and press the remote button for the curtains. They sweep open, revealing a beautiful day. The sun is already shining brightly. I dress quickly in a pair of old jeans and a T-shirt and head for the coffee machine. After several tries I walk to the phone and call the desk downstairs.

Mr. Nair answers and immediately tells me he will be around to show me how to use it. Less than five minutes later he is at my door. He even shows me how to froth the milk for my cappuccino. He explains that he used to work in a coffee bar in his younger days.

'Do you want one?' I offer.

Mr. Nair's eyes shine. 'Are you sure, Miss Bloom? We only have instant downstairs and I'd love a real coffee.'

'Of course I'm sure,' I say and take down another saucer and cup.

'Ah,' Mr. Nair says delicately. 'I am a Brahmin and I am not allowed to drink from other people's cups. I have my own mug. I will bring it up.'

And he does. He brings his own I Am The Boss mug, and I open a tin of biscuits and offer it to him. He takes two. I raise a that's-it eyebrow, and he grins and helps himself to two more.

'Any time you want a real coffee, call me, and if I am in, feel free to come up,' I say.

'Thank you. Thank you, Miss Bloom, you are very kind indeed.'

After coffee I go to my mother's house. We have a busy day ahead. We pick up her wig from Selfridges and spend some time shopping for things she will need. My mother chooses a burgundy trouser-suit that looks very good on her, two pretty pastel dresses, and some new underwear. Afterwards, I watch while two women give her a pedicure and manicure. They paint her nails coral. My mother smiles at them shyly when they tell her she has beautiful hands.

Afterwards, we take a quick trip to the doctor's surgery. We spend the rest of the afternoon at the flat. By five the flat is clean and my mother is ready. She stands before me in the living room in her burgundy trouser-suit and her new wig. She looks wonderful.

I cry. So does my mother.

Billie shoos us both out of the flat. I watch my mother and Billie get into a mini cab and head for Heathrow. Then I go back to our empty home, fall on my mother's bed and cry my heart out. It is nearly six when I wash my face and leave for the apartment.

I am surprised to see that Blake is already in. He comes out of the dining room when he hears me.

'Has she gone?'

I nod, feeling very distant from him.

'That's good. I thought you might not feel like going out tonight so perhaps we can have a Chinese takeaway?'

'Not for me.'

'Don't you want any food?'

I shake my head.

'Would you like to lie down and rest for a bit?'

'Yes. That's a good idea.'

'OK, sleep for a bit. It'll do you good.'

I nod and he retreats into the dining room. As I pass him in the corridor, I notice his briefcase is open and there are papers spread out on the long dining table, and he appears to be concentrating hard on them.

I lie down on the bed and fall asleep almost immediately. My sleep is restless and full of dreams. A noise wakes me in the middle of the night. I realize instantly that I am alone in bed. I listen again. It is coming from the kitchen. The little bedside clock says it is two a.m. My mother and Billie will still be in the air. I get out of bed, and pad towards the sounds.

I stand at the doorway dazzled by the light, pushing hair away from my eyes. Blake is toasting two slices of bread and does not see me. My mind takes a picture of him—gorgeously shirtless and wearing only his low-slung jeans—to be kept for later, when he is no longer around. When he spots me, he leans a hip against the work counter, and looks at me, his arms crossed, his eyes unreadable.

'Did I wake you?'

'No. What are you making?'

'I was working and I got hungry. Want some toast?'

I shake my head, but come into the room and sit on a stool. I put my elbows on the island surface amongst the butter dish, knives, plates and open jars of foie gras and caviar. There is also a half-drunk glass of orange juice. I slide my body along the cold granite surface and pull it over to me. As I sip at it I watch him work.

He produces a spoon from a drawer. It is the smallest spoon I have seen. He scoops a tiny amount of caviar and holds it out to me.

I crinkle my nose. 'Fish eggs?'

He shakes his head in disgust. 'Philistine,' he chides.

I open my mouth and he inserts the spoon. Little salty balls explode intriguingly in my mouth.

'Good?'

I smile. 'Tastes better than it looks. A bit like you,' I tease.

He throws back his head and laughs.

'You work very hard, don't you?'

'All rich people do.'

I watch him spread pâtè on a slice of toast. Watch his even, strong teeth bite cleanly into it.

'You should eat something,' he says.

I stand up and make myself a jam sandwich. While I am eating it, I think Rosa was right. Jam sandwiches should be made with white bread.

They simply don't taste the same with healthy bread.

'What do you feel like doing now?' he asks.

'Don't you feel like sleeping?'

'Eventually.'

'Shall we play a game?'

A smile curves that straight mouth. 'What kind of game?'

'Let's see who climaxes first.'

His eyes flash. 'What are the rules?'

Hmm...Billie didn't mention anything about rules. 'It's quite a simple game really. We take turns to make each other come. We time ourselves with an egg timer. The one who lasts the longest at the hands of the other wins.'

'What's the prize for winning?'

'The winner gets to ask the loser for anything they want?'

'What if the loser is unable to provide that thing?'

'Within reason and nothing dangerous, obviously.'

'OK, do you want to go first? Or shall I?'

'I will. You can do me first.' I stand up and swipe the egg timer off the counter. He stares at me as if he is unable to understand me. We go into the bedroom and it is easy for him to make me come. Then it is my turn.

'Why did you let me win?' I whisper.

'How do you know I did?'

'Because you've never come before me.'

'So why did you want to play this game then?'

'Because I had something special up my sleeve, but I didn't even get a chance to use it.'

He laughs. 'Something special? Is it another technique from Billie?'

'As a matter of fact, yes, but you haven't answered the original question.'

'Because I wanted to know what you would ask for.'

'Why?'

He shrugs. 'Well, what do you want?'

'I want you to cook for me.'

He lies on his side and props his head on his palm. 'Why?'

'When I was fourteen, I read a book where the hero sent the heroine to have a long soak in the bath while he cooked for her. He grilled two steaks and tossed a salad. It was really romantic. He wore a black shirt and washed out blue jeans. I remember he had just had a shower and his hair was still wet. Oh, and he was barefoot.'

'And what did the heroine wear?'

'Er...I can't remember.'

'Dinner tomorrow?'

I smile. 'Dinner tomorrow. You won't burn it, will you?'

'Maybe just the salad.'

Twenty-One

The next day drags slowly. Mr. Nair stops by at ten a.m. with his mug. We have a little chat and he tells me about his family in India. Before he worked in the coffee shop, he was a Hindu priest in a temple in India. He is interesting, but his break time is quickly over and he leaves.

I am required to idle away my days, but idling alone in a sumptuous flat, I am quickly realizing, is no easy thing. There is not much activity in the part of the park that my balcony faces, and daytime television has always bored me. How many times can one watch reruns of *Wonder Woman*?

I am also terribly lonely. Without my mother, Billie or Jack I feel quite lost. I wander around the large flat alone and bored. Idling, I finally decide, requires thoughtful planning and effort—diligent effort. I begin by ordering some books from Amazon.

It is nearly five o'clock when I am able to Skype Billie. I sit cross-legged on the bed and look at Billie's dear, excited face come alive on the screen.

'Guess what?' Billie shouts enthusiastically. 'We flew first class.'

'What?'

'Yep, we arrived at economy check-in and we were bumped up to first class. Both your mum and me!'

'How can that be?'

'Must be banker boy. They said it was all arranged and paid for.'

I am speechless. Could it really have been Blake who paid the difference? But he didn't even know which flight they were on.

'Anyway,' Billie says, 'it was bloody brilliant. They called us by name and acted like we were celebrities or something. I drank nearly two bottles of champagne, and your mum got to sleep most of the way.'

'How is mum?'

'She's here. I'll put her on.'

'Hello, Lana,' my mother says shakily. She looks so white and fragile that I almost burst into tears. When the call is over I lie on the bed and wonder why Blake did that. He is a strange man. So cold and distant sometimes and so incredibly kind and generous at other times.

At seven o'clock, Blake arrives. I run out to meet him at the front door.

'Did you pay for my mum and Billie to fly first class?'

'Yes.'

'Why?'

He shrugs casually. 'I like your mother,' he says shortly, and sends me into the Jacuzzi bath.

'Dinner is at seven thirty sharp,' he says. 'Don't come out before.'

I climb into it and close my eyes. It is heaven. Blake comes in with a glass of red wine.

'To get you in the mood,' he says.

'This is not in the scene, but impressive improvisation,' I say as I accept it.

I take a sip and open Philip K. Dick's *Do Androids Dream of Electric Sheep.* Fifteen minutes later, I smell it. Burning. Before I can wrap myself in the toweling robe, the fire alarms go off. I rush to the kitchen dripping soapsuds.

Blake has opened all the windows, and is standing on a chair desperately waving a magazine at the smoke detector in the corridor. His hair is slightly wet, he is wearing a black shirt with two buttons undone, and a pair of stone washed jeans. He is also barefoot.

I begin to laugh. 'Did you burn the salad?' I shout above the racket.

He scowls down at me.

I go into the kitchen and bin the blackened pieces of meat. Shaking my head, I pop a piece of tomato from the salad into my mouth, and immediately spit it out. Mega salty. The salad goes the way of the steaks. The alarm finally stops blaring. I look up and he is standing at the doorway.

'You've never cooked, have you?'

'No,' he confesses. 'Do you want to go out?'

'Why don't we just have some chip butties instead?'

'Chip butties?'

'Oh. My. God. You've never had a chip butty? You don't know what you're missing. You have to have one.'

'OK.'

'Let me get ready and I'll pop over to the shop and get the ingredients.'

'I'll come with you,' he offers.

We walk together to the local fish and chip shop where I order a big bag of chips.

'No fish?'

'No fish. Now we need to go into the corner shop for some bread.'

'Don't we have some back at the flat?'

'Nah. We've got the good stuff back there. This is poor people's food. For this we need a loaf of cheap, white bread.'

I pick out a loaf of sliced white bread and Blake pays for it.

'That's it,' I say.

'Are those *all* the ingredients you need for our meal?'

'The rest we have at home,' I say, and with horror realize what I have said. I called the flat home. But he says nothing and I just hope he did not notice.

In the kitchen, Blake sits on the counter and watches me liberally butter four slices of bread, load two up with chips, squirt tomato ketchup in a zigzag pattern over them, sprinkle salt, and close them into two chunky sandwiches.

'Voilà. The famous chip butty.'

'That's it?'

I push a plate towards him. 'Taste it.'

He eyes it without desire.

'Go on. I tasted caviar for you.'

'That's true.' He takes a tiny bite and begins to chew cautiously.

'No, no, that's not how you eat it. You have to attack it. Like this.' I open my mouth and take a huge bite. He follows suit. It is strange watching him eat with such abandon.

'Well?' I demand.

'Not bad actually. Kind of satisfying.'

'This is what a lot of kids on the estate live on most of the time.'

'Did you?'

'No, my mother never had a drinking or a drug problem so she didn't have to dip into our food money to finance her habit.'

'Did you have a happy childhood?'

'Yeah, I guess so. Until my mother got sick I was very happy.'

'How come you never had a boyfriend?'

I wipe my lips on a paper napkin, swallow, and grin. 'All the boys were scared of Jack. And after my mother got sick and my father left, any thoughts of boys were gone.'

'Who's Jack?'

'He's the closest thing I have to a brother.'

'Why were they scared of him?'

'Because Jack was not only big and strong, he was also utterly fearless. When we were growing up there was nobody he was scared of. Everybody knew Jack had taken me under his wing, and nobody wanted to mess with him. Once Billie, Leticia, Jack and me went to a club, and a guy there wanted to dance with me. He wouldn't take no for an answer so Jack said, "You heard her. Now scram." Of course, he didn't take that too good so he waited with his mates for us outside the club.'

I stop to pop a fat chip into my mouth.

'And surrounded us. One of them had a knife. I was so frightened. I remember Jack looked at me and said, "Shhh…you know I got ya," and then he smiled. That Jack smile. And I knew it would be all right. I walked out of the circle and they closed in on him. I can still see them now. Tattoos, broken teeth, rings where there should be none. But what shocked me was Jack. He was like a stranger. I couldn't recognize him.

'All those years I thought I knew him, warm and friendly, an unshakeable rock, and suddenly I see this fiend turning on himself, snarling, "Come on then. Who's first?" They advanced in a group. He kicked the one with the knife in the throat and another he punched in the nose, bled like crazy. Then he felled another two guys, I don't know how, it happened so fast, and then it was over. The last coward ran away. It was like watching a movie. And you know what the first thing Jack said to me was? "Are *you* all right?"'

'Unusual guy,' Blake says quietly. 'Did you never want to go out with him?'

'No, he is my brother. My safe harbor. I'd do anything for him.'

He nods. There is no expression in his face. 'How long has your mother been ill?' he asks, and takes another bite of his sandwich.

'Just before I turned fifteen. And that was also when my dad left. I was so scared she was going to die. If not for Jack, I don't know how things would have turned out. He came around every day and did what my father should have done.'

'And you've never seen your dad since he left?'

I shake my head.

'Did you not want to?'

'No. I heard he married again and had more kids, but he really doesn't interest me anymore. He ran out on us. He thought my mother would die and he would be saddled with me.'

'Hmmm...You've never had an orgasm until you met me, have you?'

I am certain my face must be astonishingly red. 'Was it that obvious?'

'A bit. You never had a boyfriend but you must have masturbated while growing up.'

'You don't know what my life was like. For most of my life I've been terrified of losing my mother. Whenever she was ill, I slept with her. And when she was not—which was not often, and I returned to my own bed I could never do anything—my mother is such a light sleeper. She will wake up if a pin drops.'

Blake takes his last bite and pushes away from the stool. 'Got some work to do. Can you amuse yourself for a bit and meet me in an hour's time in the bedroom?'

'OK.'

In the bedroom I reach for his trousers. I want to give him pleasure the way he taught me.

'Easy, tiger,' he says and spreads my legs. Watching me intently he latches onto my clit covered in its juices and begins to gently suck it. The sensation is indescribable—delicate ribbons of pleasure rise from his mouth and enter my being. I tremble against his mouth. I forget to think and become an extension of my sex, my core. He is teaching my sex, what it can be. Soon my nails become claws that dig into his shoulders. My mouth opens and my muscles begin to contract with anticipation of the explosion that is coming.

But when he judges the train wreck is almost upon me he deliberately slows his movement, brings me back down only to begin again on that velvet-soft swollen flesh. His eyes monitor my reaction. Again and again until I am holding his head in my hands and begging him to let me climax.

'I can't take it anymore,' I plead.

And this time he relents. He lets me come and it shocks me by its intensity. I scream his name, but strangely, he refuses to take his mouth away from my painfully sensitive blood-engorged sex. I try to wriggle away but his grip is steel. Then, suddenly I am no longer pushing his head away and begging him to stop, but pulling him back in; the waves of ecstasy are coming back. And again. Three times in total I jerk, shake, tremble and soar before I fall from my great height.

My hands flop to my sides, spent.

I feel him take his watching eyes away from me and lay his cheek for a moment on my stomach and listen to my ragged breathing.

Then he bounds up, full of coiled energy and picking me up lays me on the pillow. I am so spent I look at him with hazy, passion-filled eyes. I want to tell him that I have never experienced such a thing before. I want to tell him how beautiful and awesome it has been, how complete he has made me feel; perhaps I might even have blurted out that I am in love with him and have been for some time now.

There is no one but him for me—I would take the bad, the good, even the indifferent—but he places a silencing finger on my lips. He does not want words from me. He wants only claim of my body and only when he wants it.

All he was doing was defining me as his. As my eyes flutter shut I hear him step out of his trousers and feel the mattress give under his knee.

Ah, it's not over yet.

Twenty-Two

Blake Law Barrington

It is late, nearly twelve, when I slot my key in the door and enter the apartment. The sliding doors to the balcony are open and a gentle breeze plays with the curtain. I see her asleep on the sofa and feel a frisson of some strange emotion. I stand over her and watch her.

In the soft light, the pattern on the lavender wallpaper looks like thorn vines that the prince from *Sleeping Beauty* has to hack through. I can still remember reading it for my sister. So many times. It was her favorite. I fucking hated it. Corny nonsense. I sit next to her and her sleeping body tilts twenty degrees towards me. I run a finger along her cheek and she opens her eyes.

'You smell of whiskey. Where have you been?'

I chuckle. 'Doing my rounds.'

She puts a hand to my cheek. 'You're cold.' She moves the hand to my chest. Through the shirt material, her fingertips register the beat of my heart.

'You reminded me of Sleeping Beauty.'

'That must make you Prince Charming then.'

A cloud of sadness settles in my chest. My hand gently traces the line of her cheek. 'Don't deceive yourself, Lana. Our liaison can only ever be temporary. I am spoken for.'

My words stab her like a knife. I see the pain spread through her eyes. Her wounds are whispers. 'Who is she? Where is she now?'

'She's from an old family like me. She has to finish her education. She is only twenty-two. Next year I will be thirty-one and she will be twenty-three. Then we will marry.'

'Are you in love with her?'

The thought is almost amusing. 'No.'

'Is it like an arranged marriage?'

'Something like that. There is some leeway, there has to be some attraction, but marriage for us has always been a merger of two great families. The Lazards marry their sons to Rockefellers and the Rockefellers marry their daughters to Hapsgoods. It works well.'

'Is love ever a part of the equation?'

'Love is vastly overrated. We consolidate our wealth and position and make arrangements to cater to our specific tastes.'

'Specific tastes?'

'Some of us are gay; others are pedophiles.'

She looks at me in shock. 'Are you condoning pedophilia?'

'I'm not condoning anything. I'm stating a fact.'

'So you wouldn't report a pedophile who was abusing a child?'

I shake my head. 'That is a matter between the pedophile and God as God made him that way.'

'What about the child?' she demands.

'Time's march is a web of causes and effects, and asking for any gift of mercy, however tiny it might be, is to ask that a link be broken in that web of iron. No one deserves such a miracle—Jorge Luis Borges.'

'What an unkind world you live in.'

'Your tragedy is that you live in the same world as me only you do not perceive it, and that makes you careless.'

'And your tragedy is your fatalism.'

'On the contrary. It means I recognize the threat. Cause and effect. Unlike you, my wife and I will guard our children in such a way that they will never be exposed to dangerous situations.'

She gazes at me with horror at the calm and shamelessly way I discuss my bride to be with her. 'If you are already engaged to be married why are you never seen together and why are you being touted as the most eligible bachelor alive?'

'You will never understand us. Don't try.'

'Is it the same reason your family doesn't appear in the Forbes rich list?'

My lips curve. 'That's better. Now you are beginning to understand. The greatest fortunes are all secretly earned, ferociously guarded.'

'So…You are the most eligible bachelor because…'

'The impression of meritocracy must be maintained at all times.'

'Ah, the taint of elitism.'

'No, but close.'

'Why so evasive? I am bound by contract. I couldn't speak even if I wanted to.'

'If you controlled eighty percent of all the wealth in the world...Wouldn't you want the status quo to carry on? We prefer to trade anonymously behind a façade, behind the public faces. Kings, prime ministers, tsars, sultans, and emperors come to power and lose it to the jealously and dissatisfaction of the people. We have, uninterrupted, ruled from behind the scenes for centuries. Our secrets are precious.'

'What time is it?' She sounds defeated.

'Time you were in bed,' I say, and lift her into my arms. Her hands go around my neck.

'You're getting long, Bloom.'

'Too long for you, Barrington.'

'Never too long for me, Bloom.'

She turns her head and sees our reflections in the mirror on the opposite wall. Her long nightgown trails behind her and in the soft light from the nightstand she really does seem like a princess in need of rescuing.

'We look like the romantic hero and heroine of the black and white movies my mother likes to watch.'

I don't say anything.

'Only we are not,' she adds sadly. 'All your plans don't include me.'

The thought is depressing. It makes me feel sad when she buries her face in my neck.

'To sleep?' she whispers.

'Not quite, Bloom,' I reply quietly.

I drop her in the bed with a plop and look down at her tousled hair on the white pillows. In the shadows her eyes are unreadable.

'What is it?' she asks.

I bring my mouth towards her and her mouth lifts to meet me. This time our kiss is special. I feel myself heat up at the answering purr of her body. It is as though we are drinking from each other. Our bodies meld together.

And when we are lying sated in the dark I become fearful of her and have to spoil it. 'I love it when you come and your pussy grips my cock.'

She shuts her eyes and turns her face away from me in despair. She understands what I am doing.

Always, she must be reduced to an orifice.

Twenty-Three

Lana Bloom

Today, I feel happy. Billie called to tell me the good news. The antineoplastons that my mother is on are working. The tests are back—the tumors are regressing. My mother will have to carry on her treatment for another three months, but she can return in two days' time to England and carry it on here.

I am so happy I start sobbing.

To celebrate, Blake takes me out to dinner at Le Gavroche. I have already dined on the most delicious cheese soufflé cooked in double cream followed by grilled scallops, and my dessert, a raspberry mille-feuille in praline-flavored chocolate, has just been put in front of me.

Blake has ordered the Le Plateau de Fromages Affines and I watch him cut a slice of strong cheese. It is almost transparently thin. He places it on a small square of cracker and slips it into his mouth. I imagine the flavors building up in his nose, the cheese melting on his hot, silky tongue, and cheesy liquids traveling down the back of his throat. I watch the movement in the strong column of his brown throat. The entire operation is fluid, elegant, almost a ceremony. It is his education. There is no greed in him.

Not even for me.

I look away and meet the eyes of another diner, a man. He is looking at me with the same expression I must have had in my face while I was looking at the banker. Now I know what lies in the belly of all those men who have ever gazed at me with desire in their eyes. I look down at my dessert, dip my finger into the praline-flavored chocolate and place it on my tongue.

I raise my eyes and Blake is watching me. 'You are in bad trouble,' he says.

I don't take my finger out. 'What kind of trouble?' I mumble.

He smiles and is about to answer when a flash of surprised annoyance crosses his face. Its appearance and disappearance is swift. Very quickly his face resumes its neutral expression. I turn curiously to see what caused the disturbance. A silver-haired man is walking towards our table. When the man arrives, he totally ignores me, and looks only at Blake.

Blake's lips twist. 'Father, meet Lana. Lana, my father,' he introduces.

His father glances at me. His eyes are pale blue stones. He pushes his glasses up his nose. He looks quite mild and harmless. If I had seen him in the street, I would have smiled at him.

'Run along to the ladies and powder your nose or something. I need to speak to my son,' he says.

His impatience and rudeness is so unexpected it makes me gasp. I pick up my purse automatically and make to rise, but Blake's voice is like a whiplash. 'Stay,' he commands.

Surprised I meet his gaze. He is staring at me, his eyes forbidding and stern. I put my purse down, and he shifts his eyes from me to his father.

'When I have finished dinner I will come to you,' he says softly, and stands.

The old man says nothing. It is obvious that he is livid, but he turns around and leaves the restaurant.

Blake sits. 'Sorry about that,' he apologizes. 'My father can be brusque sometimes.'

'It's all right,' I say, but the incident has changed him. He has become remote and preoccupied.

He looks at my uneaten dessert. 'Do you want coffee?'

I shake my head and he calls for the bill. He puts me into a cab and watches as I am driven away.

Blake Law Barrington

After putting Lana into a cab I hail another and tell the driver to head to Claridges. I check my phone: my brother has called. I call him back.

'What's up, Marcus?'

'Have you seen Dad?'

'On my way to him now.'

'Any idea why he suddenly decided he must see you?'

'Nope,' I lie. We chat a bit more and then he hangs up.

I don't immediately to go up to my father's rooms. I stroll into the bar and order myself a large whiskey. A girl comes up to me.

'Hi,' she says. She is very expensively dressed and very seductive. A call girl. I can tell a mile off. 'Want to buy me a drink?'

I sigh and raise my hand. Instantly, the bartender comes to my side. I move my thumb in her direction. 'Get her a drink too,' I say.

The girl smiles at me. Ah, the clothes were bait, the hook is her smile. She is very beautiful. She has long, shining blonde hair that I can see is natural and pearly teeth. I so want to be distracted.

'You must be very rich and powerful,' she says.

'Why do you say that?'

'The way the bartender left what he was doing to serve you first. It's always a good sign of big money.'

'Where are you from?'

'Russia.' I nod and almost smile. Cliché of clichés. Of course, she is Russian.

'And you? You are American?'

'Yeah.'

'You are a very beautiful man. I'd really like to spend the night with you.'

I have never paid for sex. And then it hits me suddenly. I am paying for sex! It makes me laugh out loud.

'What is so funny?' the Russian asks.

'Why did you become a hooker?'

Her eyebrows arch. She is pure sophistication. 'Because I like nice things.' Then she deepens her voice until it is like hot caramel. She is very good at this. 'And I love a hot fuck with good-looking strangers.' She eyes my crotch greedily. She does it well and if I didn't know better I would think she was desperate for my body and not the contents of my wallet.

Lana's white face when my father ordered her to leave the table flashes into my mind. I down my drink and signal to the barman.

'Charge everything to my father's room,' I say, and leave a fifty-pound tip. My father is tight and actually goes through his hotel bills.

'Enjoy your drink,' I say to the Russian beauty, and make my way to the lift.

Upstairs, my father is waiting for me. As I expected the meeting does not go well.

'Do you think you are the first Barrington to be tempted?' my father asks me coldly.

'Tempted?'

'Tempted to throw it all away for a bit of flesh.'

'I don't want to throw it all away.'

'Really?'

'It honestly hasn't crossed my mind.'

'Do you think I am a fool? Do you think I cannot see what she is to you? Each one of us has a personal siren summoned from some demonic place, who enters our lives in the most mundane way, leads us to the very edge, and sings as we fall to our destruction. I had mine. Many years ago.'

I stare at him. A memory struggles to surface. A voice in my head, 'Don't go there, boy.' So I do not. Instead, I turn almost gratefully to my father's story. Even the thought of my father being in love is foreign, impossible.

He smiles frostily, his voice is calm and unemotional, but the memories must have been bitter for his mouth is a tightly controlled slash in his face. 'She was a redhead, a fledgling star. Every time I saw her, I could have ruined everything for her, but I fought it with every ounce of my being.'

'Where is she now?'

'Dead.'

'What happened?'

'It got so bad your grandfather paid a man to run off with her. She became a drug addict and died in a motel room. I saw the pictures and even then I felt an indescribable loss. But now, when I think back, I realize that my father was right. She was the enemy carefully chosen for me by fate. A beautiful butterfly. After she had destroyed me, after I'd lost everything, she would have carelessly moved on to the next flower.' He looks intently at me. 'What would happen if I paid your girl to leave you?'

Despite myself, I flush with anger. I turn away from him and start walking towards the door. 'I'll thank you to stay out of my business. I don't want to leave everything for her. It is only a fling. A temporary thing.'

I am so angry at my father's suggestion to pay Lana off that I walk the streets of London for almost an hour feeling strangely confused and lost. The only thing I know for sure is that I ache for her. With every fiber of my being, I ache for her.

I tell myself it is just lust. But I know, I know it isn't. It isn't lust when you want to reach out and wipe away her tears and press her body against your own. I don't just want to fuck her, I want to hold her after that. She fills the void inside me that has never been filled by the best schools, the most beautiful women, the fastest cars, the most expensive champagnes, or the most glamorous parties.

I take a cab back to St John's Wood and let myself in quietly. For a moment I stand at the mouth of the corridor. The living room is dim. Then I walk towards it—my feet soundless on the thick carpet—and stop at the threshold. Only the lampshade by the sofa is lit.

She has fallen asleep on the couch. Her fingers are slack and trailing down. There is an empty glass that has rolled away from her. I go to her and gaze down at her sleeping form. She is unbearably, impossibly beautiful. I put my hand under her neck and the other under her knees and lift her up. She moans softly, and I smell the alcohol on her breath.

'Don't leave me,' she mumbles.

I freeze. For a time I am completely still, but she does not awaken so I carry her to our bed and put her down. I bend down and kiss her soft lips. She is half-asleep, but she opens her mouth and I deepen the kiss. Her hands come up to my hair, her fingers entwine in the silky strands. She moans and arches her body towards me. I support her body with my fore-arms, and lifting her towards me begin to suck at her exposed throat.

'Please, Blake…' she gasps and molds her body into mine.

I let my mouth trail lower. At the soft swelling where her breast begins I stop and suck again. This time longer. I will leave my mark on her. She groans with pleasure. I take my mouth away and look at the red mark possessively. I feel like an adolescent again. She is mine. Mine to mark. I put my mouth on another part of her creamy skin and suck diligently.

Her hands are moving towards my belt. They are urgent but useless against the metal buckle. She is more than half drunk. I put my hand into her pajama trousers, slip it under her panties, and touch her between her legs. Her sex is wet and tingling for me. She has never begged me to enter her before. I want her to. I rip open her pajama top. A button hits the mirror in the room and makes a sound. She does not hear it.

I grab the ends of her trouser legs and tug. They slide off her and I fling them behind me. I tear at her panties. Then I latch my mouth on her nipple. Her head falls back and she sighs with abandonment. I gaze at the body exposed to me, mine to do with as I please. I have never felt the need to sexually possess anyone like this before. But she I must. She is like a craving. An addiction.

'Tell me you're mine,' I order hoarsely.

'I'm yours,' she says.

'Beg me to enter you,'

She obeys instantly. 'Please Blake, enter me. I want you to. Badly.'

'Open your legs and show me your pussy.'

She opens her legs and I see how wet and glistening her open flesh is.

I take off my shirt and my trousers while she watches from the bed. Her eyes are huge and strange with desire. I have never seen her like this. I want this woman so bad it feels like a forest fire is raging in my dick. I stand a moment longer savoring the way I feel. Hard, ready and so horny. That feeling of animal passion. This is my mate.

I own her.

I climb on the bed—the mattress gives under my weight—and enter her sweet flesh. She cries out, and then she is gripping me so hard, her nails dig into my flesh. I let her climax before I allow myself to. She falls asleep almost instantly and I lay my palm, the fingers spread out to full on her stomach. I recognize the possessiveness of the gesture. I turn to look at her sleeping face.

An image of my father flashes into my head. What the fuck am I doing? This is my fuck doll. Not my mate. Victoria smiles in my head. I cannot ruin my father's plan. They are also my plans. Soon. Soon I will tire of driving my dick deep into her sweet pussy.

Some deep part of me knows it is a lie, but I go to sleep snuggled against her warm, soft body, pretending to feel good. There is still time. Plenty of time to sort it all out.

Twenty-Four

Blake has a business dinner that he expects to run late, so Billie and I are going to a wine bar that has just opened in Seymour Place. I wash my hair and dress in a pair of tight jeans and the top that Fleur had called basic even though it is rather grand. It has lace and pearl buttons down the front. Tom is on holiday and Blake has left strict instructions for me to take a taxi to and fro. I go to visit my mother first.

The pouch with her supply of antineoplastons is strapped around her waist, but she looks well. She is steadily gaining weight, there is color again in her cheeks, and she seems in good spirits.

'My, don't you look nice,' she says, bustling me into the kitchen. She puts a skillet on the stove. 'You can't drink on an empty stomach. We are having grilled chicken and salad.'

She sprinkles nuts on a bowl of salad.

We sit to eat and it is like old times. Afterwards, she refuses all offers of help with the dishes and shoos me away. 'Go. Go and have a good time, you. Call me in the morning.'

'OK, OK,' I say laughing as I am bodily pushed out of her door.

At Billie's, I am ordered to lose the lace top and slip into one of Billie's skinny tops. I have to admit the red top looks hip and a whole lot sexier.

The taxi drops us outside the entrance of Fellini's. We open the wooden door and enter the dimly-lit interior. It is all green walls, chrome fittings and framed black and white photos of movie stars from the forties and fifties. The clientele is quite a mixed bag, but seems to be mostly office folk.

We find a table and I buy the first round. When it is Billie's turn, she goes up to the bar, and a guy sidles up to the half-circle seat that I am sitting on. He is wearing a suit and must be in his mid or late twenties. He smiles at me. Friendly face. I will also remember later that he looked clean and trustworthy. There is nothing about him to suggest otherwise

'Hello, doll,' he says. 'Can I buy you a drink?'

'Thanks, but my friend's gone to get me one.'

'Mind if I join you girls?'

'As a matter of fact, yes,' interrupts Billie rudely. She is standing behind me and actually glowering at the man. She looks quite tough and fierce.

'No problem,' he says immediately, and with a wink to me, gets up and goes back to join his friends, who are gathered at the bar. He says something to them and they slap him on the back and laugh uproariously. For some reason, their laughter disturbs me and makes me think it is somehow connected to me. But Billie is saying something and I turn my head to listen.

Blake Law Barrington

I feel my phone vibrate in my pocket and instantly perceive that it is from Lana. Why, I cannot say, for she has never called me before. I take my phone out of my pocket and look at the screen. Her number flashes. I excuse myself, walk away from the table, and lay my phone to my ear.

'Hi,' says a voice I do not recognize.

'Yes,' I reply, my voice is strangely abrupt. Some part of my brain registers surprise at the state of my voice.

'This is Billie, Lana's friend. Don't panic, but some wanker has slipped a roach into her drink, and she's gone down.'

Her accent is hard for me to understand, and I have never heard the term roach, but I guess instantly that Billie must be referring to a date rape drug. 'Gone down?' I repeat.

'Look, I've had to leave her at the table with one of the bar staff to come outside and call you, so could you hurry here, please?'

'Where are you?'

She gives me the address.

Without going back to the table to make my apologies, I rush out of the restaurant and drive like a mad man through speed cameras. I double park outside the entrance of Loren, and bound into the crowded bar. I stand at the entrance and let my eyes scan the room. A young girl with extremely white hair is waving at me. Lana is slumped against her and her head is lolling on the girl's left shoulder.

As soon as I reach them she stands up and tries to keep Lana up with her hand, but Lana flops over it.

'It's not as bad as it looks,' Billie says. 'Almost all my friends have had it slipped into their drink before, and we've all survived.' She jerks her eyes towards a group of men. 'I think it's them over there, but over my dead body will they be taking this girl home with them.'

I glance over at the men. Six lads. Youngish. Their idea of fun. As soon as they sense my eyes on them, they quickly turn away and I experience a fury that I have never known. The urge to go over and punch their smirking faces burns my guts. I turn towards them, raging uncontrollably. A hand on my arm stops me. I look at it. The nails are painted to look like slices of watermelon. The sight has a strange effect on me. I lose the edge of my anger.

I drag my eye upwards.

'If you prop her up on one side, we can walk her out,' she urges. Her voice is surprisingly strong and purposeful. I had dismissed her, the spiders and the boiled-egg white hair, but she is more. No wonder Lana held her in such high regard.

'No need,' I say, and scoop Lana up easily.

'Oh!' Billie exclaims. Turning around she aggressively flicks her middle finger at the group of guys who have turned to watch, and follows me out of the restaurant. Outside, Billie opens the passenger door and I deposit Lana into the seat. I close the door and turn to face her.

'Thank you for calling me.'

She shrugs. 'No problem. Thanks for coming. Couldn't take her home. Her mum...you know how it is?'

I nod. 'How will you get home?'

'Oh, don't worry about me. I'll just hop on a bus.'

That makes me frown. 'Is that safe at this time of the night?'

Her eyes widen. Suddenly she seems so much younger. 'It's only ten o'clock, Mr. Barrington.'

I take my wallet out of my pocket, pull two fifties out, and hold them out to her. 'Here, take a cab.'

'Uh...taxis don't cost that much, Mr. Barrington.'

'Call me Blake, and please, don't argue with me,' I say impatiently.

She reaches out and takes the money, then shifts from one foot to another. 'It's not as bad as it looks. Tomorrow will be the killer. She'll think she's dying, but she'll be OK. Give her lots of water to drink.'

'Thanks again.'

'Oh, and if you want to do anything kinky to her now's the time. She won't remember a thing in the morning.'

For a moment I stare at her shocked, and then I realize that it is her attempt at a joke. I shake my head. Strange girl. She pulls Lana's phone out of her pocket. 'Here's her phone. She'll need to call her mum before twelve or there'll be trouble.'

I take it distractedly. 'OK, I'll make sure she does.' I walk over to the driver's side of the car and get in.

Billie Black

I watch his car roar powerfully into life, pick up great speed almost immediately, and take the corner at an alarming speed. Then I stuff the money into the back pocket of my black jeans and casually amble over to the bus stop. At the bus stop I sit on a cold plastic chair and replay the moment when Blake picked Lana up.

I will never have that, but instead of that usual tinge of envy because someone else has more than me, my little heart is soaring for Lana.

Yay! Banker boy cared.

Blake Law Barrington

Lana moans and I take my eyes off the road to briefly look at her.

'Ooh uuugggg why uuuuuuggggg,' she says, and covering her face with her hand, mumbles unintelligently. I don't try to talk to her. When I reach the apartment block, I take my keycard from the dashboard and go out to Lana's side. The night porter's eyes are round with curiosity when I carry Lana through reception towards the lift. He stands up, but I shake my head, and he sits down again. I elbow the lift button and it opens almost immediately. I slot in my card and we are transported upwards. The movement of the elevator makes Lana stir in my arms.

'Sorry, Mummy,' she says. 'Oh it's you'...more gibberish...then clearly, 'where's Mum?'

'She's home safe.'

But she appears not to hear, and seems to be trapped in some nightmare of her own. 'Don't die, Mummy. You promised to come to my wedding.'

I watch her with a frown.

'You said you would.' She begins to cry. 'Mum, it's cold. I'm so cold.'

I curse. The lift door opens and I carry her into the apartment and deposit her on the bed.

She grasps my arm and looks into my eyes, frowns, and does not seem to recognize me. 'Where's my mother?' She shivers.

I cover her. 'Shhh...'

'I'll tell you now. You won't break me, Barrington,' she slurs and turns on her side. 'I'll tell Jack what you did. He'll sort you out. Jaaaaccccckk,' she wails.

It makes the hair on my neck stand to see her this way, but it is only when she starts talking gobbledygook in earnest that I get worried. I go into the kitchen and phone my doctor.

After a few minutes I end the call and stare at the granite top. I am simmering with anger with her, for being so careless, so naïve, and with those pigs that thought they could drug a girl and rape her. My hands clench. I close my eyes and breathe deeply. They didn't get her. They didn't get her. My hands unclench. I take another full breath. It is not her fault. She is as innocent as a child. Grimly, I go to sit by the bedside and listen to her ramblings. In all of them, I am the enemy. The one who wants to use her for sex.

I clasp my hands tightly and remain silent.

The porter brings the doctor up. Dr. Faulks is very quick with his analysis. There is nothing much to do. Wait it out. Fluids are the key. Tomorrow will be bad. She will have memory lapses, most likely won't remember a thing.

'Oh, plastic sheets might be a good idea. Sometime incontinence can occur.'

After the doctor is gone, I undress her.

She sighs elaborately. 'Oh! It's you again.' She seems confused, sad.

I pull the duvet over her and she pushes it away. 'I'm hot. Really hot. I thought you wanted to fuck me, anyway.' She grabs my hand and kisses it. 'Thank you. Thank you for what you did for my mother.' Then she moans and falls into a stupor. She sleeps for half an hour and wakes up retching. I bring a large salad bowl that I find in the kitchen, but it is only dry heaving.

I lay a cold towel on her forehead. Her fingers come up to push it away. She pulls my face towards her. Her breath smells strange and stale, but I don't care, I kiss her back.

Suddenly she turns away and begins to cry.

For hours I sit beside her as she goes from comatose to babbling idiot to crazed sex fiend, all the time wondering when it will be over. Finally, when the sky is beginning to lighten, purely from exhaustion she falls into a restless sleep.

I text Laura to reschedule my morning appointments and get into bed beside her. I put my arm around her narrow waist and close my eyes with relief that her suffering is over for the night, and hope that she won't remember this long and terrible night. My nose hovers over the crook of her neck and finds the faint but familiar scent of her perfume.

I register in my tense body a sense of victory that they did not get her, and then, a strong sense of possession. I tighten my hold on her.

She belongs to me until I say otherwise.

Twenty-Five

Lana Bloom

While we are having dinner on the balcony I say, 'We've been invited to a party tomorrow. Do you want to go?'

Blake looks at me strangely. 'It's my birthday tomorrow.'

'Oh,' I exclaim, surprised. 'You never said anything.'

'No, it's not something I am looking forward to.'

'You will be thirty.'

'Yes.'

'Do you want to come to the party then?'

'I can't. My family is flying over to be with me. They've arranged something for me in a hotel. It will be insufferably boring, I'm sure, but I am obliged to attend.'

"Of course, of course.' I try my best not to show how his news has affected me. Was he never going to tell me? 'I'll just go to the party with Billie, then.'

Only this morning I tasted the name Lana Barrington on my tongue. The whisper is my secret.

It felt right. Or as Billie would say, very fucking right. So I said it louder.

'Lana Barrington.' Daring the fates.

Mrs. Lana Barrington. Your husband has been delayed. Would you like to wait for him at the bar?

The fantasy was so perfect I wanted to cry. What a fool I have been. How on earth did I manage to fall in love with such a cold and heartless man, a banker for God's sake?

'Let Tom drive you there and back,' he is saying.

'It's OK. I'll just take a taxi.'

"I'll feel better if Tom drives you, waits for you and brings you back.'

'Will she be there?'

'Yes,' he says very quietly.

'Well, that's that then. I hope you have fun.' My voice sounds high and too merry.

'I won't,' he says, but that doesn't soothe me one bit.

That was yesterday. Today I am in Billie's bedroom wearing a pair of white shorts, a cut off, sleeveless, white T-shirt that leaves my midriff bare and white trainers.

'Wow, you look seriously hot,' Billie comments.

'You don't think it's too slutty?'

'Are you kidding? It's white. You look like a wet dream. Besides, it's Jerry's party. It's always full of working girls.'

Billie is wearing combat boots, a fur trimmed, green beret, and a clinging black cat-suit.

'Well, you look very Miley Cyrus,' I say.

'Thanks. I was going for rock chick, but obviously I'm not ever going to say no to Miley,' Billie replies with a grin. 'Now get in front of the mirror.'

I sit on the edge of the bed and Billie picks up a curling iron and takes up position behind me. With meticulous care she begins to put corkscrew curls in my hair. She is concentrating so hard she does not speak, so I let my mind wander to Blake. I wonder about his world. So entirely different from mine. At a hotel, he said, careful not to mention the name of the hotel, as if he feared there was a possibility that I might turn up and embarrass him.

In a little while Leticia comes to join us. She is wearing a plain gray T-shirt, ripped jeans and a surly expression. Her hair is gelled to spikes around her head. She is a big, butch girl.

'How's it going, Let?' I greet.

Leticia grunts moodily.

Suddenly, an image of Leticia tied spread eagle on her bed with a chocolate bar stuck between her legs pops into my head and I press my lips together to hide my amusement.

Leticia turns towards Billie. 'You told her, didn't you?' she accuses.

Unfazed, Billie takes another small section of my hair and carefully coils it around the curling iron. 'Be thankful I didn't tell her what I did to you last night,' she says, and crusty, cross Leticia squirms.

When we are ready, we walk over to Jerry's place. It is such a warm evening we don't even need coats.

The music is loud and there are many people there, but Billie, who is always the centre of any party, gets immediately pulled to the middle of the dance floor. When my mobile rings I almost do not hear it. I look at the screen. It is ten o'clock and it is Blake.

'Hi,' I say, but it is so loud it's impossible to hear him. 'Wait one moment,' I yell and fight my way out of the crowd. 'What's up?'

'Nothing. My party was rather flat, so I left. Can I come join you, after all?'

'Of course.' Suddenly my heart feels light and happy. He wants my company.

I am sitting on the stairs waiting for him when he arrives.

'Where's Tom?'

'Sent him home.'

He locks his car and walks up to me. 'What are you doing sitting here?'

'Waiting for you.'

He turns to look at a group of youths. They are swearing loudly and holding beer cans. 'It looks dangerous.'

I laugh. 'I grew up here. I know those guys. They're Jerry's mates. If you want to score some coke, they're the ones to go to.'

'You don't take drugs, do you?'

I laugh again. 'No.'

He sits beside me, and takes a curly lock of hair in his hand. 'What's this?'

'Billie did it. It's not permanent.'

His hands move to the white shorts. 'And this?'

'I can hardly wear the fancy dresses you bought me here. I'll stick out like a sore thumb.' I look at him hungrily: the man looks good enough to eat. A soft breeze teases his hair. I have a desire to flirt with him. 'Don't you like it, then?'

He looks at me expressionlessly, a master of disguise. 'What do you think?'

'I think yes.'

'Go to the top of the class, Miss Bloom.'

I laugh.

He watches me closely. 'I don't think I have ever seen you laugh.'

'And?'

'I like it.'

I giggle. 'Good. Let's go find you a drink.'

'Is my car safe there?'

'It's not Detroit, you know.'

He jerks his head at the group of youths with the beer cans. 'Are you sure?'

I look around and further away notice Kensington standing with a group of boys watching us. I point my thumb over my shoulder. 'See that boy in the green baseball cap? If you give him a ride he'll watch your car for you.'

Blake looks over at the boy.

'That black boy?' he says doubtfully.

'Be careful, you might reveal your hand as not being an equal opportunities employer.'

Blake crooks a finger in the boy's direction. Kensington doesn't need any further encouragement. He jumps on his bike and tucking his head into his shoulders races towards us. He screeches to a stop dangerously close to Blake's feet.

'Oi! Watch it,' I warn.

'Sorry,' he apologizes with a cheeky grin.

'What's your name?'

'Kensington Parish.'

'Want to watch my car for me, Kensington?'

'Yeah,' Kensington agrees enthusiastically. He looks at the car admiringly. 'This car was made by God, man.'

'Here's fifty.'

Kensington's eyes sparkle. 'Fifty quid?'

His thin hand reaches out for it, but Blake pulls his hand back slightly. 'If I come back and find the car exactly as I left it then there's another fifty for you.'

Kensington's face splits into an almighty grin. 'Thanks, Mister,' he says and snatches the note. Unceremoniously, he drops his bicycle on the ground and hops lightly onto the bonnet of the car.

'You're generous,' I say.

'Not at all. A single scratch can cost thousands to repair.'

We go up the stairs and find Billie. Billie makes a licking gesture behind his back, but she is very polite. 'Forget about good Scotch here,' she says, and goes to get Blake a beer. As we are talking, Jack walks in. He has a pretty girl on his arm and he introduces her as Alison.

'Hello, Alison. Great to meet you,' I say warmly, and turning to Jack, widen my eyes to say well done. He pretends he has not seen my gesture and, briefly shakes hands with Blake.

'Right, I want you lot on your feet and dancing,' Billie orders bossily, as she thrusts a bottle of beer into Blake's palm.

'I don't dance,' Blake says, as Jack and Alison quickly move off in the opposite direction.

A couple vacate one of the battered sofas. 'Perhaps you would like to join me on one of these lovely sofas,' Blake says, and collapses into its creaky springs. I laugh and fall next to him. A young man who looks the worse for wear comes and sits next to me on the sofa. He has a tattoo of men in a tug-of-war on his shaven head. Blake mutters something indecipherable and scoops me up and deposits me on his lap.

'What are you doing?' I squeal.

'Don't want you catching anything off him,' he whispers in my ear.

I feel the hard muscles of his thighs. Flirtatiously, I look at him from beneath my lashes. He puts his big hands on my bare knees and pulls me until my rear is in close contact with his groin. I can feel how hard he has become.

Blake pulls me closer and captures my mouth. He smells of caramel and tastes divine. I slip my hand into his unbuttoned shirt, and find a man's skin, hot, taut, muscles rippling underneath. It makes my lips part.

'I want to take you home now,' he growls in my ear.

'OK,' I agree instantly, and we stand to go.

'Leaving so soon,' Bill moans moodily.

'It's not really my scene,' Blake says.

'Call me tomorrow,' Jack says, as I kiss his cheek.

'I will.'

I turn to Alison, who is holding onto Jack possessively, as if she fears something is going on between Jack and me. 'Take care of my brother,' I whisper in her ear and see her relax and smile warmly for the first time.

Then Blake and I are leaving, holding hands, as if we are real lovers. As if he has not paid me to have sex with him. As if I am not the living, breathing doll that he expects to get bored with in a few weeks.

Outside, Kensington hops off the car bonnet when he spots us.

'Good job,' Blake says and slips him the other fifty.

'Cool. What about a ride, then?'

'Another time,' replies Blake, opening the passenger door for me.

Blake is very quiet in the car. Suddenly he reaches past me to the glove box and takes out a velvet box. He tosses it into my lap. 'I got you a present.'

'On *your* birthday?'

'I thought it would look great on you. Besides, what's the point of having a rich lover if you don't unearth expensive baubles out of him.'

I release the catch on the box. It opens and I gasp. On a bed of satin lies the most beautiful seven strand pearl necklace with a large oval sapphire centre.

'Oh my!' I say, staring at it.

At the next red light, he takes the necklace from my stunned hands and puts it around my throat while I hold my hair up. I feel his warm fingers on the back of my neck. Then the light changes and his fingers are gone. I turn around to face him, full of anticipation.

He takes his eyes off the road. 'Beautiful,' he says.

I look at myself in the visor mirror. Even in the dim light, the diamonds set around the large sapphire sparkle like stars. I didn't get him anything.

'I didn't get you anything.'

His eyes drift away from the road and rest on me briefly. 'I didn't expect anything from you.'

'Did you get lots of presents from your family?'

'We don't do presents. We already have everything we could want. When we were younger we did give each other joke gifts. But how many times can you give someone a blow-up doll or a penis enlargement gadget? It was a relief when that stopped.'

When we get to the apartment he picks me up in his arms, throws me on the bed and lunges in after me.

'This is a dangerously sexy pair of white shorts, Miss Bloom,' he teases. 'Do you have the necessary license to operate such a weapon?'

'It's not mine. It belongs to Billie,' I answer primly.

'Ah, Billie of the ear biting fame. Do you think she might let me buy it from her?'

'Oooo I don't know. It did come from a very exclusive market stall in Kilburn. There are only five hundred thousand others like it.'

His eyebrows rise, his lips curve. 'That rare?'

'That rare.'

'I better make my bid good then.'

'Good idea, Mr. Barrington. Kill the competition in one fell swoop.'

'As her agent, what do you suggest I offer?'

'I believe she is hankering after a pink car.'

His eyes gleam. 'Are you sure, Miss Bloom, that I am not better off approaching the market dealer directly?'

'Of course you can…But it will not have the Lana Bloom scent,' I say daringly.

His eyes widen and fill with delicious longing. 'You never said a truer word, Miss Bloom.'

His long fingers very deliberately pop the top button and pull down the zip. The sound is exciting in the silence. I can hear my own ragged breathing. He slides the shorts off.

'Ah, these legs…So long…So silky… I swear I never met a girl with skin such as yours.'

The shorts slip over my ankles and end up clutched in his big hands. He crushes them, brings them to his nose and inhales deeply. 'The Lana Bloom scent. I'll miss it,' he whispers, almost to himself.

And suddenly I tense. All this will end soon.

This apartment, this bed, these clothes, this delicious banter, this *man*...will all disappear into nothing. I will be left only with memories. I clutch his forearms, pull his mouth down to mine, and kiss him desperately, opening my mouth, begging him to be inside me. He has already left his mark on me. I must leave my mark on him. I lie under him naked but for my necklace, and realize I don't know how to.

When the desert wind blew it covered everything in sand.

Twenty-Six

'Remember when you said you wanted to be part of my world? Do you still want to?' he asks me.

'Yes.'

'It is very ugly.'

My answer is instant. 'I don't care. I want to know.'

For a moment, he hesitates, there is doubt there, and then an indescribable expression flashes in his eyes. 'All right. Let's go.' He leads me to a BMW parked up the street. I look at him questioningly.

'Hired,' he says briefly.

'Where are we going?'

'Somewhere in the New Forest.'

We drive in silence, the atmosphere in the car, taut and foreign, and come to a stop outside what seems to be a lodge of some kind. The building is small and unremarkable. There are other cars parked in the car park, but something feels off key.

'They are all hired, aren't they?'

'Yes,' he says shortly. 'Come.'

While I look around me, he gets out of the car, opens the boot and takes out two boxes. I look at my watch. 10.00p.m.

We go into the low building and enter a large empty room with many doors. All the doors are open except one. I shiver. Something about the place doesn't feel right. We enter one of the rooms and Blake closes the door behind us. There is nothing in that room except a table and a mirror. Blake puts the two boxes on the table.

'You wanted to come into my world. Here's your chance. Are you sure?'

He looks different. His eyes and voice are cold. He is hoping I will say no, but I want to enter his world. So badly, I throw caution to the wind. I lick my suddenly dry lips, swallow, and nod.

He holds out the box tied with a red ribbon and I take it from him. It is not heavy. 'What's in it?'

'Open it and see.'

He watches me untie the ribbon and lift the lid. I push aside the tissue and find a mask. White and pretty. I raise my eyes to his. 'Do I put it on?'

'Not yet.'

I put the mask aside and take out the bulky red garment inside. It is a cloak with a hood. I look at him, my expression begs the question, 'What? What is this all about?'

He ignores my unspoken query. 'Wear it.'

I slip into it and he steps forward and does the large button at my throat. The cloak is thick and voluminous and covers me entirely. Deftly, he pulls the hood up, and fits the mask on my face. He stands me in front of the mirror.

'Remember,' he warns. 'Do not take this ensemble off after we leave this room. No matter what happens the mask and the robes do not come off. Do you understand?'

My mask nods in the mirror.

He opens his box and dresses himself in the black robes that are inside. His mask is gold with a beaked nose. Unlike mine his seems sinister and forbidding.

'Ready?'

'Yes.'

He puts his hand in the small of my back and guides me out of the room. We cross the large empty space and go through another door. It turns out to be the back door of the lodge. A man sitting on a horse-drawn coach is waiting. He does not turn to look at us but stares straight ahead. The bizarre and forbidding alchemy of the moment causes me to blankly note the white socks on the horse. We climb in and the coachman immediately sets the horse to a trot. We follow a path that snakes through woods until we suddenly come upon a grand mansion perched on higher ground.

My breath is swept away by it. Made of cut gray stone, it is like something found in a windswept ghost story. Awestruck, I stare at the roaring gargoyles and the many soaring gothic spires that pierce the purple sky. Hundreds of windows stare out like glassy dead eyes. Unless I am very much mistaken one of the windows blinks, a flash of yellow iris, before it snaps shut. Someone was watching our arrival.

The coach comes to a stop on the entrance stairs and we climb out. I feel Blake's hand on my waist as he helps me out.

'Remember, the mask does not come off, even in the ladies.'

'OK.'

'And don't tell anyone your name.'

'OK.'

'Don't speak unless spoken to.'

'Right.'

'I'm serious, Lana.'

I look up into the eyeholes of his mask. 'You're making me nervous, Blake.'

'It's important.'

'Then don't leave my side.'

'I've no intention of doing that.'

We go up the shallow stone steps. When we reach the top, I turn to look down upon the magnificent garden maze. In the purplish light it is very beautiful. At the entrance, a totally expressionless, bone-thin man, dressed in black coat-tails, nods at Blake and slowly waves his hand towards the interior of the house.

There are more ushers and silent staff dressed in black who nod at us and wave us deeper into the interior. The funereal garments and the silence begin to seep into me. I recognize them to be poisonous.

Finally, two men open a pair of double doors and we enter a large hall full of masked, robed people standing around and talking in whispers. There is a stage at one end with a throne on it. The room reminds me of an old-fashioned theater with balconies. There are also many doors that lead away from the hall. A strange throbbing music is playing into that odd air of expectancy and waiting.

I look up at Blake. 'This reminds me of *Eyes Wide Shut.*'

'Yes, Stanley Kubrick's movies are filled with hidden messages.'

A waiter brings a tray. Blake shakes his head. When I try to reach for a glass, I feel the subtle pressure that he exerts on my hand. I shake my head and the waiter moves on silently. It is at this point that I realize that there are other women besides me who are wearing the exact same robe and mask as me.

'Hello,' a man's voice addresses us from behind.

We turn. A stocky man in an odd gray and silver mask is standing about a foot away from us. 'You brought…someone,' he says, his eyes glittering blackly through the eyeholes of his mask. I feel Blake tense beside me.

'Yes.'

'Will you be going into the main room?' the man asks.

'Of course,' Blake says smoothly, but I feel the tremor that goes through his body.

'Good, I will see you there. If I don't, tell your father I send my regards.'

Blake nods, and the man turns on his heel and disappears into the crowd of robes and masks.

'Come,' Blake says urgently, and leads me towards the entrance. The large doors open, and we retrace our steps out into the evening air. We go down the shallow steps and into a waiting coach.

When I turn to Blake, he puts a finger to his lips. The coach drops us off outside the lodge house, we traverse that strange empty room, and go back out to where the hired car is waiting. Blake unlocks the car.

'Take your cloak off and drop it on the ground,' he orders as he takes his own cloak off and chucks it into the back seat.

I do as I am told and get into the car. My hands are trembling. Blake's fear and tension have transferred themselves to me.

Blake starts the engine and the car screeches away. He says nothing and drives very fast.

'Chuck the mask out of the window,' he says when he has been driving for about five minutes. He takes his mask off and flips it onto the back seat where it lands on his black cloak.

'Why did I have to throw mine away but not you?'

'Yours is generic; my cloak has my family insignia sewn into it and my mask is distinct to me.'

Ten minutes later, Blake pulls off the road and, turning around, takes me into his arms. 'I'm sorry,' he says. 'I shouldn't have taken you there. I don't know what I was thinking of. You're just a baby.'

'It's OK,' I say, confused. 'Nothing happened.'

He looks into my eyes. He is full of secrets. 'Yes, nothing happened.'

That night he jerks awake in a cold sweat and sits upright. The movement wakes me.

'Did you have a nightmare?' I ask, my hand reaching for his back.

'I dreamed I took you into the main room,' he says. His voice is hoarse with horror.

'What happens in the main room?'

He turns to me and in the dark his eyes are tormented pools of terror. 'Oh, Lana, Lana, Lana,' he whispers in my hair.

'Tell me,' I urge, but he shakes his head.

'My world is ugly and corrupt. It only looks good from the outside. When our time is over, I must return you the way I found you, pure and innocent.'

Gently he opens my legs. 'Let me hide a little while longer in your world,' he rasps and buries his mouth in my sex.

His mouth is warm and soft. My body responds, arches; my hands come out to grasp his hair; my legs entwine like ropes around his head, and I come with a gasp while I am wonderfully full of him, but through it all I never forget what he said—*when our time is over.*

Twenty-Seven

I wake up and turn around to look at the man beside me. In the dim light I stare at him. He is so heartbreakingly beautiful when he sleeps he makes me want to cry. That hard mouth softened, the thick, stubby eyelashes dark-blue smudges on his face. I slip out of bed quietly. I am ravenous these days. I smile to think it must be all the sex. I close the bedroom door softly and pad into the kitchen where I switch on the light and head towards the fridge. My hands reach for the tin of caviar and a jar of marmalade. I go to the bread-box and cut two slices of nutty bread. Those I pop into the toaster and stand by the counter, yawning.

When they are ready, I spread a thick layer of caviar on one slice of toast and spoon a dollop of marmalade over the other. I slap them together, and popping myself on a stool, bite into my creation. It is so delicious I close my eyes to savor it. I open my mouth eagerly to take a second bite.

'Is this another terrible combination that you Brits have conjured up?' Blake teases from the doorway.

My eyes snap open, my mouth closes, and my eyes move over the food I have prepared. Marmalade and caviar. Slowly my gaze lifts to him. He is lounging against the doorframe nude as the day he was born.

'What's the matter?' he asks.

I close my mouth and try to smile. 'It's my own thing,' I say weakly. My heart is beating so loud in my ears that I feel as if he must be able to hear it. I put the sandwich down and look at him. 'Can't you sleep?'

'Come back to bed and put me to sleep,' he invites, his eyes darkening.

'OK, I'll finish my sandwich and come join you. Go ahead.'

I smile at him, willing him not to enter the kitchen, but go back to the bedroom and wait for me. He looks at me and as if he has heard my unspoken wishes he nods and, turning around, leaves. The air escapes my lungs in a rush. I put my elbow on the surface of the counter and lean my forehead against my hand. I actually feel sick. I open the sandwich and really look at what I have concocted. At the smeared caviar and marmalade. It is revolting.

My mother ate anchovies and marmalade when she was pregnant.

I cover my mouth.

I am pregnant.

I look at the clock above the door. It is two in the morning. I close the sandwich, my appetite totally gone. Oh God, what now? I begin to count backwards.

Yes, I am definitely two weeks late.

Twenty-Eight

Blake Law Barrington

I open the door to the apartment and instantly *feel* that she is gone. Not gone out shopping or gone to see her mother, but gone away from me. Forever. Her presence seems to have evaporated into thin air. I push down the sensation of horror and walk down the corridor to the living room.

The curtains are drawn shut. It is dim and cool. I move to the coffee table. It is empty. In the bedroom, I glance towards my bedside table then hers. Nothing. I go into the kitchen and look at the island top, my eyes scanning the room quickly.

No, she has left no note.

I go back into the bedroom and open the cupboard. Handbags, shoes, clothes. It is all there. She has taken nothing. I key in the combination and open the safe. The velvet box is in there. I open it and the necklace lays nestled on its satin bed. I sigh with relief, put it back and close the safe.

On my way to the living room I pass the dining room, my eyes skim the long table and fall on her purse. For an odd moment, I find myself staring at it. The thoughts in my brain are foreign. I shake my head and walk away. Three steps down the corridor, I stop and go back. Like a sleepwalker I drift to her bag. I put a hand out and lift it by its strap, a metal and black leather interlaced affair.

I raise the flap and look inside.

Lip gloss, ballpoint pen, compact mirror, sparkly eye shadow and...a small maroon wallet. I fish it out, run my finger along the leather and open it. I look at what appears to be a collage of photographs cut out from different photographs and carefully, lovingly stuck together: her mother, Billie and Jack. The child-like innocence of her handiwork causes me pain.

I do not know why it should. I close the flap, return the wallet to her handbag, and walk away from the dining room. I have never done such a thing before. My shoulders feel tense with worry and confusion. What is the matter with me? I have never been curious about the contents of any other woman's purse before.

She must have gone to visit her mother.

I ring her number and wait, but on the second ring I hear another ring coming from the living room. I follow the sound; her phone is lying on the sofa. I cut the connection and pick up her phone.

Last caller, me, last call, her mother.

I ring her mother's landline. It rings out. I go through her address list and ring Billie. When her cocky recorded voice comes on I leave a message for her to call me back urgently. Then I ring Jack. He answers on the sixth ring just as I am about to give up.

'Jack, do you know where Lana is?'

'No, why?'

'Just trying to find her. She's gone out without her cellphone.'

'It's raining here. Is it raining there?'

The question throws me and there is a slight pause before I reply. 'Yeah…It's raining here.'

'I wouldn't worry, mate, she's probably just gone out walking in the rain.'

'Right.'

Jack laughs. 'She'll come home looking like a drowned kitten. It's something to behold.'

'Right. Thanks, Jack.'

I go out onto the balcony. It is pouring with rain. A jagged flash of lightning splits the sky and I wait for the thunder. It comes deafeningly loud almost immediately. I frown. I don't like the thought of her in the rain. I go to the edge of the balcony and reach a hand out to catch some rain. Strange. I lean over the edge and turn my face up to the shower. I have not felt rain on my face since I was a child.

I try to imagine what she must be feeling, thinking. The rain is cold and I am quickly drenched. I peel off my shirt and as I am balling it in my hand I hear the key in the door. It opens and we stare at each other. Both wet. Both lost.

Instantly I know she is not the same anymore. There is such hurt in her eyes. I stride toward her. She is almost blue with cold.

'Come,' I say quickly, and taking her to the bathroom, guide her shivering body under the shower spray.

Lana Bloom

The water that pelts my cold skin is perfectly hot. I hear him moving away and I close my eyes and savor the pleasant sensation. Almost immediately I feel life and warmth coming back into my fingers and limbs. I have walked too long. I lean my forearms against the tiles and lifting my face to the water, abandon myself to it. I hear the shower door slide and my eyes open to him.

He is nude and standing outside.

My eyes rove over him and settle in fascination on his manhood that is already half erect before I suddenly realize what I am doing, and flushing with embarrassment, turn away.

He catches me by the chin and brings my eyes to him. 'I want you to look at me. Look at me.'

I return my eyes to his growing shaft. It is no longer at half-mast but standing proud. I lift my eyes back to his face and he steps into the shower. I move back to make space for him and watch him through the drops of water and steam. He chuckles and, finding the soap, slips it across the skin of my chest.

'Lift your arms.'

I obey and he soaps me under my arms. His touch is light and unticklish. He swipes the soap along my shoulders and then down to my breasts. Here he is rhythmic and meticulous. The mounds get much attention. So much that I long to have him take my nipples in his mouth.

The soap travels downward. To my stomach and lower still to my bare-skinned sex. He doesn't have to ask. Willingly, I spread my legs and the soap slides between them. The water sluices through his hands.

'Turn around.'

I turn. The soap slides sensuously along my back and down my spine to my hips and finally enters the crack of my bottom. I feel him kneel to wash my legs down to the soles of my feet, which he lifts and does one by one. Then he stands. In my line of sight I see him return the soap and pick up the shampoo bottle. I hear it squirt into the palm of his hand.

Then he is washing my hair.

The bubbles run down my body and heat collects between my legs.

He moves closer until I can feel his hard body slipping and sliding against mine. My legs begin to tremble. He turns me around and sucks my nipples while his hands slide down my stomach and boldly without warning grab my hips.

I gaze into the storm clouds in his eyes. His jaw is clenched tight. He lifts my body and penetrates me. I curl my legs around his hips and cry with animalistic pleasure. The deeper he buries himself inside me, the more my body cleaves to his.

Afterwards he carries me to the bed and dries me carefully.

I look up to him. 'What are you thinking of?'

'Your body.'

'Hmm.'

'Why did you walk so far in the rain?'

I stare into his eyes. They are unreadable. 'I like the rain. I've always walked in the rain.'

'But the rain in England is cold.'

'I don't know any other type of rain.'

He brings the hairdryer and a brush and sits on the bed with them beside him. Then he calls me to sit on the floor against the bed between his knees and begins to towel dry my hair. He is careful not to rub hard. Afterwards, he runs his fingers through my hair and gently untangles any knots he finds. Only then does he switch on the hairdryer and begin to dry my hair.

When he switches off the hairdryer I say, 'You can't cook but you can blow dry hair.'

'I used to dry my sister's hair for her.'

I swivel my neck around. 'You don't have a sister.'

Firmly he turns my head to face away from him. 'I've told you before, don't trust everything Wikipedia says.'

The brush glides through my hair in long, slow strokes. 'Why is she not known to the public?'

'She was born with a genetic anomaly. She's not like you and me. She lives in her own world. Most great families have such relatives—they just don't acknowledge or advertise them. It's an unfortunate effect of interbreeding.'

'So she is locked away?'

There is a pause. 'Something like that.'

'Do you still see her?'

'No, she is in our Buckinghamshire property. She has a whole wing and sectioned off grounds. Nurses and servants to care for her twenty-four hours a day.'

'What's she like?'

'A four-year-old child. She communicates by pointing and smiling.' His voice is sad.

'Why did you stop going to see her?'

The brush stops for a second, then starts again. 'The last time I saw her was when I was twelve. I was brushing her hair and my mother walked into the room. She was horrified. "Are you going to become a great man like your father or a sissy like your great uncle George?" He is another family member that we all pretend doesn't exist. I never went back after that.'

I turn around and catch his wrist. 'I don't care what anybody else says, you are a good man,' I say.

'Don't fool yourself, Lana. We're all no good. Don't trust any of us. Not even me.'

'Is there no one you trust?'

'No.'

'Not even your dad?'

'Dad?' he repeats sarcastically. 'My father's a sociopath.'

'Isn't he a great philanthropist?'

'Naïve little Lana. My father's a trillionaire. And there is no such thing as a philanthropist trillionaire. Do you know what one has to do to become a philanthropist trillionaire? Spend your whole life crushing as many people as possible for profit and then donate a library? I don't trust him and neither should you. It would cause him the same grief to obliterate you if you stood in his way as it would if he trod on an ant in his path.'

'Do trillionaires exist?'

The brush stills mid-air. 'Think, Lana. What is the debt of the United States alone? Who are all those lovely trillions owed to?'

'The Federal Reserve?'

He laughs. 'And who do you think owns that? The Federal Reserve is a private company just like the Bank of England, and every central bank throughout the world. Through a network of holding companies, the old families own vast controlling portions of not only their stocks, but all the too-big-to-fail banks that you hate so much.'

I frown. I need time to think about the true meaning of what he has revealed to me. 'What about your mother?'

'My mother threw us to the wolves a long time ago. My brothers and I grew up in stifling conditions.'

I shake my head. 'And there I was, wishing I was rich, while I was growing up in stifling conditions.'

'You don't understand, Lana, and perhaps you never will. We are different. We are not merely rich.

We don't own tracts of land, we own countries and politicians. We have different responsibilities. We have an agenda.'

Then his face closes over.

Twenty-Nine

Blake Law Barrington

Your hands are inside my heart.

I stand on the embankment watching the water rushing by and think of Lana...and feel confused. There is a room inside her that I cannot enter. It is like the room inside me that she is not allowed in. It is where she keeps all the hurts I have caused. There are other things in that room, too. She has secrets now. I try to imagine what else could be hidden there.

A man talking loudly on his cell phone in some European language intrudes on my musings. I glance away from the water and see the tramps sleeping rough. For the first time in my life I perceive them as people. People who have fallen on hard times because of the things that *my* family is doing. They are not the real parasites. Lana was right that night when she accused us of being the real parasites. Of course, I have always known that we are the disease that they are ill from. You have to be blind, deaf and dumb not to see that. I just never cared before.

My phone rings. It is Marcus.

'Hello Marcus.'

My brother gets to the point immediately. 'Morgan just called me. *Why* is his loan still pending?'

'Morgan is a crook.'

There is a shocked silence and then my brother sighs heavily. 'What's going on with you, Blake?'

'Nothing. It bugs me to approve the loan. This green energy thing is such a scam.'

'Of course it is. And so what?'

'Why do we have to be part of everything crooked?'

'My God, you're beginning to sound like Quinn,' my brother says referring to our youngest sibling. Quinn turned his back on the family fortune and ran off to Europe to be an artist.'

'I'm beginning to think Quinn had the right idea.'

'It's a big account—government approved. We're just facilitating the funds.'

'We're always only facilitating the funds.'

'Father worked hard to get us on board. The other banks will kill for an opportunity like this.'

I sigh heavily. 'Yeah, I'll sign off on the papers in the morning.'

'I don't care about the loan—what I care about is what's happening to you? You're still in training. You can't get soft, Blake. These are shark-infested waters you're swimming in. They'll eat you alive.

The entire system is corrupt. You can't fight it. If you try to, it will only break you.'

'Just having a bad day, I guess.'

'Have you spoken to Victoria?'

I frown. 'No, why?'

'Nothing. Her father was telling me you haven't called in some weeks. It's not a good thing to leave these things for too long.'

I do something I have never done before. I confide in my brother. 'I think I might have found someone.'

There is a shocked pause. 'Someone? What do you mean someone?'

'I think I'm in love.'

'What?' The burst of sound is so explosive and sudden that I have to pull the phone away from my ear and hold it away.

'Hell! Blake! Have you lost your mind?'

'I don't think so.'

'Who is it?'

'Not one of us.'

'Set her up in an apartment and visit her every day until you are bored of her.'

I smile in the dark. 'Done that.'

'You've fallen for a gold-digger!'

'She's not a gold-digger.'

'They all are.'

'Well, she's not.'

'Look, Blake, don't fuck this up. This is your future. You have to marry Victoria.'

'I don't have to do anything. I don't want to end up like you. A wife you detest, three kids you never see, and cold fucks with models and movie stars in luxurious apartments and hotel rooms.'

'What's wrong with that?'

It was a mistake to tell him.

'You're going to fuck this up, aren't you? This is not a club, Blake. You can't terminate your membership and walk away. There are consequences.'

'Quinn did.'

'You're *not* Quinn,' he says, his voice heavy with meaning.

'Look, I got to go. I'll call you soon. Bye, Marcus.'

I cut the call and stand looking at the cold, black water.

'Spare some change, mate,' someone says from behind.

I turn back and look at the tramp. He is probably my age. Change? I never carry 'change'. I open my wallet. There is nothing there but fifty-pound notes. I pull one out and hold it out by the corner. The man's eyes bulge.

'God bless you, sir,' he cries delightedly, and staggers away to spend the money on more booze. I look up and a star tumbles from the sky. I watch it and take it as a blessing.

I want desperately to go back to the apartment and get into bed beside her, but I won't. That will be a bad idea. She will be asleep and I will only wake her and want to get into that beautiful body. No, I want to do this properly. I will go back to my own apartment tonight and tomorrow I will meet her and tell her I am madly, madly in love with her.

I send her a text.

Meet me for breakfast outside the café? 9am. X

Lana Bloom

I am not asleep when his text comes through. I read his message and even though the very thought of breakfast makes me feel sick, I know I will go to him. Perhaps I will have some black coffee and pretend I am on a diet or something. I wonder where he is. Why has he not come to me? Has he begun to lose interest? So quickly? Alone and deeply sad, I go to sleep and sleep badly, tossing and turning. Eventually, when I do fall into a deep sleep, dawn is in the sky.

My alarm goes off at eight a.m.

I dress hurriedly in a long shirt and navy and white trousers. There is no bump yet, but it seems like a good idea to start dressing in loose attire. Carelessly I pull an Alice hair band on. It doesn't match my outfit, but I can't bring myself to care. Suddenly, I am wrecked by a wave of nausea. I lean against the mirror and fight it. I shouldn't have agreed to go, but I don't want to make him suspicious.

Downstairs, I wave to Mr. Nair and walk out of the building. The café is only down the street. As I walk my thoughts wander. What will become of me and the little life growing inside me? I put my head down and make a decision as I step onto the road. An urgent shout jars me out of my own little world.

'Watch out!'

My head jerks up. In that split second, I see Blake running towards me. He is no longer shouting. His face is ashen. As if in slow motion I turn and see a car speeding towards me. I should run, but my feet are rooted to the spot. Even far into the future I will remember how I saw everything so clearly it was like looking through a very clean glass. How Blake, his eyes full of desperate fear reached me and with both hands pushed me back with such force that I was thrown backwards and out of harm's way.

The car ploughs into him instead.

I lie on the ground and watch him flying in the air like a rag doll. He lands on the other side of the street. Even from my prone position I can see the stream of blood that starts running away from his head into the gray asphalt. I scramble up on my hands and knees and run to him screaming. He is lying on his front, but his head is turned in my direction.

'Are you all right?' he mumbles vaguely in the direction of my voice, but his eyes seem unable to focus.

'I'm fine,' I sob, and he closes his eyes and falls into some deep, dark place.

Someone calls the police and the ambulance is quick to arrive. They take him to the nearest emergency room, but I am keenly aware that his family will want him to be taken to the best hospital money can buy. I look through his mobile and find Marcus's number.

'Hello,' I say. My voice is strangely calm. It must be the shock, I guess.

'Who's this?' comes the suspicious reply.

'Blake has been in a road accident.' My voice shakes on the word accident. 'He's been taken to the Hospital of St John and St Elizabeth. I just thought you should know.'

'How bad is he?'

'It looks like a head injury, but there might be other internal things that I don't know about.'

'Are you at the hospital right now?'

'Yes.'

'Will you wait for me? I'll be right there.'

I sit on a chair feeling totally numb. There is blood on my wrists and hands. Blake's blood. Suspended inside my cloud of shock I stare at it blankly. Slowly as if in a daze I drag a finger through it. It feels sticky. *I'm not dreaming, this is really happening,* my brain says. I wipe my hand on my stained, torn navy and white trousers, take out my own mobile and call Billie.

Billie is quicker to arrive than Marcus. The sight of Billie's worried face hurrying towards me undoes me.

'Oh, Billie,' I sob. 'It was my fault. I wasn't looking where I was going. If he had not pushed me out of the way it would have been me that the car hit.'

'Banker boy threw himself under a car to save you?' Billie's eyebrows are almost in her hairline.

I stop crying, as I register what I have not with the shock. He is cold and unemotional. He hardly ever touches me unless he wants to have sex. Why?

'Why would he do that?' I whisper.

'People only do that for the people they love,' Billie says.

'He doesn't love me. If you knew what kind of relationship we have you'd never say that. He must have acted instinctively.'

Billie says nothing. Her eyes are on the door. 'Here comes big brother.'

I turn in the direction Billie is looking at and indeed, it is Blake's brother; he has the same superior air. He is standing at the door scanning the room. As soon as he spots us he comes over. His surprised eyes slide quickly over the spiders climbing on Billie's neck, but he only addresses me, as if he instinctively recognizes the type of woman his brother would be interested in.

'I'm Marcus. You must be the one who called me.'

'Yes.'

'Thank you. Where is my brother now?'

I point towards the desk. 'They won't tell me anything.'

'What happened?'

'He pushed me out of the way of a speeding car and took the hit himself.'

Marcus's face is incredulous. 'My brother did that?'

Tears begin to roll unchecked down my face. I feel like a complete fool crying in front of that disapproving stranger, but the tears refuse to stop.

He looks at my tears unemotionally. 'It will be the shock,' he says.

I nod through the tears.

He glances quickly at the two ladies behind the reception desk, obviously eager to talk to them. 'Look, if you give me your name and address, I will be happy to compensate you for what you have done.'

His words are like a slap. I take a shocked step away from him. I remember Blake saying, *we are not like you.* 'That won't be necessary,' I say.

An expression passes across his face. Irritation. He is irritated with me. 'Well, thank you for calling me, anyway.' He turns away from us and begins to walk towards the enquiries desk. Then he remembers, stops and comes back to me. 'Can I have my brother's phone back, please?'

Silently I put the phone into his outstretched hand.

'Thank you again for what you did for my brother,' he says awkwardly.

I nod and feel Billie's supportive hand come around my waist.

Marcus strides away. After the fear, the guilt, and the worry, the shock of his brother's utter rejection finishes me. I sag weakly against Billie.

'Fucking heartless, rude bastard. Fuck them and their pissy billions. They can keep it,' Billie says angrily. She leads me outside and hails a black cab. We get in and do not speak during the journey, but Billie tightly holds my hand in hers for the entire duration of the trip.

When we get out of the cab, I retch and am sick by the side of the road. An old biddy walking on the other side of the road stops to stare and Billie asks her if she has a tissue.

'Oh dear, oh dear,' she says, and crosses the road. She fishes a handkerchief from her handbag. 'What's the matter with the poor child?'

'She's pregnant,' Billie says.

My eyes swing around to Billie and Billie claps her hand over her mouth. 'Oh my God! You're pregnant, aren't you?'

'Can I have the handkerchief back?' the old biddy whines plaintively.

Billie takes the soiled cloth from me and ungratefully stuffs it into the woman's hand. 'Thanks, love. You want to stock up on tissues in future. More hygienic.'

The woman leaves with a sniff and Billie turns to me. 'Why didn't you tell me?'

'I just found out myself. Besides, I can't keep it.'

Billie's eyes open wide. 'What?'

I blink back the tears. 'It's in my contract. If I don't terminate I will forfeit all rights to it. I'm not going to give up my baby to that cold bunch.'

Billie's eyes flash. 'They can't do that.'

'They can, Bill. The way they feel about crushing us is the way you feel about killing a row of ants heading towards your jam jar.'

'Who do they think you are? Fucking Oliver Twist? Please, sir, can I have some more, sir? You know what? I haven't used any of the money that you gave me. Let's give that back to them and work out some plan where we pay the rest back with interest.'

I shake my head tiredly. 'Oh, Bill, they don't want the money back. It's all about their precious bloodline. The purity of the great Barrington line must be safeguarded at all costs. And any bastard children must go back to the Barrington care. They don't trust the likes of us to bring up children properly.'

Billie looks as though she is about to go into one. A very long and loud rant.

'Not now, Bill. Please. I just want to go somewhere I can sit.'

Billie holds out her hand. 'Come. I'll take you home.'

'I don't want my mum to know.'

'It's OK, we'll go to mine and you can clean up there. We don't have to tell anyone.'

'Remember when you said you didn't know whether you would share your lottery money with me if you ever did win?'

'Yeah.'

'Now you know, don't you?'

Billie smiles sadly. 'Yeah, now I know.'

Thirty

Victoria Jane Montgomery

I walk up to the nurse.

'Good afternoon, Miss Montgomery.'

'Good afternoon. How is he today?'

'He seems better. I just looked in on him a few minutes ago and he was asleep, but he was conscious for a few minutes this morning, and seemed desperate to know if someone called Lana was all right? It would be good to reassure him that she is all right.'

I can't stop the pure rush of shock that invades my body. I shutter my beautiful green eyes and smile. 'If he asks again, tell him not to worry about her. She is fine.'

'I certainly will, Miss Montgomery.'

I nod politely and walk down the corridor. My heart feels as if it is breaking. I enter his room and shut the door behind me. It is quiet and full of flowers. My eyes move to his face. His eyes are closed and he is very still. I walk up to his bed and stand looking down on him. He looks so helpless and pale under his dark tan that I feel an odd rush of emotion inside me. I know it is very dull of me, but I love this man. I can't even care that my friends call me Sticky Vicky behind my back.

'Oh, darling,' I whisper. 'What a perfectly awful fright you gave me.'

I take his big hand in my small dainty ones and caress the inside of his wrist. Ever since I met him at my garden party when I was ten years old I have loved him.

'I'm going to marry that boy,' I told my father.

My father threw back his head and laughed, but his eyes had gleamed strangely. He approved. And over the years he had quietly encouraged my total dedication to 'that boy'. When the families decided that it would be a perfect match I celebrated quietly. While Blake indulged in his meaningless affairs and liaisons I laid low. Of course, my father did not and would never know about the drunken one-night stands.

Those don't count.

I let my finger trace a vein. There is nothing I will not do for this man. I bend down and kiss that straight mouth—his lips feel cool and dry—and I remember that other time I pressed my lips to his. Then, he was fifteen. He wiped his lips with the back of his hand and looked at me scornfully. 'You're just a baby. Lip kisses are for grown-ups,' he chided.

Very gently I push back a piece of hair that has strayed onto his forehead and smooth it down. I know he is not in love with me. But I can live with that. I will take him on any terms. I want his seed in me. I want to see him in my children's faces. I want to watch the gray appear in his temples. I want to sit out in my father's French seaside villa when we are both old and gray watching the sunset together. But for now a fond look, an affectionate smile, a caring touch from him will be enough for me.

For a long time, I am content to simply sit with my cheek pressed against his hand. Eventually, there is a noise at the door and Marcus enters. He stands awkwardly in the middle of the room for a moment.

'Hello, Marcus,' I greet with a smile.

'How are you?' he says politely, and coming over to me, lightly kisses both my cheeks.

'I'm fine, thank you.'

He nods distractedly. 'The nurse told me he regained consciousness for a short while. Were you here? Did he say anything?'

I shake my head. 'I wasn't here.' He's never going to know about the slut Blake has installed in a penthouse in St John's Wood. 'How did it happen?' I ask instead.

'I don't know...exactly,' he says evasively, and moves to the other side of the bed.

Ah, so he knows something that he doesn't want me to know. Blake's accident must have something to do with that whore! I feel a new clutch of pain in my heart. All this while I thought it was not serious, that it was a strictly sex thing. I saw the contract, after all. The pain is so strong I feel like howling.

'I guess I'll come back in the evening,' I say. My voice sounds strange.

I close the door and quickly walk along the corridor. I hate the smell of hospitals. It always reminds me of the many months my grandmother spent in her sick bed before she died. As I round the corner I come to a dead stop. The nurse at the desk is talking to Blake's tart and a ghoul-like creature covered in tattoos.

Anger bubbles inside me. These low class people. How dare they? How dare they show up at this hospital where my father could very well come to? The cheek of it. I hear the nurse very firmly enforce the instructions I left.

'I'm sorry but I have very strict instructions not to let anyone in, but the family members on this list.'

For a while it appears as if the ghoul would fight it out but Blake's tart takes a step back and the ghoul says loudly, 'You're right, Lana, lets leave these stuck-up, la di da shits to get on with it.' Then she grabs the slut's hand and pulls her away. They do not see me.

Now I know. Something has to be done.

Thirty-One

Lana Bloom

The doorbell rings and I start with surprise. There is always somebody at my mother's door wanting to borrow a hairdryer, a pen, red lipstick, a sparkly handbag, or something. But here? None of my friends are allowed to visit. Besides…unannounced by Mr. Nair?

I walk to the door and look out of the eyehole.

There is a woman standing outside. She looks to be in her early twenties. Her skin is very good, her lipstick is pale, and her glossy brown hair is held back by a black velvet band. She is dressed as if she is going to a lawn party. In an elegant linen dress and black pearls.

I know who she is.

I open the door and, oddly, note that I would never have thought to combine black pearls with such an outfit. From every pore of her flawless skin she exudes good breeding and finishing school class. She is pure style.

You can live in a fine home, wear the right clothes and even go to the right parties but you will never be one of us, her very being seems to say.

Her mouth curves into a smile. 'Hello, I'm Victoria. May I come in?'

I cannot stop staring at her. So this is the woman that Blake is going to marry. This is the woman who will have his babies and live with him.

'Please,' she says.

I open the door wider and stand back.

She enters and looks around the room curiously, but refrains from commenting. I precede her into the living room and turn around to face her.

'You are prettier in real life.'

I don't know if I should acknowledge the compliment. In the end I don't. It is not sincere.

'May I sit?'

I nod and she perches at the end of a sofa. Her movements are all dainty. She transfers the small pink purse from her hand to her lap and crosses her slim ankles.

Then she looks at me and smiles again. 'Will you sit too?'

I flush and sit. This is not the woman's territory and yet it seems she has somehow taken charge.

'I know you are shocked to see me here and even more shocked to see that I neither hate nor feel angry with you. You see, our ways are different. You'll probably never understand so I won't try to explain too much. Suffice to say that I don't think it is ideal, especially from the women's point of view, but I am willing to concede that men must sow their wild oats before they settle down, so I allow it.'

My lips part.

'I know what you are hoping for.'

I make a strangled sound in my throat. 'Really?'

'You are hoping for exactly the same thing that every woman who has signed one of these sordid agreements and who then falls in love dreams of. You want Blake to fall in love with you and marry you.'

I cannot help it, wild color rushes up my throat.

Her eyes flash. 'But he never will. Men like him have been taught since they were knee high how to take, how to have their cake and eat it in every situation.'

She stops to make a little face.

'Marrying you or staying with you will not be that. This agreement with you, until he gets bored, and then, marrying me, will be the option most desirable to our men. And that is what Blake will do too.' She looks at me innocently. 'Has he in any way suggested more than this arrangement? Perhaps given you hope for a different future with him?'

Woodenly, I shake my head.

She smiles with great satisfaction. 'I thought so. You see, the most important thing for us is to secure the right bloodlines for our children and ensure our wealth is not dissipated away into careless hands. Blake knows where his loyalties lie. Consequently, I fear nothing from you. If anything, I feel sorry for you and want to be fair to you. I can see that you are in love with him, and in the end, you will be left with nothing more than a broken heart.'

I had been staring at the carpet but at her words my head snaps up. 'What do you want?' I blurt out.

'Well, I guess I might as well come to the point. Nobody knows I'm here and Mummy would scream blue murder if she knew I was.'

'So why are you here?'

'I know your contract will expire in six weeks.'

'How do you know that?'

'I have my ways. It is not important to our discussion today. Strange as it may seem, I am now your only friend.'

I cannot imagine a scenario where this condescending, utterly self-obsessed woman could be my friend. Let alone my only friend.

'What is important to you must be that you are adequately compensated at the end of your time here.' She pauses meaningfully. 'Of course, there is a possibility that Blake will extend or renew the contract for another three months. Then again there is the distinct possibility he will not. I am here to offer you a hundred thousand pounds for you to leave... not at the end of the contract, but today. Since there is no punitive action allowed in your contract if you end it earlier than its term you are within your rights to do so.'

I look at her with shock. I glanced through the contract so fast I did not even register that clause. Yet this woman has perused the contract carefully and is here to bargain with me.

'I will increase the amount to two hundred thousand pounds if you will leave the country. No note. No goodbyes. No explanations. Just gone.'

No note. No goodbyes. No explanations. Just gone.

Wow! I look at the young woman who sits so brazenly before me and feel a bubble of hysterical laughter forming in my throat. Unsteadily, I stand up and walk to the glass wall. Far below there are small children playing with a dog in the park. With my back to the woman, I close my eyes and try to think, but my mind is blank with horror.

'Did you think that the billionaire's son would marry the poor girl from the council estate?'

I flush. 'Of course not.'

Except for that once when I tasted my name joined with his, I have not really thought that. Always from the start it has been made clear to me that it is a purely temporary arrangement based solely on sex. He has only ever wanted me for one thing and he has been brutally honest about it. There have been no protestations of love or flowery words. Just an animal craving for my skin.

As if the woman opposite me has heard my thoughts she remarks quietly, 'Cravings go away.'

'Please leave,' I say, without turning around. I am glad to hear that my voice is firm and strong. I hear the woman stand.

'You will regret this one day,' she says. There is no malice in her voice. She is simply stating a fact. Unemotionally. 'If you change your mind, my card is on the table. Please don't mention my visit to anyone.'

I nod.

After I hear the door close I stand before a beautiful gilded mirror and look at myself. How changed I am. My eyes are full of pain. There are bruises under my eyes where there were none. My hand moves to my belly. Soon I will be showing. I think of the woman. At the heartless determination hidden within the beautiful exterior. Between them, they will kill the life growing inside me. I love Blake with all my heart, but for him I am only a wild oat.

I must stop being selfish and think only of the little one inside me now. Secure his or her future. I press my hand to my mouth and stop the cry that threatens to escape. Tears are streaming down my face. I wipe them with the backs of my hands and run out of the door. Victoria is waiting by the lift. She turns to look at me and for that one pure moment, I understand how murderers feel. I want to steal this woman's heartbeat, take her life and the man that fate has so arbitrarily assigned to her.

'I'll take…' my voice breaks. I force myself to spit out the words,…'the money.'

She smiles. It is not the smile of a victor. It is not malicious. It is not unkind. Neither is it pitying nor condescending. It is simply the lucky smile of a woman who has never been refused anything her heart desires.

Thirty-Two

Victoria Jane Montgomery

I am Victoria Jane Montgomery, daughter of the fourth Earl of Hardwicke and I will have my way.

I enter the large conservatory built on the east wall of my father's home. In my opinion, it is the most beautiful part of the house, with its old Victorian stained glass and its profusion of citrus trees, tropical palms, and orchids. When I was younger there was even a banana tree. But Geoffrey died some years ago and this new gardener has other ideas, newer ideas.

My mother, she has pink cheeks, soft blue eyes and a small pink mouth, is reading a book. Another cheap period romance with a swashbuckling man clutching a buxom woman with flowing hair on the cover. I have never understood why a woman of her age should read romances. Surely, the instinct for romance dies when one reaches a certain age. In fact, I have never understood the allure of romances. They bore me. You see, I have the real thing in my life. I have Blake, all six feet three inches of him.

And all I have to do to make my toes clench is to think of him. But when I think of him with that hussy, my stomach actually knots and I have to stop myself from doing the bitch bodily harm. In fact, in a dream I once had I tore her eyes out. The feeling of hate is so strong that sometimes I have to clench my hands, so hard my nails bite into my flesh and leave half moon marks.

My mother looks up from her book. 'Oh, daahling. Have you just come from the hospital? How is Blake doing?'

Her King Charles, Suki, jumps dementedly at my feet. I pick it up and, tickling the fur next to its pink crystal-studded collar, sit on a chair opposite my mother.

'He hasn't come around yet,' I say, as the dog tries to lick my mouth.

'Oh dear, what are the doctors saying?'

'It's a matter of time. The swelling needs to go down. They expect to be able to operate tomorrow.'

'I'm sorry, my dear.'

'Actually, Mummy, I've come to talk to you about a different matter.'

'Oh?' My mother puts her book down.

'Well, it is about Blake, but it's not about his accident, well maybe it is, a little bit. Anyway, I found out that Blake has a mistress.'

'Oh,' my mother says again. I bite my lip. It is a blow to my pride to tell my mother this.

'I went to the apartment where he keeps her and paid her to leave the country and never see him again. Her mother is Iranian or something, and I suggested she live there for a while until everything blows over.'

The foolish look suddenly drops from my mother's eyes and her voice loses that simpering softness that I grew up with. My mouth drops open in shock. In that moment I realize I have never really known my mother. This woman is nobody's fool.

'You have taken a huge and unnecessary risk by doing that. These types of women will grow in such soil as ours and wither quickly, but when you force one out by the roots the way you have done, they leave a mark, an ugly scar that some men will mistake for a lost love.'

The wisdom in my mother's words makes undeniable sense and I look at her worriedly. 'But he took her to the Craft ball!'

She looks at me with narrowed eyes. 'How do you know that?'

I look away and gently lower Suki to the ground.

My mother sighs and throws an imperial mint to the floor. Immediately Suki catches it in her mouth and crunches it. 'You've had him followed. You are playing a dangerous game, Victoria. What does she look like?'

'A slut.'

My mother looks at me steadily.

'All right, she's very beautiful and young,' I spit out.

'But dirt poor?'

'Poorer than dirt.'

'Oh dear. Perhaps you did the right thing then.'

'But what do I do now?'

'Nothing much. Persuade your father to talk to Blake and take the blame for paying the girl off. It will appear less sordid if such a thing is done by a father to protect his daughter's interest. You must remain spotless. Go and see your father. He is in the study. He never could resist a tear or two from you.'

I stand and my mother says, 'You do know that this will not be the last woman that will come into your life, don't you?'

'Yes.'

'Are you sure you want this life?'

I did not hesitate. 'Yes.'

My mother nods sadly. 'Remember this. I married beneath me. So will you. All women do.'

I stare at her in shock.

'Well, run along then, daahling,' she simpers and picks up her lurid novel.

Thirty-Three

Lana Bloom

The first person I call is Jack. He answers on the fifth ring just as I am about to give up.

'What is it?' he asks, instantly alert.

'Oh, Jack,' I cry.

'Where are you?'

'Going to Mum's.'

'I'll meet you there.'

'You don't have to meet me there, Jack. I only wanted to hear your voice.'

'What happened?'

'Nothing.' But my voice breaks.

'Fuck nothing. What happened?'

'I have to leave. I'm taking Mum back to Iran.'

'What?'

'Just for a year.'

'I'm coming over.'

'Please don't, Jack. I was feeling weak, but I'm all right now. Funny, just hearing your voice did it. I know now what I have to do. I'll email you when I get settled. It's a bit primitive over there, so it might take a bit of time, but you and Billie will be the first people I write to.'

'Don't you want to see me before you go?'

'I'll be gone by the time you get here. Someone else is making the arrangements and they don't mess about. I'm afraid I kinda jumped from the frying pan into the fire, but I think it will be OK when I get to Iran.'

'What about Blake?'

'He's history. He must never know where I am.'

'Has he hurt you?'

'No. He's still unconscious in hospital.'

'You're not going of your own free will, are you?'

'No, but it is for the best. I've got to go now, Jack. I will write as soon as I can.'

'Goodbye, Lana.'

'Goodbye, darling Jack.'

Thirty-Four

Victoria Montgomery

It is a rich room in which I find my father. He is sitting in a large armchair reading the newspapers, and his favorite foxhound, Sergeant is curled up on a rug at his feet. At my entrance, Sergeant does no more than swivel his mournful eyes in my direction and wave the tip of his thirteen-year-old tail.

'Daddy.'

My father tilts his head so his washed out blue eyes can peer over the tops of his glasses. 'Hello, pet,' he welcomes genially.

'Daddy, I've done something rather dreadful.' I clasp my hands in front of me

He lowers his paper and narrows his eyes. It is amazing how different his eyes now appear.

'Sit down,' he orders.

I walk over to the chair opposite him, making sure my face is troubled and unhappy.

'Well?' he prompts.

I look down and twist a black pearl on my bracelet. 'I found out that Blake was keeping a woman. A horrible woman from a council estate.' I stand suddenly and move a few feet away. 'He was paying her.'

My father wisely says nothing. I glance at him. He is watching me carefully.

'Anyway, I went to see her and it was awful. Just awful. Ghastly woman. There she was in all the designer gear that he had bought her, and she was so arrogant about it too. She challenged me to take him away from her. I was so desperate I offered her money to leave him.' I turn around and look him directly in the eye.

My father's face is deliberately expressionless. 'Did she agree?'

My voice is instantly hard and cold. 'Of course. I had Martin draw up the papers and I transferred the money from my Gibraltar account. I've checked and she's gone. Left the country.'

'It appears you've taken care of your little problem. What do you want me to do?'

'Daddy, I love Blake, he is a good, strong man, and I know that once we are married he will be a good husband and a fine father. I can forgive him for this little indiscretion.'

My father nods carefully.

'But I know that he will never forgive me for interfering with his affairs if he finds out it was I who offered her the money. Mummy had a brilliant idea. She thought it would be better if you tell him that it was you who offered her the money. Surely, he will be able to see what a little tramp she is to leave him while he is still in hospital.'

'But that will surely ruin my relationship with him.'

'Does it really matter? You will still be his father-in-law and in time he will come to recognize that you did it for his own good.'

'You are certain you want this man?'

'I have never been more certain of anything in my life.'

He turns away from me and looks out of the window. 'Do you have a copy of her signature?'

'Yes.'

He nods. 'Of course, the contract.' A thought occurs to him. 'What about a sample of her writing?'

'Yes.'

He raises a bushy, enquiring eyebrow.

'I have a copy of her application form from the temporary agency she used to work at.'

He smiles. I can tell he is impressed. 'Give them both to me. I will work something out with Jason.' I have never met Jason, but I know of him. He is a master forger.

'Thank you, Daddy,' I say and running up to him snuggle my softly perfumed cheek against his. My father's arm comes around my shoulder and he gives me an affectionate squeeze.

'Oh, my pretty, pretty little viper—what that man doesn't know about you!'

I move away from him and look up into his eyes.

'Daddy?'

'Yes, darling.'

'Is it very wrong what I have done?'

'You should have left it alone, Victoria. He is a man and men, my dear, have needs, but these needs do go away.'

'He took her to the Crafts ball.'

My father's eyes narrow to slits with disapproval. Immediately I feel bad that I told him that. I want my father to think well of Blake.

'He's a good man, Daddy. He's just a bit lost. She has bewitched him. He has never done anything like this before.'

My father says nothing but it is obvious he is unimpressed.

I cannot leave it alone. 'Are you angry with me, Daddy?' I ask, my eyes misting over.

'Of course not. You did what you thought was best, but there is a very important lesson that a woman can learn from a dog. When a dog finds another dog's scent on his master, he does not panic, feel threatened or hurl abuse, but merely finds it interesting. If you can cultivate that habit you will have a very happy marriage.'

Lord Hugo Montgomery

When my daughter leaves, I look out of the window at the rolling green fields of my estate and the beautiful Van Gogh clouds in the sky. Shame Victoria had not been born a boy. I could have used her at the helm of the family instead of being a tool of consolidation.

I have known about Blake's woman. Seen photos of them together. Something about the pictures make me worry that this might not be the end of the matter. Still, my daughter is an intelligent, cunning little viper. And to date there is nothing she has wanted that has eluded her.

To be continued…

Forty Days 2

The Billionaire Banker Series

GEORGIA LE CARRE

Forty 2 Days

Book Two

"I hurt myself today
To see if I still feel.
I focus on the pain
The only thing that's real."
—Hurt, Johnny Cash's version
http://www.youtube.com/watch?v=SmVAWKfJ4Go

One

Lana Bloom

I edge up to the counter, my hands clammy, my stomach in a tight knot. The woman manning it smiles efficiently. She is wearing the bank's uniform; a striped shirt, a navy blazer and matching skirt. Her black name-tag has Susan Bradley printed in white.

'Thank you for waiting.' Her voice is iceberg lettuce crisp. 'What can I help you with today?'

I run my hands down the skirt of my gray suit. 'I have an appointment to see an officer about a loan. The name is Lana Bloom.'

She consults her computer screen. 'Ah! Miss Bloom.' Her eyes move upwards. Meet mine. No smile there. Just avid curiosity. 'Take a seat, and I'll let someone know you are here.'

'Thank you.' I walk towards the nest of gray-blue chairs she indicates. I perch on the edge of one and watch her.

'She's here,' she announces into the phone, and returns it to its cradle. Then she does an odd thing—without turning her face in my direction, sneaks a look at me from the corners of her eyes, catches me watching, and looks away quickly, almost guiltily.

I feel the knot in my stomach grow tighter. Something is wrong. Perhaps the manager has looked at my business plan and decided against the loan. It shouldn't be too surprising. I have no experience and no collateral and, as my mother used to say, banks will only lend you an umbrella when it is not raining outside.

I clutch my bag in sweat-slicked hands, take a deep breath and very firmly urge myself to be calm. There is always Plan B—Billie and I will simply start small and build the business brick by brick. Our progress will be very slow, but we will survive, and perhaps if we work extra hard, one day we will thrive. With or without their money we will get by. My chin goes up a notch.

An Asian lady in a dark suit comes out of a closed door. She looks at me, eases into another smile that doesn't quite reach her eyes, and asks, 'Miss Bloom?'

I stand nervously and smooth down my skirt. Here goes nothing. I touch my hair self-consciously. Hope the wind outside has not wrecked it too much. In an attempt to look older and more professional Billie scraped my hair back into a severe bun and colored my lips a dark plum. She said it has the effect of making me look like a sophisticated flamenco dancer, but I think it has simply made me look pale and gaunt.

'This way please.' The woman waves her hand in the direction of the stairs and starts walking towards them. I frown deeply. All the other people waiting with me have been shown into one of the cubicles downstairs. Upstairs, I have not seen anyone go. Why am I going upstairs? The woman's clunky heels make a hollow sound on the uncarpeted stairs. The sound reverberates in my chest. The feeling of dread in the pit of my stomach increases.

We go through a door that requires a code, and I realize that we have entered the area that only staff members are allowed into. Another employee passes us and glances at me curiously. We walk down a corridor of offices. Near the end of it the woman turns around and faces me. There is an oddly speculative expression on her face.

'Ready?' she asks. It seems a strange thing to ask.

Bemused, I nod.

She knocks once, pulls open the door, and holds it ajar for me.

I enter, a sunny smile plastered all over my face, and freeze. My jaw drops, my stomach lurches in my body. I am in a nightmare. *Ah, but haven't you waited for this for a long time?* Always my heart knew it was not over. One day I would see him again. I didn't know how or when or why—just that I would.

And I have rehearsed this scenario in my mind countless times but in different circumstances. Where I am dressed seductively and have run into him in a nightclub or while I am accidentally, purposely loitering outside One Hyde Park where he once told me he lives. But never, never here at my local bank. Not in a million years. I am so shocked my mind actually goes blank. I blink.

Oh! But to be caught this unprepared!

'Wait,' I want to scream to the Asian lady, 'there has been some mistake,' but my mouth is frozen open, and even my slow-moving brain knows there is no mistake. I have not been shown to this room by accident. I am here because this man wants me here.

The door closes quietly behind me.

Two

'Hello, Lana,' Blake says from behind a desk.

His voice is still the same. Jack Daniel's on ice. Smooth. A bite hidden somewhere in its amber depths.

A shiver runs down my spine.

He looks at me with a tight jaw and unreadable eyes. He is even more beautiful and raw than I remember. An impossibly splendid, impersonal god. But there is something different about him too. Some harshness that wasn't there before has crept into those hooded, intensely beautiful eyes. Some faint lines about his mouth.

The shock to my system of seeing him so unexpectedly is so great I am unable to say or do anything. Robbed of all coherent thought I simply stand there slack-jawed: a fool, greedily drinking in the sight of him. For I, have spent many a long, lonely night, the heat of the desert all around me, trawling the net looking for any mention of this man.

For months nothing.

Then one day on a conspiracy site—a brief article that he got engaged to Victoria Montgomery, daughter of the fourth Earl of Hardwick. I sat back, my body in an unbelievable turmoil. Insane jealousy is like red-hot lava. It poured into my gut, carrying with it the terrible, terrible sensation that I had lost something irreplaceable.

There was a small picture of them taken at a restaurant. So grainy there was nothing to be gleaned from it, but I had stared at it for a long time that day, and gone back to it again and again. As if it held some clue to a mystery I didn't understand. Slowly, I began to notice things, the coffee cup, his hand on the table close to, but not touching hers. Victoria's face upturned to him, hard to tell her expression, but there was the impression of great devotion and determination. I had rubbed my seventh-month belly slowly. The circles my hand made comforted me. That life is not yours. That man is not yours. Has never been. But this baby is all yours. The molten lava cooled, formed its black crust. The fan droned on. In the next room, my mother slept, blissfully unaware of my deep sorrow.

'Have a seat,' he invites smoothly.

But I dare not move. My legs are pure jelly. I close and then open my mouth, but no words come. I swallow and try again. The song 'Baby Did A Bad, Bad Thing' starts playing in my head. Shit. I am in trouble. Bad things always happen when that song starts playing in my head.

'What are you doing here?' My voice is barely a whisper.

'Processing your loan application.'

'What?' I know my expression must be without intelligence, like those worn by beasts of burden, at the very least slow, but I cannot stop the slackness.

'I'm here to process your loan application,' he repeats patiently.

Sounds logical, but his words are rocks in my brain. Process my loan application? I shake my head to dislodge the rocks. 'You don't work here. You don't process tiny little loans.'

'I'm here to process yours.'

'Why?' And then a stupid thought occurs to me. Later I will think back and slap my forehead at my own naivety, but at that moment it fires me into action. 'So you can turn me down? Don't bother. I'll show myself out,' I say hotly, and begin to turn.

He stands. 'Lana, wait.'

I look all the way up at him. Strange! He even seems bigger, taller.

'I am the one in the entire banking industry most likely to extend you this loan.'

I continue to stare dully at him. How I have longed to set eyes again on this man. And how I have missed the sight of him. How truly beautiful he is.

'Please take a seat.'

Dazed I look at the two chairs facing him, but I do not move. My thoughts trawl through treacle. Nothing makes sense.

'How did you know I would be here today?'

'A nifty little software that flags your name if it matches your date of birth whenever it comes up in the banking system, and, of course, the fact that you began using your account again less than a week ago.'

I can't think straight.

'Is all money in the Swiss account gone?'

I nod. 'But why are you here?' I ask, even though I already know the answer to that.

'Same reason as before.'

'For sex.'

'Sex?' he hisses. 'God, you have no idea, have you?'

He is angry. Angrier than I have ever seen him. I stare at the transformation in disbelief. What shocks me the most is the expression on his face, drawn, hard, his jaw clenched so tight the muscles in his neck stand out. His eyebrows are two straight lines. The urbane man who fed me caviar and quietly upgraded my mother to first class is gone, vanished, replaced by this stranger with furious, mistrustful eyes. His breathing seems to grow harsher as he advances towards me. He stops a foot in front of me.

At that moment he emits tremendous power. Electricity crackles between us. He holds my gaze steadily for heart stopping moments and I see the battle in his eyes. The emotions that wage for control. I flinch as he draws even closer. Until we are inches apart and the scent of him invades my senses. Nobody else I know smells like him. The smell of old money, Rupert called it. For one unguarded instant carnal lust glitters in his eyes. Then he lowers his lids and masks it. But I have already seen it, the potency of his desire for me. It heightens my perceptions. Drenches me with wanting and lust.

I feel my skin tingle in response. My lips go numb and my throat becomes so dry words would scratch it. What could I have said anyway? *Oh, Blake, I'm so sorry?* I reach out a trembling hand to him.

His reaction is instant. 'Don't,' he rasps, stiffening.

Shocked, I retract my hand. I have damaged him. The knowledge spreads like a dull ache in my chest. 'Please,' I whisper, stupidly, helplessly.

He bends his head towards my face. My eyes are riveted on those sinfully sexy lips. I remember their taste, their passion.

'Dishonest little Lana,' he murmurs, his breath hot against my skin. He runs his hands down the smoothness of my neck into the collar of my blouse.

I begin to tremble. He watches his own fingers slip a button out of its hole and then another. He spreads apart the joined material so my throat, chest and the lacy tops of my bra are exposed. His cold furious eyes return to mine. The breaths that escape my lips are suddenly shallow and quick. He smiles possessively. He knows the effect he has on me.

'You were by far more when you squeezed into that little orange dress and your fuck-me shoes and went looking for money. Look at you now; you're flapping around inside a man's jacket. Two hundred thousand and you don't even buy yourself a nice suit.'

He tuts. 'And this…' He raises his hand to my hair. 'This ugly bun. What were you thinking of?' he asks softly, as he plucks the pins out of my hair and drops them on the blue carpet. Bit by bit my hair falls around my shoulders. Without moving his feet he reaches back to a box of tissues on the table. Takes one and starts wiping away my lipstick. Meticulously. From the outside in. He throws the stained tissue on the ground.

'That's better,' he pronounces.

I stare wordlessly up at him. He looks as if he wants to devour me. All the time we have been apart is wiped away. It is like we have never been away from each other. This is the man I belong to heart and soul. Without him I have been an empty shell going through the motions.

'Lick your lips,' he orders.

'What?' I am horrified by the cold command, and yet electrified by the sexual heat his order arouses in me. My nerves scream.

His jaw hardens; his eyes are steely. 'You heard me.'

The tension in his body communicates itself to me. It simmers between us. Desire ripples through me. My thighs clench tight with excitement and my heart flutters like a crazy thing. This is how he is in my recurring fantasies. Demanding, possessive, taking, raging with sexual need. But the sane logical part of me doesn't want to comply. The argument between my brain and body is pure torture. In the end, yeah right, as if there was ever any doubt, my body wins. So what if I slip and fall on that slick road. It is only for a moment.

I lick my lips slowly.

He eyes the journey my tongue undertakes avidly. 'That's more like it. That's the mercenary bitch I know.'

One moment he is standing there cold and insulting, and the next he has thrust a rough hand into my hair and pulled my head back. I gasp with shock, my eyes wide, his dark. Like a desert storm he descends on my parted mouth. There is no time even to pull one's cloak about oneself. So sudden. So unexpected. He tastes wild, the way the first drops of rain in the desert taste. Full of minerals. Bringing life to all it touches.

He kisses me, as he has never done. Roughly, painfully, violently, purposely bruising my lips, his mouth so savage that I utter a strangled, soundless cry. The change, the extent of his anger, is impossible to comprehend. He is different. There is no longing. Only an intense desire to hurt and have his revenge. This is not the same man. My actions have unleashed something uncontrollable. Something that wants to hurt me. Alarm bells go off in my head. It occurs to my fevered brain that he is ravenous, starving. Then for some strange reason an image of him eating thin, almost transparent slices of cheese on biscuits flashes into my mind. How civilized he was. Then. Before I betrayed him.

I taste the fury in his kiss: blood.

And my mind screams—this is abuse. A moan gets caught in my throat, struggles vainly, and then escapes. My hands reach up to push him away, but my palms meet the stone wall of his chest, and as if with minds of their own, push aside the lapels of his jacket and grip his shirt. I know what once lived beneath the shirt and I want it. I have always wanted this man. As if my hands splayed across his chest have communicated my total submission, the kiss changes. His tongue gentles, but demands more surrender.

The fingers grasping my hair hurt my scalp. I feel the pain vaguely, but more than that I feel myself begin to drown in that vortex of sexual desire. The violent, throbbing need between my legs finds its way into my veins and flesh. Every cell in me wants him inside me. I am on fire. One year of waiting has made me hungry for him. I want him. I want him thrusting that enormous dick of his deep inside me. For a year I have dreamed of him inside me, filling me. I know how good he can make me feel. My body tries to burrow closer to him, but I cannot get closer; his grip on my hair is relentless. Desperately I push my hips towards him towards what I know will be delicious hardness.

As if that is some silent signal he puts me casually away from me. And I am thrust back in a shitty back office in Kilburn High Street. What the fuck am I doing? He casually props himself against the desk, folds his arms across his chest and looks at me calmly.

I cannot return the insult. I am a mess. I stand there frustrated beyond belief, breathing hard, the blood pounding like an African drum in my head. My knickers are wet and between my legs I ache and pulse for him. With every weak and trembling part of me I want him to finish what he started. I want him so bad it is shocking. I clench my hands at my sides and try to get myself under control. I look at him, how cool and collected he is, as he watches me struggle to regain some measure of composure.

Then he smiles. Oh! Cocky. He shouldn't have done that. I feel maddened by the taunting smile. How dare he? He just wanted to humiliate me.

And then I see it. Not so fast, Mr. Blake Law Barrington.

I take two steps forward, reach my hand out and put a finger on that madly beating pulse in his throat. It drums into my skin. The frantic beat is carried away by my blood up into my arm, my heart and into my brain. Years later I will remember this moment when we are connected by his beating pulse. We never break eye contact. His eyes darken. Now he knows that I know—my need may be obvious and easy to exploit, but he is not as unaffected as he pretends to be. He was testing his own limits of control, but it hasn't been as easy as he expected.

'Is it sex when I want to see you come apart?' he asks bitterly.

A breath dies in my chest. I take my finger away from his throat. 'What do you want, Blake?'

'I want you to finish your contract.'

I drop my face into my hands. 'I can't,' I whisper.

'Why not? Because you took the money and ran, while I lay in a hospital bed.'

I take a deep breath and do not look up. I cannot look up. I cannot face the condemnation in his eyes. I did not keep my word. But I had a reason, one that he can never know about.'

'I was cut up to start with,' he says.

I look up, shocked, mesmerized. Contrary to his words his face is detached, calm, cold, so cold.

I shiver. 'You were cut up?'

'Funny thing that, but yes I was.' He shakes his head as if in disgust. Whether it is with me, himself, or both of us, I cannot tell.

'I thought it was just a sex thing for you,' I murmur. My world is all wobbly. He was cut up! Why?

'If you wanted money why didn't you ask me?' His voice is harsh.

'I...' I shake my head in defeat. I cannot redeem myself.

'You made a serious miscalculation, didn't you, Lana, my love. The honey pot is here.' He pats the middle of his chest. I look at the large male hand. Something inside me twists. Once that beautiful hand with its perfectly manicured nails roamed my body, swept my legs apart and entered me. Dear God!

'But not to worry. All is not lost.'

My gaze lifts up to his mouth. It is thin and cruel and moving.

'You did me a favor. You opened my eyes. I see you now for what you were...are. I was blinded by you. I made the classic mistake. I fell in love with an illusion of purity and loyalty.'

I raise my face up to his. Blinded? In love? With me?

'If I had not bought you that night you would have gone with anyone, wouldn't you? You are not admirable. You are despicable.'

'So why do you want me to finish the contract?' I breathe.

'I am like the drug addict who knows his drug is poison. He despises it, but he cannot help himself. So that we are totally clear—I *detest* myself. I am ashamed of my need for you. '

'The...The...people who paid me—'

'They can do nothing to you. My family—'

I interrupt. 'What about Victoria?'

A sudden flash of anger gleams in his eyes. 'The fact that I need the feel and taste of your skin is my shame and private hell. Don't ever bring her into our sordid arrangement. Her name on your lips makes me feel sick. She is the one pure thing I have in my life. She stood by me through...everything.' He pauses, his lips twisting. 'I actually told her about you and gave her the option of leaving me, but she refused. She is wiser than me. Far wiser than I gave her credit for. She said you are just a sickness and one day I will wake up and the sickness will be gone. Until then...you owe me 42 days, Lana.'

My God, he really hates me. I close my eyes unable to look into the censure or revulsion glittering in his. He cannot know how much his angry words have cut and wounded me. I had guessed he would think badly of me, but I never imagined he would so utterly loathe me. I never realized that I had hurt him so deeply. I honestly thought it was a sex thing for him. That I was just another in a line of many. In my defense he had never given me to understand otherwise.

Now he hates me with a passion. And there is not a single thing I can do about it. Victoria has shown herself to be a formidable foe. I can never tell him what really happened. I am on very shaky ground. I will have to be very careful. I have too much to lose. I hang my head. I need to think.

'Name your price.'

My head snaps up. 'No,' I hear myself say. This time my voice is very strong and sure. 'You don't have to pay me again. I will finish the contract.'

'Good,' he says, but he frowns, and for one second I see not just confusion that I refused his money, but something else—relief? No, that would be too weak an emotion for the wild thing leaping into his eyes. Then it slips away seamlessly. A seal that leaps and disappears into the blue ocean.

'Back to business then,' he murmurs, and, turning away from me, goes around the desk, and takes his position behind it. Back to the way I found him.

Three

I watch his toned, powerful frame slide smoothly into the black swivel chair and open the file in front of him.

'So, you're setting up a business?' The sudden professionalism in his voice is like a bucket of cold water in my face. I take a shocked backward step. We were somewhere totally different a moment ago. Awareness of his potent masculinity in that small utilitarian room is still prickling across my skin. So, he wants to play. Cat and mouse. First the cheese and then the claw and teeth.

I go forward. Position myself in front of one of the chairs facing the desk. When I feel the edge of a chair against the backs of my knees I sink into it. 'Yes, Bill...Billie and I are.'

'Ah, the inimitable Bill,' he says, looking up, the hot gaze completely replaced by a remorseless mask. 'Why didn't she come with you?'

'She thought her tattoos might put the loan officer off.'

He smiles lopsidedly. 'You girls have it all covered, don't you?' he says, but I can tell straight away, he has a soft spot for Billie. It twists my heart. I wish my name would soften his face like that.

'That reminds me. How is your mother?'

The breath gets sucked out of me. 'She passed away.'

He stills, his eyes narrowing. 'I thought the treatment was working.'

I swallow the stone lodged in my throat. 'The treatment worked.' The words catch in my throat. 'A car. Hit and run.'

His eyes flash. For an instant I am looking back into the past. We are all sitting around my mother's dinner table. There are fresh flowers on the table and our plates are full of Persian food. Chicken with fruit and rice. My mouth is full of the smoky flavor of dried chilies. Blake is being charming and my mother is laughing. Her laughter fills the room and my heart. Hardly I heard her laugh in my life. I did not realize how happy I was then.

'I'm sorry. I'm so sorry to hear that, Lana.'

His pity is my undoing. The scene before me blurs. I blink furiously. I am not going to crumble in front of him. I can feel the waves of grief beginning in my body. I have not yet cried. Oh shit. Not now…please. I stand suddenly. So does he. I put out a hand, a warning—do not come any closer—and I run to the door. I need to get outside. My only thought is to escape. Not let him see me break down, but he is already at my side. He grabs my arm. I twist away from him, but his grip is too firm. He doesn't know it, but he is part of the great pattern of my terrible grief.

'This way. There is a staff restroom,' he says quietly, and opening the door leads me down the corridor. He does not look at me, and I am grateful for that. Hot, uncontrollable tears are streaming down my cheeks. I did not cry when my mother died. For three whole months I could not cry. There was so much to do, but now the silent tears are flowing unchecked, and the huge sobs are on the way. I can feel them shaking my innards, threatening to burst out.

He holds open the toilet door and I rush in. The door closes behind me. Inside are white tiled walls and cubicles made of plywood. An ugly place. Perfect for what I have to do. I grip the ceramic basin, stuff my fist into my mouth and, doubling up, wait for the screaming sobs. They don't disappoint in their ferocity. They are long and hard and ugly. Full of regret and recrimination and blame. For so long I believed that my mother would die of cancer. Year after year of watching her suffer and still not being able to let her go in peace, and then when she is bright and full of life again, and, when I am least expecting it, she is gone. Just like that. Without warning. I never even had a chance to say goodbye. In the end she was cruelly snatched away from me. I don't know how long I was in there, but I buried my mother there.

Alone, in a toilet reeking of industrial bleach.

Finally, I lean against the sink exhausted. I look in the mirror. What a right mess. I look horrible. I blow my nose, wash my puffy face. My eyes and lips are red and swollen. I straighten. I button my blouse to my neck. I know it is cowardly, but I decide at that moment to scuttle away. Just walk down the corridor and leave. The bank has my address and he will find me, but by then I will be different. I will have repaired the walls of my fortress. I will be strong. He cannot hurt me. But then I remember Billie waiting at home.

'Well, did you get it?' she will ask.

I close my eyes. I'm not going to let her down. I'm going to say, 'Yes, I got it.'

I pull open the door and he is standing in the corridor outside, staring at the floor, his hands rammed deep into his trouser pockets.

It is the oddest thing. It reminds me of the first time we met. When I had bawled my eyes out in a toilet and come out to find him waiting for me. He looks up, still frowning. The door shuts behind me as he strides towards me. The last time I had six inch heels that lifted me to almost his eye level. Now I am left staring at his brown throat.

'Are you okay?'

I nod.

'Tom will take you home.'

I lift my eyes up to his. They are strange, liquid with some emotion I cannot comprehend. 'No,' I say. My voice comes out oddly terse. I had not meant for it to be like that. 'Let's get this loan business out of the way.'

A shutter comes over his face. I realize then I have just confirmed his thoughts about me. I am the gold digger who will do anything for money. Anybody else would have exploited this opportunity for softness. I am filled with regret, but it is too late. He is the tide that is going out and cannot be recalled. His eyes return to cold and distant.

He nods and we go back to the clinical office. I sit opposite him and he takes the swivel chair. It is a parody. He knows it and so do I.

He looks down again at my loan application form. 'Baby Sorab?'

Oh. My. God. What the hell am I doing? I am playing with fire. I feel my heart thump so loudly in my chest he must surely hear it. The fog in my brain clears. It is no longer just me. Cat and mouse? I can play this game. He has nothing to lose. I have everything to lose. So I will be the winner. He will not beat me. I school my features, shrug carelessly. And then the lies begin to drop from my mouth so smoothly even I am surprised. Until today I never realized what an accomplished liar I am.

'Yes. We thought it was a good name for our business.'

'Why baby clothes?'

'Billie has always been good with colors. She can put red and pink together and make it look divine, and since, Billie had her baby this year we decided to make baby clothes?'

'Billie had a baby?' he asks, obviously surprised.

I look him in the eye. 'Yeah, a beautiful boy,' I lie straight-faced.

His lips twist derisively. 'You girls sure have it figured out. I suppose she is now being housed courtesy of the British taxpayer?'

I say a silent apology to Billie. 'I believe we have had this conversation before.'

'OK,' he says.

'OK, what?'

'OK you got the loan.'

'Just like that?'

'There is one condition.'

I hold my breath.

'You do not get the money for the next 42 days.'

'Why?'

'Because,' he says softly, 'for the next 42 days you will exist only for my pleasure. I plan to gorge on your body until I am sick to my stomach.'

I swallow hard. 'Are you going to house me in some apartment again?'

'Not some apartment, but the same one as before.'

I lick my lips and surprise myself. I never knew I could think so fast. That lies would come so easily to me. 'There is one small complication. Billie goes to see her girlfriend three, no actually, four nights a week and I take care of her son.'

He doesn't miss a beat. 'Tell Laura what you need for the baby—cot, pram, bottle warmers whatever. The baby can stay at the apartment.'

I stare at him. 'Are you serious?'

'Do you have a better plan?'

I pause. My mind racing. 'One more thing. Billie must be able to come to the apartment.'

'Done.'

'And Jack. He is the baby's godfather.'

He looks bored. 'Anything else?'

'No.'

'Fine. Have you anything planned for tomorrow?'

I shake my head.

'Good. Keep tomorrow free. Laura will call you to go through the necessary arrangements with you.'

'OK, if there is nothing else…'

'I'll walk you out.'

Heads turn to watch us. Their eyes slide off when they meet mine. I feel my face flushing. Hell, I'll never be able to come back here again. I see the bank manager hurrying towards us, the material of his trouser legs slapping against his ankles. Blake raises a finger and he stops abruptly. Blake pulls open the heavy door and we go into the late summer air. It is a gray day, though. Drizzling slightly.

We face each other.

'Why did Billie call her baby Sorab?'

'It's from the great epic Rustam and Sorab.'

'Yes, I am aware where it is from, but why did she choose it?'

'It was a tribute to my mother. It was my mother's favorite story.'

'Hmmm…That is the most admirable quality in you. Your unshakeable loyalty towards your mother.'

For a moment we look at each other. I realize that I have never seen him in the light of day. Not even in this dull light. Strange. We have always met during the day at the apartment and only ever gone out at dusk or at night. And in the light of the day his eyes are storm-blue with moody gray and black flecks. A gust of wind lifts his hair away from his head and deposits it on his forehead. Unthinkingly, I reach a hand out to touch the unruly skein, but he jerks his head back as if dodging a wasp.

'This time you won't fool me,' he bites out.

We stare at each other. Me, astonished by how close to the surface his fury lives, and he, contemptuously. My hand drops. I feel exhausted. There is a ton of bricks inside my chest. Cotton wool inside my head. I can't think straight. I look down the road at the bus stand. 'I'll see you tomorrow then,' I say.

'Here's Tom,' he says, as a Bentley pulls up along the curb.

I shake my head. 'Thanks, but I'll take the bus.'

'Tom will drop you off,' he insists, and I have a flashback of him from the first night we met at the restaurant. That same inbred sense of confidence and superiority.

'No,' I snap. 'Our contract doesn't start until tomorrow. So today I'll decide my mode of transport,' and I swing away from him.

His hand shoots out and grasps my wrist. 'I will pick you up and put you in the car if necessary. You decide.'

I feel anger bubbling inside me. 'And I'll call the police.'

He actually laughs. 'After everything I have told you about the system—that's your answer?'

I sag. 'Of course, who will believe me if I claim that a Barrington tried to force me to take a lift.'

'Please, Blake.'

'Very well. Tom will go with you on the bus.'

I don't argue. I simply turn around, open the car door, get in, slam it shut and stare straight ahead.

'Good morning, Miss Bloom. It's good to see you again,' Tom greets, pretending not to notice my puffy face.

'It's good to see you too, Tom.'

'How have you been?' he asks as the car pulls away.

'Fine,' I reply, and twist my neck back to look at Blake. He is standing on the sidewalk where I left him. His hands are hanging by his sides and he is staring at the moving car. On the street teeming with some of the most dispossessed people in Britain he stands out. Tall, impressive, separate from the crowd, a ruler; and yet he looks alone and abandoned. I remember what he told me a long time ago.

I trust no one. No one.

Four

The traffic is bad and the car crawls slowly down Kilburn High Street. I stare blankly out of the window. I know I'm not dreaming this. This is actually happening and yet...it has a dreamlike quality. The street looks the same only there are many people staring at the car and into it, at me. Their eyes seem unfriendly. The rich are resented here. I feel restless and disturbed. I need a bit of time to think. Walking always helps. I ask Tom to drop me off by the shops.

'Are you sure, Miss? I don't mind waiting, while you pop in. I'm free until much later.'

'Thanks, but I'll be fine, Tom. I'll probably see you tomorrow, anyway.'

Tom nods. 'All right then. Mind how you go.'

I enter the newsagent and buy a bottle of vodka and a packet of cigarettes for Billie. Then I walk home slowly, taking the long way home so I pass by my old house. I stand on the street in the drizzle and look up at it. At the blue door where we once lived, my mother and I, for so many years. Some of them happy, but most of them filled with stress and worry and fear. Now she was gone.

For a moment I stand there, my face upturned, pretending that my mother is still there. That I could, if I wanted to, simply go up those stairs, put my key in the door, open it, and find her in the kitchen. Bald and thin to the point of skeletal, but happy to see me. Then the blue door opens and a child about seven years old comes out. She has brown hair cut very short.

From the interior a woman's voice yells, 'And I want change from the fiver.'

The girl doesn't answer. Simply slams shut the door and runs to the top of the stairs. She is so cocky she reminds me of Billie. I hear her shoes clattering down the stairs. She runs past me, dirty stained top, yellow shorts and brown legs. And suddenly, I am racked by a sense of deep nostalgia for those times when Billie and I ran free. Summer days. Fingers sticky with ice lollies. Not a single responsibility in sight. I watch the girl turn down the road towards the shops. Then I slowly begin to walk towards the tower block flats where Billie and I now live.

It is a horrible place, far, far worse than this small, friendly block. If Blake saw where we live now, he would literally have a heart attack. All his worst nightmares are realized here. Prostitutes work the underpass and there are fights and stabbings when the pubs clear at night. Their drunken shouting and cursing floats up to our flat. Inside our block it is no better. The lifts perpetually smell of stale urine and the stairwells are littered with blood-filled hypodermic syringes and used condoms. Kids play among the needles in the morning.

I live here, but in my heart I am absolutely determined that it will only be temporary. I intend to work hard, make our business work and, hopefully, by the time Sorab is old enough to walk the three of us will be out of here. A sign says no ball games and no dumping of rubbish. In defiance the place is littered with empty cans and someone has simply tipped a badly stained mattress over one of the long balcony walkways of the tower.

I pass the children playing on the concourse.

'Hey, Lana, we saw you get out of a big car by the shops. Whose car is it?'

'Never you mind,' I tell them tartly.

'Somebody's got a sugar daddy,' they sing, and I am surprised anew by how clued up these kids are. At their age, my innocence was complete, my childhood totally unsoiled by any adult knowledge.

One of them breaks from the group and sidles up to me. 'Go on, give us a pound to buy some sweets,' she cajoles. She has a head full of bouncing brown curls.

I look down at her. 'Does your mother know you are begging for money?'

'Yeah,' she pipes up immediately, standing her ground without the least trace of embarrassment.

I look into her eyes and feel sad. I know her mother. A hard-faced woman with six kids. Each one from a different father, all dirty and unkempt. For a split second I consider teaching her not to beg, to have pride, and then I give up. I know in my heart it is pointless. I wish a different future for her, but she is already infected by the generation before her. In her round, beautiful face walks the shadow of a drop-out, perhaps even an alcoholic. A blight on society through no fault of her own. I reach into my purse and give her a pound. She grasps it in her small, hot palm and runs off in the direction of the shops, calling after her. 'Thanks, Lana.'

I skirt the weeds and step onto the cracked concrete. Moodily I kick a Coke can out of my path and round the block. I look up to the second floor of the ugly gray block and see Billie standing on the long walkway balcony outside our door. She is smoking a cigarette and leaning against the metal railing. One of her bare feet is curled around a metal bar. Her hair is no longer white, but flaming red. She changed the color and the style last week when she broke up with Leticia. It is now cut very close to her head on one side and falls longer on the other. She must have just got out of the bath, for her hair is still wet and slicked to her head. She does not see me.

I run up the smelly stairs and step on to our level. She looks up from her contemplative stare and watches me. I step over discarded toys, a tricycle, a plastic bucket and spade, and then I am standing in front of her.

I grin. She kills her cigarette on the metal railing. I fish out the vodka. She grins back. Hers is real, mine is not.

She takes the bottle from my hand. 'Really?'

'Really,' I say.

She puts the bottle on the ground, grabs me around the hips, and sweeps me off my feet, laughing. Her joy is so infectious I have to laugh.

'Put me down before you drop me over the balcony!'

Instead of setting me back down she whirls me around a couple of times, carries me over our threshold and kicks the door shut like a man, before setting me down on the dining table.

'You. Are. A. Fucking. Genius,' she says. Then her face undergoes a sudden change. 'Oh, shit,' she cusses and dashes outside. And she is just in time too. 'Oi you,' I hear her shout. 'Touch that bottle and you're dead.' There is the sound of little feet scuttling away and Billie comes back into view cradling the vodka bottle.

I slip off the table. 'How did it go with Sorab?'

'The usual, you know, eat, shit, sleep, repeat,' she says, and thumps the bottle on the table.

'Let me have a quick peek,' I say, and go into my bedroom. I stand in front of his crib, my heart heavy with sadness. He has no one, but me. He will never know his father. I have denied him his father and a life of unimaginable riches. I push the guilt away. Not now. Not yet. For a moment I think of Blake standing alone in the crowd. We are all of us alone trapped in our own version of hell. I gently trace my finger on his sleeping arm and go outside.

Billie is sitting at the table. The vodka bottle is unopened.

I slip my jacket off. It is too big for me and swings from my shoulder. I open the fridge. 'I'm going to make some pasta. Want some?'

'No, had a couple of Turkish Delights.'

'Bill, you can't survive on leftover pizza, jam, and chocolates, you know.'

'It's not me who looks like a walking skeleton.' She stares at me daring me to contradict her.

I close the fridge door and face her.

'You know, when I saw you walking home with the plastic bag from the newsagent I didn't dare believe, because I could see that you had been crying. I'd like to think you cried because you were so happy but that's not it, is it? Want to tell me what really happened?'

I sit opposite her. 'Blake was there.'

Billie pulls forward with a frown. 'There where?'

'At the bank. He processed our loan application.'

'Don't. You're going to make me cry.'

'Can you bite back the sarcastic remarks for one moment?'

She raises her hands, palms facing me.

'Apparently he has been monitoring my account with the intention of making contact.'

Billie opens her eyes wide. 'Wow! That's tenacious.'

'He wants me to finish the contract.'

Billie closes her eyes in a gesture of extreme exasperation. 'Oh God! You agreed or we wouldn't have got the loan, would we?'

'Yes,' I say, but before I can tell her more she leans forward, her chin jutting out aggressively.

'Lana. Are you completely crazy? Have you forgotten what that bloodless troll he is engaged to and those reptilian entities masquerading as his family did to you the last time? They closed ranks and kicked you out of the fucking country. Anyway, didn't she make you sign in blood never to go near her man again?'

I flush. 'No, simply that I must never make contact with him again. I didn't.'

'Yeah, she'll appreciate the difference.'

'As a matter of fact, Blake said that he has told her about me and she is prepared to wait until he is over his infatuation with me.'

'And you believe that?'

'Well, it *was* something like what she told me.'

'If you believe that then you definitely should stay away from him. You are not equipped to deal with such lethal cunning.'

'I won't come into contact with her. It's only 42 days.'

'We don't need the money, you know? We can always start small. We talked about this. In fact, it was unlikely that you were ever going to get the money without collateral or business experience. It was only an off chance. We'll do without it. In fact, that might be more fun.'

'I didn't do it for the money,' I say very quietly.

There is a moment of shocked silence. Billie looks at me as if I have lost my mind. And in a way she is right. I am risking everything.

'Fuck me, Lana. Have you forgotten how difficult it was for you to get over him?'

'I'm not over him.'

'Exactly. So why walk into the lion's den *again*? Look at you. You are already just a shadow of yourself. Why put yourself through it? Besides the spectacular sex, that is.'

I try to smile and don't succeed. I feel my chin and lower lip begin to tremble. I press my lips together. 'You don't understand. I *owe* him. He was good to Mum and me, but I didn't keep my word. I should never have taken Victoria's money. It was wrong. I knew that the moment I saw it sitting all fat and jolly in that Swiss bank account. I'm not a Swiss bank account person. It was only when I gave it all away to that hospice that I felt better. I will only feel right again when I finish what I started. Until then I will never be able to close this door.'

'And Sorab? Are you going to tell him about *him*?'

'Of course not. They would take my son away and turn him into a cold-eyed predator, like Blake's father and brother.'

'So what happens to Sorab then?'

I squirm a little. 'I told Blake Sorab was yours.'

'Right,' she says slowly, obviously unable to get her head around such an idea.

'He thinks you did it to jump the welfare queue and get a flat.'

Billie grins suddenly. 'So you didn't tell him that as a child I wanted to have my entire reproductive system removed and replaced with an extra set of lungs so I could smoke more.'

I shook my head.

'What does all this translate to then?'

'You keep Sorab here for three days of the week and I keep him at the apartment for the other four days.'

Billie draws a deep breath. 'What does he imagine I am doing for the other four days?'

'Spending the night at your girlfriend's place.'

'Jesus, I'm a shit mother, aren't I?'

'Do you mind terribly?'

'I don't give a monkey's what he thinks of me, but are you OK with being apart from Sorab three days a week?'

My little heart is breaking at the thought but I put on a brave face. 'Well, it *is* only for 42 days and I was thinking that three weeks of that time I could say you are on holiday and Sorab is too young to go with you.'

'And you think he'll believe that?'

'Quite frankly, I don't think he cares enough to ponder the matter too deeply.'

'I don't want to take the philosophical upper hand here, but if it'll all be over in 42 days, isn't this all a bit…unnecessary?'

I trace my fingernail along the wood grain of our kitchen table. We bought it in a charity shop for twenty pounds. It has two cigarette burn marks on the surface, but I rather like it. It has character, a story to tell.

'I know you think I am being foolish, but have you never had someone touch you and you go up in flames? Or that odd sensation as if your bones are melting and your ears ring like bells in your head?'

'No,' she says flatly. 'And judging from what it has reduced you to...No thanks. I enjoy my self-control. My ability to say no and walk away from a situation that screams danger or abuse ahead.'

'Don't you miss Leticia, Billie?'

'Yes, I do, but... 'She looks at me meaningfully... 'Unlike you I have never had to crawl around the floor with missing her.'

I lower my eyes. Once many months ago when I first left the country I was reduced to crawling on the floor, but that intense pain passed. His reappearance, though, has awakened new realms of need and craving.

'I can say no, but I still miss him, Bill. I miss him like crazy. Even if there is no hope, I still want whatever I can have. I want him on any terms. I actually find it impossible to resist him.'

She sighs elaborately. 'OK, it is your life. When does this charade start then?'

'Tomorrow.'

'I guess we won't need a babysitter for Friday night, will we?'

I make an apologetic face. 'Sorry. Can you babysit tomorrow?'

'While you bang Banker Boy? Sure, why not. I hope that kid remembers what I have done for him when he grows up.'

I smile gratefully.

She fills two glasses with vodka and pushes one towards me. 'Here's to Sorab.' I don't want a drink. I am all churned up, but we clink and down. The alcohol burns the back of my throat. This is no celebration. Not for me and not for Billie. When our eyes meet again, hers are unsmiling; they warn me I am making a dreadful mistake.

Five

By nine o'clock the next morning, Sorab is fed and bathed and I am nervously checking my mobile to see if the battery is low, but it is fully charged and the reception is good. Blake's secretary's brisk, efficient voice comes through at 9:05.

'Good morning, Miss Bloom.'

'Hi, Mrs. Arnold.'

'Is this a good time to talk?'

'Yes.'

'Good,' she says briskly, and then falters for a second. 'I…uh…How have you been?'

'Fine, thank you.'

'That's good. Are you still on contraceptives?'

'No.'

'Oh!' It is clear she cannot understand why I have come off them.

Again the lies trip off my tongue so easily they surprise me. 'I have been in Iran. There was no need for them. Besides they are difficult to buy over there.'

'I will schedule an appointment with the nurse for a repeat prescription.'

'OK.'

'Next you will meet with the lawyer and then Fleur will take you shopping, and afterwards you have an appointment with the hairdresser, followed by appointments at the nail and wax bar.'

Suddenly I am swamped with a sense of déjà vu. I've done this before. Definitely. First time I was naïve. Stupid. That first kiss, it had blown me away, but now I know…I am the 'unnecessary, unwanted thirst'. The man who thirsts for me also despises me.

But then I thought it was all a fantastic adventure. A romantic dream. How I had jumped in with both feet. All I knew about him and his family was what Bill had read out to me from the Internet. Now I have done my research, sitting alone and pregnant by a window in Iran and I know a lot, a lot more about the great Barrington clan.

I know for example that there are no fewer than a hundred and fifty-three species or subspecies of insect which bear the name Barrington, fifty-eight birds, eighteen mammals and fourteen plants including a rare slipper orchid, three fish, two spiders and two reptiles. Numerous streets around the world and dishes have been named after them too. The only dish I still remember is the one with prawns, cognac, and Gruyére on toast.

They are the twenty-first-century Medicis, offering patronage to artists, writers, and architects. I learned about the houses they have donated to the people and the staggering amounts of money they have expanded into beneficiaries ranging from universities, hospitals, pubic libraries, charities, non profit institutions and archaeological digs. But Blake had already explained how the very rich play the philanthropic game to me. Steal from millions over a long period and give a small portion back as a taxable gift.

Over the weeks I came to realize that Blake's words were true. *If you see it in Wikipedia or a main-stream news outlet then we have planted it.* That everything I read and saw about the Barrington family and history was part of a picture, a false picture. They wanted the world to believe the bogus biographies that they themselves had commissioned, all of which declared their family as a once great dynasty that had since lost most of its wealth and influence. It was the picture of a benign, powerless house that jealously guarded its privacy.

Then I came across a Youtube video of Blake's father. There he was not the cold-eyed man who wanted to arbitrarily dismiss me to the toilet so he could talk to his son. Dressed in an expensive cashmere coat and metal rimmed glasses he worried about the world economy in a mild mannered way. His opinion: more austerity measures should be implemented worldwide before any recovery could be achieved. His silver hair made him look like someone's grandfather, but as I watched him I felt a cold shiver go up my spine.

At his transformation.

At the benevolent role he had so easily and effectively slipped into. If I had not seen the frosty arrogance with which, the blue stones had snubbed me I would never have believed these two men were the same person, but it gives chilling credence to Blake's warning that nothing in his world is as it seems to those in mine. That was when I began to search through the conspiracy sites. And they were rife with 'information'.

The Barringtons were blamed for everything from secretly starting the American Civil War in order to capture the monetary system, precipitating the American bank panic of 1907, to duping Congress into approving The Fed in 1913, to funding the Bolsheviks and Hitler. They were even accused of having a hand in the assassination of Kennedy. I gave up after a while.

There was one thing they got right, though.

They refused to believe the fairy tale that the Barringtons were a declining dynasty, whose members could not even make the Forbes rich list. As far as they were concerned the Barringtons were one of thirteen old families. Through complicated structures of off-shores companies they owned all the debt of all the countries. They were trillionaires and the true rulers behind governments and world organizations. To be a Barrington is to be a modern Croesus, a twentieth-century Midas.

'Is it all right if Tom knocks on your door at 10:00 am?' Laura Arnold asks.

The state of the lift flashes into my mind and I feel ashamed. 'No. Just ask him to call me on my mobile when he gets close to the flat. I'll come down.'

'All right then. Have a nice day, Miss Bloom.'

I thank her and end the call. As I place the phone on the dining table Billie walks in. Her eyes are half-shut. She goes to the fridge, takes a mouthful of orange juice straight from the carton and turns to face me. Her face is unsmiling.

'What time are you leaving?'

'Less than an hour.'

'Right,' she says.

'What would you do if you were me, Bill?'

'I don't know because I don't have all the facts, do I?'

'What do you mean?'

'You took the money and disappeared on him, no note, no goodbye, while he was unconscious in hospital after he had risked, if what you tell me is true, his precious life to save your lowly one. So in his eyes you must be the worst kind of gold digging slut that ever walked English soil. Instead of wanting to jump your bones shouldn't he just put it down to a lucky escape and thoroughly detest you by now?'

I put my head down. I feel ashamed that I have not told Bill the whole truth. 'You're right, he does detest me, but I'm like an itch that must be scratched.'

'Hmmm... There's something wrong with this explanation too—scratched itches get worse.'

'OK. He called it a disease.'

'For fuck's sake, Lana. What are getting yourself into?'

I close my eyes. I am making it worse. 'Look, Bill, it is not as bad as it looks.'

'Make it look better then.'

'I can't. All I can say is, I have to do this. I know I left him, but I have never ever stopped wanting him. There is not a single day that has gone by when I have not thought of him and longed for him. I don't fool myself that I can have him. I know I can't, but these 42 days are mine and nobody and nothing is taking them away from me. So he wants to punish me. Let him. A slap from him is better than nothing.'

Bill's mouth is hanging open with shock. She looks at me as if she has never known me. 'Are you going into some kind of sick sado-masochistic relationship?'

This time it is easy to meet her eyes. 'Blake doesn't know how to hurt me. Even if I asked him to, he couldn't. He believes he can, but he can't. I know that. You've met him. What do you think?'

Bill sighs. 'I liked him,' she admits finally.

I smile, but inside I am incredibly sad. I feel as if I can never touch real or lasting happiness. Everything gets taken away. 'Yes, I got the impression he likes you too.'

Bill turns red.

'Are you blushing, Bill?'

'If he ever tries anything funny, you're out of that sick contract in a flash,' she says gruffly.

I nod. She has just ensured that I will never tell her the whole story.

Six

The appointment with the nurse is quick and painless.

Next stop: the solicitor's offices. I get shown into Mr. Jay Benby's room by his secretary. He stands in greeting. I look around. Everything is exactly the same.

'How are you, Miss Bloom?' he says, half-rising from his chair, the same trust-me-I know-what's-best-for-you smile slowly slithering into his face like he is showing off his pet snake.

I drop my eyes to his turquoise ring and ask, 'Where do I sign?'

He draws himself to his full height. 'I must remind you, Miss Bloom, about the importance and the serious implications of what you are about to sign,' he begins with sanctimonious arrogance, but I cut him off. Last time I was the young thing that came into his office all big-eyed and intimidated by his legal jargon. Not this time.

'Mr. Benby, we are both being paid to be here. We can pretend you are better than me, but why waste our time?'

His eyes narrow dangerously.

Ah, I have offended him. Good.

His movements are sharp and jerky as he opens the contract on his desk to the required page, puts a black and gold fountain pen on top of that page, and pushes the whole shebang towards my end of the desk. Truth is we both know that I don't have to be here. The contract I have already signed is for life. Of course, he can't figure out why I am here, I see that in his speculative eyes, but I know exactly why I am here.

This is part of my humiliation.

I take the pen. It is cool and smooth in my fingers. I unscrew the cap, sign and date the document, then push it back towards him.

'Are we done here?'

He nods stiffly, his anger very firmly held in check. I am Blake Law Barrington's woman, at least for the next 42 days. Untouchable. I turn around and leave.

A small Boots paper bag is sitting in the back seat of the Bentley. I thank Tom , stuff the contraceptives into my rucksack and turn my head to look out of the window. London has a different air from Kilburn. Less desperation, more bustle. The people are different too. They haven't given up. They still believe in their pursuit. It makes their eyes hard. The way all city people's eyes are. I press my hand to my stomach. I am nervous. I don't know what tonight will be like. So far it seems as if Blake has recreated the day of our first night together. Our first night together still burns in my memory. I replay it in my mind and it causes my thighs to clench together with a mixture of excitement and anticipation.

This time, I think, I will hold my own.

Fleur is waiting in the reception area for me. She walks towards me, smiling, polished and elegant, exactly as I remember her. She embraces me warmly. Then she holds me away from her and says, 'It is wonderful to see you again, but you have become so thin. Have you been all right?'

Suddenly I want to cry. I couldn't cry at all for weeks, but since yesterday the smallest acts of kindness make me want to bawl my eyes out. I bite my lip and blink back the tears.

For a moment Fleur registers an expression of surprise, but she is not a PR executive for nothing. She smiles brightly and making a crook out of her left arm invites me to slip mine through hers. We walk together out of the glass doors. 'Shall we start with some cosmetics?'

'I don't need new cosmetics, Fleur. I've hardly used the stuff you got me the last time. Not much call for it in Iran.'

She turns her face towards me. 'It is bad enough that women have to put chemicals on their faces, at least let it not be old and toxic. Six months is the maximum that you should keep your cosmetics once opened,' she says firmly, as we exit into the weak sunlight.

We get my cosmetics on the ground floor of Harvey Nichols. Besides the nudes and soft pinks Fleur picks out a scarlet lipstick. 'I am informed that you will be going to the opera. This will be perfect for the black dress I have in mind.' She passes a credit card over to the sales assistant and turns to me. 'Have you been to the opera before?'

I shake my head.

Fleur smiles. 'Well, then it will be a new and wonderful experience for you.'

We get into the lift.

'There is a dress here which you absolutely must try on. It is a dream.'

We are passing a glass showcase when Fleur stops so suddenly I slam into her. Grabbing my hand she yanks me down into a crouched position with her. I stare at her without comprehension as we hunker down behind the showcase. She puts her finger to her lips, smiles weakly and to her credit manages an insouciant shrug.

My first thought is that she has spotted someone she wants to avoid, but the next moment I hear a snooty accent ask, 'Don't you have it in cerise?' An icy claw of horror clutches my stomach. I must have paled or looked scared because Fleur's fingers tighten on my hand and her eyes shoot out a silent, but clear warning to make no sound.

I swallow hard.

The voice is saying something else I do not catch, but it is moving away. Fleur tugs at my hand and starts crawling away. If I was not so shaken it would have been funny. Both of us on our hands and knees in Harvey Nichols! Once when Billie had come barefoot here in the height of summer security had her forcibly ejected. But Fleur is not just anyone. Fleur represents big business, repeat business.

A matronly woman looks at us with widened, disapproving eyes, but then she recognizes Fleur who gives her a small wave. She nods almost imperceptibly and stares ahead. As soon as we reach the end of the long showcase Fleur stands and, pulling me with her, walks quickly out of the department. We go down the stairs and exit the store. Outside Fleur doesn't wait for Tom, but hails a black cab. We get into it and she tells the driver to take us to Kings Road.

Then she sends a text message to Tom to meet us there and turns to me.

'I'm really sorry about that, but it is better that we did not meet her. I take it you know her?'

My hands are trembling. I nod. I am in a state of extreme shock. Of all the millions of people in London I could have to run into, why her? And on the first day of my contract. I understand it to be a bad omen, a warning that I am making a horrible mistake.

Fleur's beautifully manicured hand grasps mine. 'Don't worry about it. It was just bad luck. We will shop in Kings Road instead. There are wonderful places there too. In fact, sometimes I think I prefer it.'

I shake my head. 'I don't want to shop anymore, Fleur. I just want to go home.'

Fleur's eyes change. I see pure determination shining between her extravagant lashes. This is a woman who will not allow anything to stand in her way. I start to admire her anew. She is resilient in a way that I am not.

'You can't go home, Lana. You are committed to this day. We have appointments that we must keep. Victoria is not as powerful as you or she believes. She cannot take away from you that which is really yours.'

'What do you mean?' I ask shakily. I am actually filled with fear. I have lost so much. All I have left is Sorab and if I am careless in any way at all he will disappear like a mirage in the desert.

'My position does not allow me to say, but do not underestimate Blake Law Barrington. He could surprise you yet. Besides, don't you think that women who blame the other woman are stupid? The other woman owes them no allegiance. Look to your own man. He is the one who has betrayed you. Get angry with him, if you dare.'

I nod. Fleur is right. I have done nothing wrong. I kept to my agreement. I left the country for a year. I did not approach Blake. He came looking for me.

'Good,' Fleur says with an encouraging smile. 'Here is what we will do. We will go to my friend's boutique and find something for you to wear tonight and tomorrow I will have some clothes that I think will be perfect for you sent to your apartment? And you can choose what you want and return the rest, OK?'

'OK.'

'I will reschedule your hairdresser's appointment and Laura will push all the other appointments up accordingly.'

In a daze I hear her call the celebrity hairdresser and effortlessly get him to come into the salon four hours earlier than scheduled. People bent backwards to accommodate a Barrington's needs. After that she calls Laura.

'Slight change of plans,' she says. 'Mmnn. Tell you about it later. We are going to the hairdresser's at 1:00 pm. Push all the other appointments up accordingly.' A pause while she listens and then she says, 'Right. That's fine with me. Speak later.' She turns to me. 'All right?'

'All right.'

'Lunch first?'

I am not hungry, but I nod unhappily.

She takes a deep breath. 'If you promise you will never tell anyone what I am about to reveal to you then I will tell you a secret.'

I promise quickly.

'It is very important that you do not tell anyone, especially Blake, or you could drop both Laura and me into some extremely foul smelling stuff.'

'I won't tell anyone. Especially Blake.'

'You are more important to Blake than you think. Sometime after he met you last year, when he was about to go into an important meeting, he called over his shoulder and told Laura to hold all his calls. But then he turned around and said, "except for Lana".'

'Laura was very surprised by the request. You see, never before had he given her such an instruction. Not even for his father or brother. "Is that for just this meeting or for all day," she asked. "Until I tell you otherwise." But here is the most surprising thing of all: Blake Barrington has never told her otherwise.'

The first thought in my mind. That was before.

'Don't make the mistake of thinking that is because he has forgotten. Blake never forgets anything. Not even the smallest details.'

I nod. Perhaps he did care. Perhaps he will learn to care again.

'I did not want us to meet Victoria not because I am afraid of her, but because I think it is unnecessary. It is unnecessary for you and unnecessary for her. She has overestimated her importance; you have underestimated yours. Be confident. Things are not always what they seem.'

A business call comes through for Fleur. She asks if I mind her taking it. I say no and spend my time looking at the shoppers on the street, my stomach rolling with anxiety.

The car comes to a stop outside a brightly painted corner shop called Bijou.

Fleur pushes open an old-fashioned door and a quaint bell tinkles. A waft of carpet deodorant rushes out to greet us. The small shop is so crammed with clothes, jewelry, hats, bags and shoes and so different from the usual pared down designer shop that Fleur usually takes me to that I actually have the impression of having stumbled into Aladdin's secret cave.

A well-preserved small woman of indeterminate age stands from behind an ornate desk and comes forward to greet and air kiss Fleur on both her cheeks. Her laughter is a sophisticated, heavy smoker's rasp. She has that sort of European chic that comes from teaming box jackets in bold colors with numerous ropes of pearls.

I am presented to Rêgine.

She smiles at me, gives me the once-over, and bustles Fleur and me towards a couple of red velvet chairs. When we are seated, she turns the sign on the door to closed and begins running around her overcrowded shop humming to herself. She comes back with three different outfits.

'Try that one first,' suggests Fleur pointing to a fabulous knee-length white dress with a high mandarin collar, three jeweled cut-outs in the shape of leaves in the chest and slits up the thighs. I take it from Madame. The material is the softest wool.

'Only girls with very slim arms can wear the cheongsam,' says Fleur.

'Qui,' agrees Madame Rêgine.

I go behind a heavy velvet curtain, where there are three full-length mirrors. We have no long mirrors at home. Billie goes to Marks and Spencer's changing rooms to see herself nude. I strip down to my undies. I can see that I am too skinny. My ribs and hip bones are showing. Not a good look. I used to look better before. Immediately I begin to worry if I will please Blake. I remember how attracted to my body he was. How he used to tell me to take my clothes off, and watch me. Simply watch me with hungry, fascinated eyes as if I was the most beautiful thing he had ever seen. What if my body no longer excites him?

'Hey, we want to see,' calls Fleur with a laugh.

'Coming,' I say, and slip into the dress. I zip up and stare at my reflection. Wow! I cannot believe how well the dress flatters me. It makes me look like I have curves. I turn my head to look at my side—the slit that comes to mid-thigh is at once subtle and sexy. Feeling reassured, I pull back the curtain.

'Magnifique!' sighs the throaty voice.

Fleur grins like a Cheshire cat. 'You look beautiful, Lana,' she says and I know that she is being sincere.

'But wait... I have the perfect shoes,' calls Madame, and rushes off to the back of the shop.

She returns with a pair of shoes that are encrusted with similar stones as the ones that edge the leaf-shaped holes in my chest. They are like Cinderella's glass slippers. Only the right girl can fit into them. I take them from her and step into them. The shoes fit perfectly—she must have an excellent eye.

The powdered face smiles cunningly. 'Aaa...but wait.... You must have your hair up.'

She plucks from a large vase three jeweled pins and expertly holding my hair up inserts the pins into it. The European madam, whose age I am slowly having to revise upwards, claps her hands and declares with finality that it is, 'Absolument fabuleux.'

I look into the mirror and I have to agree. Absolutely fabulous. The dress is truly amazing. I have never felt so glamorous or sexy in my entire life. I look at Fleur and she is smiling.

'No one can take what is truly yours away from you,' she says, and I smile.

We come out of Bijou and Tom is waiting for us. He puts all our packages into the boot and takes us to the celebrity hairdresser.

'You let your fringe grow out,' Bruce the celebrity hairdresser accuses.

'I was living in Iran. Women are not allowed to show their hair in public. It was easier to let it grow and pull it all back into a bun and throw a scarf over my head,' I explain.

'Ah, that takes excellent care of my next "have you been anywhere nice?' question.'

I laugh. I like him. He's a rare one, a tough guy hairdresser with a good British sense of humor. And he has a strong determined jaw and eyes that are subtle, but surely undressing me. If I am not totally in love with Blake I could fancy him.

'But honestly,' he continues, 'what the devil possessed you to go live in that godforsaken country?'

'My mother hails from there.'

'Ah! I hear it has very beautiful tiled baths.'

'It has.'

He puts a hand out and touches my cheekbones. 'You have lost weight. A fringe alone will be too harsh. I will feather your hair from your mouth onwards to return that lost softness.'

And he does.

Fleur gives the jeweled pins to the girl who takes over the job of drying my hair and instructs the girl to put my hair up. 'But no hairspray,' she says and winks at me. 'Men don't like hard hair.'

The girl is finished and I am a marvelously different.

It is also time for Fleur to say goodbye. I feel almost tearful. She is the only one who seems to be on my side, rooting for me. She kisses me on the cheeks. 'All will be well. Just be yourself and nothing can be more beautiful.'

Back at the waxing salon I learn that Rosa has moved back to Spain. A stout German woman with reddened hands and nails bitten to the quick takes me into the treatment room. There is no talk about jam sandwiches consumed in front of the TV or a clever son who is in art school, only a silent, ruthless dedication to bald skin. Gertrude strips every single hair from my body. When I am all over a sharp shade of red and the last offensive hair is gone she heaves a large of sigh of satisfaction. Unlike Rosa she does not offer to do my eyebrows for free. That was from another time. When life was generous to me.

My nails are too short for a French manicure. The girl asks me if I would like acrylic nails and for a moment I am tempted—I have never had them and they seem rather fun—but then I think of accidentally scratching Sorab's tender skin while I am changing his nappy and I refuse. She waves towards a shelf full of nail varnish.

'Choose your color.'

'White,' I say. 'I will have the white nail polish.'

In the car I admire my nails, how pretty and clean they look. 'Tom,' I say. 'If you give me the key to the apartment you can drop me off at my place, and I'll take a cab later to the apartment.'

'Oh no, Miss Bloom that would be more than my job's worth. I got an ear bashing for dropping you off at the shops the last time. I can take you to your place and wait downstairs until you are ready to go to the apartment.'

He drops me off at the entrance and parks by the dark staircase to wait for my return.

Seven

Billie is sitting at our dining table when I enter. The baby's basket is sitting on the table beside her. Surrounded by pens, watercolors, and crayons, she is bent over a large sketchpad in deep concentration. Hair is falling over her forehead and I feel a great surge of love for her. She looks up and smiles.

'Wow! That's a seriously cool hairstyle,' she exclaims, and springing up comes to hold my hand and twirl me around.

'So you like it?' I probe, self-consciously touching my fringe.

'Yeah,' she says emphatically. 'If he won't have you, I will.'

I laugh and go towards the basket. 'Is he asleep?'

'Nope.'

Sorab is waving his little arms. I reach into the basket and lift him into my arms. He is wearing something Billie designed and made from scratch, a bright red and yellow romper suit with big blue cloth buttons that look like flowers.

'Hello, darling,' I say, my face creasing into the first joy-filled smile since I left the house.

He stares at me with his intense blue eyes for a few seconds before he breaks into one of his deliciously toothless grins.

Over my shoulder Billie says, 'Shame he will have to grow up to be a man.'

I turn around and look at her meaningfully.

'What?' she asks.

'Your dad's a man.'

'That remains to be seen,' she says, and moving towards her drawings, says, 'Come and see this.' I follow her around the table. I put Sorab into the crook of my arm to get a better view of her work. She has drawn a girl's dress. It is not in the usual pale pink normally reserved for baby girls, but banana yellow with green apples all over it. I have never seen anything like it in the shops. She truly has a unique talent.

'Well, what do you think?'

'It is so cute, I almost wish Sorab was a girl.'

Billie smiles. 'You got time for a pot of tea?'

'I do,' I say. She puts the kettle on and we sit and talk. We never mention Blake. Until four thirty when I kiss Sorab and walk out of our front door. Tom gets out of the car and opens the back door when he sees me come down the stairs. I look up and Billie is standing at the balcony looking down at me. She shifts the baby to one hand and waves. I wave back, a feeling of dread in my stomach.

I do not let Tom carry my bags for me or take me upstairs. I know the way. Besides, I am dying to be alone with just my chaotic thoughts. I go through the glass door and Mr. Nair leaps to his feet from his position behind the reception counter like a startled meerkat. He comes towards me beaming.

'Miss Bloom, Miss Bloom,' he cries. 'You are back in the penthouse. I saw all the cleaners and bags and new furniture going upstairs and I wondered who it would be.'

'How nice to see you again, Mr. Nair.'

He holds out his hands. 'Here, let me help you with your bags.'

I pull the bags out of his reach. 'It's OK, Mr. Nair. They are very light. I can manage. Why don't you come up tomorrow morning for a coffee instead, and we can have a nice chat, then.'

'Oh yes, Miss Bloom. That will be wonderful. It hasn't been the same ever since you left.'

I smile. In truth I too have missed him and his fantastic stories of an India gone by. 'I'll call down tomorrow.'

'Goodnight, Miss Bloom. It really is good to have you back.'

I bid him goodnight, enter the lift and slip my key card into its slot. The doors swish close and I am borne up. Strange, I never thought I would be coming back here again and yet here I am. The doors open and it is all the same. Nothing, but nothing has changed.

I unlock the front door and open it. The same faint fragrance of lilies that I always associate with this apartment wafts out. Such a feeling of nostalgia rushes over me that I feel my knees go weak. I close the door, put my packages on the side table, and walk down that long enameled corridor. I run my fingers along the cool smooth wall the way I had done more than a year ago.

I don't go into the living room, but turn off and go into the bedroom. A sob rises in my throat. Nothing has changed even here. It is as if I was here yesterday and not more than a year ago. I go into the room next to it and, as Laura promised, it has been set up to function as a nursery. There is a beautiful white and blue cot, all kinds of toys, a very swanky-looking pram and tins of baby formula. I go to them. I recognize them. I have seen them advertised, all natural and made of goat's milk, but I could not afford them. I pick one up and look at it and experience a shaft of guilt.

I have denied Sorab all this. Am I really doing the right thing by him? Will he thank me one day for depriving him of a life that 99.99 percent of people can only dream of? The answer is confusing and I don't want to go there. I know I will go there, it is too important not to, but not yet. Not today. It is already six o'clock.

I close the door and go into the bathroom and switch on the lights. In the immaculate space I am a stranger with a beautiful hairdo. I stare at myself. The night stretches out in front of me. I am excited and fearful of what it will bring. I sit on the toilet seat for a moment to compose myself.

I take my dress out of the exclusive-looking bag Rêgine packed it in and hang it up in the bedroom.

Then I run a bath, add lavender oil, step into it, and, lying back, close my eyes, but I am too nervous and excited to relax and after a few minutes I get out and, wrapping myself in a fluffy bathrobe that smells of squashed berries, I go into the kitchen.

In the fridge there I find two bottles of champagne lying on their sides. I remember the last time when I stood in the balcony and drank to my mother's health. This time champagne doesn't seem appropriate. I close the door restlessly and go to the liquor cabinet. There I pour myself a very large shot of vodka. Standing by the bar I knock it back. It runs like fire into my empty stomach, but it has the desired effect of almost immediately settling my nerves. I look at my hands. They have stopped shaking.

I go back into the bathroom and carefully apply my make-up. Two layers of mascara, a touch of blusher, and nude lip gloss. I move away from the mirror.

'Not bad, Bloom. Good job.'

I go back to the alcohol counter and pour myself another large vodka, down it and, feeling decidedly light-headed and, devil may care, go to the bedroom. I take my beautiful white dress off the hanger and change into it. As I gently ease it over my head a hook catches on my hair and pulls a lock out of place. I stare in horror at the dangling lock. Cursing, I try to twist it and push it back into place. My efforts are somewhat successful and I sigh with relief. I zip up and step into my shoes and look at myself in the mirror.

A sophisticated woman with glittering eyes and high color stares back. Too much blusher. With cotton wool I remove it all. The heat and the alcohol have tinged my cheeks pink. No need for blusher. I dab my finger with perfume and touch it behind my ears.

There I am, ready for the great Barrington.

Eight

I kill ten minutes pacing the balcony tiles in my Cinderella shoes. At 8:05 exactly Tom rings the bell. His eyes widen when I open the door.

'That's a beautiful outfit, Miss Bloom,' he says, with an embarrassed cough. He is holding a long cardboard box, which he awkwardly slips onto the side-table. I look at it and feel the color rush up my neck. Oh my God! Blake really means for this to be a re-creation of our first night together.

As the lift descends I already know where Tom is taking me.

Madame Yula is filled with the same sort of people that had populated it the last time I was there. If this is a re-creation of our first night together then I know exactly where I will find Blake. Waiting at the bar. I turn towards it and even though I know what I will see, my heart stops. He is wearing a charcoal suit, black shirt and a white tie, and he is the most beautiful man in the place…but that is not it… I am being eaten alive by his eyes. For a long moment I stand frozen, simply caught and staring back at the *hunger* in his stormy blue eyes. It is so naked and raw it shocks me.

'Mademoiselle,' someone says, close to my ear. I turn in the direction of the voice, my expression blank, distracted, perhaps even confused. 'Can I help you?' the waiter queries.

Before I can answer, Blake is there.

'She's with me,' he says smoothly, and the waiter slips away, the way waiters in movies do. I turn my head and look up into Blake's face. In the glow of candles and soft lighting he seems dark and impossibly mysterious. For a moment neither of us speaks. We never broke up. It's all there crackling between us. The sex-rumpled sheets, the slim hips wrapped only in a towel, the hungry mouth, and the hours upon hours of fucking. I shiver with the memories. My lips part. An invitation that cannot be missed.

But a shutter comes over his eyes.

'How complete is the illusion that beauty is goodness,' he murmurs.

Vaguely it registers that it is quotation, but my stunned brain cannot locate the source. A hand reaches out to take that escaped lock of hair that has worked free of my efforts to keep it up. Gently he twirls the strands in his fingers and carefully reinserts them into place. His hand drops off.

'Would you like a drink?'

It occurs to me that I am already a little drunk. 'No, I had some back at the flat.'

His eyes flash. 'Champagne.' He remembered.

I shake my head. 'Vodka.'

He nods. 'Food for you then,' he says.

We are shown to the same table. I look closely at him. Try to see beyond the mask, but his face is deliberately blank. In a daze I order food. It arrives. I pick up my knife and fork. Slip it between my lips. Taste nothing. I lift my eyes to him and catch him watching me. His eyes are ravenous. His food untouched. Between my legs I ache. I swallow the food in my mouth. It becomes a lump that sticks in my throat. I reach for the wine glass and take a gulp, but that only makes me choke. I start to cough. My eyes fill with water. Fuck. Trust me to do something so sexually unappealing.

'Are you all right?'

'Fine,' I say flushing with embarrassment. I need to go to the Ladies and sort myself out.

'Excuse me,' I croak, putting the napkin on the table and standing up.

He stands when I do. I leave the table and feel his eyes boring into me until I round the bend. I go into the Ladies and look at myself in the mirror. And again I am surprised by my reflection. I honestly can hardly recognize myself, the new hairstyle, the clothes, the make-up, but more than all of that is the look in my eyes. Wild. 'I am Lana from the council estate, mother of Sorab,' I say aloud.

That piece of hair comes loose again. I carefully pull one of the pins out a little and wind the hair around that pin. It seems to do the job. I take a deep breath and go back out to the restaurant.

While I have been away Blake has not touched his food. Instead, he has finished his whiskey and ordered another. He looks at me from above the rim of his glass.

'Aren't you hungry?' I ask.

He puts his glass down and catches my fingers. His hands are exactly as I remember, firm, warm, strong. He turns them over and looks at my nails.

'Very nice,' he says softly, and bringing them to his lips kisses them. It is a mocking gesture, but at the touch of his cool lips I tremble with anticipation. I remember them smiling with sexual invitation. He lets his fingers run up the skin of my wrist. 'Pure fucking silk.' His eyes rise up to meet mine. Between the thick lashes they are potent, compelling. 'Have you missed me even a little, Lana?'

For an instant, I forget myself and respond to the emotion I see simmering in his eyes. 'There is not a day that has gone by where I have not longed for you,' I whisper.

As if I have slapped him, he snatches his hand away and begins to laugh bitterly. He shakes his head as if in wonder. 'I see now why I was fooled by you. You're downright lethal. A very, very dangerous seductress indeed I have caught in my net.'

He drains his glass and, looking away from me, gestures to a waiter for another. When he turns back to face me, his eyes are glittering. 'So how much did my father pay you?'

I pause. I am in dangerous territory. My contract with Victoria does not allow me to reveal the sum or even tell anyone that I have been paid by her. The waiter arrives with his whiskey and sets it down in front of him.

'Another,' Blake barks.

The waiter nods discreetly and clears his empty glass in one smooth movement. Blake does not take his eyes off me.

Billie is right. My position is untenable. In his eyes I must be the worst kind of slut. Ahead lies only more misunderstanding and pain for both of us. The pain has already begun, a physical ache. It fills my chest. I can never tell him the truth. In his mind I will always be his bad romance. Lady Gaga singing, 'I want your ugly. I want your disease.'

'I'm sorry, but I had to sign a non-disclosure agreement,' I say, with the full knowledge that without the truth he will always despise me. I lean back in my chair feeling soiled. I will never again be clean in his eyes. And there is not a damn thing I can do about it. The waiter returns with more whiskey.

'I know you're angry but—'

'Shut the fuck up. You have no idea,' he grates through gritted teeth.

I close my mouth. I have never seen him so openly angry. He is always so controlled, so smooth. Even when he was once angry with someone on the phone his fury was so tightly leashed, so frighteningly quiet that I stood stock still behind the door listening.

He shoots his whiskey aggressively, and turning the empty glass on its edge rolls it on the tablecloth. 'Do you want more food?'

I shake my head miserably. This is turning out to be nothing like I imagined.

A muscle in his jaw twitches. He calls for the bill.

Someone in a suit comes rushing to his side. 'Is anything the matter?' he enquires worriedly.

'Everything is fine.' He looks at me hard and deep.

'But your main course…'

Blake does not take his eyes off me. 'I have unfinished business to take care of, Anton.'

I flush badly and Anton slips away with impressive speed from that which has nothing to do with him. Another waiter, his face schooled into impassive professionalism, comes bearing the bill. Blake signs for it, unfolds himself out of his chair and comes to stand by me. I get to my feet and he leads me out of the restaurant. We do not touch except for his hand splayed on the small of my back. Possessive, the way only a husband's hand should be.

Not a word is spoken by either of us in the car, but every cell in my body is responding to his nearness. My desire for him is such that my hands are clenched tight against my thighs and my sex is actually throbbing. In fact, the need is so excessive it is almost violent. I sneak a look at him. He is staring ahead, the chiseled cheekbones like stone, but that muscle in his throat is ticking like a time bomb. I know that tick. It tells me what he cannot, how hard and deep he wants to fuck me. He is well and truly snared inside his bad romance.

'What happened to all the clothes I left behind?' I ask in the lift.

'You enquire about last season's fashions? What about the people you left behind, Lana? Why don't you enquire about them? Me for instance.'

'How have you been, Blake?'

'You're just about to find out,' he replies with a nasty grin.

Nine

I hear the soft, thick click of the door behind me, and turn around to face him. He stands there, tall, dark and throbbing with sexual tension. God! How I want this man. A rough sound rumbles in his throat. I recognize it. Blind, earth-shattering desire. It has been a long time since I heard it. Makes me rock on my feet. He shoots out a hand and pulls me hard towards him. My body slams into his.

I have the impression of stone—unmoving. It will break, but it will never bend. But I can bend. I mold my hips into his. His erection is thick and hot against my stomach. The rawness of it awakens that great beast inside me. Greedy, relentless thing. It wants more, it wants it all, and it wants it right now. Intoxicated by the smoldering fire in his eyes my hands snake up his chest and twine around his neck, but his strong hands come up and untangle mine. He catches them in his and takes them behind my back. His clasp is a firm handcuff.

Very deliberately he holds me away from him and lets his half-lidded eyes rove my parted mouth, my breasts—thrust out towards him and heaving, down my body, to my legs. His eyes lift again to meet mine. I am impossibly aroused.

'I had half a dozen fantasies of what I wanted to do to you when I got you naked. Tame sex is not one of them,' he says, as he plucks out the pins in my hair and flings them away. Released, my hair falls all around my face and shoulders.

'My beautiful whore. Once I was good to you and you kicked me when I was down; now you get what you deserve.'

Without warning he grips the two sides of the high collar of my lovely dress and rips it into two. I clutch the torn ends of my ruined dress together and stare at him in shock.

He looks down at me, breathing hard. Strangely, he is as cold as ice. My mind is in unbelievable chaos. I have misjudged the extent of his fury. Underneath the façade of calm he is seething with anger at what he perceives to be my duplicity. I want to cry at the wanton destruction of something so beautiful, but in fact I am too shocked to cry.

'Dress only in what's in the box and meet me in the bedroom,' he commands curtly, and walks away from me.

I stand there a little longer, too dazed to move. I glimpsed the fierce hunger, and need; now all I see is the iron control in his tense shoulders. He stops in front of the bar and pours himself a whiskey. I pick up the box by the side table and go to the bathroom.

Quickly, I take off the torn dress and stuff it into the chrome bin under the sink. As the lid closes over it a sob escapes my lips. I had never owned anything so fine before. It had suggested curves where there were jutting bones and made me feel so elegant and sophisticated. I could still see Fleur grinning with delight and Madame Rêgine rasping, 'One of a kind. You will not find another like it.'

I press my hand to my mouth and avoid my reflection. I will not cry. I will be strong, I tell myself while, another part of me stands appalled by his violence. I know what is in the box. I pull the satin ribbons and lift the cover of the box.

And frown.

It is not white lingerie and shoes.

As if in a trance, I pick up the familiar velvet box and open it. Under the yellow lights of the bathroom the diamonds in the sapphire necklace glitter like the bling on a rap singer. The next thing I find in the box is even more surprising. Billie's shorts, the ones I borrowed to wear to the party. I must have left them behind. I had totally forgotten them. I remember that night again. What did it mean? That he himself has gone through all my stuff and kept these? That this item of clothing means something to him? I open the last item—a shoe box. A pair of snake skin orange Christian Louboutin shoes, but startlingly similar to the ones I wore the first night we met.

I try to imagine how he came upon them. Did he describe them to Laura? Did she then search the net and give him a list to choose from? I undress quickly. I consider leaving my knickers on, but I remember his eyes when he held my hands behind my back and told me everything I should be wearing is in the box.

The necklace is cold on my skin. I pull the shorts on, zip and button them. I get into the shoes and look at myself in the mirror. Oh dear. The shorts hang about my hip bones and my rib bones show. I look gawky and awkward and as sexy as a pole in shorts. I console myself that the lights in the bedroom will be muted. I stare at my breasts. The nipples are erect. This morning I could have covered them with my hair, but now that the front has been feathered that option is gone.

I touch the light switch and kill the light, in the hope that he will not see the silhouette of my skinny frame, or my half-naked exit from the bathroom. My steps falter and I stand uncertainly by the wall in my high heels. Half-hidden in the shadows at the edges of the room, I stand and stare at the magnificent specimen sitting shirtless, in a pool of light on the bed.

His legs are crossed at the ankles and his arms are folded across his chest. The muscles of his arms seem even more defined than I remember. He must have taken his frustrations out in the gym. He moves slightly and the action ripples the golden row of thick muscles in his stomach. My mouth dries. Suddenly I feel exposed and ashamed of my body, my arousal.

My hands rise up to cover my breasts. My nipples are hard pebbles against the palms of my hands.

'Come in,' he purrs. His voice is silk, but his eyes are shadowed and his face is a blank wall. Expressionless. Impenetrable.

He begins to unbutton his trousers. I stare at the flat stomach, the beautiful body that I have longed for. The trousers slip to the floor. Black briefs. The bulge is clearly, clearly visible. Dear me, but it's been so long. I feel my own body producing its juices, getting ready for the sweet invasion. He steps out of his briefs. Wow! Nothing has changed. He is as gorgeous as ever.

But I don't move. I can't. My soul refuses to allow me to go forward. Not towards that demeaning drill again. I remember it like yesterday. Go to the middle of the room, strip, turn around, spread my legs as wide as they will go, and bend down to touch the floor. Then it had been strangely exciting, but now it seems sordid. I'm not here because he paid me to be here. I'm here willingly. I am here to atone for a wrong I did him. I'm here because, even though he doesn't believe it, I'm crazy in love with him.

'New games, Lana?' he mocks when I make no move towards him, but his voice is different. The silk is gone. It is sinuous and alive with the kind of unthinking lust that only a man knows how to feel.

I watch him bound off the bed, and come towards me, tall, dark, dangerous, and looking for trouble. He stops in front of me. Heat comes off his body in waves. The air thickens. I want to taste that golden skin. I blink to break the spell. *Take control, Lana.* The blackness of what I have made him become envelops me like a bleak shadow. His vengeful eyes bore into me.

A strange fascination with danger slides down my spine. I want to shut my eyes and try to picture him as he was, but I don't. One wrong move and he'll take me now, roughly, and the chasm between us will become wider, impossible to breach. But a woman is never without options, my mother always said. Start the way you mean to carry on. I need not be powerless. I can be as powerful as Billie, as powerful as my mother.

I take my hands away from my breasts and slip the copper button of my shorts out of its eye. Slowly I unzip my shorts. His eyes do not follow my fingers but watch my face. Even so my fingers are trembling with a kind of feral excitement. I don't have to push them down my legs. They are so loose they run down like water. For a while I stand there in my necklace and my high shoes.

When I lift one leg to step out of the shorts, he catches my leg firmly under the knee and forces it up high so I am spread open to him. I feel air in places that have never seen the sun. My gesture of submission has done nothing to lessen his cold regard. His eyes are deliberately barren. I wonder how someone can be as turned on as he obviously is and still look so cold and distant.

His other hand cups one bare buttock possessively and my pussy, already wet, floods and clenches with anticipation. He plays with the wetness he has aroused. Pleasure and delicious release shimmer between us. It has been so long. My body doesn't care how he does it or why he wants to do it. It just wants him inside. It has always been like that for me. My body weeping for him. He lets his fingers sweep along my open sex and brings it to his mouth. He sucks his fingers.

'Mmnnn you still taste like heaven.'

I whimper and that sound has an electrifying effect on him. With a growl he thrusts his fingers into me. Again. And again. Harder. Faster. A sound escapes my lips. My head presses against the wall and my hips thrust towards his hand. He is rough, but after all this time I welcome it. My pussy creams with the force. I feel the excess fluid trickle down my thighs.

But it is not enough.

I rock my hips mindlessly. Looking to fill that ache. Where his fingers cannot reach. Begging him with my body, with every jerk and every gasp, but he will not give me that. His fingers pump with a steady, forceful tempo, pushing me towards a rough, humiliating climax.

Which comes while I am standing on one foot like a stork, my body twisted open. The rapture is explosive. My muscles lose all their strength and I sag against the wall behind me. The dizzying roar of my own blood abates to a dull thud. He looks at me with frosty eyes. He wants me to lower my head in shame while he pretends he has felt nothing. But I know different. My eyes defiant, I lift a hand and cup his hard erection.

'You are as aroused as I am.'

He smiles. 'Sure,' he drawls. 'I want to fuck you. What man wouldn't? To tell you the truth, babe, I'm drowning in lust.'

He lets go of my leg and with rough hands grabs me by the upper arms, whirls me around, and pushes me forward. My palms and forearms hit the wall. My right cheek is pressed against the cold surface of the wall and my breasts are crushed into it. He takes the hair that covers my face from his gaze and hooks it behind my ear. He wants to watch me. My eyes swivel desperately to the side to look at him, but I cannot see him.

"You taste and smell the same, let's see if you feel the same,' he says, and, lifting me slightly off the ground, grasps my thighs and spreads them wide apart. My shoes fall off with a dull thud. He returns my bare feet to the ground soundlessly. His large hands grab my hips and tilt my lower body so it is perfectly aligned with his cockhead. For a second I feel him tease me by running it along my clit and then he drives into me.

The impact makes me shudder and my breath catch in my throat. My mouth opens in a soundless cry. I draw a breath quickly. Prepare myself for the next swift thrust of pleasure. It comes before I am ready. This time I cannot help it, I utter a strange cry, but my muscles are already clenching him and sucking him even deeper into my body.

He sets up a rapid pace. Every wild plunge into my depths has me jerking in response. Slowly I am lifted higher and higher until I am standing uncomfortably on the tips of my toes, my hips tilting higher and higher, wanting more and more of the gloriously thick invasion. My thighs and calf muscles are so tense they start to ache and my heart is beating so fast I feel it thudding like a drum inside my ribcage. My sex becomes a greedy, hungry mouth sucking at him.

I force myself to hold my body in the same position while he hammers into me until, with one last painful thrust that I register at the base of my womb, he calls my name and finds his climax. His cum is slick and hot inside me. For a second his nose nuzzles in the crook of my neck and then he rouses himself and pushes away from me.

I don't turn to face him, but slowly set my heels down to the ground and push myself away from the wall. I will gather myself a tiny bit more before I turn again to face his condemnation. I feel weak, raw, bruised, abused, vulnerable, but…satisfied. I should have felt shame, but I don't. I love this man.

I turn around slowly.

He is dressing quickly. While buttoning his shirt with his back to me, he says, 'I will get Laura to send you a morning after pill.'

A stray thought. *A bit late for that, mate.* If he knew. If he only knew. I say nothing, suddenly feeling my nakedness. Soon he will be dressed and I will be the only naked one in the room. I begin to walk to the bathroom.

'Wait,' he orders. I long to cover myself, but I do not. He cannot humiliate me. I will not allow it.

When he is fully dressed he turns and looks at my exposed body. It is masked well, but it is still there, the hunger. Still now. When he has just been satiated. So much remains that my eyes widen. It is the same for me: I want him again. I am just as helpless to the call of his body.

But he turns away from me.

I watch him go to the side cupboard and pull out a book. It is covered in leather. Looks like a journal. He tosses it on the bed next to me. 'This is for you. I want you to keep a record of everything I do to you.'

'Why?' I whisper.

'For my reading pleasure?'

'That's just sick. I'm not doing it,' I say.

As if I am a life-size doll he picks me up and tosses me on the bed. I land on my back with a bounce, but I stare up at him defiantly.

He stands over me. His face is hard and forbidding. Very gently he touches the necklace.

'You're nothing but skin and bone,' he says, almost to himself. His hands reach for my ankles and lifting them up he opens my legs into a V. Turning his head to one side he kisses my right ankle and runs his hot, velvety tongue along my calf. My breathing quickens. At my knee he stops and sucks the tender skin at the back of it, and then that cunning tongue licks on to my inner thigh.

'How much do you want me to taste you?' he whispers.

As an answer I moan and try to push my sticky legs further apart.

'No, ask me nicely.'

'Yes, please,' I beg.

'Please what?' he asks enjoying his dominance and control. His finger lightly circles my wet opening.

'Oh God...please, please...Taste me,' I beg shamelessly.

'Will you write your journal?'

'Yes, yes, I will.'

He straightens his arms and holding my trembling legs open wide he looks at my sex, swollen and drenched with both our juices, a glistening treasure.

'Cunt,' he dismisses, and letting go of my legs leaves the bedroom.

I had heard him tell Tom to wait downstairs, so I knew he was not going to stay the night, but I still flinch when I hear the front door shut. I cup myself between my legs. Slick and sore and unsatisfied. I want more.

Ten

That night I dream of my mother. In my dream we are in a shop. It is very similar to Madame Rêgine's boutique, but it is full of wedding dresses. My mother points to a long dress that is ripped in half. 'That's perfect for you,' she says.

'But it's torn,' I say.

'That's how Victoria likes it,' she says sadly.

I wake up disturbed and unhappy. I have never spent a night away from Sorab and I miss him terribly. It is four in the morning and it is dark outside. I get dressed in the jeans and T-shirt that I arrived in and leave the apartment. I exit the lift and the night porter nods at me. I return the gesture and open the doors.

The air outside is crisp and fresh. I walk along the side of the block, cross the road and enter the park. Then I begin to run. There is no one else around and I run until I am breathless and so weary I can barely walk. Then I stumble onto a park bench and watch the sun come up. My thoughts are jumbled. I refuse to put them in order. I am actually afraid of them. Afraid of the future.

A man and his German shepherd come into the park. It is off the lead and it runs at great speed up to me.

'Don't be afraid,' he shouts. 'She won't harm you. She's just a puppy. She wants to be friends.'

She jumps up on my knees and starts licking my face. Her exuberance is such that I break out in laughter. Oh, if only life were so simple. I look into her gold-brown eyes and run my fingers through her silky coat feeling the wild life that is coursing through her body. In contrast, I feel drained and jaded. As if I am a husk left on the mill floor. After a while the man whistles and she bounds away, but the exchange has left me lifted as I walk back to the apartment. The night porter is getting ready to go home. Soon Mr. Nair's shift will begin.

I stand in the shower for ages. When I come out my mobile is double blinking. Fleur has left a message that two racks of clothes, shoes, and accessories will be arriving at 10:00 am. I am to choose whatever I want and somebody will come and pick up anything I don't want at 5:00 pm. I am to call her if I need any help. I text back to thank her. Then I text Billie.

Are you awake?

Billie calls back. 'Hey.'

'Oh good, you're awake,' I say, happy to hear her voice.

'Yeah, the little monster got me up early.'

'Is he all right?'

'Shouldn't you be asking *me* if I'm all right?'

I laugh guiltily. 'Hey, you want to come around about tenish. Fleur is sending some clothes for me to try on. You can help me decide which to keep.'

'That'll be fun.'

'I'll call a minicab for you for ten.'

'Got to go. The creature has just started wailing again,' she says. 'But see ya tenish.' I hear Sorab's cries in the background just before she terminates the call and feel a sharp pang of loss. That should have been me. That's my life. Not stuck all alone in an empty apartment. I know that Billie is enjoying her time with Sorab. With her, true affection is masked by insults. Hello, Repulsive, she will say to her lover. I realize that I already miss him too much. Maybe tomorrow I will tell Blake it is my turn to babysit Sorab. And have him with me for two days.

At nine thirty I invite Mr. Nair up for a coffee. He comes through the door holding his *I'm the Boss* mug, his eyes bulging with curiosity.

We sit at the kitchen counter. 'What happened to you, Miss Bloom?' he asks.

'I had to go to Iran suddenly.'

'Oh! No wonder. Poor Mr. Barrington. You broke his heart,' he states, enlarging his eyes dramatically. I watch him bite into a biscuit. Crumbs land on his jacket. I look at them, but my mind is spinning.

'Why do you say that?' I ask as casually as I can manage.

'Because,' he says, 'I was the one who gave him your letter.'

'My letter?'

'Yes. Have you forgotten, you sent your friend with a note instructing the porter on duty to give the envelope to Mr. Barrington? It was a strange note, very formal, not at all like you, but I knew it was you because I always recognize your handwriting.'

I take a sip of coffee, swallow and lick my lips. 'What did Mr. Barrington say when you gave it to him?'

'I tell you, Miss Bloom, it was the oddest thing. He practically snatched it out of my hand, tore it open and read it right in front of me. The contents shocked him so very much I saw his eyes go back to the top of the letter to read it again. Then he crushed the letter in his hand and walked out of this building...and I have never seen him since.'

I bite my lip. The past. I can never change it, but then would I? How can I regret it? Sorab came out of my sorry past.

Mr. Nair pops the last bit of biscuit into his mouth and hops nimbly off the stool. 'My ten minutes are up. I'd better go.'

'My friend Billie will be coming this morning. Will you call me to let me know when she does?'

'I can do better than that, Miss Bloom. I will show her up myself.'

I thank him and close the door.

An hour after the stuff that Fleur sent arrives Billie breezes in with Mr. Nair in tow.

'Thanks, Mr. Nair,' I say relieving him of a large bag of baby things.

'I'm very happy to help you, Miss Bloom.' He nods happily towards Sorab. 'He looks exactly like his father. A very handsome boy, indeed.'

I freeze.

But Billie is quick off the mark. She grins broadly. 'Sorry, mate, but this one here is my baby. Don't you think he looks like me? Everyone says so.'

Mr. Nair's dark, confused eyes look to me.

'I'm only his godmother,' I say weakly, filled with a sharp sense of pain. I am terribly proud of Sorab, and not being recognized as his mother is far more difficult than I expected.

'Oh, I'm very, very sorry. I spoke out of turn,' Mr. Nair apologizes. Poor man. He looks embarrassed and flustered.

'Please don't worry about it, Mr. Nair. I know you meant no harm.'

'Better be going. The desk is unmanned,' Mr. Nair mutters awkwardly and hurries away.

I close the door and turn towards Billie. 'Oh my God, Billie. He knew.'

'Of course he did. He is Indian. They are into astrology and all that shit, aren't they?'

'Billie,' I wail. 'Recognizing a family resemblance has nothing to do with astrology.'

Billie crosses her arms. 'I know that! I was being sarcastic. For God's sake, Lana, what's got into you? Sorab is a three-month-old baby and *all* babies look alike. I wouldn't even be able to pick him out from a line-up of six babies.'

I frown unconvinced. I believe that Sorab is one of those children who have very definite features. 'He *does* have his father's eyes.'

'Look, you said Blake's secretary sent a whole list of baby stuff, including pram and cot, to the apartment, right? So he's obviously seen it all go into the lift, put two and two together and come up with four. Unfortunately for him, the correct answer is five. Now, quit fretting over things you don't need to worry about and give me a tour of this awesome flat.'

I smile. I am such a paranoid fool. Of course, she is right. I give her a grand tour.

'Wow!' she enthuses. 'Guess how much this crib costs?'

'I don't know. Five hundred quid?'

'Add another zero and you're almost there.'

'Really?'

She pulls the price tag off and holds it out to me. 'Five thousand five hundred and fifty-nine pounds for a fucking crib when a third of the world is starving.' She shakes her head. 'Still it is dead cool to be so stonkingly rich, isn't it?'

My phone rings. It is Laura. She is calling to tell me that Tom is on his way with my morning after pill and to tell me to be ready for 8:00 pm. She has made a dinner reservation for Blake and me at The Fat Duck.

'It sure looks good from the outside, though,' Billie says, having listened to my conversation with Laura.

Billie finds a box of chocolates in the kitchen and then lunges headlong into the bed and, lying sprawled on it like a sultan, makes me try all the clothes on, one by one. She insists I keep a pair of pink leather pants. 'You got to. They make your bum look all ripe and trapped and in need of saving. Blake is an ass man, right?'

'How do you know?'

'Just a guess. Now go try on the long black dress,' she orders.

The black dress makes her gasp. 'Very, very sexy.'

I grin.

'How many are you allowed to keep?'

'As many as I want, I think.'

'Really? What's that like?'

For some reason I think of the white dress. 'Nice, I guess.'

'What happened last night?'

'He's angry with me, Bill. Very angry.'

'He didn't hurt you, did he?' I can hear the protective anger come into Billie's voice. She is such a firebrand.

'No,' I say, but I find it almost impossible to discuss how I feel about Blake with Billie. For Billie sex is fun, something to do when she feels horny. For me, and I suspect for Blake as well, it is a clawing need. I know it is the reason why he is angry. He hates losing control. Control is important to him. In fact, if I am given only one word to describe his personality, I would have to use the word controlled. His whole life is about control of himself and others. He is controlled in everything he does, what he eats, how he eats, all his dealings, the precision of his time keeping, his immaculate appearance. I don't think I have ever seen a single scuff mark on his shoes.

Until I came everything was perfectly in order, compartmentalized. There was room for a fiancée and a mistress. Now it is all a mess. I am like the lock of hair on his head that will not be tamed. He wants to walk away and feel nothing but disgust for me, but he can't. I look Billie in the eye.

'His real anger is not directed at me, but at himself for still wanting me.'

'I've no beef with him. I only fear it will all blow up and he will not be able or willing to protect you against his family and the bitch.'

I do not tell her about my near run-in with Victoria in Harvey Nichols. That would be putting the cat among the pigeons. She stays until the five o'clock rush hour traffic abates at six. I send her home with a heavy heart and a couple of tins of the goat's milk formula.

At seven I come out of the bath and slip into a blue dress. It is long and straight with a demure neckline, but it dramatically deepens the blue of my eyes and suggests the curves that I no longer possess. I am stepping into a pair of peacock blue shoes when I hear him come in. I look at my watch. He is early. I turn in surprise when he comes directly into the bedroom. For a moment we look at each other. He is wearing a silver-gray suit, a white shirt, and a black and red striped tie.

'I hope you haven't dressed in a nun's habit on my account, because it is coming off the first chance I get,' he says.

Once he might have come up to me and told me how beautiful I looked. My hands flutter upwards uselessly and settle down to my sides. Now he will not accept anything except that which suggests I am a slut. He goes towards the bed. The journal is lying on the bedside table. He picks it up and opens it to the empty first page. He comes towards me expressionless. He reaches a hand into his jacket and emerges with a sleek black fountain pen. Swiss. Very expensive. He holds the journal and the pen wordlessly out to me.

I take the offered items and go into the dining room. I sit at the long, polished table and write.

Day 1

Blake ripped the first dress that I have actually loved into two and fucked me hard against the bedroom wall. Then he threw me on the bed, didnt deliver on his promise, and used the C word on me.

I go back into the living room where Blake is pouring himself a shot of whiskey so large my eyes actually widen. I hand him the book and his pen. He opens the book, reads the two sentences I have written and looks at me with amusement.

'The C word. May I remind you that you come from a council estate where the...er...C word is almost an adjective?'

I lift my chin. 'I first heard that word in the playground when I was six years old. A mother had sat on one of the benches by the swings and described her toddler daughter as a 'clever little cunt'. So I came home and used the word in front of my mother. She didn't scold me or wash my mouth out with soap. "I have obviously failed in my duty as a mother that you feel comfortable to allow such a vile word to sit on your tongue. I will not eat until I realize where I have gone wrong," she said. She put dinner on the table and refused to eat. "Of course you have to eat. You have done nothing wrong," she told me. I had to sit there and finish all my food. She would not let me leave a single pea behind. She did it again at breakfast. By lunchtime I was so distraught I could not eat a single mouthful. I promised her I would never use the word again. And I haven't until today.'

He steps away from me, as if knowing that little bit about me is poisonous to his sanity or well-being. 'If you are ready we should leave now.'

Outside he remote unlocks a white Lamborghini. The wings lift upwards. It is the kind of flashy car I associate with the spoilt sons of Saudi Arabian oil sheiks. I settle in. 'What happened to Aston?'

'Wrapped it around a tree.'

I swing my head around. 'With you in it?'

'Yes, cracked a couple of ribs, but, as you can see, I emerged unscathed. It's hard to hurt me.'

There is an edge to his voice. Of course. He is telling me I have hurt him.

The Fat Duck is the same as I remember it. Great service and divine food, but there is a large difference that I cannot not notice. Blake is drinking far more than he used to. He orders the obligatory bottle of wine that perfectly matches our meal, but hardly touches it. Instead, he goes for the whiskey. I have already counted seven.

'You were completely drunk when you had your accident, weren't you?'

'Yup. Miss Marple solves yet another mystery.'

'Didn't they do you?'

The alcohol has relaxed his tense shoulders somewhat. He laughs and I want to press my mouth against those hard lips. 'Have you forgotten everything I told you, Lana dear? The Barringtons are above the law. Cream always floats to the top.'

'So does shit.'

He raises his glass and chuckles without mirth. 'Let's see how bright you can be when you are naked in my bed.'

'Depends how full my mouth will be,' I retort unwisely.

'To bursting, darling.'

I feel my cheeks heat up. 'Are you planning to drive home tonight?'

He picks up his glass and shoots it. 'I wouldn't risk your pretty face on my windshield for anything. Tom is coming to pick us up.'

In the car we do not touch each other. Our conversation is stilted and shallow, unsustainable.

What did you do today?

Billie came around with her baby.

Fun?

Yes.

Both of us are already thinking of the time we will be alone. When only our bodies will speak. There is something about this man that makes my hands itch to touch his skin, suck that firm mouth, meld with him...forever. Desire fogs my brain.

I pretend to drop my purse. He bends to retrieve it, but I reach out for it and brush his clothed thigh. Immediately I feel him tense.

'Don't push me, Lana. I am already on the edge,' he warns.

We are like tinder and kindling.

Eleven

In the lift I raise my eyes to meet his.

Fuck. What the hell?

The door whooshes open.

He takes my hand and drags me behind him. Opens the door and pulls me through, and leaning back against it tugs me to him so I fall smack onto him. My purse finds a quick path to the carpet, opens its guts, spills. His hot mouth finds mine. The kiss is rough, crazy intense, and full of urgent need. It is what I saw in his eyes. I go astray. I don't want to come back from this. His hand locates the zip at the back of my neck. That hapless zip flies down and the nun's habit pools around my shoes.

His hands expertly release the clasp on my bra. One tug and it is gone the way of the dress. I am so lost in the jaws of desire that I barely hear the sound of light lace tearing. Once again, I am naked and he is fully dressed.

For a moment he holds me at arm's length simply looking at me, the way he used to do in the beginning. Then he takes me to the gilded mirror on the wall.

'Look at you,' he snarls. 'Your pupils are searching for someone to pleasure you. Anyone would do.'

I want to back away from what I see. My eyes are glazed with lust. I look...hungry, feral...electrified. Yet he is wrong. Anyone would not do.

He strokes my heated cheeks then he bends his head and his strong white teeth nibble at my earlobes. 'Cream and sugar and venom,' he says and bites my neck.

In the mirror my eyes widen with shock and pleasure. The sensation is exquisite. The rush of it makes me feel reckless. He begins to gently suck my skin. I moan. His mouth moves to my nipple. The skilled precision of his mouth starts an aching that travels into my core. I am in a sex-induced frenzy thirsting for him to enter me. The taste of true desire is sweltering. I push my ass into the thick, hard snake between us and yearn for it driving inside me. He puts a finger on my lower lip and lets his finger enter my mouth.

'Suck it.'

I take the finger between my lips and suck it gently at first, and then harder. He starts to unbuckle his belt.

I get on my knees. The carpet digs into my skin. I open his fly, pull up his shirt, and kiss that hard, tight stomach. He becomes very still. My tongue flicks out. Tentative, but not for long. I lick the golden brown skin, find the line of fine hair and follow it all the way to the elasticized band of his shorts. My teeth grasp the material and pull. His cock springs free and hovers, swollen and angry over my mouth. I take the throbbing ready meat in my hand. The head swells, surges, pulses, and comes alive in my hand.

I use both my hands to quickly pull the briefs down his thighs while my mouth takes in that gorgeous, rock-hard cock. I look up at him and watch him draw his breath sharply. Slowly, I move forward and let him witness every inch of his dick sliding between my lips. He pulses in my mouth and that pushes me into sucking greedily at the head of his erection. I devour him, taking him deeper and deeper into my mouth.

He thrusts his hips forward, jamming himself down my throat. It makes me gag, but it still feels right. His cock should always be inside me. It is where it belongs. Anything else would be wrong. I am struck by the potency of my obsession.

'Yes. Yes, like that… Exactly like that.'

He keeps my head in place with his hands as his thrusts become more and more urgent until with rigid muscles and a fierce groan, he buckles, and I feels his hot seed jet to the back of my throat. It is slick and leaves a tang on the back of my tongue as I swallow. He stays in my mouth, his head thrown back for a few moments more. My eyes look up at him, waiting for what I do not know. His face drops down, shadowed, to look at me, my mouth stuffed with his meat.

'Very pretty,' he says softly. 'You were born to suck dick. I'm surprised I never realized it before.' He pulls out of me. 'Now go and sit on the bed.'

I stand and simply look at him. He wants to humiliate me. It will be a cold day in hell before I allow him to succeed. Naked and barefoot, but head held high I walk to the bedroom. I go up to the bed and as instructed sit on the edge. He appears at the door. Again he is fully clothed and in control while I am naked and defenseless.

'No, with your back against the headboard.'

I scoot up and lean against the plump pillows.

He comes and sits on the bed beside me. His voice is casual, conversational. 'What did you do for sex in the past year?'

I flush.

Some hardness barely leashed has crept into his voice. 'Did you take a lover?'

I shake my head.

'Did you go without?' Curious.

I shake my head again.

'Show me what you did?'

'I can't,' I whisper.

'Show me.' An order.

I open my mouth, but he silences me with a finger on my lips, his head shaking gently. 'You obviously don't understand how this works,' he explains. 'The only words I want to hear pass those delectable lips are yes, please, and more.' He takes his finger off my lips. 'Was it any of those words or a combination of them?'

I shake my head slowly.

'I thought so. Show me,' he says, and now his voice is coldly authoritative.

I press my lips together. I feel that flash of defiance return. That's what he wants. He wants to watch me masturbate in front of him. Fine. Let him see that. He has seen everything else. He folds his arms. Slowly I open my legs. He smiles slightly at my submission. I bring my fingers to my clit and close my eyes.

'Open your eyes.'

My eyes snap open. Locking my gaze with his glittering ones I move a finger into the opening of my sex. The folds are covered in slick juices, and collecting some from the opening I move my fingers around the sensitive nub, slowly teasing it to attention.

His carefully guarded eyes never leave me. 'What did you think of while playing with yourself?'

'You.'

His expression doesn't change, but his eyes flicker. 'Didn't you miss my dick inside you?'

'Very much.'

He makes a small disbelieving sound and reaches over to what had always been his bedside table. He opens the drawer and I am surprised to see it full of sex toys. All of them still in their packaging. I even catch the glimpse of a pair of handcuffs. Rummaging around he finds and fetches a vibrator to our bed. It is black and bright orange and large. Scary large. I close my legs in horror. This has nothing to do with sex. This is him punishing me. Filling me up with a large black and orange object. Reducing me to a piece of meat. Letting me know I'm nothing to him. My resolution to be strong and my conviction that he can never humiliate me if I don't allow it crumble into dust.

'Don't worry. This won't hurt a bit,' he promises, and switches it on. It makes a whirring sound.

I open my eyes and look at it humming in his hand. 'Don't, Blake. Please don't,' I beg.

'Open your legs.'

I shake my head. 'Please. If you insist on punishing me like this… I'll run away.'

'No you won't. Remember I paid for this. Mine to do with as I please. We had a deal. I give you want you want and you give me what I want. I gave you what you wanted. Now it's your turn to give me what I want. And I want to see this big black and orange machine buried inside that sweet, tight pussy of yours.'

I swallow a lump in my throat and lick my lips. 'Why do we need that when we have your cock?'

'Because,' he explains patiently as if he is talking to a particularly obtuse child, 'you won't always have my cock.'

I look into his eyes. I am looking for the passionate lover I adore, but his eyes are purposely blank. I know I will do anything to bring him back to me. From deep inside me I find the strength. He wants to push that inanimate object into me. Let's give him what he wants and see what comes up. Let's see how he fares!

'All right,' I say and open my legs wide.

If he is surprised by my defiant submission he does not let it show. He lets the vibrator touch my clit. I jump.

'Too sensitive?' he queries softly, and moves it slightly away.

He runs the vibrating tip along the wet folds, and very slowly while watching my face he inserts it into me. While I gasp with shock at its size he pushes it into me up to the hilt.'

'Good?' he asks.

'Good,' I reply, my chin lifted, my eyes widened, my fingers grasping the silk duvet underneath.

So he fucks me with it and even though I beg him not to look at me as I crack apart, he stares at me possessively as I come.

Then he gets up and leaves me.

I lay there spread-eagled with the vibrator still inside me staring at the ceiling. The gadget makes a soft muffled sound that I have not noticed during my humiliation. I want to pull it out of me, but my limbs feel like lead. I am in love with him and he just hates me. If he had cared anything for me I would have seen in his eyes, but nothing! I finally understand. I am just a demon that must be exorcised before he marries the daughter of the Earl. I hear the front door close and the first sob escapes me. I try to be brave, hold them back, but they will not be stopped.

Suddenly he is standing at the door. Through swimming eyes I watch him come to me. He sits beside me, pulls the vibrator out; it makes a sucking sound. He switches it off and bending his head licks a tear from my cheek.

'Damn you, Blake,' I whisper.

He buries his face in my hair. 'I'm sorry,' he says.

I stare at the ceiling. I am sadder than I have ever been. The doctor, the solicitor, Fleur, Madam Yula, The Fat Duck. 'Are you re-creating everything so you can destroy it, Blake?'

'No.'

'What do you want?'

'I thought I knew, but I don't anymore,' he confesses honestly.

'What did you want?'

'Revenge. I wanted to punish you. I had all kinds of humiliations planned for you, but I can't hurt you without hurting myself. Maybe you are what my father said you are. My greatest enemy.'

Automatically, my hands come up to wrap protectively around him. I know he is hurting too. I just don't know how to make it better. I want to tell him about Victoria, but what good would that do? She would make a new and supremely dangerous enemy. 'I'm not your enemy, Blake. I never meant to hurt you.'

He laughs. Again it is bitter. 'So what are you? A friend?'

I sigh. Such sadness is in that sound. Does he hear it? Possibly not. In his mind I am a gold digger. Took the money and ran. Now I represent dirty sex. There is a chasm between us. It seems impossible to bridge. From her ivory tower Victoria smiles triumphantly and tells me I am not embedded in his life plan. I will never be.

'Where do we go from here?'

He doesn't respond. Instead he gathers me in his arms and hides his face in the crook of my neck. Slowly he starts to suck. Automatically, my head twists away. Not in rejection, but in invitation. The dedication of his soft lips on my skin is delicious. His tongue burns a trail to my nipple. He takes it into his mouth and my humiliation, my hurt dissipates to nothing. Everything that happens between a man and a woman is a sacred journey, my mother once said.

She said that when my father left her.

A sound escapes my mouth. Silently, solemnly, he goes to the other breast. His teeth catch the nub and pull slightly. I writhe under the expert manipulation. He raises his head and looks at me as his palm skims the hardened tip. I am aching for him. Suddenly he is on his elbows and with consummate ease he pushes the entire length of his tongue into my aching folds. I grip the silky hair as his heated tongue thrusts in and out of me in sure practiced stokes. And then he begins to suck...

Ah, the pleasure, the pleasure!

He pinches my swollen clit in his fingers suddenly, and an intense pleasure like an electric current stabs me. I scream and come in a mindless explosion. Waves crash on the rocks below, but I fly high. When I come back to the bed and the room,

Blake is still licking the wet walls of my sex. There will never be another after him, I think lazily, drowsily, sadly. He has done what he set out to do. Ruined me for all other men.

I am so drained and exhausted I close my eyes and fall asleep with the sensation of his silky head on my thighs.

Twelve

I wake up with the duvet pulled over my naked body, but alone. I turn my head and gaze at the vast expanse of bed that is spread out on one side of me and the unused pillows and sigh. Pushing my legs free of the duvet I dangle them out of the bed and savor the cool air. Then I slip out of bed. I can hear the fain sounds of Francesca, Blake's personal shopper, rummaging around in the kitchen. She is always as silent as a mouse. I pull on some clothes, brush my teeth, and go to the kitchen. She is updating her list on her iPad.

'Ciao,' she greets brightly. She is from Naples. 'I remember, you like jam and I bring you two extra bottles.' She holds them up in her expressive hands. 'You like?'

I go forward and take them in my hands. 'I like. Very much. Grazia, Francesca.'

She dimples prettily.

Tom drives Billie, Sorab, and me to The Royal China in Bayswater. We find a table and order our dim sums.

I take the bottles of jam out of my rucksack and stuff them into the back of Sorab's pram and Billie grins. 'The perks of pimping you out,' she says. 'By the way, Jack called mr looking for you. Your mobile must have been switched off.'

'Oh! What did you tell him?'

'The truth, of course. You were with Blake.'

'What did he say?'

'He went dead silent for a while, and then he asked me if I thought you were safe. I said I didn't know, but that you thought you would be. Then he hung up.'

I bite my bottom lip.

'You should call him. He worries about you.'

'I will. This afternoon.'

'So how's it going at casa Blake?'

I expel my breath in a rush. 'I don't know, Billie. I might as well be a blow-up doll for all the use I am to him. It's really just sex. He's so remote, so angry, and so hurt. I don't believe I'll ever be able to reach him. He wants revenge, but he doesn't have the stomach for it.'

'What kind of revenge?' An edge has crept into Billie's voice.

'Sexual humiliation. Last night he used a... vibrator on me.' I flush bright red. The words were almost impossible for me to get out.

Billie laughs. 'You are so weird. That's not sexual humiliation. Everybody uses them. If anyone offers to use one on me I'm going to lie back, open my legs as wide as they will go and ask them to knock themselves out.'

'You don't understand, Billie. He did it because he understands that I'm sexually repressed.'

'Oh for heaven's sake. You cried, didn't you?'

I nod and play with a chopstick. 'What would you do if you were me, Billie?'

'First off, I'm not you. I don't think I could ever be in such a fucked up situation.'

'But if you were,' I insist.

'Then I would drink at least half a bottle of vodka and challenge him to do his worst. Press all his buttons and push him mercilessly until he loses his tightly reined sense of control. And then it would all be over and done with. Mind you, I wouldn't if I thought he was capable of truly hurting me. But you're a thousand percent sure Blake is not, right?'

'A thousand percent. He is cold, not cruel.'

I pay the bill with the new Platinum credit card that I have not applied for, but arrived for me this morning. Billie raises an impressed eyebrow but says nothing.

Afterwards we spend a pleasant afternoon in Whiteley's Shopping Centre. There is nothing I want, but I treat Billie to a really cool pair of cowboy boots, which she adored, and we buy some divinely soft bedding for Sorab. Stuff I could never afford before.

Everything goes on the new card. It has a ninety thousand pounds credit limit on it.

After Tom drops Billie and Sorab off I phone Jack.

'Are you all right?' is the first thing that Jack utters.

'He's not capable of hurting me, Jack,' I reply.

'It's not him I'm worried about.'

'Victoria won't do anything to me.'

'Lana, she paid you two hundred thousand pounds to get lost. You took her money and now you're back with her guy and you don't think she's going to retaliate?'

Oh God! Put like that it did seem I was being stupid in the extreme. 'I didn't go looking for him, Jack. He found me. Besides it's only for 42 days.'

'42 days?'

'He just wants me to finish my contract. There's 42 days left of it. Well, forty-one now.'

'Lana, I'm a man and I'm telling you no man wants a woman for just 42 days. It's not going to end in 42 days. I can give that to you in blood right now. You're going to be his mistress until the day comes when he is finally bored with your body. Is that what you want for yourself?'

That feels like a low blow and yet it is the truth. 'I don't know what I want anymore, Jack. All I know is at the moment I am with Blake for forty-one days. I'm playing it by ear.'

Jack sighs heavily. 'All right, Lana, but promise me you will take care of yourself, though. The first smallest sign that something is not right you will call me.'

'I promise. Jack?'

'Yeah?'

'Please don't worry about me. I'm a big girl now. I can take care of myself.'

'Just be careful, OK,' he says gruffly, and then he is gone. I lean back, but I do not think of Jack and his warning. Something else is bothering me.

As soon as I get into the apartment I go to my computer. Into the browser I type in the word cunt.

And I am shocked to learn that the word cunt is the most offensive word in the English language with the highest power to shock, but that it only became obscene around the time of Shakespeare. Before that it was actually the root word for the words queen and cuneiform, the most ancient form of writing. The word itself derives from kunta meaning female genitalia in Sumerian.

So: when a man calls a woman a cunt he is actually calling her the queen who invented writing and numerals—one of the finest compliments a woman can be given. The Irish apparently even use it as an endearment!

I also learn that cunt is the only word in the English language that describes the whole of the female genitalia. Vagina refers only to the inner entrance and vulva to the clitoris, outer labia majora and minora. To talk about a woman's entire incredible sexual orchestra in all its stupendous glory one needs the word cunt!

At that moment I claim the dreaded word for myself.

When Blake called me a cunt I had only pretended to be offended. The real truth is that years of avoiding the word, and despising others for allowing something so foul and disgusting to sit on their tongues, fled and all I felt was its raw sexual pull. *Yes, I am a cunt and I want your rigid hot dick deep inside my cunt.* I realize that no matter what Blake said his actions were teaching me that my body is my temple. That between my legs is an altar called cunt where he comes to worship.

And now I have a plan. A plan that involves my cunt.

Thirteen

Blake sends a text to say that he will be around at 8:00 pm.

By seven thirty I am showered and standing in my new black stockings and garters. Carefully, I slip into the black dress that Fleur sent for me to wear to the opera and fasten the row of black pearl buttons. I look at myself in the mirror and marvel at the intricate beauty of the dress. It must have cost a small fortune.

The chest and the entire back is made of black patterned lace and lightly sprinkled with rhinestones, but the lace is so delicate it appears like a tattoo on my skin. I adjust the material into place around my body and hips, and then turn back to see the effect of the plunging back. It looks really cool and perhaps even sexy. I fluff out my hair and sit down to do my make-up. When I am done I slip into black stilettos and walk into the living room, the dress swirling gently around my shoes.

I pour myself a triple vodka and swallow it neat in four gulps. Wow! That makes my veins sing. I pour another double, top it up with orange and walk onto the balcony. I am actually very nervous. Make that very, very nervous. Tonight I will see him without his mask. I will provoke him into holding nothing back from me. I look at the time. 7:59 pm. I turn to find him standing at the door. He is watching me silently. Trying to figure out the scene he has come upon.

I turn fully. 'Hello.'

'Are we going out or are you dressed like that just for me?'

'We're not going out.'

An eyebrow rises. A mocking smile. He comes towards me. 'We're not?'

I shake my head slowly. 'I need a favor from you.'

'Are you allowed to ask favors?'

'You'll like this one.'

'You've got my attention.'

'I want you to hurt me.'

He becomes very still. For a moment neither of us says anything. We simply look at each other. And then he says, 'No.'

'Why not? I thought you wanted revenge.'

'I've tried rough sex and I didn't like it.'

I am shocked by the intense flash of burning jealousy that rips through me. He has already done this with someone else. There is no new territory that I may claim for my own. 'Maybe I do.'

His eyes narrow. They become like stones. Cold. Unreachable. They remind me of his father's eyes. I shiver involuntarily. Feel afraid. What if I am wrong? What if he is capable of really hurting me? 'What do you know about rough sex?'

'Show me what there is to know.'

'Is that what you really want?' His voice is soft, dangerously soft.

'Yes.'

His hands come up to my face. I cannot help it. I flinch and he smiles. A cold, knowing smile. Gently he brushes my cheeks with his hands. 'You're a baby. You don't know what you want,' he says, and he is about to turn away when I swing my arm with all my might and let my palm crash into the side of his face. I hit him so hard his head jerks away, and my hand is stinging painfully. The alcohol has made me strangely light-headed. I even feel removed from my own actions. I stare with dull fascination at his cheek, at the white imprint of my fingers. My eyes travel to meet his. They are stormy and furious.

'Feeling better?' he asks.

As an answer I swing my hand clumsily out again, but he is prepared this time and he catches my hand easily. I rush towards him and bite his neck. Hard. His growl is annoyed.

'You inherited all this money so everybody treats you like some kind of god, but you're just a little coward hiding behind a façade of superiority; a spoilt rich kid who has to do anything and everything Daddy tells him to do.'

He begins to laugh, really laugh, and suddenly I realize I have never seen him happy. Never seen his head thrown back and his throat open and vulnerable.

'I wonder what you would be without great-granddaddy's money?' I taunt.

'I'd still want to fuck you senseless.'

'Fuck you,' I shriek and as if possessed by some crazed demon I begin to kick at his legs and punch his hard body with my free hand. Like a sack of potatoes I am lifted up by sheer male strength and thrown over his shoulder. For a moment the shock of being turned upside down stills me and then I continue to pummel his back as he takes me into our bedroom. 'You don't trust anyone, you don't love anyone, you're just an emotional bonsai,' I scream.

He hurls me on the bed. I fall on my side, winded but unhurt. My head is still, but fuck me, the room is spinning around like a merry-go-round. Still, the important thing is I have lost all fear and apprehension. My only goal is to goad him into losing that tight control that dictates his every move. I look at him, my eyes taunting him. 'Scared of a cunt, Barrington?'

His head jerks slightly with surprise. 'You really want rough sex?' he asks.

I nod.

His mouth twists. He unbuttons his shirt, yanks the ends out of his trousers. Opens his fly, flings his underpants behind him and takes a step to the edge of the bed.

'Here it is, my love,' he grates.

In one smooth moment he hauls me up, catches the hem of my long dress and flicks it over my head. He stands looking at me, upper body and head covered, but lower body obscenely sprawled with garters, stockings and inelegantly splayed legs. Then, before I have even recovered my balance, he grabs my hips, his fingers digging painfully into my flesh, and brings me to my hands and knees. He grips my ass and very roughly spreads apart the cheeks, kneading them as if they are two pieces of dough, and drives his dick into my wetness, so savagely that I actually cry out with the shock of it. That stops him cold as if he too is shaken by the ferocity and violence of his own thrust.

'Don't stop,' I hear myself say, in a voice I do not recognize.

And he slams again into me. This time he does not stop even when I cry out. My entire body becomes a rag doll shuddering and rocking to the deep thrusts. I want to scream, but I dare not for fear he will stop. His stomach continues to pound my spread ass. His hands travel up my sweat-slicked body, digging, grasping in an effort to push as deep into me as he can. He grinds my rear so hard into his groin that I feel him to the very ends of me.

Every thrust is torture, but in the hurt there is a strange and exquisite pleasure. After he comes, he bends forward, kisses my shoulder blades and slowly eases out of me.

My slit is so sore it stings, burns and throbs painfully as he withdraws. It is over, I think. Then I feel his mouth lightly licking the reddened, raw skin around my cunt. He slips his velvet tongue gently inside, but even that hurts like hell. I moan and he takes his tongue away, starts lightly sucking my clit. I forget how sore I am and come in a moment, white with shockingly intense pleasure. As if my nerves have been made more alive by the pain, the pleasure is far more powerful than anything I have experienced before.

I fall forward on my face. My body is aching everywhere and so tender, I don't think I will be able to sleep on my back. My last thought as I drift into blackness is that I haven't had dinner yet and he never lost control. Despite all my efforts not once did his cold exterior crack to reveal the real man inside. Now I know whatever he guards so carefully inside must surely be truly precious or ugly beyond words.

Fourteen

I wake up, my mouth sour, aching, and stiff—getting out of bed is a slow belly crawl. I can barely walk to the bathroom. A disheveled mess greets me in the mirror. I stare with fascination at my reflection. Very slowly and with great difficulty I unhook the row of black pearl buttons at the back of the dress and shrug out of it. I go to the end of the room where two mirrors meet and gasp in shock at the dramatic sight that greets me.

My back, hips, buttocks, and thighs are blue black. It looks like I have been run over by a truck.

I gingerly lower myself down on the toilet seat. The urine flow burns and the entire area is so sore I can hardly clean myself. Drinking without having consumed food has also left me with a throbbing headache. I step into the shower. Good move, Lana. It relaxes my muscles and makes me feel a little more normal. Afterwards I dose myself with two 500mg paracetamols. In fifteen minutes Mr. Nair and I are sitting at the kitchen counter having coffee. I feel pretty normal.

After coffee I call Tom and tell him that today I am bringing Sorab to stay with me. I go downstairs at 9:30 am and Tom puts down the newspaper he is reading.

'Good morning.'

'Good morning, Tom.'

He opens the car door, but getting in draws a wince from me.'

'Are you all right?' Tom enquires with a look of concern.

'Just stomach cramps,' I say.

He nods and goes around to the driver's seat.

Billie is drying dishes. She throws a dishtowel over one shoulder and turns to me. 'You look a bit constipated,' she says by way of greeting.

'I tried your advice. Drank half a bottle of vodka and pushed his buttons last night.'

'Oh yeah?'

'He didn't want to play ball.'

'So why are you all scrunched up with pain?'

'I mean, I got the rough sex, but nothing else,' I say. 'He never said a word he should not have or retaliated in any way that would fall outside of rough sex.' I lower myself slowly onto one of the dining chairs while Billie looks on with an expression I cannot quite fathom.

I stay with Billie the whole afternoon making plans for our new business.

Blake texts to tell me he will be late so I leave after the rush hour traffic at six. I have dinner on my own. A simple meal of grilled cheese on toast with a slice of smoked salmon on top. It is wonderful to have Sorab with me. The flat doesn't seem so foreign and lonely. Afterwards we have a grand old time in the bathroom, him shrieking happily and splashing lustily and me laughing. It is at this moment that Blake appears at the door.

'Hi,' I say. I am actually very nervous. In my mind I still think Sorab looks a lot like Blake.

'Who do we have here?' he says, and comes into the room. I look at him in surprise. He stands over us looking at Sorab for a long time. Sorab is waving his hands at the new face excitedly, but my heart is in my mouth. What the hell is he looking at? Surely, there is no way he can tell it is his son? When he turns to look at me his eyes are neutral. We look at each other.

'Does he cry a lot?' he asks finally.

'No. Most night he will sleep right through,' I say quickly, my breathing, returning to normal.

'Good,' he says, and turning around goes out. I throw the sponge into the water. Shit. For a moment there I was really worried. I mean really. I take Sorab out of the water and as I dress and powder him I can hear Blake in the dining room. He is talking to someone on the phone. He works steadily on and by the time he comes into the bedroom I am almost asleep.

I feel the mattress next to me depress with his weight and I open my eyes sleepily. He is sitting in the dark. He bends his head and kisses me. I am so startled I come awake. The kiss is gentle and soft. I open my mouth and the kiss deepens. Raw hunger starts eating my brain. I am aching and sore and yet I am still gagging for him. I feel his fingers slide down my body and tug at the rim of my knickers. His fingers press flat against my crotch.

'You are so wet,' he whispers and inserts a finger into me.

It burns all the way in, and I tense involuntarily.

Immediately he stills. 'What's the matter?'

'Nothing,' I mumble and light bathes us. I blink and squint. Blake's hands are lifting my gown. My knickers are being taken off and I am being turned over. 'Jesus Lana,' he gasps. Gentle hands turn me back to face him.

'I did that?' His face is shocked, pale, draped in regret. I would never have believed that he could look so shaken. This is a new Blake. One I cannot reconcile with the man I know. The change in his face and eyes is so great, it is like night and day. Could a few bruises really have such a grand effect on a man like him? I did not like the answer. There was more to this change. What, I did not know yet.

'I bruise easily,' I explain warily. 'It's not permanent.'

He doesn't answer. 'I'm sorry… I'm so very sorry. I can't believe I've done that to you.'

I shrug, still very suspicious of his niceness. 'It's not as bad as it looks. Hey, I pushed you to it, remember?'

He looks at me with a creased brow. 'Why did you?'

I look down. 'You know that song 'Wrecking Ball' by Miley Cryus. That's me. I wanted to break down your walls. You were so cold and distant with me all the time. I guess I used my body as the wrecking ball…'

'There are many things you don't understand, but you must believe me when I tell you, you are my sustenance, my oxygen. I need you desperately. In fact, right now, what I feel for you is the only part of me that feels human.'

I look at him in shock. 'What do you feel for—'

He lays his fingers flat against my mouth. 'Shhh. Please trust me that I have your best interest at heart, always…and it is not in your best interest to know any more than you do now.'

I am unhappy with his mysterious reply, but I nod my agreement. What choice do I have?

'Now I need you to make me a promise.'

'What sort of promise?'

'That you will not leave me before your 42 days are up. No matter what you hear or see, no matter who asks you to, you will not leave me.'

'Why?'

'Because I am asking you not to. Will you do this one thing for me?'

I shrug. 'OK.'

'No, say the words. It is very important that you understand the importance of the promise that I am asking for.'

'I promise not to leave you until the 42 days are up.'

'Do not forget this promise you have made to me.'

'I won't, but what happens when the 42 days are up?'

He smiles. It is a sad smile. 'That will be your decision.'

'My decision? What do you mean?'

'No more talking tonight. Move over to your side of the bed.'

My eyes widen. 'Are you staying the night?'

'Mmnnn.'

Instead of scooting over I gently roll over and end up on my side, propped on my elbow. 'Do you want me to blow you?'

He shakes his head.

'Are you holding out for my ass?' I tease cheekily, daringly.

'I will have your ass, soon. I want to own every part of you. But not today. Today I just want you to curl up against me and sleep.'

And that is what we do. We go to sleep entwined, like two wise snakes.

Fifteen

By the time I wake up Blake is gone. I bring Sorab into the bed and lie watching him drink his milk while my brain incessantly replays Blake's intriguing and confusing words from the night before.

You must believe me when I tell you, you are my sustenance, my oxygen. In fact, right now, what I feel for you is the only part of me that feels human.

Other than my failed attempt at being a wrecking ball, nothing I can see has changed between us, and yet the coldly furious stranger who could barely stand for me to touch him is suddenly professing an emotion so deep that it makes my toes curl. And what was the insistence that I promise never to leave him until the 42 days are up all about? What were the things that I do not understand that he referred to and he obviously did not want to tell me about? I remember again his intense eyes. He seemed to be begging for something from me, and yet what was he begging for? Another thirty-eight days with me? Why? Nothing makes sense.

Jack's words come back.

No man wants a woman for just 42 days.

When Blake said it would be my choice, did he mean the choice to be his mistress? And what of Victoria, his patient paragon of spotless virtue? I have dealt with her and I know without any doubt that she will not allow such a scenario.

I kiss Sorab's head. 'What's Daddy up to, Sorab?' I ask, but he only sleepily sucks at his milk bottle.

The day passes lazily without incident. My movements are slow and languorous. The pain is beginning to subside. When I use the toilet there is no burn. I am excited by the idea of Blake inside my body again. I recognize that I am in a state of constant arousal.

Laura calls to say that Blake will be home for dinner, but not to prepare any food. She is ordering in for us. Chinese. 'Anything you particularly want?'

'Crispy Peking duck,' I say.

I hear the smile in her voice. 'Yes, that's a particular favorite of mine too, Miss Bloom.'

It is a fine day with only a little wind and at four in the evening I pack a book and take Sorab out in his brand new stroller into the park for some fresh air. The seat where I had been joined by the exuberant puppy is empty so I head for it. The sun is deliciously mild, but I do not put the hood of the pram down. Next summer he will be ready to play in the sun.

I eye him proudly and he blows bubbles and shakes his rattle violently. I am so incredibly in love with him. I look around. There is hardly anyone about and after a little while, I take my book out and begin to read. No more than ten minutes could have passed with Sorab contentedly playing with the little toys hung up on the hood of his pram when a woman comes up to us.

'Oh, but he is a daahling,' she croons.

I look up from my paperback smiling. 'Thank you.'

'What's his name?'

'Sorab.'

She swings her head suddenly towards me and I am stunned by the flash of alarm in her eyes. 'Why did you name your son so?'

I remember myself. 'He's not my son. I am baby-sitting for my friend.'

'Oh,' she says and straightens so I get to see her properly. She has medium brown hair, pink cheeks, and blue eyes, and is wearing an understated, but obviously very expensive coat. Her accent is very upper class, but there is something shrill about her eyes. It makes me itch to stand up and put myself between her and my son. I stand up and we are facing each other.

'Why did she give him such a name?'

'It is after the legend of Rustam and Sorab.'

'Do you know the story of Rustam and Sorab?'

'No,' I lie, immediately.

'It is the legend of a very great warrior who accidentally kills his own son in the battlefield, because when the boy was born his mother lied. She told the father he had no son, that she had borne a girl.'

I stare at the woman trying to control my horror, but by the expression on her face I am not succeeding. The irony had not hit me before. What have I unthinkingly done? Who is this woman? What is she to Blake, my son, and me?

'Who are you?'

'Who I am is not important. Do not be tempted to stay longer than your allotted time. You and your son are in grave danger. It may even already be too late. Don't trust *anyone.*'

'What are you talking about?'

'Beware of Cronus,' she says, her voice as dry as dust, and begins walking away.

'Hey, come back,' I call out, but she increases her speed, and quickly disappears from my sight. I sit back down because my knees will no longer support me. I know that woman. An evening breeze rushes past me. I force myself up and push the pram as quickly as I can back to the apartment. Inside, I rush to the computer and Google images for the fourth Earl of Hardwicke and his family. Up pops a picture of the woman.

I sit back. The memory of her perfume drifts past me. The rest is a blur of real fear. Of course, I recognize her. The resemblance is small, but noteworthy. She is Victoria's mother, but there is something pitiful about her. She has lost something precious. True, her shrill eyes betrayed extreme fury, but beneath the rage, she was essentially telling me that she has had to suffer, and intolerably. But unlike her daughter she was not threatening me, but warning me so I could avoid a similar suffering in my own future. *Beware of Cronus.* Turn back now, Lana. Before it is too late.

My phone rings. It is Blake.

'Hi,' I mumble.

'You sound strange. Is everything all right?'

'Yes, I'm fine,' I say.

'I'm coming home early. Wait for me.'

'I'm here,' I say.

By the time Blake gets home I have stopped restlessly pacing the floor and stilled the tremor in my hands, but not the terrible fear in my heart. I am standing in the middle of the living room lost to some unknown dread, when Blake appears at the doorway. I turn towards him and suddenly I am filled with a new fear. Can I even trust him? I feel confused and frightened of what I do not know.

In a few strides he has covered the ground between us. 'What is it?'

I shake my head. 'Why are you back so early?'

'We are going to Venice.'

'Venice?' I repeat stupidly.

'Would you like that?'

'I can't. I have Sorab.'

'He will come with us. Laura has arranged five nannies for you to interview tonight. They come with the highest recommendation from the best nanny agencies in London. The nanny can help you here too until such time as you no longer need her.'

Why did no one warn me about this? My hands rise to my temples. 'A nanny?' The word is foreign on my tongue. The idea intimidating. Another woman taking care of Sorab.

'The first lady will arrive at seven and one every half hour after that until you find one that you think is suitable. I thought we could have an early dinner. Laura has ordered us Chinese for six o'clock, I believe.'

I nod distractedly and notice the relief that washes over his face and tense shoulders, but I cannot imagine why he is relieved.

'Can I fix you a drink?' he asks, and moves to the bar. I stare at his turned back. Suddenly I have the distinct impression, he is worried about something. Something important. Something about me. But he doesn't want to talk about it. Not yet. It's part of those secret things I do not understand.

'A large brandy,' I reply.

He pushes a goblet into my hand, kisses me softly on the forehead. 'I'll join you after a shower. Just relax. Be back soon.'

'Why are we going to Venice?'

'You are going to the opera to experience Venetian music in its original setting. Pack your black dress,' he says, his eyes smoldering.

He has planned a Venetian adventure for me. I drop my eyes to the floor. *I dare not look in his eyes, not yet.* I plan to tell him about Victoria's mother. Not today, though. Not until I figure out who Cronus is. And who I can trust. Who is friend and who is foe?

The nannies arrive punctually. When the third woman comes through the door I know she is the one. She has a pleasant face and laughing, soft eyes. Her name is Geraldine Dooley. She is from Ireland. I put the baby in her arms.

'All right, lad, what's the story?'

Sorab babbles back at her.

'T'be sure,' she agrees solemnly.

The last two candidates I am able to cancel by calling their mobiles, but the next candidate is already waiting for me in the living room. I go out to meet her.

'I'm so sorry to have wasted your time. I have just found the nanny that is perfect for my son.'

She smiles and pulls on spotlessly white cotton gloves. 'You haven't, my dear. I have been paid a considerable amount for attending this interview on such short notice.'

A thought occurs to me. 'What time were you contacted?'

'I couldn't say for sure. But perhaps 4:30 pm.'

'Oh.' That was just after Victoria's mother approached me in the park. Can it be a coincidence that I am suddenly being whisked off to Venice? Her words, 'trust no one,' still reverberate in my head. Perhaps it is naïve of me, but I am unafraid. I believed him when he asked me to trust him to do what is in my best interest. And I still do.

With his hands spanning my waist just above the bruises and his eyes never leaving mine, Blake gently lowers me onto his throbbing hardness. The muscles in his jaw twitch and betray his lack of detachment. I know he is worried about hurting me, but I am so slick and wet and ready that the first inch slips in easily, filling and opening me beautifully. It feels so good I drive myself down and suddenly he has pierced me too deeply, stretched the swollen hole too much. I cry out involuntarily and I feel his hands bodily lift me off the shaft I am impaled on.

'Jesus, Lana. Take it easy,' he bites out.

But now that the first flash of pain is gone I am afire with need. I want to forget about Cronus and Victoria and all the confusing things I have not yet figured out and I know no better way. I place my hands on either side of him and slowly push my trembling, clinging sex down until the bruises on my rear touch his thighs. I stop and move upwards. This exquisite pain-pleasure is what I have been craving all day. This time I go down that bit faster. My soaked sex hovers an instant at the tip of his shaft and then comes down too hard. I cry out. He tries to hold me up.

I shake my head and say, 'No, this is fine. I can take it.'

He tightens his grip around my waist.

'No. No more pain for you,' he says firmly, and gently rolls me onto my back. He covers my entire body with daddy-long-legs kisses until I feel as if I am floating. And when I do come, I feel as if I am a pond on a day when the sunlight is so white it is impossible to look at it. And someone goes and throws a stone into the pond of my very core, the shimmering ripples spreading out and out and out.

Sixteen

I stand on the prow of the black boat that traverses the Grand Canal to catch the full opulence and majesty of the white domes of the church in the bright sunlight. Such decoration, such grandeur. A funereal gondola passes us. I shiver and touch the blue ribbon that Blake has put in my hair. Here even decay and death are beautiful. Rotting houses stand next to glorious palaces.

Blake extends a strong arm down to me at the Piazza San Marco stop. He is dressed in a black denim shirt rolled up at the sleeves, blue jeans and lumberjack boots, and is head and shoulders taller than most of the locals. Devilishly sexy dark sunglasses do not allow me to see his eyes. I look up at him with that same sense of awe that he is with me. He helps me off the boat and keeps my hand as we walk up to the piazza.

I immediately fall in love with the regiments of arches that surround the impossibly splendid square. The great flocks of pigeons that roost in the stupendous roofs fly down to interact amiably with the tourists clutching guidebooks and cameras. They flutter around us and make me smile.

We stop for coffee. The waiter brings biscotti with our coffee. Blake pushes his sunglasses over his head, stretches his long legs out in front of him, and closing his eyes turns his face up to the sun. I dip a biscotti into my cappuccino. The dunked biscotti reminds me of the tide marks on the stained, crumbling walls.

'The lagoon is eating the city alive,' I say.

Blake looks at me. 'It submits with pleasure to the tide. It's a willing consummation. The way I have been crumbling into you from the first night I laid eyes on you.'

For a moment we are both lost in each other's gaze. And then I simply can't leave it; I whisper, 'But what happens after the 42 days are up?'

A strange emotion crosses his eyes. Pain? Sorrow? 'I don't ever want to lie to you. The truth is I don't know. There are powerful forces at play, predictable only in their ruthless ability to accumulate and recreate the world in their image. And I am part of that image.'

I frown. These riddles. What does he mean? 'What forces?'

'Forces that are unaccountable, unprincipled, and extremely dangerous. The less you know the safer you will be. I may never tell you about them. I take them on willingly for you, but I might lose. The only way you can help me is to keep your promise. No matter what you hear, see or whatever anyone tells you, do not forget your promise.' Then his mouth stretches into a brilliant smile. And that smile takes my breath away. 'Will you trust me that even if I lose, I will ensure that you will be taken care of for life?'

Money! I don't want his money. I want to know what he knows. I want to have him, forever.

I let my gaze drop and he reaches forward and covers my hand with his. His hand radiates warmth. I turn my palm upwards and entwine my fingers with his. I realize that this is a moment of great import. I look up. I am looking into the eyes of a man who almost appears to be drowning and I am the straw that he has found to clutch onto. For the first time I realize that beneath the cold, aloof exterior there is so much, so much more depth. I smile suddenly.

'All right,' I say. 'Let's live as if all we have left are thirty-seven days. Let's not waste a second.'

'That's my girl,' he says, and standing up tugs my hand. 'Come on,' he urges. 'To know Venice one must wander its narrow bridges and bewildering alleys on foot.'

We leave the winding alleys to stop for lunch in an old ostaira that apparently has been around since the nineteenth century. Blake and I both order the pasta in squid ink to start, followed by baked swordfish and polenta, which the waiter tells us are the house specialty. Pasta in squid ink is something I have never tried before, and I enjoy it very much, but the portions are very large and I leave nearly half of my main course behind.

Blake frowns. 'Your appetite was better before. You have lost so much weight. Why?'

I shrug. 'I'm sorry. The food is delicious, but I really can't have any more.

'He looks at me, his fork neatly laid at the four o'clock position on his plate, waiting for an explanation.

I glance down at my hands. They are clenched tight. 'For weeks after what happened to Mum, I couldn't eat at all. Every time I thought about food I saw that breakfast table again. It is almost as if my stomach has shrunk and I can only eat small amounts.'

'What breakfast table?'

I unclench my hands and flex my fingers. I haven't spoken to anyone, not even Billie, about that day when I opened the front door and even the walls were silently screaming for my mother. I look up.

'I had an appointment with the doctor that day. My mother wanted to come, but I said to her, "No, I'll be fine." God, I wish I had never said those words. If only I'd kept my mouth shut and let her come with me, she might be alive today.'

I shake my head with regret. 'I can still see her face. "Are you sure?" she asked. Even then I could have said, "All right, come. You can keep me company." But I didn't. Instead, I said, "Absolutely. Stay at home and have a rest. Hospitals are full of germs."

'When I came back, I opened the front door and called to her. She did not answer so I went into the kitchen, and I knew immediately that something was very wrong when I saw the kitchen table. It should have been ready for lunch, but it was full of leftovers from our breakfast. Sliced tomatoes, pita bread, olives, oil. And…flies.' I cover my mouth. 'Flies were buzzing around the congealed fried eggs.'

The startlingly clear image makes me feel nauseated again and I push the plate of food away from me and take a deep, steadying breath. I do not tell him that that day too my milk dried up. No a drop was left for Sorab. A kindly woman, two doors away became his wet nurse until the day I left Iran.

I look up into his eyes and they are soft and pained. In his world of unlimited funds almost everything can be made better with a little application and cunning. This one cannot. Even he is helpless in the face of death.

'She was such an incredibly clean person. I knew something terrible had happened. My mother had gone out to the shop opposite to buy some sugar for her coffee and had been run over while crossing the road outside our house. For many weeks I would wake up having dreamt of flies in my food. Perhaps it was the shock of how quickly they had taken over my mother's kitchen, after her relentless efforts of keeping them away.'

My chest seizes up. A small sob escapes. Oh no, surely I'm not going to bawl again. I swallow while the tears run down my cheeks. I feel the waiter's eyes on me. Blake reaches for my hand.

'I'm sorry,' I apologize, squeezing his hand. 'I know, this too will pass, and all that, but I just can't seem to get over my loss.'

After lunch we return to the palazzo that belongs to Blake's family. Iced with a filigree of white stone and built on three floors it reminds me of a wedding cake. Inside, it is as beautiful as any palace with glittering mosaic, marble statues of human beings, golden statues of beasts, detailed frescos, decorated ceilings, priceless antiques, bell pulls made of rich gold and red braids, and liveried servants

Gerry is sitting on the balcony under an umbrella. Sorab squeals with delight at my appearance. The afternoon is spent on the balcony with Sorab. Pleasant. Rare. I won't ever forget it.

That evening I go to the top floor. A strange place. Smooth marble steps right in the middle of the huge space lead to an antique clawed bath with gold taps. I take my dressing gown off and step into the scented water. Here the servants are light-footed and like ghosts. Secretive and almost unseen. I rest my head against the warm marble.

High above my head looming out of the dark of the vaulted roof space is an iron chain from which a glass chandelier of unsurpassed beauty is suspended. Its many glass arms twist and turn into delicate cristallo cups that hold real candles. Blake told me that it was once made for the Church of Santa Maria della Pieta, but one of his more flamboyant ancestors acquired it for himself. He wanted to look up at the work of art as he bathed. At the hundreds of diamond fruits and crystal teardrops.

I gaze at them with awe. Each droplet, because of its position on the chandelier and its distance from each candle, has been blown a slightly different shape in order to transmit the same luminescence from every angle as they capture the flickering flames inside their prisms.

Blake appears at the door. He stands in the enormous shadows cast by the candles. Silent, full of some wild emotion that makes my cheeks burn.

'I've dreamed of seeing you in this bath under this chandelier,' he says huskily, and, coming forward into the light, takes the washcloth out of my hands and proceeds to wash my back.

I feel his mouth on the back of my neck; the evening stubble of his unshaved face rasps my skin. Goose pimples rise on my exposed skin. Instantly my head arches back exposing my entire throat to him. He kisses my neck softly, delicately. His large hands catch my breasts. Immediately, the desire for him grows in my being. I want him inside me, but he shakes his head lightly.

'No, no, I have other plans for you.' He stands up and brings the towel. I stand, soapsuds running down my body. Hoping he will change his mind. His eyes darken, but he wraps the towel around me carefully and turns me around in his arms.

'I love you,' I say.

He stills. Something indescribably beautiful comes into his eyes. 'I know,' he says gently. 'It is what keeps me going.' But he does not say I love you back. Instead he helps me into my dressing gown. 'Fabiola is waiting outside to do your hair.'

'Oh.'

Someone outside to do my hair. I look at him in wonder, at the precision of his plans. Is there anything he has not thought of? Fabiola enters with a rosewood box. In its compartmentalized interior she keeps all her accoutrements. She is young, keeps her dark eyes lowered for most of her time with me, and does not speak English, but she is nothing short of a hair genius. She twines blood-red rosebuds into my hair. It is the kind of hairdo that you see on Oscar night. I will be sorry to see it come down.

When she is gone I dress in the black gown. There is only one yellowing bruise that shows through the net on my lower back. I twist up the scarlet lipstick and apply it to my lips. I get into my tall shoes and in the mirror a woman looks back, highly colored, wild-eyed, and more than a little wanton, but at the same time, rather beautiful. I am still looking at my reflection when Blake comes into the room. My breath catches. He is dressed in a black tux. I have never seen him look so vital and handsome. His hair gleams. With that aristocratic nose...he looks like he has just stepped out from a painting.

He is carrying two packages in his hands. He comes and stands behind me. Inside the looking glass we make a stunning couple. I don't make any sudden movements; I don't want to spoil it for the woman in the parallel universe. Perhaps she will get her man. All day long, people have been staring at us. Now I know why. He opens the first package and takes out a necklace. It is stunningly simple. A band made of rubies with an oval black centerpiece.

'It's a black diamond,' he says.

'It is beautiful,' I breathe, raising my eyes to meet his.

'Something for you to remember Venice by.' He sets it around my neck. The red stones encircle my throat like ribbons of fire. He stands back and looks at me. There is a glint of possessive pride in his eyes. And I feel owned.

Then he opens the next box.

I tilt my head forward curiously. 'What are they?' I ask. I cannot make them out. On a bed of black material are some colorful gadgets made of plastic or silicon.

His answer is succinct. 'Spread your legs.'

My body's reaction is immediate. A wave of sexual arousal. Those things fit into my body. I obey. He bends and, lifting the long dress, inserts one of them into me, adjusts it so the cup-like end fits snugly around my clitoris, and pulls my knickers up over it. It feels strange and smooth inside me. From his trouser pocket he takes out a small device. It is no bigger than a remote control car key. He presses it and the thing inside me starts vibrating.

'Oooo,' I giggle. As he turns the dial the vibrations become more violent until I squeal, 'Hey.'

He turns it right down.

'Venetian music in its original setting *and* the latest vibrator,' I tease, but I am fascinated with the idea of putting total control of my sensations into his hands.

'It is the perfect touch,' he says softly. 'Music is passion. We are going to watch L'Incoranazione di Poppea. The coronation of Poppea is a Venetian opera of unbearable sensuousness, and the frissons you will experience on the outside will be reflected inside your body.'

Seventeen

The sun is bleeding into the lagoon as we go down the steps and climb into the gondola. It is a cool evening and his arm comes around me. I revel in his touch. I know Cronus is waiting for me in England, but this is my night, my adventure. He is not allowed here, in this sinking city.

The theater is very old and full of faded charm. There are no tourists present. The other patrons who have turned up are mostly elderly and dressed in fine clothes. They have a kind of grave dignity that reminds me of a time gone by. Everyone seems to know everyone else and one or two of them even nod gravely to Blake. It is almost as if it is a private showing. We take our place in one of the boxes.

'This theater affords better acoustics than some of the more glamorous ones,' Blake explains, before the curtain goes up, and the vibrator begins its almost constant throb. At first, I squirm awkwardly, judging it as an unwelcome distraction that is going to reduce my enjoyment of the experience of being at the opera, but then I begin to look for its rhythm.

It soars with the music.

The opera is sung in Italian, but I have Blake whisper in my ear each scene and even point out the significance of some arias. The coronation of Poppea charts the opulently atmospheric journey of Poppea, the mistress of the Roman emperor Nero, who in pursuit of her desire to be Empress of Rome forsook love for the power. As Blake warned, the story is erotic and decadent. Combined with the vibrator between my legs the experience is indescribable and has me not only incredibly aroused, but also emotionally drained, and perhaps confused too.

During the rapturous love duet when Nero holds Poppea in his arms while she caresses her jeweled crown, and the vibrator has been turned to full, I turn to look at Blake wondering why he has brought me to see an opera where the virtuous are punished or put to death and the greedy and unscrupulous rewarded. Is it an unsubtle hint to me? Am I the greedy woman of his world?

As if he has read my mind he says, 'Glorious music goes beyond human frailties.'

It is true I feel excited and light-headed. The experience has been profound. I need to go the toilet and see what I look like. It feels as if I have been altered this evening. I touch his wrist lightly. 'Going to the toilet. Meet me at the bottom of the stairs.'

He nods and stands. Between my legs I am throbbing. I don't know if he can see the desire in my eyes. I don't want to go to dinner. I just want to go home and have him inside me.

In the faded mirror I meet myself. My eyes are strange. I am changing right before my eyes. I touch the slightly protruding cup on my clitoris and think about taking it out, but in my heart that privilege belongs only to Blake. He put it in there and he is entitled to take it out when it suits him.

Coming down the curving marble stairs from the toilets, I witness him in conversation with one of the ushers. A raven-haired girl. His back is to me and he is speaking to her in Italian. I see her animated face and a strange unfamiliar fear clutches at my stomach. Immediately, I grasp the wrought iron and brass banister, unsteady suddenly, my heart knocking painfully against my ribs. Whatever he has said has made her laugh self-consciously, and, as I watch, her large, dark eyes kindle with fiery interest.

I lay my palm flat on my stomach almost in disbelief. I am jealous. I am unreasonably, insanely, uncontrollably jealous of a man whom I cannot even publicly lay claim on. But the thought of him with anyone else makes me feel sick to my stomach.

Will it always be so from now on?

The most innocent encounters ripe for worry and painful inner speculation while I play blind, deaf and dumb outwardly? Then he turns, his eyes searching, looking for me, and I step forward, a silent sigh escaping my lips, relieved to be back in the warm, wonderful light of his gaze. And everything is fine again; the fear slinks away, momentarily.

'I didn't know you spoke Italian?'

He grins. 'Nope, but I studied Latin in school, so it's not difficult to figure out how to ask for directions.'

With the dark water lapping at the steps of the Palazzo, I whisper, 'Blake can we go upstairs first… before we eat.'

He shakes his head with a smile. 'Not yet, Principessa.' He puts his hand into his pocket and the little machine buzzes into life. But now the suction cup is licking me almost like a tongue.

'Oh, Blake,' I gasp. 'I can't take much more of this.'

'Yes, you can,' he says.

I swallow hard. How can I think of food while my pussy is throbbing and a silicon tongue is licking my clit? The only thought on my mind is release. I am already very close to climax.

'What if I have an orgasm at the dinner table?'

'You won't. I'm switching it off while you eat. Nothing comes between you and food.'

I gape at him.

'Have I ever told you, Miss Bloom, you're a sight to behold,' he says cheekily, and pulls me up the steps.

He goes through the double doors of the salon and I go upstairs to check on Sorab. Mercifully the vibrator stops as I am walking up the stairs. Sorab is fast asleep. Gerry's door is slightly ajar and light is coming through. I knock softly.

'Come in,' she says.

I enter. She is in bed reading. Her kind face is wreathed in a welcoming smile.

'How was he?'

'As good as gold.'

'I'll keep him tomorrow morning and you can take some time off. Do some sightseeing.'

'No need for that, Love. I was here twenty years ago. Broke my heart on a glass blower.'

And it occurs to me that it is impossible to tell the nuances of anyone's history by looking at them or knowing them for a few days. My mother used to say, 'You can eat salt with someone for five years and never know them.'

I find Blake in the cavernous, gorgeously painted red dining room. He is standing by the fireplace looking up at a massive portrait of a haughty man in fine clothes. He turns at my approach. The resemblance between him and the man in the portrait is striking. It is immediately apparent that he is an ancestor. It is there in the aristocratic arch of his cheek, the set of his jaw. The same way that I found Victoria in her mother. These families that do not mix their blood easily carry their genetic footprint clearly in their faces, their bearing.

The humming between my legs begins as I walk towards him.

'Have your family always owned this house?'

He frowns. Discussions about his family always distance him. 'Yes, we are descended from the Black Venetians. We branched out into Germany before crossing the Atlantic.'

'It's very beautiful. Do you come here often?'

'I haven't been to this house for years,' he replies, and switches on the licking function.

I squirm.

'Shall we eat?'

Dinner is served by a dour, mostly silent man in a white jacket called Enzo. I find it almost impossible to eat. True to his word Blake has switched off the gadget, but by now I am so aroused I can hardly wait for the meal to be over. I taste nothing. When Blake pushes away his coffee cup I spring up.

'What's the rush? You'd only be exchanging the silicon tongue for mine.'

I make a strangled sound and turn pleadingly towards him. 'Please, can we go up *now*?'

'No, I want to see you completely laid to waste tonight,' he says, lifting the champagne bottle and filling our glasses. 'I am going to make you come harder than you have ever done before,' he promises as the licking and vibrating in my knickers increase in tempo.

I sit down and lift the glass to my lips. It is a beautiful, hand-blown work of art. The long slender stem rises into a decorative figure of the lion of St. Mark's before it meets the delicate flute.

'Mmnnn.' He takes my wrist in his hands and runs his finger lightly along the inside, up to the crook of my elbow. The sensation is unbearably sensual. The desire to straddle him in that vast red room is undeniable.

'I have never met a woman with skin like yours,' he purrs. He looks into my eyes. 'Do you have any idea how desirable you look right now?'

I clench my thighs and shake my head.

We go up the curving staircase to our bedroom. Moonlight is flooding in through the tall windows. There are long rectangles of light on the floor.

He turns to me and gently takes off my dress. He throws it behind him and it lands on a squat green and gold brocade chair. He drops to his haunches, bends forward and kisses the tightly bound mound of my sex. The gesture is so unexpectedly charged with erotic possibilities that my body screams for him. He slides my knickers off.

'Spread your legs.' I obey instantly. He removes the gadget and I actually feel my body sag with relief. He lets his fingers graze the sticky opening. 'You are so, so wet,' he says.

I nod helplessly. My hands are frustrated fists, waiting for him.

'What do you want, Principessa?'

'You.'

He shakes his head gently. The eyes looking up at me are almost black. 'I need more details. The low-down of what you want.'

'I need you inside me,' I mutter.

Again his head moves negatively. 'Details, Lana. Details.'

And in this way he persuades me to describe in minute detail exactly what I want, to use words that would have at any other time made me blush furiously. That thick prick of yours, your dirty big, cock, deep into my cunt, suck it, fuck me hard…

He gags me. 'The walls are thin and may even have ears,' he whispers. It jars in my head, but only a little; I am too far gone to search for hidden implications.

His large hands grab my hips and impale me on his dick.

The pillar of solid meat is thrust far into my body. Instead of moving me up and down the hard length, he pulls me to and fro, making me ride him like a bull. I grind myself on him. My body is thrust far forward like one of those cyclists in the tour de France race, so that his mouth has easy access to my breasts.

He latches on and sucks hard and my sweaty thighs slip and slide against his muscular hips, the thick cock inside me acting as my brakes. It is too intense to last. In seconds I lose it. Screaming like a banshee, I come fast and hard. Thank God for the gag. I have lost it. Completely. Even my teeth, fingertips and toes are vibrating.

I rest my lips on his damp forehead. Sated. He is still hard as a rock inside me. My nipples are still pinched between his thumbs and forefingers. They throb painfully, exquisitely. Now it is his turn. And then it will be mine again. The day will come when all I will have are memories of what we have done together.

I am awakened in the early morning hours. Must be the unfamiliarity of my surroundings. It is two o'clock and it seems all of Venice is asleep. I get out of bed and walk barefoot across the highly polished dark wood floor, towards the windows overlooking the interlocking canals and cobblestone pathways. Shivering slightly I stand in the cool night listening to the sounds of the murky waters lapping against mossy, old stones. The sulfuric smell like that of slowly rotting eggs rises from the canals and slips into my consciousness. Not that that bothers me. For me being with Blake in this city with its crumbling glory and beautiful stonework is a dream.

And then a thought—clawed and dangerous. Who or what is Cronus?

I hear a rustling and, turning my head, see Blake, raised on his elbows and watching me. In the silvery moonlight he is Atlas or Mars or Apollo. A god. He gets out of bed, nude, and with the lithe grace of a beautiful animal, prowls over to me. He bends and kisses me. I luxuriate in the warmth emanating from the length of his body. But my thoughts make me kiss him a touch too desperately.

He lifts his head and looks at me. In the moonlight his eyes are dark wells of curiosity.

'What's the matter?' he asks, crouching beside me.

'Nothing,' I lie. 'I think I'm too excited to sleep.'

He sighs and persists, 'What's wrong, Lana?'

'What did you say to the usher at the theater?'

He sits back on his heels. 'What usher?'

'You know, when I went to the toilet.'

'Ah...I was asking if there was an ice cream bar nearby. Why?'

I look down, unable to meet his eyes, unable to help the sadness that creeps into my voice. 'I just wondered if you...if you found her attractive.'

'What?'

I look up at him.

He takes my cold fingers in his large warm hands. 'Shall I tell you a secret?'

I nod. That will be a first.

'From the first moment I saw you I wanted you. Not in the compartmentalized way I wanted the others, the length of leg, the jut of a butt, or the strain of material caused by a well-shaped chest. When I saw you I had to have all of you as mine. I would have paid any price that night to buy you.'

'Oh, Blake,' I sigh. I want him to say he loves me, even if it is just a little, but I won't push anymore, I might hear something I don't want to. It is always cleverer to quit while still ahead.

'Shall I show you just how much I want you?' he asks quietly.

I nod and he stands up. I stretch my arms out to him as if I am a child, and he picks me up and carries me to the kingly bed. I sigh deeply with pleasure under him. For a time there is only the soft rustle of white linen and the occasional gasp. Then a fierce, rapid rhythm. Until a shudder like a silver explosion shivers through me, and I am back among glittering stars. Here I can hide from Cronus. I hold onto the exciting firmness of his buttocks as he finds his release and spills his seed inside my body.

Dreamily I snuggle deeper into his body and am soon as deeply asleep as everybody else in that stinking, sinking city.

Eighteen

After a trip to the glass blower's we return the way we came. By private plane: without queues, passport control or waiting for baggage. Blake does not get into the car with us. He has a business appointment that he must keep. He tries to convince me to let the nanny go back to the apartment with me, but I refuse. She is put into a taxi.

I hold Sorab in my lap and stare out of the window. I cannot help feeling a little depressed. While I was away I had temporarily put away the things that Victoria's mother had said, but now they have all come crowding back. Their whispers are loud in the quiet apartment. I feel very alone and frightened.

When Jack calls I immediately invite him to come around.

'You've just come back from holiday. You must have a thousand things to do. I won't disturb you. I'll come tomorrow,' he says.

'No, not at all. Do please come today, now if you can. I'd love to see you again.'

'Is everything all right, Lana?'

I laugh. 'Of course. I just want to see my son's godfather again. Is there anything wrong in that?'

He laughs. The sound is familiar. 'No, but you will tell me if there is, won't you?'

'Yes, yes, yes. Now how long will it take you to get here?'

'Half an hour.'

'See you then.' I terminate the call and feel relief.

'Mr. Jack Irish at reception for you, Miss Lana,' Mr. Nair calls thirty minutes later.

'Brilliant. Send him up,' I say, and opening the front door go out to wait by the lift. The lift opens and there is Jack. He doesn't look comfortable. I can see he is overawed by his surroundings.

'My, my, Jack,' I say, 'is that a new shirt? I don't think I've ever seen you in red.'

He flushes. 'Alison picked it out,' he mumbles, and steps out of the lift.

'Hey, it looks good. Really. Actually, very dashing.'

'And you're playing fast and loose with your compliments today.'

'I am,' I agree, and go into his arms. It is so familiar. So good. I love Jack. I truly do. He is like that first ray of sunshine after a particularly heavy downpour. A delicious uncomplicated invitation to go out and play. I step away. 'Come and see the place.'

I push open the door and turn around. 'Wow,' Jack says. 'This place must have cost something.'

'Yeah, wait till you see the view.' I pull him by the hand towards the balcony.

'Startling, isn't it?'

'Vistas like this must surely induce attacks of megalomania,' he says softly. We stand in silence for a minute, and then he turns to me. 'Where's the brat then?'

'Sleeping.'

'Again?'

I laugh. It is so easy with Jack. 'Want some real coffee?'

'What kind of question is that?'

'Come on then.'

I put on some music and we sit on the sofa with our cappuccinos.

'Just off the top of your head, what do you know about Cronus?'

'That's a strange question.'

I take a sip of the hot liquid. 'Just heard it the other day and realized I didn't know anything about it.'

'My Greek mythology is very shaky, but I believe he is the god who ate his own children. It is also another name for Saturn, or Father Time.'

'The god who ate his own children?'

'Yeah, it was to stop a prophecy that his own child would overthrow him. Something like that, anyway.'

I nod unhappily. Don't like the sound of any of it. After Jack leaves I intend to do my own research.

'Are you happy, Lana?'

'No,' I say before I can stop myself.

His coffee cup freezes on its way to his lips.

I cover my mouth with the tips of my fingers. I can't tell him about Cronus so I start making it up. 'No, wait. That came out wrong. I'm not actively unhappy.' I clasp my hands under my chin. 'But you know how I feel about him. It's a kind of torture to be so in love with someone who doesn't love you back. I'm the dead wasp floating in his glass of champagne. I ruin his perfect life. His perfect plans.' And yet this too is true. Blake is not happy. There is something that is tearing his insides, but he won't tell me what it is.

Jack puts his coffee cup on the low table. 'You poor duck,' he says with such compassion, I am suddenly filled with morbid self-pity. I blink back the tears. Jack puts his hand out.

'Don't touch her.'

The violence in the words startles me. I swing my head around and find Blake standing at the door of the living room. We had not heard him enter. The thick carpets, the music.

His face is a thundercloud. I jump up guiltily, my face flaming. And then I realize I have done nothing wrong. We have done nothing wrong. My innocence makes my voice strong. 'We were just talking, Blake. Jack is my brother.'

Blake does not look at me. 'He's not your brother. He's in love with you.'

'Oh! For God's sake,' I burst out angrily, and turn to Jack in exasperation for support against such a distorted view of our relationship, and then I freeze.

Jack is looking at me with so much pain in his tortured, artist's eyes. Why, Blake is right. My Jack is in love with me. Deeply. Hopelessly. Perhaps for years. It seems impossible. It is me who has been so blind, so stupid. Both our mothers knew it.

'Jack?' I whisper. I want him to deny it so it can all be as it was before—uncomplicated, beautiful, but he presses his lips into a thin line and starts walking towards the door. Blankly, I follow his progress past Blake, their shoulders almost brushing but not quite. He is in the corridor when I find my legs and begin to run after him. Blake catches me by the arm.

'Let me pass,' I hiss.

He looks at me. Implacable, his eyes glittering. 'I don't share,' he rasps.

'Please…He needs me now'

'Your pity is the last thing he needs.'

'I wasn't offering pity. I was offering friendship.'

'He doesn't want your friendship either. He wants you in his arms, in his bed. Can you give him that, Lana?'

We stand there staring at each other, the air bristling. Then he releases my arm and backs away from me. I drop my head. As I stand there crushed by my loss, he puts his arms around me and draws me to his body. 'I'm sorry, baby.'

I lay my cheek against his hard chest. Dry-eyed. When the loss is that big tears don't come. I know from the time I lost my mother. Tears come when you release that person and I refuse to release Jack. He will fall in love with someone else. He will forget this love he has for me and then we will be brother and sister again. I feel Blake's lips on my hair.

And I begin to cry. Not for the loss of Jack because I will never lose Jack, but for the loss of Blake, because I know in my heart of hearts I can't keep him. Because of Cronus; because everything I really love is always being taken away from me. Blake doesn't understand why I am crying or clinging or why I am insatiable. I am drinking the last of the summer wine. That night I let myself get drunk as a skunk.

Nineteen

When I go to visit Billie she has a surprise for Sorab. A beautiful rocking horse from Mamas & Papas.

'OMG!' I exclaim. 'You shouldn't have. That must have cost a fortune,' I go to it and touch the soft brown material of the horse's mouth.

'Nah, I nicked it.'

I whirl around to face her. Trying to imagine how on earth she walked out of the store with such a big item in her arms. 'Why, Billie?'

She shrugs. 'It's not a big deal. These big corporations make allowances for pilferage. It's part of their operating costs.'

'When we have our business are we going to make allowances for pilferage too?'

'Hell, no.'

I raise my eyebrows and cross my arms over my chest.

'All right,' she says. 'But I'm not taking it back.'

I laugh. Billie is incorrigible. Sometimes I wish I was like her. Life is such an abundant adventure. She takes everything with both hands.

'Listen, Billie, I know why you did it, but you don't have to compete with Blake. You're Sorab's aunt. You'll always be there,' and the words stick in my throat, but I spit them out, 'Blake will not.'

'I'm sorry, Lana.'

'You don't have to apologize to me.'

'I'm sorry that you can't have Blake.'

'Yeah. It's a bummer.'

'I got a bottle of vodka,' she suggests brightly.

I smile. 'No, but I'll have a cup of tea, though.'

We are sitting at the kitchen table having our tea when the doorbell rings.

'Expecting someone?'

'Yeah, Jack said he might come around.'

'Oh!'

She goes to open the door. 'Hey, you.'

'Hey, yourself,' Jack says and comes in.

'Hello, Jack,' I greet softly.

'Hello, Lana.' He is surprised to see me. His eyes seem sad. So sad. I don't think I have ever seen him like this. Now that his secret has been unmasked he seems purposeless, empty and defeated. He looks like a man who has had all his dreams and hopes shattered, and he is simply standing there looking at the shards in disbelief.

I move forward and he looks at me with a tortured expression.

'I'll leave you two alone,' Billie says and walks quickly to her room.

'We have to talk,' I say.

'There is nothing to say,' he replies. His eyes are burning in his face, though. There is something he wants to say. Badly.

'Tell me,' I urge.

'I am leaving for Africa soon. I volunteered. I'll be working for a medical charity.'

I gasp. There are already tears prickling the backs of my eyes. 'Where in Africa?'

'Sudan.'

'For how long?'

He shrugs. A half smile. The old Jack poking through. 'Until I feel better, I guess.'

I nod. I'm not going to cry. I'm going to be strong for him. Make it easy for him. I'm going to wish him well.

'Before I go will you...kiss me, Lana?'

My mouth gapes. I stare at him. First thought: I love Jack. I can't refuse him such a small thing. Second thought: my mouth belongs to Blake. I think of Blake saying, 'I don't share.'

'Forget it, forget it,' he says, and whirling around makes for the door. For a few seconds I am frozen, and then I am running out of the door calling to him. He turns in the corridor and looks at me.

'Yes,' I whisper.

I owe him this. This is my Jack. He would give his life for me. I love him. I have loved him all my life.

One parting kiss. What harm can it do? The kiss is already doomed.

He strides towards me, broad-shouldered, confident, sure. The old Jack in every line. He stops in front of me. I look up into his bright blue eyes, totally different from Blake's or mine. 'Old blue eyes,' my mum used to call him. He could have had any girl. All the girls in school used to call him Mr. Happening and he was in love with me the whole time.

He puts his hands on either side of my cheeks, butterfly light. There is no fire in his eyes. There is no lust. There is only the light of love, such love that the breath catches in my throat. It pours out of his eyes, drowning me, leaving me speechless, parting my mouth. He smells of soap and some cheap aftershave. But clean. And good. And wholesome.

Gently, gently his lips descend.

And when they arrive I tremble at the surprise that is Jack. All my life he has constantly surprised me, by the unfathomable depths of him. Like that time he was shirtless and turning on himself like a wild animal, growling 'Who next?' to his attackers. He is truly unknowable.

His kiss begins gently and without any hope, but there is such skill and technique that on a purely physical level my body begins to react to him. *Where did you learn to kiss like this?* My shocked mind wonders distractedly. And suddenly I am not standing in a concrete corridor in a council block of flats kissing my brother. I am making love to a beautiful, surprising man who is in love with me, and who I could have fallen in love with if only he had kissed me like this a year and a half ago.

Shit, what the hell am I doing?

I put my hands on his chest to push him away. Immediately he moves back.

'Why didn't you tell me?' I whisper.

'I didn't think you were ready,' he says bitterly, and begins to walk away.

'Jack.'

He turns slightly.

'Please take care of yourself.'

He doesn't answer. Simply walks away. I watch him until he disappears down the road. Then I gently shut Billie's front door and begin to walk. Sorab will be safe with her for a few hours. I don't have a destination. I simply walk in the general direction of St. John's Wood. I feel ripped apart. I truly never suspected. Now he is going to a dangerous war-torn country and he may never come back. I don't know how long I walk, but suddenly I am very close to the apartment and mind-numbingly tired. I cannot face the walk back to collect my son. I realize my mobile phone and my handbag are in the pram.

I find a phone box and make a collect call to Billie and she agrees to keep Sorab for another hour. I will go back to the apartment. Rest for half an hour and then go back to Billie's. I wave to Mr. Nair and go into the lift. In the lift I sag against the wall. I used to be able to walk for miles and never feel this tired. Billie is right. I am only a shell of what I used to be.

I open the front door of the apartment and Blake is standing in the corridor. I stop and stare at him. Why is he home? There is an expression on his face that I have never before seen.

In a flash he crosses the room and closes the door. He bends his head to kiss me and rears back as if burned. His eyes blaze into mine. Then things happen so fast they are blur to my tired mind. He grabs me by the upper arms and the next moment I have been lifted off the ground and I am lying dazed and flat on my back with him crouching over me like a predator, his eyes so ferocious I do not recognize them. He pulls my skirt up and tears my knickers open. Then he grabs my legs by the kneecaps and opens them wide. He jerks his face between my legs, and to my eternal horror, *sniffs* me. Like an animal.

I am so shocked and humiliated, I freeze.

When he raises his head and looks at me I am staring at him, speechless, horrified. The wild, aggressive expression on his face is gone as quickly as it had come. I look at him almost in disbelief. *I have just seen him lose control.* I find my strength, my fight, and raising myself on my elbows, I place my feet on the carpet and push hard and away from him. He grabs my foot. I kick out with the other. He grabs that one too and pulls me toward him. I slide helplessly along the carpet, like a rag doll towards him.

'Don't,' he growls. 'I smelt a man on you.'

I am flat on the ground. His face is very close to mine. I close my eyes. 'I kissed Jack.'

'Why?'

'Because he is leaving for a war-torn country. Because I may never see him again. Because he asked me. Because he has never asked me for anything before,' I sob. The tears are running down my temples into my hair. I feel shocked and bruised. I am in love with a man who wrestled me to the ground and sniffed my sex organs for the smell of another man. Another man's scent on me has brought out dormant territorial and protective instincts in the cool banker. The instincts are destructive, feral.

He scoops me up in his arms 'Shhh… I'm sorry, I'm sorry. I didn't mean to frighten you,' he croons.

But I cannot stop crying.

'Please don't cry. You didn't do anything wrong. I just can't bear thinking of you with anyone else. I don't even want you in the same room with other men,' he confesses.

'What is happening to us, Blake?' I whisper.

'Nothing is happening to us. I just lost my head for a moment. I didn't think. It was pure instinct.'

'What's going to happen when the 42 days are up, Blake?'

He looks pained. 'I don't know, but will you trust me that everything I do is in your best interests?'

'And what is in my best interest, Blake?'

He sighs heavily. 'In thirty-one days you will know.'

Softly he starts kissing my eyelids, my cheeks. He ends on my mouth. He kisses it hard, forces my lips open and lets his tongue sweep into my mouth. Possessively, staking claim on what is his, erasing the mark, even the memory of the other man's mouth. His hands are unbuttoning my blouse, cupping my breasts. I am lifted and the bra clasp flicked open. The blouse is being pulled out of my skirt. It slips easily from my shoulders. The skirt follows.

We have sex on the floor beside the front door. The shock and the pent-up emotion make the climax explosive, and afterwards, I feel so exhausted I wish I could sleep where I am. He picks me up and carries me to the bed.

'I have to go and pick Sorab up from Billie,' I whisper.

'Tom is already on his way. Sleep.'

I sleep for many hours. When I wake up it is 7:00 pm. I see the light from beneath the connecting door of Sorab's room. I pull on a dressing gown and pad towards the door. I open it and stand for a moment unnoticed. Bands of steel around my heart. Blake is holding Sorab in his arms and rocking him. I have denied Sorab a father. I have denied Blake his son. I had never thought to see Blake so domesticated. He looks up and smiles.

'Ah, you are awake?'

I smile.

'Did you sleep well?'

'Yes, thank you,' I say, but I did not. These days I wake up unrefreshed, tired. I hope I am not sickening for something. 'Here, give him to me. He probably needs to be changed by now.'

'No need, all done.'

'You changed his nappy?'

'It's not exactly rocket science.'

I go to Sorab and put a finger into the nappy around his belly. The nappy is perfectly snug. He has done a good job.

'When did you learn to put a nappy on a baby?'

'I watched you.'

'Hmnnn…I guess I'd better prepare some formula for him.'

'No, need, I just fed him.'

'Quick learner, aren't you?'

'Like you wouldn't believe,' he says and grins, all boyish and gorgeous. As if I have not seen him tackle me to the ground and smell my sex for the scent of another man.

He puts Sorab into my surprised hands. 'I hope you are hungry. Dinner will be served in half an hour.'

'Starving,' I say to his retreating back.

The wine is an old vintage from the Barrington estate in France, the steaks are perfectly juicy and tender, and the salad is out of a bag, but perfectly dressed and salted. I gaze wonderingly at him as he sits opposite me in a black shirt, faded blue jeans and bare feet. Like you wouldn't believe, indeed.

He learnt to cook while we were apart!

Twenty

Billie calls surprisingly early in the morning. She has something to tell me.

'What is it?' I ask.

'Tell you when you get here,' she says, her voice full of something delicious, something she can barely keep suppressed.

I hurry over. When I arrive with Sorab she is in the bath.

'In here,' she calls. I go and sit on the toilet seat. There is glittery-green eyeshadow on her eyelids.

'Gosh, you look like you've had a fun night.'

She grins widely. 'I went to The Fridge last night.'

'Who with?'

'On my own.'

I frown. 'Why?'

'Just wanted to.'

'Well?'

'I let a man pick me up.'

'What?' I am so surprised my mouth actually hangs.

'What can I say? This huge man, I mean really big, with muscles coming out of his ears, came up to me and told me that the tattoos on my neck were the most beautiful things he had ever seen.'

I giggle.

'All right. It is possible that he has cornered the market on going up to girls and complimenting the very thing that everyone else has told them is ugly. But nobody has ever thought my tattoos are beautiful. Not you. Not even Leticia. And it made me curious about him.'

'But you don't fancy men.'

'I know. "Thanks, but I'm a dyke, mate," is what I told him too.'

'And?' I prompt.

'"That's only because you haven't been to bed with me yet," he said, and I was so high, I was actually impressed with that level of arrogant confidence. "I'll fuck you, but I'm not sucking your dick or doing anything else gross like that," I replied.'

'Billie!' I squeal.

'No point being coy. I'm not sucking any man's dick. Anyway, "I'm not too keen on that practice either," he said, so we went back to his place.'

'And?' I can barely believe what I am hearing.

'And it was actually very exciting. You know how I always take control. He wouldn't let me. He was very strict and masterful, and fucking strong too. I've never had anyone so...well...authoritative in bed before. It was something new, something I'm not used to.'

'So you enjoyed sex with a man?'

'I hate to say yes, it messes with my self-identity, but yeah. In the morning he brought me breakfast, ugh, sausages and eggs.'

I am almost laughing. 'What did you do?'

'I ate it.'

'What?'

'Wasn't bad.'

'Billie, you haven't had a proper breakfast since you were two!'

She laughs.

'Are you going to see him again?'

'Maybe. He took my number, but he's going to be away for a month. If I see him again, I see him again; if I don't, I don't.'

'But you want to…'

'Yeah…I guess I do. There's something intriguing about him.'

'Does this mean you are no longer a lesbian?'

'Don't get me wrong. I still fancy you more than him, but maybe I'm not just DC but AC too.'

'What's his name?'

'Rose, Jaron Rose.'

I bite my lip. 'Actually, I have something to tell you too.'

'Get on with it then.'

'I don't want you to freak out but…'

'I won't freak out. What is it?'

'Victoria's mother came to see me.'

'Bloody hell. That was quick. Let me guess. She warned you to leave Blake alone?'

'Yes, she did warn me, but the funny thing is, I think she thought she was warning me for my own good.'

Billie snorts disbelievingly. 'You're soft in the head.'

'Just hear me out, OK?'

'I'm all ears.'

'It was all very vague and mysterious, but basically she told me I was in danger.'

'Now you *are* freaking me out. What kind of danger?'

'She didn't say, but something about the way she said it made me realize that she was frightened. She shouldn't have come to see me. She came against her better judgment.'

'So what exactly did she say?'

'She said I should beware of Cronus.'

'Who the hell is that?'

'I didn't know either. But he is the god of time. Usually depicted as an old man with a grey beard. According to Greek mythology Cronus deposed his father and, in fear of a prophecy that he would suffer the same fate, he began to swallow each of his children as soon as they were born.'

'Charming. What's that got to do with you?'

'I don't know. I'm trying to work it out.'

'Why don't you ask Blake?'

'Because she said, don't trust anyone and I'm not sure—'

'You don't trust Blake!' Billie's eyes are huge with shock.

'It's not that I don't trust him. I trust him with my life, but he is definitely hiding something important from me. Besides, he has already told me that the less I know the safer I will be.'

'Jesus, Lana, what kind of shit are you messed up in?'

Twenty-One

I wake up exhausted.

In fact, last night I was so dead to the world, I did not even wake up at dawn to take care of Sorab. Blake did. Before he left for work he gently shook me awake and said, 'Shall I ask Gerry to come take care of Sorab today?'

But I had shaken my head. 'No, I'm fine.'

'OK, I'll call you mid-morning.'

I pull myself out of bed. I am so tired I feel almost tearful. I hear Sorab cry and I move instinctively towards the sound. I pick him up and put him in his playpen. He looks at me with his great big blue eyes and grizzles softly. I know what he wants. He wants me to carry him. But I can't. Not today.

Today I just want to go back to bed and sleep. I wipe my hand down my face. I go over to the tin of biscuits. Flavored with organic grape juice they are his favorite. I thrust one into his hand. He starts nibbling on it and I stumble out of the room. I have a plan. I will leave him with Billie and I will have a good sleep. I need it.

By the time I reach Billie I actually feel dizzy.

'What's the matter with you?' Billie says.

'Tired,' I say. 'Can you just watch him while I go back and sleep for a few hours?'

'Whoa,' she says. Her voice sounds far away. 'You're going nowhere like this. Come here.'

Obediently I turn towards her voice. She leads me to her bed. I fall grategully into it; it smells of her hairspray and perfume. Familiar. I turn my face towards it.

I feel a cool hand on my forehead. 'Shit,' I hear her say. 'You're burning up with fever.'

I go to sleep and when I wake up I hear Blake's voice, raised, angry.

'Why didn't you call me?'

'It's not like she's dying. She's got the fucking flu. Everybody gets it.'

'I'm calling the doctor.'

'Who's stopping you?'

I feel Blake sitting on the bed beside me. He seems odd, distressed.

'I'm all right. It's just the flu.'

'The doctor will be here soon.'

The doctor confirms Billie's diagnosis. 'Flu, but,' he cautions, 'she does seem malnourished. Perhaps even anemic. I'd recommend a full check-up.'

Other doctors come and inject me with cocktails of vitamins, C, B complex. I must admit I feel better after these injections. I am spoon-fed tomato soup that Laura has sent. It doesn't taste anything like the canned Heinz tomato soup that I am used to. I make a face.

'It's just missing the MSG,' Blake comments dryly. He makes me finish it all.

I am then moved into my old room. The sheets have been changed. They feel cool against my skin. It is a relief to fall into soft blackness, but I sleep badly. Tossing and turning through the night. Sometimes I open my eyes and Blake is always there. Awake and working. He has brought a desk into my room. The fever breaks in the early morning hours. I sit in bed and eat a cup full of jelly. The jelly tastes funny. I complain and grumble.

'You are such a terrible patient. Get it all down. It is all good stuff. You're body is crying out for minerals and vitamins,' Blake scolds.

To my absolute horror I am put into a wheelchair the next day and wheeled down the corridor and into the lift. It stinks of urine and I see Blake's mouth settle into a hard line. He hates dirt, chaos, disorder, ugliness.

For a week I am invalid, but the expensive daily injections and cups of red, green and yellow jelly are useful, and soon I am almost myself. My appetite returns and I feel good again.

But I have lost five days of my 42.

Twenty-Two

I meet Blake for lunch in Maide Vale, in a restaurant that reflects the laid-back style of the area.

'Why are we meeting here?' I ask.

'Got something to show you,' he says.

'What?' I ask curiously. His eyes are twinkling, he laughs at my impatience.

'Why spoil the surprise?'

'OK.'

After lunch, Tom drives us to an apartment block in the middle of Little Venice. We get out and take the lift to the fifth floor. Blake fishes a key out of his pocket, and with a lopsided smile at my uncomprehending frown puts the key into the door and opens it. We step into an empty apartment. I am immediately drawn to the balcony. It has a wonderful view of all the waterways and canals that make up Little Venice. Pretty amazing.

'Do you like it?'

'Yeah,' I say carefully, not sure where this is going. And then suddenly it hits me. This is my kiss-off present at the end of our 42 days. I keep a bright smile on my face, hope it doesn't look too false, and turn around.

He has taken Sorab out of the pram and is coming towards me with him in his arms. 'He'll drool all over your suit,' I say, trying to appear normal.

'Come, I'll show you the rest,' he says. He seems almost excited. That kind of annoys me. I remember Jack saying, no man wants a woman for just 42 days. You'll end up as his mistress.

Silently, I follow him around the two-bedroom flat. The main bedroom is sunny and spacious, but my heart is breaking inside. He wants to stash me away here!

'Do you think Billie will like it?'

'Billie?' I ask, confused.

He nods. 'You know her taste, do you think she will like it?'

I frown. 'Why?'

'It's for her.'

'What?' I laugh. A crazy cackle.

'Well?'

I laugh again with relief. It is tumbling inside me like an upturned bowl of marbles. The sound a joy to behold. 'She'll love it.'

'That's settled then,' he says, in a satisfied tone. 'It is in your name, of course, since I know that she keeps...er...complicated financial arrangements with the Her Majesty's government, but whenever she becomes financially independent you can transfer it into her name.'

'Why are you doing this?'

'I don't want you visiting her on that horrible estate. Every time you tell me you are going there I almost break out in hives.'

I can't stop smiling.

'Obviously it needs a new bathroom and kitchen, but you girls can redecorate it in any way you want. Just liaise with Laura and she will open accounts wherever you want.'

I am so full of joy I am almost in tears. 'It is the most wonderful thing that anyone has ever done for Billie.'

He becomes suddenly brusque with embarrassment. 'Well, I have to get back to the office. Tom will drop you off wherever you want to go. See you at home this evening.'

I throw my arms around his neck. I feel so much love for him I am almost in tears. 'Thank you,' I whisper. 'Thank you so much.' I pull back and look deeply into his beautiful eyes. 'I really, really, really love you, you know. With all my heart.'

He bends his head and kisses me tenderly. Why won't he tell me he loves me? I know he loves me. Someone who is not in love could never do something this generous and delicious.

I go with him to the door. He stops. 'Who did you think the apartment was for?'

'Me.'

'You?' He seemed genuinely confused. 'Why would you think that?'

'I thought it was my kiss-off gift.'

He caresses my cheek with the back of his hand. 'You have no idea at all, have you? The papers are on the ledge over the fireplace,' he says, and then he is gone.

I stand in the balcony and watch him leave the building, cross the road and get into the back of a waiting dark blue Rolls-Royce with a silver hood. Then I call Billie.

'Billie, what are you doing right now?'

'Watching my nails dry.'

'Can you get a cab and come meet me in Maida Vale.'

'Why, what's in Maida Vale?'

'Do you want to spoil the surprise?'

'Why would I wanna do that?'

The bell rings in less than half an hour.

I open the door with a stupid grin on my face. I can't help it. I am so happy and excited for Billie.

'I've smeared my nail polish so this better be good,' she says, waving her ruined nails in front of my face.

'Sorry,' I say and she steps over the threshold. Just like me she goes immediately to the balcony.

'Wow, this is some view, isn't it? Whose place is it?'

'Yours.'

She turns around slowly. 'Sorry?'

'It's yours. Blake bought it for you.'

'For me?' She is frowning.

'Yup.'

Her eyes are narrowed. 'Why?'

'I think he hates Sorab's godmother to live on a council estate. He was kind of put off by the syringes and the smell in the stairwells.'

'What do you mean by *for me*? What happens when your 42 days are up?'

'You still get to keep it.'

She breaks into a mad grin. 'A flat right in the middle of classy Little Venice just for little ole me? Wow. You know what, if he hasn't been straight as a die in all his dealings with you from the moment he met you, I'd never believe it.'

'Well, it's in my name at the moment, but as soon as our business picks up and you stop being on the dole, I'll transfer it into your name.'

I hand her the papers.

She looks at them. 'Wow, who'd have thought?' She lifts her face to mine. There are tears in her eyes. She blinks them away proudly.

I smile at her. 'And you know what is even more exciting? Blake has agreed to pick up the decorating tab. You have carte blanche to decorate it in any way you want.'

'I just don't know what to say, Lana,' she says suddenly.

'Is it worth messing your nails for?' I tease.

'Can you put that child down for one moment,' she asks gruffly.

I put Sorab into his stroller and she envelops me in a bear hug. 'Thank you, Lana. I know you don't pray, so every day I get down on my knees and I pray that everything will work out for you,' she whispers in my ear.

I pull back. 'You do?'

She nods solemnly.

'Thank you,' I say, and smile. Grateful that she is my friend.

Twenty-Three

Day 17

He made me lie on the bathroom floor and gave me a hot coffee enema. Twice he administered it. It was uncomfortable. And twice I sat on the toilet until there was no more to void, and I felt strangely light and cleansed.

At the edge of the bed he pushed me back and holding onto my thighs he spread my legs wide and pinned them on either side of my head. My lower body rolled up to accommodate his needs. Now nothing was hidden from his eyes. Completely exposed to him, I looked into his hooded eyes,

He laid his palm on my open sex.

'You are very damp,' he said, and immediately after sank into my wet cunt.

He buried himself deeper still. I cried out, but he only said, 'You were made for me. This body was made to take me and only me. When I am finished with you there will be no part of your body that I will not have been in or on. Every fucking inch of you is mine and mine only.'

He pulled out of me and without taking his eyes off me smeared his thumb with lubricant.

'Now lie down on your face and present yourself to me.'

I turned over and lay down with my cheek flat on the mattress and my butt rounded and pushed up towards him.

'Spread your legs more for me.' I obeyed and he slowly inserted his thumb into the ring of clenched muscles.

'I own this,' he said, dipping it in and out. In and out.

Strange, but not painful. Pleasurable even. I knew what he was doing. He was stretching me. Touching the sensitive walls, pressing on vital nerve endings until my body began to move restlessly on the bed. Now he knew I was excited and ready.

He covered his erection with jelly and began to press it against me.

This time I cried out in protest. A sharp, unfamiliar pain. A frisson of panic in my lower belly. He is too big. I won't be able to take him.

'You have to relax,' he said. 'Let me in…Pain has possibilities, holds a different kind of pleasure.' His voice was low, seductive.

I wanted to take him in, but my muscles remained clenched, uncooperative. He could not have moved an inch further.

'You have to trust me, Lana,' he said and reaching under me began to stroke my clitoris. I began to tremble. Taking advantage of my distracted state, he pushed suddenly into me.

The pain was immediate and sharp, and I screamed out, but he had become motionless, to allow my body to absorb the foreign intrusion, the strange sensation of hot fullness. When he judged my body had come to accept him, he pushed all the way in.

I moaned restlessly.

There was still pain, but more than the pain was the pleasure of being taken by him. In that position that I should have considered debased and humiliating I found decadent pleasure.

He began to move inside me and I couldn't help the strange animal sounds that came out of me. Firmly gripped by my rectum and the foreignness of what we were doing he came fast, spilling his seed deep inside me, crying out my name. He buckled against me, but he did not pull out of me. Instead he reached over and began pleasuring my clit.

'Clench your muscles,' he said and I obeyed.

The unfamiliar sensations of pressure and pleasure coursed through my body. I climaxed, shaking and trembling, as quickly as he had. For some time he remained inside. When he pulled out of me I was sorry. I wanted him back inside me. He belongs inside me.

Every part of me cries for him when he leaves.

I put the pen down and close my journal. Nowadays, I write without resentment, eagerly, because it is the only real and honest communication I have with him. I feel him distant. Moving away from me. Something is bothering him. The days pass away in a haze of sex—it seems to me more like a desperate desire to physically meld with me, to forget for a while whatever is troubling him.

Once he woke up, drenched in sweat, shouting hoarsely, almost sobbing, 'Not her, please.'

When I touched him, he turned to me with wild eyes, and recognizing me, fell into the crook of my neck gratefully, and hugged me so tightly, I whimpered. But when I asked him about his nightmare, he whispered in my ear, 'Just don't ever leave me.'

As if I would ever leave him. As if it was me that set a limit of 42 days on our time together.

Twenty-Four

Billie calls. She wants me to drop Sorab off for the afternoon. She is lonely. She misses him. I leave Sorab with her and go to Sloane Square. I want to buy a pink shirt for Blake. It's a sort of joke. He thinks pink shirts are sissy, and I think they are a turn-on—only really macho men can carry them off. I find the shirt I want and I am about to return home when I suddenly stop in my tracks.

Rupert Lothian.

There are two men with him, business types in dark suits. He must have just had lunch with them. For a moment we are both so surprised neither of us speaks, but he is first to recover.

'What a lovely surprise,' he says smoothly, and lays a heavy, proprietary hand on my arm. And grasps it. I try to shake him off unobtrusively, but he tightens his hold. He turns to the two men and tells them he will call them later. They call out their goodbyes and leave together, and Rupert turns his attention to me.

'I was wondering, just the other day, what the devil happened to you. How've you been, gorgeous?'

'I'm fine, but I'm late and I really must be going. It was nice to see you again, though.'

'What's the rush? Come and have coffee with me,' he invites. His voice is genial and wheedling, but I still have the memory of his oyster-flavored saliva pouring down my throat, his finger digging into my crotch, seeking rough entry. If only I am big enough and strong enough to be able to say, 'Don't stop, don't look at me, don't touch me. Walk on by.' But I am not big enough and I remember the sheer male strength of his rugby player's hands as he pinned me against the wall and abused me.

'Perhaps some other time.' I take a step back, but he refuses to relinquish his hold on my hand. 'Are you still with him?'

'That's really none of your business.'

'As a matter of fact, I am looking for some business. Are you available? Same terms as before.'

I twist my arm and try to wrench it free, but his grip is like an iron clamp. The fury that I never expressed before rises like bile inside me. Without thinking I bring my other arm up and hit him, and instantly he lets go of my arm, and throws a punch in my direction. It should have hit me square in the face, but it only glances my chin. I stare in surprise as he lands on the ground. Flat on his back. Out cold. I look up dazed. A man is standing in front of me. I stare at him. The blood thrums in my ears.

'Are you all right?' he asks solicitously. He is looking at my chin.

'Yes, I think so.'

'Good. You best be on your way, then.'

'What about him?' I glance at Rupert, sprawled, unmoving. He could even be dead for all I know.

'Don't worry about him. I'll make sure he is all right.'

I nod, but the whole thing is surreal. The speed with which this man arrived on the scene and the swift, totally professional move that floored a huge man like Rupert. I look again at the man. He has sandy hair, a fit, wiry body and flinty eyes. Dressed in a black shirt, leather jacket and blue jeans, he could be anybody off the street, but I know he is not. He did not appear here by accident.

His kindness is a mirage. Pay him the right money and he will just as easily break my neck. I take a step away from him.

'Don't forget your shopping,' he reminds me politely.

I turn and look at the shopping bag lying on the sidewalk. The pink shirt is poking out. I pick it up and without a word, without thanking him, I walk away quickly. As if I am running away from the scene of a crime. Perhaps I am.

I walk for God knows how long, my mind in turmoil. I come upon crowded walkways where people brush past me, but I feel nothing. When it finally dawns on me, I come to a dead stop suddenly. A woman runs into me and swears inelegantly. She loses her anger when I turn around to apologize. She looks at my chin, mumbles something and walks on.

I walk towards the wall of a building and lean against it.

Finally, one more piece in the mad puzzle. That is why Blake suddenly turned up at the apartment when Jack came to visit. And why he appeared so unexpectedly, his behavior so odd and secretive that day when Victoria's mother made contact and he suddenly whisked me away to Venice to hide, to think, and to regroup. And that too is how he knew to smell my face the day I kissed Jack.

He has always had me followed. The whole fucking time.

I feel angry and confused. Why? Why would he spy on me? He is so full of secrets. So mysterious.

By the time I reach the apartment I feel lost and unbearably sad. My entire life is a messy lie. Being secretly followed and watched seems an extension of all the other lies that my relationship with Blake entails. I open the front door and Blake comes striding towards me. Of course. He already knows about Rupert. I stand at the door and stare at him. His hair is disheveled, his tie has been pulled loose and is hanging a few inches away from his throat. But it is his eyes that I cannot look away from. I have never seen his eyes so wild with fear.

He lays a gentle hand on my throbbing chin. I flinch slightly. Immediately, he retracts his hand,

and I swear I see tears swimming in his eyes. Then he pulls me into his arms and holds me tight. I hear him take a deep breath.

'I've been sick with fear. Where have you been all this time?' he asks in a hushed voice.

'I was walking.'

'Why did you switch your phone off?'

'I didn't. My battery was low. It must have died.'

'Oh God, Lana. Don't do that to me again.'

He takes a step away from me. 'He grabbed you. Did he hurt you anywhere else?'

I shake my head, but he pulls the sleeves of my coat and examines my arms. He touches the light bruises and looks at me. There is pain in his eyes. 'I have taken care of that bastard. He will never hurt another woman in his life again.'

I love you. I love you. I love you. I love you so much nothing else matters. But I don't say it. I can't. Something is very wrong. I cannot only think of myself. There is more than just me in this equation. There is Sorab. And I will love him the way my mother loved me. I will give him everything. And everything could mean no Blake EVER. Victoria's mother's words are still fresh. 'You and your son are in grave danger.' It would appear she was right.

I swallow the lump in my throat. I am in such pain I feel sick.

'What?' he asks worriedly.

'Nothing,' I say. But I actually feel dizzy. If he was not here, I would throw myself on the bed and howl—because I cannot have this man. I grit my teeth.

'Come,' he says and taking my hand leads me to the bedroom. His plan is simple. As Billie would say—he is a man, what can you expect? He wants me to sleep. When I wake up it will be all OK.

So I let him put me to bed. I watch him with blank eyes. I know he doesn't understand. And that he never will. Men are strong in a physical way, they don't know how to be strong in an emotional way. He thinks if I have no bruises I have no pain. I grasp his hand. 'Why did you have me followed?'

He runs his hand through his hair. He moves away from me. Paces the bedroom carpet like a caged creature. Then he sits beside me. 'Do you really want the truth, Lana?'

'Always.'

'Even if it makes a liar of you?'

'Even then.'

'Because I couldn't trust you with my son. Not in that horrible place you live in.'

My jaw drops.

'Jesus, Lana, what did you expect me to do? That place is crawling with drug addicts and low-lifes. I can't even bear it when you go there let alone a helpless thing like him.'

I gasp. 'You knew all along?'

'Oh, Lana, Lana, Lana. You must take me for such a fool. Did you really think I would not know he is mine? I knew from the moment I laid eyes on him.'

I am so shocked I can say nothing. Then I remember how silent he had suddenly become when he first looked at Sorab. And then he had blanked his eyes and casually asked me, 'Does he cry a lot?'

And that was the first day he had stayed the night. That was the first day he stopped drinking heavily and the first day he began to look at me without hate. It was the day he understood that I had left him not because I had been paid, but because I was pregnant. The next day his things had arrived and he had begun to live in the apartment with me.

'This elaborate charade…It was for you. For whatever you were playing at. I wanted to know what kind of woman you were. What kind of woman are you, Lana? You lie with me every night and you never think to tell me I have a son?'

I sit up. 'I was afraid.'

'Of what? Me?'

'I was afraid you or your family would take him away from me?'

'What are you talking about? I would never take him away from you.'

'It is in the confidentiality agreement I signed. If I have your child I will have to give it up.'

He sits on the bed and leans his forehead against his hand. 'This is all so fucked up.' He turns to face me. 'I'm sorry, Lana. I was so stupid.'

'What happens now?'

'Nothing. For now.'

A thought suddenly occurs to me. 'So you were having me followed because you are worried about Sorab's safety?'

He nods, but his eyes are careful, watchful.

'I didn't have Sorab with me today.' My voice is flat.

'You have your own detail. Do you think I would protect my son and not his mother?' His gaze is hard, uncompromising, refusing to be ashamed by his underhand methods.

'I don't like being watched. Call off my shadow?'

'After today? Are you kidding me?' He stands up and puts some distance between us. He turns to look at me. 'It's for your own protection, Lana.'

'Today was an exception. I don't need to be protected.'

'What's your real objection, Lana? It's not like it's in your face, is it? You didn't even know until today when Brian had to break his cover.'

'That doesn't make it better.'

His jaw clenches. 'I can't work. I can't concentrate. In fact, I think I actually go quite crazy when I don't know that you are all right. Can't you just humor me on this one thing?'

'Why are you so paranoid? Is there something that I should be fearful of?'

He comes to me. 'I have my reasons. You and Sorab are my first priority.'

I look at him stubbornly.

'Is it really so much to ask, Lana?'

'OK.'

He breathes a great sigh of relief. 'Thank you.'

I touch his hand.

'There was a time I used think Arab men were mad to keep their women covered and hidden. Now I know where the need comes from.' He jabs his finger into the hard wall of his stomach. 'In here.'

God, I love this man so much it hurts. It actually hurts.

Twenty-Five

I wake up in the cold, bluish light of dawn. For a moment I lie in the elaborately carved four poster bed confused by my surroundings, and then I remember. We are in Bedfordshire, at the Barrington's estate where Blake's sister lives. We arrived at the wrought iron electric gates in the dark, and ran up the curving stairs in the light from the moon. It was how I imagined young lovers of ancient times met, in secret and in the dark. We fell into bed and I ravished Blake after we had drunk a whole bottle of vintage champagne directly from the bottle.

I burrow into the delicious warmth of his body. He does not wake but puts a heavy hand on my stomach. I turn my head and smell the sheets. Starched sheets. My grandmother used to have starched sheets in her house.

Blake said I could explore the house and garden as long as I keep away from the west wing, where his sister lives.

And now I long to go into the extensive garden. I lift Blake's hand and edge out from under it. The morning air is surprisingly chilly. I dress quickly. There is a large extra blanket folded at the foot of the bed. I throw it over my shoulders and slip out of the room. The entire house is dim and silent. I walk down the corridor and stand at the top of the beautiful staircase. I am drawn to a painting.

A family at breakfast scene. Probably Victorian. I go closer to it. A man with rosy red cheeks is spooning egg into his mouth; some of it is dropping off his spoon. He is holding the egg cup very close to his chin. I realize that it is not a picture that is meant to depict the family as dignified or grand, but is a parody of unparalleled and uncouth greed. It is also ironically a celebration of greed.

My hands glide down the polished banisters.

I try to imagine Blake as a boy running in these spaces as I pass the music room with its priceless antique furniture, its rare objets d'art, and its tables of exotic orchids and feel a kind of lingering sadness. Nothing truly happy has happened in this house. Not even the children who ran through these rooms were happy. The entire house is crying out for the sound of laughter.

I pass another room where the heavy drapes are still shut and enveloped in the same sort of despairing gloom. Through that room I can see the main reception room. In the foyer, which looks like the inside of a snail, hangs a Salvadore Dali, blue black with naked ritual dancers. It looks almost like an orgy to me. I cross the black and white checked marble floor and go out of the front door.

Outside it is warmer than inside the house. The sun is filtering through the trees. The vista is as magnificent as that of any old stately house. I walk around the side of the building, admiring the lay of the land. There I come upon a massive, industrial-size greenhouse. Flowers, vegetables, herbs and fruit are plentiful. Some reach the ceiling. In the middle of it is a large hydroponic pond.

At the side of the glass structure, I meet a peacock. I have never seen a peacock before and I slowly inch closer. Suddenly it opens its tail and I am shocked by how beautiful it is. A pure white peacock comes to join it. I wish it would open its tail too, but it doesn't. Instinct makes me look up and I see Blake standing at the door leading to the stone balcony outside the room we slept in.

He is looking at me.

I wave to him. He does not wave back, but opens the door and walks out onto the balcony. Shirtless, he stands looking down at me. I gasp at the sight. The way the house frames him, draws him in as part of it. I feel the privilege of his background swirl around him like an unseen hand and grasp him in its invisible clutches. He belongs here in these splendid surroundings. In every way he is different from me. I imagine what he must see. A woman wrapped in a blanket. I am not regal or imposing. I am the outsider.

After a grand breakfast Blake takes me to meet his sister.

The reception room we wait for her in has been painted in soft pink. She is accompanied some a woman in a nurse's uniform and dressed in a long dress and blue sweater. A butterfly pin sits in her hair. Her eyes are as blue as Blake's, but otherwise she is nothing like him. Her brow is low and juts out and her skin is very pale.

'Hello, Bunny,' Blake says softly.

She drops her chin shyly and points at him.

'That's right. Your brother has come to see you. Isn't that nice of him?' the nurse says.

She nods vigorously.

'Would you like to show him your zoo?'

Again she nods and smiles.

'Perhaps you'd like to show him some of the tricks you have taught your animals to do.'

She beams with excitement.

Blake walks up to her. 'Will you show your animals to my friend too.'

For the first time her eyes come to rest on me. I smile. 'Hello,' I say.

She begins to rock her head and smile shyly.

'Come on then,' Blake says and holds his hand out to her.

She puts her pale hand into it, and we go outside towards a white marquee where there are seats all around it and a sandy enclosure in the middle. We take our seats and Elizabeth goes to the podium like structure at the entrance of the sandy enclosure.

She claps her hand and a horse runs in. It gallops around the enclosure a few times and comes to a stop a few feet in front of her. She raises her hand and the horse rises to its hind legs and paws the air. She drops her hand and the horse ambles towards her. From her pocket she produces a cube of sugar and holds her hand out. The animal accepts the treat delicately and she turns around to smile proudly at us.

'Well done,' congratulates Blake.

Elizabeth claps her hands with delight.

I am truly amazed. It is very impressive to see a woman with the mental capacity of a child successfully train animals to perform tricks and obey her. Afterwards we watch Elizabeth's Indian elephant sit on a stool and turn around in a circle on his hind legs, a cute dog dance on command, and her pet monkey ride a bicycle.

When the show is over Elizabeth grabs Blake's hand and starts pulling him out of the tent. Blake gestures with his other hand for me to follow them. She takes him to her bedroom, a pink room filled with dolls, children's books and a rocking horse specially made to accommodate an adult. Taking a hairbrush from her dressing table she puts it into his hand and like a child runs eagerly to the bed and sits sideways on the edge of it.

At first Blake looks surprised that she should remember a ritual from so many years ago, but then he goes and sits behind her. With gentle hands he takes the butterfly clip out of her hair, and begins to brush her luscious, dark hair with long, sure strokes.

The girl clutches at his shirt and sobs, when it is time for us to go. She becomes hysterical when the nurse and a servant try to pry her away and they have to sedate her. In the car Blake is very silent and lost in his own thoughts. The way she had clung so desperately to him had distressed me too.

'It's great how she trained all those animals, though, isn't it?' I say, in an attempt to take him away from his unhappy thoughts.

'She doesn't train them. An animal trainer works with them and everybody just pretends that she has trained them.'

'Oh! Whose idea was it to do that?'

'My mother's.'

The brevity of his answer tells me not to go there. As ever, any talk of his family makes him clam up. I turn my head and gaze at the countryside and think of the fraught child locked away in that sad house, and the woman who won't acknowledge her child's existence, but who will go to elaborate lengths to create a private circus, which her daughter can ringmaster.

Twenty-Six

It is a Monday night. Blake has already phoned to say he will be late. He has a meeting. I am in bed reading when he comes in. He stands for a moment at the doorway simply looking at me. He seems different. Not so held together.

'What's the matter?' I ask.

'Just admiring your beauty.' Even his voice is drowsy and very appealing. This Blake is like nothing I know. He begins to walk towards me. Sits on the bed beside me and his liquored breath hits me instantly. I suck in my breath.

He nods knowingly, sagely. 'That's right...Been drinking.'

And then underneath the smell of the liquor, perfume. Expensive. Crushed flowers, herbs, musk. I have smelt this before. More than a year ago. When he came back from his birthday party. The realization hits me like a fist in the belly. Victoria. I stop thinking. Pain and fury are rushing into my brain. I raise both my hands and push him. He is not expecting such a reaction and he falls backwards, awkwardly, to the floor. I hear the thud of his body hitting the floor.

'What the fuck?' he slurs.

I fly towards his prone body and with quick hands I unbutton his fly and pull the trousers down to his hips. I tear furiously at his underwear. I bend my head and smell his crotch. But the odor is familiar. His. I sit back on my heels and look at him. He has raised his head off the floor and is looking at me, astounded.

'What's good for the goose…You were with a woman. I smelt her perfume on you.'

He lets his head drop to the carpet and sighs heavily. 'Yeah, my mother.'

Shit. Of course his mother was at the birthday bash last year too. I scramble over his prone body, and peer into his face. 'Ooops…Sorry.'

'Why don't you finish what you started, Lana?'

'Yes, sir,' I reply, and start tugging his trousers off.

'Take your clothes off and sit on me, but face my feet. I want to see my dick disappearing into you, and your pretty butt hitting my groin.'

I slip my nightgown off and ease myself on the hard column.

'Ride me hard and fast,' he says and I slam myself onto him.

'Oh yes,' he groans.

He is drunk and it takes longer than usual for him to come. By the time he does I am sweating and exhausted. I haven't come, but all I want to do is lie down beside him on the floor. I slide off him and am about to fall sideways to the floor when he catches me.

'I want you to rub yourself on my thigh until you come, but this time face me so I can see you come.'

I sit on his thigh, our juices squelching under me. The hairs on his thigh tickle me, and feel strange on my open pussy. I begin to rub myself on him while he watches me with avid eyes. The spasm of release comes quickly to my exhausted body. I slump against his body, my breast crushed against his rib bones, my cheek pressed on his chest.

'How could a woman who has had a baby have such a tight pussy?' His voice is rambling, sleepy.

I grin to myself. 'The woman doctor who delivered Sorab said she always puts in a couple of extra stitches. "For your husband" she said.'

Blake chuckles. 'That should be made standard practice.'

I rest my chin on his chest. 'Why did you get drunk today?'

He sighs heavily. 'Because today I had to make a very, very difficult decision.'

I raise my head up onto my palm and look into his eyes. 'Involving your mother?'

He brings a finger to my lips. 'Shhh…'

I sigh and drop my head back down. All these secrets. Why can't he just trust me and tell me.

His voice is a whisper. 'It's a funny thing smell, isn't it? Do you know the thing I missed most after you left?'

'Sex?'

'Sex? I slept with hundreds of women.'

I feel searing pain at his words. 'In the beginning I had them all; brown, black, yellow, redhead, blonde, you name it. Got myself wasted and bedded them all. Then I began to be a little more discerning. They had to look like you, at the very least, from the back. If I drank enough and kept the lights dim, then I could fool myself that it was you, but the second I woke up, I knew: it was not you. They all—every single one of them—smelled of stale sex. No one had your smell. And I would practically run out of the door.'

His words, if they are meant to console or flatter me, have the opposite effect. I don't like the thought of all the women he has been with paraded before my eyes. Everything he has had with me he has had with others. There is nothing special just between us.

'Fuck my smell! Is there nothing we can do together that you have not done with anyone else?'

For a moment he simply looks at me as if pleading with me to recant. I don't. A bitter expression crosses his face. He sits up. Almost I can believe that he is no longer drunk, but stone cold sober.

'Get on the bed,' he says.

I obey immediately. This Blake reminds me too much of the old Blake. Far away and distant. Cold. A stranger. I am almost regretting my request. He gets up, goes to the drawer where all the sex toys that we never got around to using are kept, and pulls out a vibrator. This one is not big like the black and orange one that he humiliated me with. It is white, shaped like a missile, and of a modest size. He shrugs his shirt off.

'Lie down,' he says. His voice is clipped and quite scary. This is not my Blake. Yet, he is mine. This Blake lives inside the Blake that I know and I want this Blake too. This Blake is my opponent, but this Blake also holds secrets. Secrets that I want. I am not all light and he is not all dark. To be whole, to know him completely I only have to embrace his darkness and make it mine.

Do I have sufficient bravery?

Of course I do.

I will take my torch and go where love takes me.

He puts the vibrator on the bedside table close to him. Then he positions himself so his cock is over my mouth. And I note the most surprising thing of all. His cock is flaccid. This does not excite him in the least. He is doing this for me. Slowly, he lowers his dick into my mouth. I have never had it half-soft before and it is strange in my mouth. But it makes me determined.

I begin to suck so hard and so well and it grows quickly in my mouth to double its size. He takes the vibrator and inserts it into my slick vagina. He twists and turns it a few times inside the slippery walls, then removes it, and puts it into my hand. I take it, surprised. It is not switched on.

'Go on. Fuck me,' he orders.

But I am paralyzed. This is neither sexy nor erotic for me. I don't want to do it, and I can see in his eyes that this is unrelished territory for him. He takes my hand and, positioning it over his rectum, pushes my hand hard upwards. There is no real lubrication. Only the juices from my own sex. I see him jerk and wince with pain.

'Suck me and fuck me hard. Use both hands,' he commands, his voice clipped, foreign.

But I cannot. It is almost impossible for me to hurt him.

'Harder,' he growls, his eyes hard, unrecognizable. This time I obey. With both hands. As hard as I can. Only when I embrace his darkness… I see him straining with the pain and the undeniable dark pleasure. I know because I have already experienced it.

I suck so hard my lips and mouth start to hurt, but I know somehow this is very important. Once or twice he pushes so deep into my throat, I gag and choke. Finally, I see that he is near. He is coming. He starts to strain and clench. I increase my speed, and he is almost there. Always, at the point of climax he calls my name. This time he does not.

'Don't, Daddy,' he cries instead. His voice is high and strange, that of a frightened child.

I freeze, my mouth full of meat.

Twenty-Seven

So does he, but the climax is greater than us; his horror, his shame, his secrets, his pride or my shock. He buckles as hot seed shoots into my throat. I extract the vibrator out of him, and he pulls himself out of my mouth. He is moving away from me. But I catch his hand. He stops, still on his knees, and looks down on me. Hauteur in every line of his face.

'Blake?'

'What?'

'I'm sorry.'

'Don't be. You wanted something I have never done with any other woman. You have it.'

'No, I mean about your father.' I still remember our conversation a year ago when he refused to condemn pedophiles, saying God made them that way and it was up to God to condemn them. 'Your father sexually abused you, didn't he?'

'My father didn't do it for sexual gratification.'

I frown. 'What do you mean?'

''He did it to cement his control over me.'

'What?'

'He has made me the person I am today. He had to teach me discipline. Our ways are different from yours.'

My mouth hangs open. Is he on the same planet as me? Teach him discipline? Our ways are different? 'What the fuck are you talking about, Blake?'

'You won't understand.'

'Damn right, I don't. Your father raped and brutalized you when you were a child, and you think that is a form of discipline?'

'My education was...vigorous and difficult, very difficult. I would not wish it upon anyone else, but without it I would not be fit to implement the agenda?'

'What agenda?'

'Without our banking services illegal drug trafficking would stop in a heartbeat. Without our economic policies there would be no poverty or starvation. Without our money wars would never be fought. By necessity we have to be cold and callous.'

For a few seconds my mind goes blank. These people are monsters who deliberate train their children to be monsters too. 'Did your father discipline your two brothers too?'

'Not Quinn.'

'Why not Quinn?'

'Quinn was never meant to lead. Only Marcus and I will take over the helm of the empire.'

'Are you planning to do that to our son?'

'No. Never.' His eyes have become pained, but again, closed to me. The secrets are swimming on the surface. I cannot understand them. There is more. What the hell is he hiding?

I play my last card. 'Is your father Cronus?'

The change in him is so instant and so violent I can hardly believe my eyes. He crouches on all fours, like a cat, his face very close to mine, and his fingers flat against my mouth, but it is what is in his eyes that causes me to feel the first real frisson of crawling fear. They are desperately pleading with me as he shakes his head. I understand the silent plea. *Say no more.* I begin to tremble with real fear. What is it that is so terrible that it has put that expression into his eyes?

What dangerous secrets is my lover hiding?

I remember again when he said in Venice the walls are thin and might even have ears. He is still looking at me with that same expression of anxiety that I might decide not to obey his silent plea. When I nod slightly, he says coldly, callously, 'Meine Ehre heisst Treue.'

'What does that mean?'

'My honor is loyalty.'

And I know instantly that those words are not meant for me. The walls have ears. I frown. Trying to figure out what is going on. And then I grab my journal from the bedside table and scribble quickly on it.

Is this room bugged?

He shakes his head slowly and I understand that it is not an answer, but a reminder of his earlier plea. *Say no more.*

'I'm tired,' he says softly, 'and the worse for wear. Let's go to sleep.' He lifts his fingers off my lips.

'Yes, let's sleep. Things always look better in the morning,' I acquiesce, my voice shaky, barely a whisper.

He smiles at me. Gratitude. For what? Why? Then he kisses me on the mouth. 'Goodnight, my darling.'

'I love you,' I mouth silently.

He smiles sadly and covers our bodies with the duvet. I fall asleep with his body curved tightly around mine, but I sleep badly. Dreams, nightmares. All broken and disjointed. I am calling for him, but he has his face turned away towards strong winds and jagged rocks. Always I am frightened for him. It is never me in danger, but him.

I wake up when Blake suddenly jack-knifes into a sitting position. Dawn is breaking in the sky. 'I have to go to work,' he says.

'All right,' I feel very small and lost.

I stand at the door of the dressing room watching him get ready for work.

'Do you know that there are only ten days left?'

He eyes me in the mirror. 'Yes,' he says and carries on knotting his tie.

'Coffee machine should be ready by now. Want one?'

'Thank you,' he says with a smile.

As I am putting the saucer under his espresso, Blake comes into the kitchen. Even today with my heart so heavy he makes my heart skip a beat. He looks a little pale, but he is so male, so gorgeous. I can almost forget what happened last night. That thin child's voice, begging Daddy to stop. I watch the movement his throat makes as he drinks his coffee. It is amazing to think that inside this accomplished totally confident man lives a damaged child, right down to the eerie little voice. But today is also different from any other day for a different reason. He is changed. I can feel it. Not in the way he feels about me, but inside him. A steely determination. He finishes his coffee and comes to me.

'What will you do today?'

'I don't know. Probably just mess about.'

He nods distractedly. Already he is elsewhere. Taken there by the steely determination. He kisses me. Then he opens his mouth as if to say something, but shuts it. 'Do you trust me, Lana?'

The little question is loaded with meaning. 'Yes, I trust you.'

He smiles tenderly. Then he is gone.

The day stretches ahead interminably. He will be gone for so many hours. I feel restless and oddly… frightened. I sit at the computer and Google Cronus. Is there something I have missed? A god who ate his own children. Father time. Another name for Saturn. What am I missing? I start delving deeper down the Google pages. Conspiracy sites churning nonsense start turning up.

I give up and type in 'Blake Law Barrington early years'. Nothing. There is not a single photograph or piece of news about him. I try to imagine him as a child. A little older than Sorab and suddenly tears appear in my eyes. Poor little thing. I have never come across it. Where a child who has been abused by its parent grows up to be a man and protects his abuser in such a loyal fashion. As if what his father had done was right. Did his mother know? The thought sickens me.

I don't understand what I am mixed up in.

I spend the morning and most of the afternoon wandering aimlessly around the apartment. The truth is I am stuck in an uncomprehending daze. I am even tempted to attempt contact with Victoria's mother. But the memory of that shrill look in her eyes frightens me. As if she is teetering on the border of madness. It is as if she is trapped in her own hell.

At four o'clock I hear the front door open. Blake is early. I run out gratefully to greet him. I have so missed him. I come to an abrupt stop in the middle of the corridor. It is not Blake standing just inside the door looking at me, but his father.

Twenty-Eight

"The world is governed by very different personages from what is imagined by those who are not behind the scenes"

—Prime Minister Benjamin Disraeli of England, 1844

'Hello, Miss Bloom.'

'Hello,' I whisper.

'May I come in?'

'You are already in.'

His mouth twists haughtily. 'True.'

'Blake's not here.'

'I didn't come to see him.'

He passes me on the way to the living room, stops a few feet away, and prompts, 'Shall we?'

I follow. I am so furious with this man that my hands are white knuckled fists. I actually think I hate him. In fact, this is first human being I have met that I could feel all right about killing. This is the man who attacked a child and molded him into cold, money-making machine. But I know better than to order him out or to show my fury. I recognize that he is at the end of the maze I am lost in.

He stops in the middle of the living room. He does not sit and I do not offer him a seat. 'What do you want?'

'You have taken something very precious to me and I have come to ask you to give it back to me.'

I shake my head. 'I don't have anything of yours.'

'Don't play games with me, Miss Bloom. I haven't the time or inclination. I want you to leave my son.'

'What is it with you people? Don't you think Blake is old enough to decide who he wants to be with?'

'I've seen you. I've watched you beg my son to hurt you,' he says softly. But the venom in his calm words shocks me far more than if he had shouted at me. I take a step back. His cold eyes are unblinking. They watch me like a snake does its prey. He takes a step forward. 'This is the first time I have seen it. A woman begging a man to abuse her. I have to admit I enjoyed it even if my son didn't deliver. Next time you want to be hurt, ask me. I know exactly how to make you scream.'

I stare at him blankly. The walls not only have ears, they also have eyes, Blake. You didn't know that, did you? My mind scrambles for a way out of this nightmare. What has this man seen? He has witnessed me with my legs wide open, the black and orange dildo buried inside me. But I don't feel shame or humiliation. I feel fear. To beat down the fear, I simulate courage. I raise my chin to a fuck you stance.

'If you think your son shouldn't be with me, why don't you approach him directly?'

He looks at me strangely. As if I am a creature of very low intelligence that he is trying very hard to communicate with. 'Because I don't have to. I have what you want.'

'I'd rather die than take a penny from you.'

He smiles. 'I wouldn't insult you with money. You are far too subtle for that. Rather I am giving you another opportunity to be selfless and do something wonderful.'

I stare at him wordlessly as he weaves the net that he hopes to catch me with.

'I see a gloriously bright future for my son, but you are in the way. Your genetic imprint, your lack of education, your...your lack of social standing will eventually drag him down. What I am offering is a place in the countryside, near a good school, a beautiful home, a car, of course money, and introduction into better society than you have known.'

'I can't make that decision for Blake. He is old enough to choose what he wants.'

He holds up a hand. 'Let me finish. I know you are in love with my son. And believe me, that is something greatly in your favor. I know how difficult it must be for you, but the consequences if you do not leave him are enormous, incalculable...for Blake.'

'What do you mean?'

'If you don't leave him, I will destroy him.'

I laugh. A wild disbelieving laugh. 'You would destroy your own son just because he doesn't marry the woman you want him to.'

'What good is a son I have no use for?' he asks. His logic is so simple, so direct, so painfully sociopathic that I gasp.

'You wouldn't.'

'I would. I would destroy him in a heartbeat.'

'You can't.'

'Name me,' he says conversationally, 'a politician, a leader of a country, an important man in any sphere, and tomorrow I will turn him to nothing.'

'I'm not going to be responsible for destroying anyone so you can prove your power.'

'If you don't choose I will have to, and that will be a little less spectacular for you because then you can pretend that I had not the power to destroy, but only knowledge beforehand of something that was already in the pipeline. Choose anyone. Of course, I would prefer it if you did not pick prime ministers or presidents of countries. It is always expensive and time consuming to maneuver them into their positions of power—and they are all, other than one or two, being good little puppets at the moment, but if that is what it takes to convince you, then so be it. Or perhaps you would prefer a billionaire who particularly irritates you. Bill Gates? Warren Buffet?'

I shake my head. 'I'm not playing your game.'

'Fine, I will choose. The head of the IMF has been displaying a little less obedience than usual. I choose him. Tell me what kind of disgrace you would like to see come upon his unsuspecting head.'

'Nothing.'

'In that case let him be accused of rape. Not just any rape but the rape of a maid in a hotel room. Let her be of Asian descent. Thai would be too common. Would you be happy with Burmese?'

I say nothing. Simply stare at him.

'Now which newspaper do you choose to disgrace him?'

He is serious. He is actually going to ruin the career and life of an innocent man to make a point. I shake my head. 'I'm not going to be part of this.'

'What about the *Guardian*? Perhaps you'd like more than one newspaper to run the story? And a television channel? BBC? Or all of them?'

And suddenly my brain kicks in. He is bluffing. 'The BBC. I want the story to be run by the BBC,' I say. Surely he cannot have influence in the British Broadcasting Corporation!

But he smiles confidently. 'Done.'

I shouldn't have spoken. Now he knows he has me.

'When the story breaks tomorrow you will understand the extent of my reach. I will do the same to my son. Here are the pictures that will grace the world media if you refuse to be reasonable.'

I realize that he has been holding an envelope all this time. He takes two steps towards me and throws it on the coffee table and it slides towards across and stops in front of me. He is so close now I notice his eyes. Eyes are usually called the windows of the soul, but in his case the windows are closed, or there is no soul to look out of them. There is not even a pencil of light from the empty interior.

I grasp the envelope with unsteady fingers. Photographs of me. With my hair tousled, my lips parted, my legs wide open. The photographs are clear and graphic. I look at them. The photos of that night when I taunted Blake into hurting me are so horrible I cannot go on. They do not reflect what really happened. They look like rape of the worst kind. I do not need to get to the end. I put them carefully back into the envelope and slide them back along the table top. My face is not flaming with embarrassment; it is numb with shock.

'No, keep them for your album,' he says.

Like a puppet I pull them back towards me.

'There are videotapes too of you and…other women. I'm afraid my son was rather indiscriminate when you left him the last time. They will be released a few days later on the Internet as supporting evidence. My son will become a common criminal. A sexual predator.'

I need to think. I am blank. My foe is too great. 'What happens if I agree?'

'You get to choose a leafy English suburb or if you prefer even another country. Perhaps you'd like to live in the sun.' I shake my head. 'No, well you get to choose. Somewhere like Weybridge, perhaps?'

'What will happen to Blake?'

'Absolutely nothing. He will mourn for you…for a while, then he will marry Victoria and have a family, and life will be good again.'

'What if he comes looking for me?'

'He won't know where to look. You will be fitted with a totally new identity. You'll have to give up your friends, of course. But you will make new ones, better ones.'

'Why are you going to so much trouble to keep me away from him?'

Something flashes in his eyes. So quickly it is almost as if in my numbed state I have imagined it. But it makes my skin go cold. It is not as simple as he makes it out to be. There is more. Much more.

I clasp my freezing cold hands together. For a moment neither of us speaks.

'There is another thing you must consider. My father was a banker, I am a banker, and my son will be a banker. '

'What do you mean?'

'May I see my grandson?'

I understand immediately and the fear of before is nothing compared to this. Oh God! He is referring to what he did to his son. He is implying that that is what Blake will do to Sorab.

'Blake will never do that to his son.'

'It is our way. If you choose to live in our world, then you must abide by our rules.'

I don't want this man anywhere near my baby. 'He is asleep,' I push through frozen lips.

'I will not wake him up. Just a quick peek,' he says with a sick, lizard smile.

Outmaneuvered I begin to walk stiffly towards the door. He follows me into Sorab's room. Protectively, I stand next to the crib. He stops a foot away from the crib and nods as if satisfied. Of what I do not know and do not ask. He turns away and I follow him, weak with relief, to the front door.

'Look out for the newspapers tomorrow morning. I will be in touch later in the day.' He opens the door.

'Mr. Barrington?'

He turns slightly towards me. 'Yes?'

'Who is Cronus?'

He turns fully towards me, and smiles. At that moment the strangest thing happens. Into those dead eyes climbs something. The most inquisitive look that you ever saw, an interest more avidly probing than you could ever have thought possible in those leaden eyes. It is as if it is no longer even the same man. A cold claw grips my insides.

'When you do your little Internet searches find the shrouded one under the name of El,' he says and opening the door exits the apartment.

Twenty-Nine

I do not walk, I run to my laptop to type El into Google's search engine.

El, I learn, is a deity dating back to Phoenician times. He is meant to be the father of mankind and all creatures. He is the gray-bearded ancient one, full of wisdom. The bull is symbolic to him. El is distinguished from all the other gods as being the supreme god, or, in a monotheistic sense, 'God'.

Through the ages he is listed at the head of many pantheons. He is the Father God among the Canaanites. In Hebrew text El becomes a generic name for any god, including Baal, Moloch, and Yahweh. Finally late in the text I come across the reference to Cronus.

Apparently it was the custom of the ancients during great crisis for the ruler of a city or nation to avert common ruin by sacrificing the most beloved of their children to the avenging demons; and those who are thus given up are sacrificed with mystic rites, arrayed in royal apparel and sacrificed on an altar. Those that follow this path are called the sons of El.

El the articles points out is the root word for elite.

I type in El and Cronus and learn that el cronus is a sex toy for men.

I type in Saturn and El and I find out that El is another name for Saturn. And Saturn is interchangeable with Cronus.

I sit back. To avert common ruin these men give the most beloved of their children as a sacrifice to their great god El. Did it mean what I thought it meant? That Blake's father would willingly sacrifice his son in exchange for more power?

I hear someone at the door and quickly click out of the pages I am on. I go to the door warily, but it is only Blake.

'Hi,' he says. He looks normal.

'Hi.'

'Everything all right?'

'Great.'

I walk up to him and kiss him. His kiss belies his casual attitude. It is the kiss of a man who is drinking sweet water from a fountain before a long journey into the desert. My hands entwine in his hair. I want the kiss to go on and on but my brain will not allow me to. Now that I have proof that walls have eyes and ears I cannot be myself. I withdraw my tongue slowly, work my hands down to his chest and give him a slight push.

He looks down at me, his eyes darkened and wild.

'Can we go out for dinner tonight?' I ask, forcing a smile.

'Sure. Where would you like to go?'

'That Indian place you took me to last year. I forget its name. The one named after the thieves' market.'

'Ah, Chor Bizzare.'

'That's the one.'

'We'll drop Sorab off at Billie's.'

'Shall we call Mrs. Dooley instead?'

'No,' I snap, and then quickly smile to take away the sting. 'Billie was just complaining that she never gets to see Sorab anymore.'

'OK.'

'Hey, I've always been curious. When you get your reports from your spies what do they tell you?'

'Just a list of your movements.'

'Have you received your report for today?'

'Yes, as I was on my way home.'

'What did it say?'

'Why?'

'Just want to know how it works.'

'OK. Today you stayed indoors until 3:50pm when you took Sorab out in the pram to the coffee shop around the corner. You had a cake and coffee and were back by 5:00 pm.'

I try hard to keep my face neutral. I never left the house!

Then it hits me. A look-alike lures the spy away and the father enters the building and comes to see me. When the father leaves the look-alive re-enters the building. Now I know. Now I know. Blake cannot protect me, or himself, from his father.

His father has outsmarted him.

Thirty

"We are the tools and vassals of rich men behind the scenes. We are the jumping jacks, they pull the strings and we dance. Our talents, our possibilities and our lives are all the property of other men. We are intellectual prostitutes."

—John Swinton, Head of Editorial
Staff, New York Times,
at a banquet thrown in his honour, 1880

Blake's father is true to his evil. *The Independent* and the *Guardian* are the first to report that the CEO of the International Monetary Fund, Sebastian Straus Khan, has been implicated in a scandal. A Burmese maid working at a hotel in New York has accused him of rape. He has been apprehended at the airport. The BBC runs the story at lunchtime. By evening every TV channel is running the story. There appears to be no investigation. Simply a story that is repeated almost word for word by all the different news feeds. Each one gleefully convinced of his crime.

That night when Blake comes home, I have painted my face and dressed in the sexiest outfit Fleur sent. The tight pink leather pants that Billie said, made my bum look all trapped and ripe and in need of rescuing, and a little top that leaves my shoulders and back bare.

His eyes light up. 'Wow, what's the occasion?' he breathes against my ear.

'We're not spending the night here,' I tell him. 'I've booked us into The Ritz.'

He smiles slowly. He has no idea. Inside I am dying. It is our last night together, a night I will never forget. We have dinner, I taste nothing, and then we go upstairs. There is champagne waiting in a silver bucket. I did not order it. Compliments of the house. I don't drink. I don't want anything to be fuzzy. I want to remember every last detail.

That night I am insatiable.

Again and again we make love until he says to me, 'Go to sleep, Lana, I don't want you falling ill on me again.' Even then I reach down and take his big, beautiful penis in my mouth and mumble, 'Use me for your pleasure. You have paid for this.'

And he looks deep into my eyes and says, 'Consider the debt paid in full.' The irony stabs me in the heart. He has no idea.

When morning arrives, I pull him close and whisper, 'I love you. I'll always love you.'

And when he is leaving, he says, his voice husky with emotion, 'I'll miss you terribly until I see you again…tonight.'

And I almost break down. He will never see me again. Tears blur my eyes.

'Hey,' he calls very softly. 'Nothing can keep us apart.'

A sob breaks through. He does not understand.

When he is dressed and leaving, I hold on tight. He looks at me with strong, sure eyes. 'Nothing can keep us apart,' he says again. And then the door closes behind him and I sink to the ground. I cry as if I will break apart. When I am all cried out on the floor of The Ritz hotel, I rise numb, but ready. This is for him and Sorab. This will keep them both safe. I get into the lift, between my legs sore and the tips of my breasts singing from being sucked and bitten all night. Tom is waiting in the lobby for me. My thick coat is folded over his arm.

'Mr. Barrington had me get this from the apartment for you. It's a cold morning.'

Again I am struck by how carefully and thoroughly Blake's mind works. Always he is one step ahead. Except for the most important thing of all. I take off my light coat and get into the coat Tom has brought for me. I turn my head and notice a man looking at me. Our eyes meet. He does not drop his. I look away. The world has changed for me. A few months back I would have assumed that he found me attractive; now I am not certain if he has not been paid to watch me.

Outside an icy wind hits me. I am glad for the coat.

In the car I stare out of the window. I am actually in a state of shock. The thought of leaving Blake is so painful I refuse to think about it. It is almost as if I am on autopilot. There is an accident ahead and Tom takes the longer route through South Kensington. We pass an old church. The door is ajar and I jerk forward.

'Stop the car, Tom.'

Tom brings the car to a stop by the side of the road.

'I'm just going into that church.'

Tom looks at me worriedly. 'I can't park here.'

'I won't be long,' I say, and quickly slip out of the car. I go through the Gothic wooden doors, and it is as if I have stepped into another dimension. It is cool and hushed, the sound of the street outside strained out. The stonework is beautiful. I see the holy water, but I do not cross myself with it as my mother used to. I follow the gleam of candles into the belly of the church. There is no one else there. My footsteps echo in the soaring space. I go to the front of the church and sit on a wooden pew.

I close my eyes. I don't know why I came here. I don't believe in God. God has done nothing for me. All he has ever done is take and take and take every fucking thing I've ever had. I feel so incredibly sad and defeated I wish I did not have to leave this quiet sanctuary. Hot tears are pricking the backs of my eyes. Life is so unfair.

Suddenly there is a gust of cold air. I open my eyes and look around. There is no one there. A draft? And then I have the strange sensation that my mother is there with me. I stand.

'Mum?' I call out.

My voice sounds strange and loud in that empty space.

'Mum,' I call out again, this time more desperately.

Nothing. I sit down again and close my eyes and presently the sensation returns that my mother is with me. The sensation soothes me. 'I love you, Mum,' I whisper. 'You left me too quickly. I never even had a chance to say goodbye.'

A feeling of peace settles on me. There are no words to describe the sensation. A timeless moment and I don't know how long I sit there. It is only the sound of footsteps that rouses me. I look behind me. Tom is standing by one of the pillars at the entrance. I stand up and go to him.

We walk silently to the car. There is a yellow parking ticket stuck to the windshield.

'Sorry,' I say.

'Laura will take care of it. My instructions are clear.'

We get into the car and Tom drives me to Billie's.

'Can we take a small walk down by the canal?' I say to her.

'What's wrong?'

I put a finger on my lips. 'I just fancy a walk.'

'All right,' she says, frowning.

'It's cold outside. Wear your coat.'

She takes her coat and follows me. When we are in the bracing air I tell her everything. Sometimes she will come to a sudden stop and stare at me mouth agape, and then I will take her arm into the crook of mine and we will continue on our path. I have never seen Billie look so white or totally robbed of her trademark wisecracks. It serves to highlight just how shocked I must be to be able to act so normally.

After the walk I kiss Billie's stunned face goodbye, and she pulls me hard against her body as if she could pass me some of her strength. Both of us know exactly how to contact each other. She is blinking back the tears.

'Be safe,' she calls as I push Sorab away from her.

Then I go home to await my next instructions.

When the call comes I leave my cellphone on the dining table and push the pram out to the front. I wave to Mr. Nair and he looks at me with confusion. I know that only a few minutes ago he must have seen my look-alike push an identical pram out of the door, perhaps to the coffee shop where she will have cake and coffee. Just outside the front door a car is waiting for me. A man jumps out of the front seat. I take Sorab out of his pram.

He holds open the back door while I slip into it. When I am settled in, he closes it with a gentle click. He folds the pram quickly, stores it in the boot, and gets into the front seat. Not a word has been exchanged by any of us. The car pulls away.

I think of my lookalike. She must have reached the patisserie by now. She has probably finished with her slice of cake. I imagine she must be an actress. Paid to play a part and then disappear. She will probably push her pram back into the building. Perhaps Blake's father has another flat where she can drop off the pram and effect a change of clothing. A hat, a scarf, a wig, before she exits the building forever.

And Blake, my poor darling love, will come home to his empty nest.

Thirty-One

We travel for many hours, stopping only at rest stops. Finally we arrive at a farmhouse in the moors. Here the countryside is wild and deserted. A strong wind is blowing as I get out of the car.

'Where are we?' I ask.

But the men simply smile politely. 'They will tell you when the time comes.'

Inside it is warm. A fire is already roaring in the fireplace. From the kitchen come delicious smells of roasting meat. I am shown to my room upstairs. It is pleasant enough, with blue patterned wallpaper and a double bed with a thick mattress. There is a crib in it too. As instructed I brought no clothes for Sorab or me. The man tells me everything I need is in the drawers and cupboards. I can already see the exact same brand of formula that I use for Sorab on the dresser.

He leaves and I go to stand by the window. The moors seem to stretch into the horizon. Not a single dwelling in sight. Fear gnaws at me. Why am I here? I know Blake's father said this is to be my temporary home until everything is arranged, but something feels very wrong.

Another voice in my head frets, *you didn't keep your promise to Blake.* But I had no choice. I protected Blake with my own body. I walk away from the window and lie down on the bed, curling my body around Sorab's sleeping one. I close my eyes and pretend I am in my bed in St. John's Wood until there is a knock on the door.

'Dinner is ready,' someone informs.

I wash my hands and freshen up before going downstairs. I put Sorab in the playpen and one of the men puts a plate of food on the table and withdraws from the room. I hear him open the front door and go outside. I eat alone. The food is wholesome and steaming hot, and I finish it all. Something tells me I am going to need all my strength.

I fall asleep while I watch TV in my room.

I am awakened by a hand over my mouth. My eyes jerk open. A man's voice urgently whispers, 'Please don't make any noise.' A small torch is switched on. 'Blake sent us,' and he dangles over my eyes, in the light of the torch, the ruby and black diamond necklace that Blake put around my neck in Venice. I gaze at it as if hypnotized, but in fact I do not need the necklace. I recognize the man. Brian, the one who felled Rupert.

'Can I take my hand off now?'

I nod.

'Take nothing. Just pick up your baby and keep him as quiet as you can,' he instructs.

Carefully I lift Sorab out of his crib and lay him across my chest. He makes a small sound, but does not wake up. We go down the stairs. The house is dark and silent. As we round the corner of the dining room, I see an inert shoe and quickly look away. I knew I had made a mistake from the moment I got into the car with those men. Now I know I am on the right path. Come what may. We get into the car and the car pulls away. I don't look back. I look down on Sorab's sleeping face and will him not to wake up, buy the noise of the helicopter blades wake him up. He screams his head off and does not stop until we touch down on a helipad in a totally different part of England.

Thirty-Two

'Put your hand out for her to smell you,' says Brian.

The German shepherd looks at me warily. There is not an ounce of friendliness in her. This is the dog version of Mr. Barrington Senior.

I put my hand out.

'Guard,' Brian orders. The dog sniffs my hand and goes back into his sit position.

'Now, hold out your son's hand.'

I hesitate. Sorab's hands are so small and there is something about the dog that I don't quite trust. It has been trained to kill on command.

Brian turns to one of the other men and says, 'Give me your shoe.'

The man takes his shoe off and holds it out to Brian. He lets all four dogs sniff it. 'Guard,' he says, and throws the shoe into the air. It falls about thirty feet away. All four dogs run towards the shoe and form a circle around it, their backs to it.

'Go get your shoe back,' he tells the man.

The man begins walking towards his shoe. Five feet away from his shoe, the dogs growl viciously and bare their teeth. Their bodies are crouched, ready to pounce in attack. The man stops in his tracks.

'At ease,' Brian says, and in unison the dogs leave the shoe that they had been guarding so ferociously and trot back to him. He praises them then gives them treats.

'Let them smell the boy.'

I bend down and hold Sorab's hand out in front of their black faces. One by one they sniff his hand and go and sit by their master.

'Guard,' their master says. Immediately their ears stand to attention. Brian disappears and the dogs stay with Sorab and me as we catch the last of the day's sun. As soon as we go through the front door, the dogs stop following us and begin patrolling the grounds.

It has been two days that we are living in this house. It is surrounded by high walls, a massive manned gate, and teams of dogs that patrol the grounds incessantly. There are CCTV cameras every few yards and security staff watching their screens twenty-four hours a day.

I wonder where Blake is and why he has not come for me, but I feel no fear. I know Sorab and I are safe here. I think about Billie. There is no way to contact her either. There is no Internet or a phone line. That evening I dine alone and go to bed early. I feel lonely but I am not bored. I know that somewhere out there Blake is executing the plans that I have seen so many times in his eyes.

It is 2:00 am when I feel the mattress depress next to me.

'Blake?'

'Who else did you expect?'

Thirty-Three

I lunge into his arms with a yelp of pure joy and rain kisses on him; his lips, his cheeks, his eyelids, his hands. 'I'm sorry, I'm so sorry I ran away. I thought I was doing the right thing.'

'It's all right. I knew you would. Once you sold yourself for your mother. I knew you would do the same for me.'

I cannot hold back the tears. He did understand. I had no choice. I had to break my promise to him.

'I love you, Lana Bloom, I love you more than life itself.'

'Oh, darling. I've waited so long to hear you say that.'

'I've loved you for a very long time. I thought you'd know. My every action screamed it. Even when I thought you left, I couldn't forget you. We have this unbreakable connection. No matter what you do, I still long for you. I always have and I always will. Could you not tell?'

'Maybe, but I couldn't be sure. Why couldn't you tell me?'

'Because I wanted my father to think the relationship was temporary. It gave me time to lay down my plans.'

'If you had told me I wouldn't have told anyone, anyway.'

'And take the risk that you would blurt it out accidentally in a conversation with Billie or Jack? No, the stakes were too high. It involved you.'

'Will you tell me everything now?'

For a moment he hesitates.

'Please.'

He nods and switches on the bedside lamp, and suddenly I see how worn he looks. There is also a look in his eyes that I wish wasn't there. It is the look of a man who has had to tell the vet to end his beloved dog's suffering. I lay my palm on his cheek. 'Are you OK?'

'Yes. I was always safe. You were the one in danger.'

'As you can see, I am just fine.'

He takes a deep breath, his chest collapsing. 'Oh, God, the thought that you might not have been.'

'How did you know where to send Brian?'

'Our apartment was bugged, not only by my father, but by me too. I knew he had been around and what he had told you.'

'So you knew when we were at The Ritz that I was leaving you the next day.'

He nods.

'Why didn't you try to stop me?'

'The only thing I had on my side was the element of surprise.'

'Where is your father now?'

His eyes harden. 'As of fifteen minutes ago, the victim of a plane crash.'

'You killed him,' I gasp, utterly horrified.

'Yes,' he admits flatly.

'Why?' My voice is no more than a whisper.

'Because he wanted to terminate the thing I love most in the world. And what my father wants, my father gets.'

'You killed your father for me?' My voice is incredulous, disbelieving. The words I waited so long to hear, tainted.

'The real test of love is not being willing to kill for someone, but being able to give up your own life for them. I think I proved my love for you more than a year ago.'

'Oh no, what have you done?' I close my eyes in horror. 'He wasn't going to kill me. He just wanted me out of your life. He was only going to set me up with a new identity.'

'My little innocent. How little you know us. It is cheaper and far less troublesome to kill someone of little value than to give them a new identity and support them for life.'

I shake my head. I am in a state of shock. Blake killed his own father. I can't take it in. Everything is screwed up. 'Will you have to go to prison?'

He smiles sadly. 'How many billionaires do you know languishing in prison cells?'

'So you killed him,' I say again. As if repeating it will somehow make it go away.

'And would again.'

'Why did he hate me so much?'

'He didn't hate you, Lana. You were simply in his way. He wanted Sorab.'

Thirty-Four

I wear this crown of thorns
Upon my liar's chair
Full of broken thoughts
I cannot repair.
—Hurt, Johnny Cash's Version
http://www.youtube.com/watch?v=SmVAWKfJ4Go

'Sorab?' I gasp, utterly, utterly confused.

'You were looking for Cronus. Did you find him?' he asks sadly.

'Your father told me I should be looking for El.'

'And did you?'

I shake my head. I can't remember the details. All my thoughts are scattered and ruffled. 'Only briefly. There was not enough time. It used to be the name of the highest god before it became a generic name for God.'

'Mmnnn.' But he is not really listening. He turns away from me, and rests his forehead on the heel of his palm. 'Remember when my father told you, his father was a banker, he is a banker, and his son will be a banker. Well, here is something he didn't tell you. My father has a dead brother, I have a dead brother and Sorab's brother would have had a dead brother too.'

I feel the blood drain away from my face. I grasp his arm and turn him to face me. 'What are you telling me?'

His eyes. His eyes. I become terrified. Not of him, but for him.

'What did your Wikipedia tell you was the demand of the highest god?'

My fingers are icy. 'Sacrifice of the first-born.' My eyes narrow. 'Are you trying to tell me that your family are Satanists?'

'No, that is for the rough and the crude. A show. We are the sons of El.'

I shrink from him, feeling like one of those boys who dive for pearls, get entangled in seaweed, and run out of breath. 'Wait, just wait for one moment. I can't take any of this in. I'm sorry I just can't. It's making me feel sick.' And it is too. I feel my stomach heave even though there is nothing in it.

'We count on people to be incredulous, to turn away because it is too terrible to contemplate. It is our protection. Do you still want the truth, Lana? Do you want to know what a monster I am, or shall we go back to what we were? We can pretend I am your knight in shining armor. That you made the right choice when you accepted my offer over Rupert's. Your choice.'

I take a deep breath. The shock made me react in that way. I want the truth. The whole truth. No more lies. No more pretenses. If I kick hard enough I will reach the surface and the light.

'I want the truth, whatever it may be,' I tell him.

'People think that they are no different from us, that we are all playing for the same stakes. That by a process of aspiration and hard work, perhaps a lucky break they can become one of us. Nothing could be further from the truth.

'We are not merely different we are a different species entirely. We are willing to go further than anybody else. Our naked ambition is a cold vise-like clamp around our hearts that causes us to align ourselves to a horrific blackness. And the blackness craves power over others and maintains itself by sucking the innocent energies of others.'

My heart is thudding so hard in my chest I can hear its roar in my ears.

'A child goes missing every three minutes in the United Kingdom alone, and around the world millions disappear every year. They are never seen, heard of or found. What do you think happens to them?'

I am too stunned to reply.

'On some days of the year, but especially eight dates, tens of thousands of children are sacrificed, not just by the sons of El, obviously, but by the Satanist and other cults around the world. On the night of the autumn equinox, September 21, three days from today, Sorab would have been ritually murdered. Like my brother, his uncle, and his uncle before him.'

My hands are clasped like a prayer in front of my mouth.

'I had to stop it,' he says, his face gray.

'Why couldn't we have just run away? Why have his blood on our hands?'

'There is no place on earth where Sorab, or you, for that matter, would have been safe. Only with me at the helm of the agenda, can the forces be held back.'

'But I don't want you at the helm of such a sick and twisted religion,' I cry.

'There is no other way. It is not a club. We are chosen to rule. I was born into it and must die in it.' I shudder visibly. 'Please,' he continues, 'don't grieve for me. I am reconciled to the knowledge that it shall be for me…a hell for all eternity. It is only important now that Sorab and any other children I father are not initiated. They will be free as my brother Quinn is.'

My skull aches. 'Is Marcus involved in…your father's death?'

'No. I acted alone. To protect what is mine.'

A desperate sob escapes me. 'Why can't we run away and let Marcus take over? He's older than you.'

'Marcus is not strong. My father always knew that. It was always going to me. At the helm of this empire of dirt.'

'Why can't you expose them? Tell the whole world the truth.'

'Who would I tell, Lana? Over the years hundreds of children who have escaped have told the same story, with the same details of underground chambers, hooded figures, orgies, and sacrificial murders, and they have all been dismissed as unreliable fantasists. Not a single figure of real prominence has ever been brought to justice.'

'But you are Barrington. You are powerful. You have inside information. You know people. You are not an unreliable witness.'

'The other families would immediately close ranks. What my father claimed he would do to me will be done. I will be destroyed and you and Sorab will disappear without a trace.'

I am frightened to ask my next question, my throat feels raw. I swallow. 'Do you also participate in these…rituals?'

'No, the rituals are not for us. We float above them. They are for the compromised and those who enjoy such perversions. I do not.'

'Can you not stop the agenda from the inside out?'

'Can *you* stop Monday from rolling into Tuesday? No one can stop the agenda, Lana. It will come to pass no matter what I do.'

Thirty-Five

I fell into a burning ring of fire
I went down, down, down as the flames went higher
And it burns, burns, burns,
The ring of fire, the ring of fire.
—*The Ring of Fire*, Johnny Cash

That night we do not make love.

We huddle together like the shell-shocked survivors in the embers of a horrific battlefield. All around us are the dead and the terrible cries and wails of the dying. His hands cling to mine.

His voice is a whisper in my hair. 'I know I should push you away, but I can't. Until you came I lived a joyless life. It will be up to you to leave me.'

Finally, I understand why the choice to stay will be mine.

It is only in the early morning hours that his hands stop clinging, relax, and fall away in exhausted sleep, but sleep never comes for me. I lie on my side, his warm body curled around me and I think of

Victoria's mother. That shrill look in her eyes that had so frightened me. She was right. It was already too late for me by the time she came to see me.

When the first light filters through the gap in the curtains I watch him sleep, his face relaxed and vulnerable, and I shiver not with desire, but with the memory of my desire for this man, for this body. It seems another lifetime ago. I think of what he has done for Sorab and I, and I am filled with sorrow at the thought of the secrets and sins that he carries in his soul. I understand that he is as trapped as I was when I slipped into a sluttish orange dress and went to sell my body to the highest bidder.

Billie, Jack, and probably even you…you thought it was too much to sacrifice for such a small percentage of success, didn't you? But I didn't. I would have done anything for my mother. Would I kill for her? If someone climbed into her bedroom and threatened her survival, yes, in a heart beat. Blake and I are worlds apart and yet we are cut from the same cloth.

I get dressed quietly and put my son into his carrycot. He smiles at me. I look into his clear blue eyes and feel like sobbing. How lucky he is. He is pure. He has done nothing wrong, yet.

I go downstairs.

Brian is sitting at the kitchen table watching TV. It is running the news of Blake's father's plane crash. When he sees me at the doorway, he switches off the telly and stands up. In his eyes something has changed. A new respect. It is in recognition of my association with the new head of the Barrington empire.

'Good morning, Ma'am.'

Ma'am? Even that's new. 'Good morning, Brian. Is there a church nearby?'

'Sure, but it won't be open yet. Bit early.'

'Can we try it, anyway?'

'Of course. Would you like to go now?'

'Yes.'

'I'll let Steve know.'

Outside Tom is carefully polishing the Bentley.

'Good morning, Miss. Bloom,' he calls.

I wave.

Brian drives me to the church, and as luck would have it, a man is locking the great doors. I run up to him, carrycot in hand.

'Oh please, please. Can I go in and say a quick prayer?'

He looks at me, glances at the child. Behind his gold-rimmed glasses his eyes are kind, innocent, unaware that I have been touched by sin. Would he believe me if I told about the secret world of the children of El? What they do for power and domination? Even to me, in the cold light of day, it all seems like a fantastical nightmare or a particularly bad film script.

He smiles kindly, and opens the door.

'Thank you. Thank you very much.'

'I'll be outside. Go with God, my child.'

Inside it is very quiet. First, I consecrate myself with holy water, then I walk down the old church.

Light is filtering in through the stained glass, a magnificent aspect in the still gloom of grey stone. It streams onto a massive icon of the dying Christ as he hangs sorrowing above the altar. Above the smell of flowers and ferns.

I stand in silent awe in the middle of the house of God. A lost sheep returning to its fold. Alone, I go to the side of the hall where there is a statue of Mary carrying baby Jesus in her arms. I open a wooden box and take out four candles. They cost a pound each, but I have no money with me. I will come back tomorrow and put the four pounds into their donation box. I light the candles and put them into their metal holders. One for Jack, one for Sorab and one for Blake and one for all the little children.

The flames cast their warm light into the shadows.

I remember my grandmother saying, Gods are not beings like people. It is only humans who have given them arms and legs and faces. They are metaphors for all the things human consciousness can aspire to. If there is a darkness called El, then there must be another metaphor to describe the consciousness of light and goodness. I will pray to that god, in every temple, mosque, synagogue and church that I find.

I fall to my knees, cross myself and pray.

'Dear God, take care of Jack while he is in wartorn Africa and bring him back to this kind land as soon as possible.'

I stand and put the carrycot with Sorab in it in front of the altar and return my knees to the cold stone floor.

'I give you my son to keep safe for always and... in return, I promise to do for the little children all that is in my power...until my last breath. I am not a cog in the machine. I am not a bloodline. I can make a difference. Nothing is set in stone. Not even the agenda.'

Then I bow my head and pray for Blake's tormented soul. With the unyielding, cold stone against my knees, I tell God, 'Dear God, this is my sincere and most fervent prayer, if Blake must burn in hell for eternity, then I must burn with him. For we are two souls that must never again be parted.'

"Some of the biggest men in the United States, in the field of commerce and manufacture, are afraid of somebody, are afraid of something. They know that there is a power somewhere so organized, so subtle, so watchful, so interlocked, so complete, so pervasive, that they had better not speak above their breath when they speak in condemnation of it."

Thomas Woodrow Wilson
28th President of the United States (1913 to 1921)

The Billionaire Banker Series

GEORGIA LE CARRE

Besotted

Book Three

The way to make money is to buy when
blood is running in the street.
John D. Rockefeller

Blake Law Barrington

April, 2014

The knock on the Lanesborough Suite's door is firm and unhesitant. I glance at my watch. Very punctual. I like that. I open the door and... My, my, she is a beauty: waist-length, straight blonde hair, gorgeous big eyes. And scarlet lips. Lana almost never colors her lips so red. A pity. She is wearing a long, white coat belted at the waist and really, really high heels. They remind me of the shoes Lana wore the first night I met her.

She is chewing gum, though. I hate that. She must watch too many movies about big-hearted hookers. I put my hand out, palm outstretched. For a moment she looks at me, clueless. I raise my eyebrows and she hurriedly takes the gum out of her mouth and drops it into my hand. Then she raises her own eyebrows and cheekily stretches her hand out.

'Don't you want to come in first?' I ask, amused but not showing it.

'Of course,' she says and walks past me. Her accent is odd. She must be making it up as she goes along.

I close the door and watch her walk ahead of me. She has a good walk. I like a woman who can walk with grace. She stops in front of the low table where there is a platter of fresh fruit and a bottle of champagne cooling in an ice bucket, and turns around to face me. For a moment I am distracted by the picture she makes standing in the agreeably English decor of traditional prints and chintzes teamed with bold choices of acid greens and Schiaparelli pinks. I put the gum on the sideboard.

'I'm sorry, what's your name?'

'Rumor.'

I smile. The name suits her. She looks like a rumor. Couldn't possibly be true.

'Would you like a glass of champagne?'

She lifts one foot and lets it swing back. It is impossibly erotic. 'I'd like to be paid first.'

I don't react to the provocation. 'The money is by the lamp.'

She glances at the neat pile of money as she works the two buttons on her coat. The coat lands on the sofa behind her. She is wearing a very short white dress. Wordlessly, she turns away from me and bends from the waist, so her ass is pushed out and her skirt rides up to where her smooth thighs indent and I glimpse the other thing I had specified—a freshly waxed pussy. The lips are already swollen and reddened, and as I watch moisture starts to gather.

Immediately I am hard as hell.

Slowly, holding that position, she counts the money. The desire to ram her while she is counting her money is strong, but I resist. She puts the last note on top of the pile she has counted, and turns to face me.

'All there?'

'Yeah,' she says slowly, her acquired accent undergoing another change. 'All there.'

I move towards her and put my hand between her legs. Obligingly, she parts them and my fingers start to play with the soaking flesh.

'So Rumor, what shall we do with you?'

'Mr. Barrington—'

'Blake,' I say persuasively, as I continue to explore the silky, wet folds.

She takes a steadying breath. 'Blake, we can do anything you want to do, so long as you remember anything kinky is extra.'

'What kind of kinky things are on offer?' I plunge my middle finger into her.

She gasps and sinks her teeth into her bottom lip. I watch with amusement.

'You're the customer. Tell me what kinky things you want and I'll do them.'

'Have you been on many callouts?'

'Not really. Just one other time.'

'Tell me—what did he do to you?'

'He fucked me really hard.'

'How hard?'

'So hard I was too sore to go to my next appointment.'

'Have you got another appointment after this?'

'No.'

'Good.'

She turns around, lifts the heavy curtain of golden hair and offers me her zip. I pull it down and she wriggles out of her dress. It falls on the pink carpet. I run my hand along the nude flesh. She shivers. I turn her around to face me. Her body is very beautiful and her pupils are so dilated that her irises are almost black. I lift her up—she is as light as a feather—and carry her into the lavish, blue bedroom. I lay her down gently on the king-sized, four-poster bed. I look down on her pale body. I have bought her. For the next hour she is mine to do anything I please with. The thought electrifies me.

'Open your legs,' I command.

Immediately she lifts her knees and lets them fall open so her swollen reddened sex is exposed to me. I have one hour to fuck, and that is exactly what I do. I fuck her until she is panting, her slim young body slipping against mine. Until she screams. She lies on her back, her eyes closed.

I cup her breast in the palm of my hand. It fits perfectly. 'That was great. Thanks.'

She sits up. I watch the curve her waist and hips make and I feel like pulling her down and having her all over again, but I have an appointment in less than thirty minutes. She goes into the bathroom.

'Don't wash,' I tell her.

She says nothing. Just nods.

I hear water running. By the time she comes out I am already fully dressed.

'I'll book you again next week,' I tell her.

'Sure. Arrange it with the agency.' She seems oddly shy.

'OK.'

'I need to use the toilet.'

By the time I come out she is fully dressed and waiting in the sitting room.

'Do you need a ride back? The hotel offers a complimentary chauffeur-driven Rolls-Royce.'

She shakes her head.

A thought. She is wearing nothing under the dress. 'Lift your dress.'

She doesn't appear surprised, just quietly parts her coat and lifts her dress, and exposes her sex to me. My seed is still leaking out of her. I walk up to her, gently cup her buttocks and drop to my knees. I look up at her. She is watching me curiously. Bending my head I lick her slit, puffy with engorged, glistening flesh. She moans. I could have her again if I wanted to. I pull her dress back down and walk her to the door.

'See you then,' she calls.

I close the door and go to stand at the triple-glazed, floor to ceiling window. It has a marvelous view of Wellington Arch. I look at my watch and I catch sight of the pile of money sitting on the low table. I pick it up and put it into my jacket pocket, then I take my mobile out, and call her.

'You forgot your money.'

She laughs. 'Give it to me tonight,' she says.

'You're spoiling my fantasy,' I tell her.

'Oh yeah?' Her voice is challenging, full of life.

'Yeah, but nice touch—the blonde wig.'

'Thought you might like a change.'

'I love you.'

'I love you too,' she says softly. I imagine her sitting in the back of the Bentley.

'Text me when you get home.'

'I will.'

She makes a kissing sound and then she is gone.

I look at my watch. Ten minutes left before my next appointment with the Crown Prince Muqrin Bin Abdel-Aziz of the House of Saud. I ring the twenty-hour butler service and ask them to summon housekeeping. The Head Butler, Daniel Jordan arrives in less than five minutes with three foreign-looking chambermaids in tow.

In two minutes they have put right the bed and bathroom and out of the door, smiling broadly, their tips snug inside their tight fists. Daniel discreetly removes the gum from the sideboard, and perfumes the air with attar of roses. Afterwards, he takes up his position in the dining room, which is actually my favorite part of this particular suite. Soon food arrives on trolleys and waiters start gathering in the kitchen. Laura calls—His Highness and his entourage are in the lobby and on their way up. The butler starts walking towards the door.

I shoot my cuffs.

October, 2013

We build our temples for tomorrow,
strong as we know how,
And we stand on top of the mountain,
free within ourselves.
—Langston Hughes

One

Lana Bloom

When I come back from the church, Blake is awake. He must have heard the car in the driveway. He is standing in the living room waiting for me. There are bluish shadows under his eyes, which make his eyes seem as if the entire sky has been boiled down and rendered in those two small points. He smiles faintly, like he does not quite know how to react to me, and my heart breaks for him. I remember reading George Orwell: *You wear a mask and your face grows to fit it.*

I go up to him and lay my cheek on his chest. He has had a shower and he smells clean and fresh. Like my idea of heaven. I feel him nuzzle my hair. It is like a prayer for which there are no words, and my love increases and ripens, the way fruit does in the autumn. He will never again have to pretend to be anything he is not. Or wear his mask with me. I think of Beauty dancing in the great ballroom with Beast. I am madly in love with Beast.

'I woke up and found you gone,' he said. His voice is different, softer.

'Did you think I'd run away?'

'You can never run away from me, Lana. I would journey into the underworld to find you. You are mine.'

'I went to church.'

'Yes, Brian said. I thought you didn't believe in God.'

I look up at him. He is heartbreak in a shallow basket. 'For short there is tall, for sad there is happy. For dark there must be light. I wanted to align myself with the God of goodness. I wanted to ask his help.'

'Oh, Lana. You and all the believers of this world. You pray and you pray and all your billions of unanswered prayers are like wailing cries somewhere. Your God doesn't exist.' His voice is so sad.

'How do you know?'

'Because if he did the world wouldn't be the way it is. And even if he does exist he is definitely not the lord of this world.'

I look up into his face. Already the weight of being the head of the Barrington dynasty is changing the shape of his face.

'Why do you say that?'

'Look around you, Lana. The entire planet—land, air and sea—has been poisoned by sheer greed, your food is toxic, you are governed by sociopaths who wage war after war with impunity while promising peace, and humanity itself is poised on the brink of extinction. Who do you think is in charge? Your God of love and light, or mine?'

There is a tap on the door. Blake closes his eyes and sighs. 'Maybe this conversation can wait till later,' he says. He looks so tired, so burdened, I wish I could take him away from all this.

I nod and move out of the circle of his arms.

'Come in,' he calls. And I see the transformation in him—the way the mask of power slips back into place—and lament it. Vulnerability has no place in the world of gaudy wealth.

By the time Brian opens the door and comes in the mask is firmly in place. The man who had nuzzled my hair has dissolved.

'Your brother is on the line.'

'Marcus?'

'No, Quinn.'

I notice the look of surprise on his face. He takes the phone and Brian leaves, closing the door behind him.

'Quinn. Yes. No. You will come? Three thirty p.m. Of course, they'll be there. But you have nothing to fear, I will be there.' I feel the strength flow back into his voice. 'While I am alive they can do nothing. Have you spoken to Marcus? You should call him. This has affected him greatly. He was very close to…Dad. When will you come? Good I'll send someone to pick you up. Goodbye Quinn.'

He ends the call and looks at me. 'If ever anything happens to me, the only one you must trust is Quinn.'

Fear like l have never known slams into me. And a pain takes root so deep inside myself that I find myself gasping the next breath. 'Why do you say that? Are you in danger?'

'I don't think so, but it is always wise to be safe. I have made extensive plans to protect you and Sorab in the event anything does happen to me. You will be safe. You will have money and a new identity.'

I gaze at him in horror. At that moment he becomes my greatest enemy. Money? Is he mad? 'Fuck you!' I scream suddenly. 'Extensive plans to protect me and Sorab? If you die on me I don't want a fucking penny from you. It's blood money.'

He strides towards me and crushes me tightly against his broad chest. I crumple inside his arms. 'Nothing is going to happen to me. I just said that as a precaution. The way other people take out life insurance.'

'You are my angel,' I sob. 'I cannot go on without you.'

'I cannot lie to you, Lana. If I have to I will sacrifice myself for you, over and over. But you must be strong. You have Sorab.'

'Has it become hot in here?' I feel feverish, as if I could faint.

Immediately he tilts my face up to his. 'You're pale.'

'No kidding,' I say, but my voice seems to come from far away. My eyes burn.

'I'm not trying to scare you, Lana. I'm trying to make you feel safe. I could die tomorrow in a car accident. I want you and Sorab to be safe and well. That's all.'

'Fuck you.' I wish I could wrap my arms around him and tell him not to go anywhere.

'Stay here. I'll go get something—'

'No, no, you won't come back. Don't leave me, please.'

'It's OK, OK. I'm not going anywhere.'

There is a sound from below. We both turn to look at him. He gazes back at us with large, curious eyes and for an instant, for a disconcerting instant, it is as if he can see through us, right through to our tormented souls. Blake releases me and goes to his son. Sorab makes a shrill sound of delight as he picks him up. The child lays both his hands flat on his father's cheeks as if he is trying to get all his attention. And when his father nods, he laughs. His father throws him up into the air and catches him while he laughs uproariously.

Oh God, oh God. If only he was just a normal person, if we could just live a normal life, but here he is. Trying to be normal. Trying his best to give us all he can. Yes, I do not know him. There is much left to be done, but this, this can be the prelude to our life. For I am determined to be there each morning when his eyes flutter open.

Two

Sorab and I leave after breakfast with Tom. Blake kisses us goodbye. He will not be coming with us. He will be going the way he came, in a black hawk. I tell Tom to stop by Billie's. Then I call her.

'Are you all right?' she asks me urgently.

'We're fine. We're on our way to you.'

'Who's we?'

'Sorab and me.'

'How long before you get here?'

'Two hours.'

'I'll be waiting for you,' she says, and ends the call abruptly. I look at the phone in my hand with surprise. Strange. I thought she might want to chat, find out more. Oh well.

I knock on her door and it is suddenly flung open. Billie snatches Sorab out of my startled hands and runs with him towards the room Billie and I have together decorated as Sorab's. Slightly bewildered, I close the front door and follow them. I walk into the blue and yellow room in time to see her deposit Sorab in his cot, shove a toy into his hands, and turn towards me with a contorted face.

'What?' I ask and she launches herself at me. She hugs me so tight I can hardly breathe.

'Hey,' I say. 'It's going to be OK.'

That only makes her go stiff in my arms. She pulls away from me. 'Don't lie to me, please.'

I stare at her. I am speechless with shock. Even though her voice is utterly normal, tears are escaping from her eyes and running quickly down her face.

'It's never going to be OK, is it?'

'Of course it is.'

'No, it's not,' she mutters darkly.

I open and close my mouth without having said anything. I have never seen Billie like this before. It shocks me. She's always so cool, so sarcastic.

'The old rat's dead. You're not going to tell me *that* was an accident.'

I shake my head slowly.

'See,' she says, fresh tears slipping down her cheeks.

'Yes, but it is over now.'

'Over? Can't you see that it will never be "over"? I wish to God you had never gone into that fucked up family of reptiles.'

I grip her by her arms. 'But I did, Bill. I'm in it. I love Blake with all my heart. And he is Sorab's father.' I turn and look at my son. He is gazing at us again with those big, innocent eyes; not crying, not upset, but aware that something is not right.

'Have you chosen wisely?'

For a moment the words are like thorns in my heart. I close my eyes. Then I open them and face Billie. 'I cannot be without him, Bill. I simply can't.'

Billie wipes her nose on the sleeve of her oversized T-shirt.

'Let me go get you some tissue.'

'You can't. I ran out yesterday.'

'Oh, Bill! Wait here.'

I go into her bathroom and tear off some toilet paper. When I go back to the room she is standing exactly where I left her. I fold the toilet paper, clip it around her nose, and say, 'Blow.'

She cracks a smile, takes the toilet paper from me, and blows her nose noisily. 'I've been so frightened and confused these last few days.'

'Come on, let's discuss this over a cup of tea,' I cajole.

'All right,' she agrees and reaching into the cot picks Sorab up. Together we go to the kitchen. She closes the door and puts Sorab on the ground. Immediately he starts crawling very fast across the floor.

'My God look at him go,' Billie exclaims, for the moment her earlier worries forgotten.

I laugh. 'He changes from day to day. Sometimes I wake up in the morning and I swear he has grown in the night.'

I fill the kettle with water while Billie lays a plastic mat on the floor and throws some toys on it. Sorab squeals and moves quickly towards them.

While Billie sets about preparing Sorab's milk, I drop tea bags into two mugs and three-quarter fill them with boiling water. I look into the cupboard where the biscuits are usually kept and it is empty. I open the fridge and peer into its impressive bareness.

'Want some milkie, banker baby?' I hear Billie ask Sorab.

Sorab lifts both hands and waves them in the air.

'Good baby,' she praises, and, gently pushing him down to the plastic mat, puts the teat into his mouth. She holds the bottle in place with one finger until he grasps it with both hands.

'Don't you have any food at all in this house?'

Billie gets off the floor and turns towards me. 'Nope,' she replies, totally unconcerned.

'Want some of Sorab's grape biscuits?'

'OK.'

I shake out a couple and we sit next to each other.

I watch her put six spoons of sugar into her tea and stir it morosely. She takes a sip. 'Well?'

I tell her everything I know.

She frowns. 'It's all a bit hard to believe, isn't it?'

'I'm sure it was far more difficult for the people who thought the world was flat to accept that it was actually round. Wouldn't people on the bottom half be falling off? But the world is round. From young we have been trained to unquestionably accept what we are told from our parents and teachers. They taught it to us just as they had learned it. What if they, too, had been deliberately taught the wrong thing?'

'OK, I get that they want to cull the 'useless eaters'. I even get that they start wars not because they are promoting democracy and freedom, but because they want the country's oil or gold or whatever. But why are they poisoning the land, water and air? Don't they have to breathe the same air and live on the same land as us?'

'I don't have the answers, but I intend to find out.'

'What really worries me is how safe are you?'

I sigh. 'I haven't really had a chance to speak to Blake about many things, but one thing I do know is that if Sorab and I were not safe now, I wouldn't be here talking to you.'

'So is Blake the new head of the Barrington empire now?'

'I guess so.'

'What about his older brother? Shouldn't he be the next in line? And if he isn't, wouldn't he be jealous and plotting Blake's downfall?'

I cover my eyes. 'I don't have any answers, Bill. I am scared. The future frightens me, but Blake is nobody's fool. He plays his cards very close to his chest. He never once let on that he knew his father was watching. He let it all unfold in precisely the manner he had decided it would.'

Three

I know that Blake will be home very late because there is so much for him to organize. Even while I was with him the phone calls never stopped. As I promised to do, I call him when we reach the apartment building. We don't talk for long—he is busy. I put my key through the door and realize that this is now home for me. It is where I live with my little family.

So much has happened here.

I play for a while with Sorab, then feed him and put him to bed. I prepare some food—grilled cheese on toast, and, eat it alone—I clean up after myself and wander about the place. From room to room I go switching on lights. It all feels so still and silent. Tonight I cannot bear any shadows. I see ghosts everywhere. I wish Blake would come home. When the phone rings I grab it with relief.

'Hello.'

'Hello, my darling. I'm missing you.' His voice is like velvet in my ear.

'Me too.'

'What are you doing?'

'Nothing. When are you coming home?'

I feel almost tearful. So much has happened that I do not understand. My head is so full of questions and worries. We haven't made love since that night at the Ritz, and I long to feel him on my skin, and deep inside me. I am desperate to forget, to purr, to lose myself and ride that wave of ecstasy. I decide to have a bath, a really long bath, with bubbles and scented oils. I lay my head back and try to relax.

Everything will work out.

Everything *will* work out.

But I am unable to relax. I get out of the bath, dry myself down, lather my skin with some lotion that has honey and extracts of avocado in and lie on the bed reading. By ten Blake is still not home. I go to the fridge and pour myself a glass of white wine. I should put some music on. It feels so deserted and strange. I check on Sorab. All is fine there.

I stand for a while in the balcony. For some reason I think of Jack. Ever since that last time I saw him I have not heard from him. I wonder where he is and what he is up to. I look up to the stars and say a silent prayer for him. Wherever you are, be well. The night air is cold and makes me shiver. Eventually I return to the bed and my book. I want to wait up for Blake, but I fall asleep while reading.

Something wakes me. He is home. I see the glow of the little moon-face lamp under Sorab's door. Softly, I open the door and freeze in the doorway.

Blake is standing by the cot staring at Sorab as he sleeps. His hands are gripping the cot so hard, his knuckles show white. He has opened a window and the night outside has become coal black. No stars. No moon. A soft breeze blows in. I feel it on the bare skin of my arms. Goosebumps scatter. The room is full of clinging shadows. My heart hitches.

He whips his head around suddenly, and I am face to face with him. I see his eyes. For a moment it is as if he does not recognize me. I do not recognize him. It must be my imagination in overdrive but it is as if I have interrupted a powerful predator. His eyes burn through me, angry blue.

'I regret nothing I would do it all again in a heartbeat, if I had to,' he whispers. The sound is fierce and heady with male dominance.

We are locked in a stare, neither of us blinking.

I am mesmerized by his gaze. Here is the man who has a hold on me, on my soul. And he has the keys to secret rooms I have yet to open. They are full of dark secrets. I am scared. Scared for us. Scared that the secrets will defeat me. That he will not give me the keys. The breath catches in my throat. My heart skips a beat. My head is flooded with so many unanswered questions.

He makes a sound, husky, unintelligible.

And suddenly he is beautiful beyond anything I have seen. He is my man. Mine forever. I love him. I open my mouth and words flow from my heart.

'I know our lives will never be the same again. I know you are trapped in a world that is like nothing

I have ever known, but I am willing to climb mountains, cross rivers, and travel barefoot over thorns and rocks if it takes me to you. I will find you. I promise,' I whisper.

'I hope you never find me in the place where I exist, Lana.' The words are ripped out of him.

A chill runs down my spine. I shiver. Words bubble up in my throat. 'Why are you always so harsh with me?'

'I'm not being harsh with you, Lana. For you, I'd die a thousand times. You'll never know how lonely I was without you, but you have to understand that I am only strong when I am certain you are safe. And you are only safe when you are innocent. You can never come to me. Always I will make the journey to you. The knowledge you are looking for is poison. It will seep into your very essence. Just this once allow me to act with beauty and courage, for you and Sorab.'

He is a broken soul. I walk up to him, and immediately he sweeps me into his arms and presses me against the hard expanse of his chest. I breathe in the scent of him, and feel again that passionate desire to be one with him. When our bodies are so fused together that our souls touch. I need to feel complete again. I have been for so many days unwhole.

'Oh, Blake.'

He lifts me into his arms, I wrap mine around his neck, and he walks me to our bed. 'Your fingers are freezing,' he says.

'Sorry.'

'Don't be.'

God, hot tears are trickling down my cheeks.

He bends his head, his shadows spilling over me. I hear the blood pounding in his temples, and he kisses my tears. 'Dew drops,' he whispers. 'I never thought it could ever be like this.'

I swallow and try to stop the tears but they won't halt.

He lays me on the bed. 'It always surprises me how silky your hair is,' he says softly to himself.

This has to be enough to pull us through. This must.

'It feels like a dream. As if you are unreal. I couldn't bear it if I woke up and you were gone,' he murmurs.

'It's not a dream. Do you believe that two people can share a love that is so deep that nothing can ever take it away?'

He doesn't answer me. Instead he looks into my eyes with so much love my heart quivers. The look changes. My tears stop, the blood begins to pound in my head.

'No need for words, Lana.'

He is right. There never was a need. His finger lightly strokes my throat. I draw breath sharply. I have been starving for his touch. He lets his finger rest on the desperate pulse. The tenderness in the gesture captivates me and starts the red-hot ache between my thighs. His mouth moves in closer and closer until his lips meet mine. I open my mouth to taste him. Ah…

He enters my soul.

In the shadows of our bedroom, time stills.

Four

I wake up in total darkness, shivering and realize instantly that I am blindfolded and naked. My hands are tied behind my back, but my legs are free. My nostrils are full of the smell of damp soil and dead leaves. Rocks and branches are digging into my back. It is eerily silent. I have no memory of how I got here. Where is Blake? Where is Sorab?

Suddenly, the air is pierced by a wail, despairing, monotone, and distant.

What the hell is that?

I freeze, bewildered and petrified. Precious seconds pass, with me holding my breath, staring into the blackness of the blindfold. Then: the knowledge, something's coming. An abomination—stalking, circling.

My lips move. 'Oh God!'

It is coming for me. It is almost upon me. The terror is indescribable. Frantically, I rub my face against the ground, gouging my cheeks on sharp stones. The blindfold shifts fractionally, but enough for me to make out that I am in a dark forest.

I scramble to my feet, swaying, my hands tied behind my back, and lurch away into the spooky shadows. The cold wind whips my face. Branches and leaves slap my bare body. I slip on moss, sprawl on the ground, pick myself up, and run blindly. In a panic, I glance backward, but it is impossible to see anything. The blackness is so thick. But I know it is still coming. I feel it in the chill that goes out like long tentacles before it to envelop me.

I take great gasping breaths: my lungs are on fire. Suddenly I hear men's voices chanting, low and guttural, and I immediately start running towards the sound. They are gathered around a large bonfire in a clearing not far away. All of them are in long black and red robes with hoods, which are pulled so low down over their faces, it is impossible to see them. There is an air of menace about them. I remember them. I have seen them at that party. They all know more than they will tell.

They are the brotherhood of El.

Far away in the distance I see a lantern. I should have gone towards the lantern. But it is too late. They have all turned to look at me. I stare at them, appalled, and terrified, and consumed with horror. They begin to advance. I turn around and run. I hear them behind me. They are faster than me. I hear them closing in, their heavy grunts. They are almost upon me.

I stumble and fall on the ground among roots and creepers. They surround me. I look from one faceless figure to the other with abject fear.

'You cannot escape.'

I freeze. Oh God. No! That voice. I know that voice. I look into the darkness inside his hood. There is movement. Shiny black eyes moving to look at me. I recognize those eyes.

'But you are dead.'

An unpleasant wet, rasping sound comes from him. The rest of the group fall on me. Hands everywhere, on my breasts, between my legs. I kick and struggle, but it is no use. The clawing and yanking are impossible to resist. They make a whispering sound. Insidious and unspeakably horrible.

They are taking me down, down into the freezing pits of hell.

Suddenly I hear a cry. A baby. My baby. My Sorab.

The hands still, and they turn towards the voice. It is not me they want…It was never me.

I see Blake standing there with Sorab.

No, no, no. Quick, quick, do something. Run. I open my mouth and scream to warn him but no sound comes. They have taken my voice. It's too late. I'm too late. I begin to howl silently.

I feel hands on me. 'Wake up. It's just a dream.'

My eyes snap open and Blake is peering down at me. I stare at him in confused terror, my head full of gravel and evil. Then I throw my arms around him and clutch at him desperately.

He tries to lay me back on the pillows, but I can't let go of him. I pull back just enough to look at him. 'I am afraid for you.'

'There is nothing to be afraid of.' His voice is tender. He cradles me in his arms and gently sweeps away the hair sticking to my damp forehead and cheeks. 'It's over. It's over,' he croons.

But I am full of terror. The dream had been so real. 'The men. The hooded men…In the woods. Who are they?'

He frowns. 'What men?'

'They want you back.'

'It was just a nightmare, Lana. There are no hooded men. You're safe. There is—'

'Your father. He was alive.'

A bleak look comes into his eyes. 'My father is dead.' His voice is flat and lifeless.

I rest my forehead against his chest and begin to cry.

Again and again he reassures me, 'It was just a dream. Just a nightmare,' until I fall asleep clasped in his arms.

When I wake up again it is with a premonition that something is wrong. Raw fear. I glance at the bedside clock. It is the early hours of the morning. A warning burns in my head. I don't dismiss it. I scramble out of bed, pull on Blake's discarded shirt and run into Sorab's room. It is still early and the child is fast asleep. Softly, I open the door and hurry down the corridor. Blake is in the dining room working, bent over a piece of paper. He lifts his head, sees me, and gets to his feet suddenly.

'What's wrong?'

'Nothing,' I say, but I run towards him and throw my arms around his waist. It is true nothing is wrong. So what is the little prickling at the back of my neck, as if someone was watching me, all about then? Is this the calm before the storm? I feel my stomach in knots.

'Don't become a slave to your fears, Lana,' he whispers into my hair.

As if by magic I feel the fear slinking away. Everything is all right. Blake is fine, Sorab is fine and I am fine. Nothing is wrong. It must be just my own overwrought senses. I know it is because I don't have all the facts. There is so much I don't know.

I look up into his face. 'Shall I make you something to eat?'

'No. The only thing I am hungry for is you,' he says, taking the lobe of my ear between his teeth. 'I simply can't seem to get enough of you. I want to devour you all the fucking time.'

It *is* tempting. Just let him fill me up. Make me forget. My lips part. 'Devour me, then.'

He lifts me by the waist and I wrap my legs tightly around hips, put my arms around his neck, bury my face in his throat, and let him carry me to the bed. I unwrap my legs and he lays me down gently. For a while he stands simply looking down at me, his eyes dark and grimly determined. Then he starts unbuttoning his shirt.

I watch him through eyelids that feel heavy and veins full of urgently pulsing, hot blood. As he rips open his button fly, unzips, and stands before me naked, my eyes move to and remain fixed on his penis: big and proud and pulsing with its own supply of hot urgent blood. I lick my lips—I crave it inside me, its length, its brutal thickness, its relentless power.

Its dark promise.

I just wanted to be fucked senseless.

But more important is the desire to be the only thing he sees, feels, wants. To obliterate everything else for him but me. To capture him inside my body. To make him mine. To watch his eyes lose focus, turn so deeply blue that it is almost violet with sexual euphoria. And to watch his powerful frame shudder and convulse as his mouth helplessly calls my name at the moment of climax.

What he does is the opposite of what I imagined.

He lands on the bed on his knees. Suddenly grabs me by the waist and turns me over, the same way someone would upend a bottle. Without warning I am folded over and positioned on my hands and knees. I feel his hands push the shirt I am wearing upwards, until it is bunched around my armpits.

While I am still finding my balance he ducks his head into the overhanging shirt and sucks one of my nipples. The other he rolls between his thumb and forefinger. The unusual position and the greedy sucking, as if I am a four-legged beast feeding its young, makes my head go back and my spine arch.

Immediately, he removes his mouth as if the only reason he had nudged his head into the shirt flap was to cause my back to arch.

I whimper restlessly, but he places his hands between my shoulder blades and pushes me face lower down, so my chin and mouth are buried in the pillow and my buttocks and pussy are horribly exposed. But even that he deems not enough for him. He yanks my hips higher up until my knees lift clean off the mattress, and with a manacle-like hold of my thighs, rams into me. I cry out with the shock of his ferocious entry and the surprising depth his shaft has gone to.

The pillow muffles my cry.

For a few seconds I hover between pleasure and pain. And then the pillar lodged deep inside me begins to journey out. I open myself to accept all of him, close my eyes, and wait...But even though I am anticipating it, the second punishing thrust makes me scream into the pillow. The wild violence of it is shocking and yet I welcome it. I want him to use me in this primitive way. To use my body to rid himself of his demons. I am in awe of his power and my ability to withstand brutality of his need. So he fucks me with ragged breath, as if with each pump he is releasing all the pent up tensions in his body.

The frenzied battering makes my sex fell raw and tender, but I squeeze his cock as if I am milking it. Suddenly he makes a sound, feral, triumphant, inexplicably male. And for the first time since I have known him he allows himself to come before me.

He climaxes as he always does, long, hard, agonized, calling my name, as if it is a prayer. His cock jerking and spurting its hot liquid into my desperately clutching cavity.

He withdraws out of me and I attempt to fall over on my side but he puts his hands on either side of my hips and holds me in that highly exposed position. He goes on his haunches. I know his seed is leaking out of me. He jams his thumb into my pussy and pulls it out, which causes his milk to spurt out. He smears his juices all over my sex and begins to rub, over and over in and around my cleft.

'Yes,' I hiss, my body clenching, feeling the orgasm building inside me, almost upon me.

But he does not allow me to climax, instead he teases me until I can bear it no more, and I lift my head and beg him to let me come.

He puts his palm flat across the soaking wet entrance of my body and simply holds it tight. Shameless, I grind my heated sex against wood-like hand, pumping and working my hips mindlessly, like some rutting animal. It does not take long. My orgasm scorched through me like a primal fire. It leaves me high and quivering like jelly.

Gently he lays me on my back and lies beside me, one hand, the fingers spread on my stomach. The hand is full of possession and ownership.

Slowly my breath returns to normal and I find myself exactly where I started. With a whole pile of unanswered questions.

'I'd like us to finish that conversation we started the other day,' I say.

'Maybe another time, Lana,' he says quietly.

We lie facing the ceiling in silence and the longer the silence stretches the more lost and alone I start to feel. I think of what we have just done—it is so vivid in my mind—and yet we could be strangers now. I have to stop myself from rolling away from him, curling up into a ball, and just crying my eyes out. I simply want to help. I am his woman. Not his toy.

Why the silent treatment? I haven't done anything wrong. As the seconds tick by I start to fume silently. If I was Victoria he would tell me. I would enter the forbidden realms with him. I become jealous and sad all at once. But more angry than sad. I sit up and glance down furiously at him.

He turns to look at me. Questioning. Slightly puzzled. His thoughts obviously elsewhere far.

I swivel my eyes away from him.

He reacts by catching my hand and pulling me down to his chest. 'What's wrong?'

There is no avoiding him while he is so in my face, and anyway I don't want to avoid him. I want a confrontation. Molded into his chest I crane my neck away from him and glare into his stare.

'You know,' I bite out fiercely, and try to twist away, but he brings his other arm around and, effortlessly, I am a total prisoner.

'If you carry on I'm going to have to fuck you again.'

'That's your answer to everything, isn't it? Out of bed I am of no use to you, am I?'

His expression changes. 'What the fuck are you talking about?'

'I don't understand you. You say you love me and you can't imagine your life without me, but you won't tell me anything. I'm sick of being locked out, Blake. Honestly, it's tearing me up inside. Do you think I am too dumb to understand? Is that it?'

'No, it's not that—' he interjects.

But I am not done. 'In your heart of hearts you think I'm not good enough, one of the unwashed masses. How stupid of me to ever think that we could be equal partners in a relationship. I'm just a doll to you, aren't I? One day you'll get bored of playing with me, and then you'll just put me away and totally forget I even exist.'

Hot tears begin to gather in my eyes. I try to blink them away. I am not going to cry, but the more I try to stop the more sorry I feel for myself and the faster they spill out.

He does a surprising thing. It stops my blubbering instantly. He fists my hair and lures my head lower until it is inches away from his face, and then he lifts his head, and licks my tears. First one cheek, then the other.

My reaction is instant and unexpected: fresh desire sizzles through me.

'Don't...Don't ever again say such things. They were true once, but not anymore. In fact, I don't believe they were ever true. From that first night I saw you, I had a reaction to you that I have never had with anyone else. You took my breath away.

'I tried to tell myself that it was because you were so extraordinarily beautiful, but I've been with so many beautiful women, some who have brazenly thrown themselves at my feet, others who have played hard to get, and then there were the truly shy ones, but never have I felt that irresistible need to brand them as mine.

'To lock them away and never let another man near them, let alone touch them. When I met you the rest of the world stopped existing. There was only you and I in my world. I wanted nothing else.'

He presses his forehead against mine, his words curling softly around us. I feel him everywhere. I love him so much it feels as if I should scream it from the rooftops. And yet I worry—my life has taught me that every time I love something, even if it be an animal, my heart will eventually be wrung out and broken.

'You must believe that I am telling you the truth. My heart was in a coffin, safe, dark, motionless... until I found you in a secret place, among the shadows of my soul. You saved me.'

He smiles softly and weaves his fingers through mine, his brows dipped low. I stare into his sad eyes. He has laid his heart at my feet. How would I have thought that he would turn out to be a gentle warrior? Love doesn't keep a record of wrongs. My heart melts. I forgive him.

'So why do you hide so much away from me, then?'

He sighs softly. 'If you knew a room was full of needles, would you let Sorab crawl in it?'

I frown. 'I'm not a baby.'

'Let me make myself clearer. I am afraid for you. I am afraid you will be taken away from me. Even the thought of losing you makes me feel sick to my stomach. You are the only person I can ever imagine myself with now. If all else—the mansions, the mines, the cars, the business, the yachts, the planes—perished and you remained, I could still continue, but if everything else remained, but you were gone, I'd be a broken man.'

His eyes are suddenly wet. He has never cried before. It breaks my heart. He is my love, my heart, my everything. I will leave it for now. I must know, but I will find out on my own. Somehow I will find out.

'Could you not sleep last night?'

'No, there is too much to do. The phones never stop ringing. People from all over the world offering condolences.' His lips twist bitterly. 'If only they knew.'

'When is the funeral?'

'Day after tomorrow.'

'Where?'

'New York.'

'When do we leave?'

'You're not coming.' His voice is suddenly hard.

I step away from him. 'Why not?'

'Because you never take your beloved gerbil to a viper's den.'

'But I want to be with you.'

'I'm only going for a day. I'll be back the next day.'

I gaze up at him. 'Blake, I want to be with you during that time.'

'No.'

I cross my arms. 'So you don't want me at the funeral?'

'No, I don't.'

'All right, I will come with you but I won't go to the funeral.'

He shakes his head. 'No. Then I'll be worrying about you in New York.'

'All right. I won't leave the hotel.'

'You'll be bored.'

'I'll read and I'll order room service.'

That takes the wind right out of his sails. 'Why do you want to come so bad?'

'Because I want to be with you during that time. I think it is important.'

'All right. But you have to promise that you won't leave the hotel without me.'

'I promise.'

'What about Sorab?'

'If it is only for one night I'll leave him with Billie.'

He frowns.

'Blake, if you don't take me with you I will fly there on my own.'

Suddenly he looks tired. 'I can never resist you. Yeah, you can come.'

'Thank you.'

'Don't make me regret it.'

'By doing what?'

'By leaving the hotel or making me worry about you.' He looks at me warningly.

'I won't. When are we leaving?'

'Tomorrow.'

Five

At first, I am amazed by the suite. Wow! This is what forty-five thousand dollars a night buys! So: top of the list are 360-degree views of Manhattan through bulletproof, floor-to-ceiling windows. I walk through the tall, spacious rooms alone, in a daze. The attention to detail is mind-boggling. The master bedroom is made from hundreds of thousands of painstakingly cut and ironed straws! Yes, very beautiful, but God!

Another room has calfskin leather walls. All the walls of the library are covered in French lacquer. The bathroom has an infinity bath and each sink is cut from one solid crystal piece. I lie on the horsehair mattress. Very, very comfortable. I open the lid of the grand piano and let my fingers trail tunelessly on the gleaming keys. I stand for ages on the balcony seven hundred feet high up looking down on the entire sprawling, throbbing city below my feet. I look at the book I have brought along and pass it by. And wonder what Blake is up to.

Eventually I get so lonely and bored I Skype Billie.

'How's Sorab?'

'Asleep. The shot of vodka did the trick.'

'I don't know that that's even funny, Bill.'

Billie laughs. 'He has to start sometime.'

'Yeah, when he's thirty.'

'So how's it going?'

'Well, Blake is busy meeting people, arranging stuff, and I am here bored out of my mind at the hotel.'

'You don't have the baby hanging around your neck—why don't you go sight-seeing?'

I sigh. 'I kind of promised I wouldn't leave the hotel.'

'What?' she splutters. 'Are you kidding me? You are in the Big Apple and you're not going out?'

'Forget it, Bill. I've promised. He didn't even want to bring me until I promised. We'll come another time. It's a bad time with the funeral and everything.'

'It's hardly a promise.'

'Don't start, please.'

'Why don't you at least go use the sauna or the pool, hmm?'

'Might do. I'm a bit hungry. Maybe I will go down and get something to eat at the restaurant. But first, do you want a tour of the suite? It's amazing.'

'Go on then.'

I end the call after the tour and go down to the lobby. I am standing at the plate glass window looking out when a man comes to stand beside me.

'You look like a child outside a cake shop,' says a strongly accented, man's voice.

I turn my head to look at him. He is tall, lantern-jawed and wearing jeans and a cowboy hat. He might be from down South.

'Texas,' he says.

'I see.'

'British?'

I smile. 'Yes, it is that obvious, huh?'

'I'm just about to fly to London on business.'

'Oh really?'

'Do you know what they say here about the difference between British accents and the hillbilly accent? When you hear a British accent add fifty to the IQ and when you hear a hillbilly accent subtract fifty.'

I laugh.

'Carlton Starr. Welcome to America.'

'Lana Bloom. Thank you.'

'Will you keep me company while I take some tea?'

'Ah…I'm actually with someone.'

He throws his head back and roars with genuine laughter. 'Of course you are. It never crossed my mind that a woman as beautiful as you would be without someone. Come on, I'll tell you all about my country if you'll tell me all about yours.'

I smile. From the corners of my eyes I can see Brian seated in one of the plush chairs. He appears to be reading a book. I know I am totally safe and I am not leaving the hotel premises.

'OK,' I agree.

Immediately, he puts a guiding hand just under my elbow. That does make me feel as if he is being a little too familiar, but Billie did say that Americans were super friendly. They can become your best friend on the first encounter, was her verdict.

I have taken no more than a few steps in the direction he is guiding me towards when I freeze. My stop is so sudden that Carlton's body nudges into me making me stumble slightly, forcing him, in turn, to grab me by the waist. All this while my eyes are caught by Blake's. He is staring at me with a look I have never seen.

Carlton whispers in my ear. 'I guess that's your someone.'

Blake strides towards me, his face as hostile and unyielding as gray granite. When he reaches us, he glances at Carlton with crushing clear-eyed contempt before snatching my wrist, and dragging me away. Blake moves at such speed across the foyer that I am forced to gallop to keep up. I am so embarrassed my entire face flames up. I feel like a child who is on her way to be punished.

At the lift he hits the call button and waits. A staff member comes to stand beside us. He lets his eyes slide off Blake and rest on me a while before lowering them to hide his expression. My dignity is in tatters and I am certain everyone is looking at me. Blake enters the lift with me in tow.

'Would you mind waiting for the next one?' Blake says coldly, when the man tries to enter behind us.

The man nods and hurriedly steps backwards. The doors close. I pull my hand out of Blake's grasp and rubbing my wrists ask, 'What the hell was that all about?'

He lets his eyes swing down in my direction. His voice is a tightly controlled don't fuck with me. 'Shouldn't I be asking you that?'

'What exactly are you suggesting?'

The doors open and, taking my wrist in his hand again, he drags me into our suite. I whirl around to face him.

'What's the matter with you, Blake?'

'What the fuck do you think is the matter with me?' he roars. 'I leave you for a few hours and you start picking stray men up in the hotel lobby?'

'Are you mad? Picking stray men up? It wasn't like that. I *told* him I was with someone. He just wanted to have some company while he was having tea.'

'You're not a child so you must be stupid.'

My jaw drops. 'You're crazy. It's not like I went up to his room.'

His eyes glitter dangerously and his jaw hardens even further.

'For God's sake, Blake, Brian was there. We were just going to have some tea. He wanted me to tell him about Britain. He's going to do business there. That's all.'

'You let him touch you.'

'On my elbow!'

He comes towards me. 'How can I put this politely? If I catch you trying to have tea with strange men or letting them put their hands on your elbow or any other part of your body again I will put you over my knees and tan your backside.'

I gasp. The unfairness of it is unbelievable. 'So I can never again have tea with any other man even under the most innocent context?'

He crosses his arms. 'Exactly.'

I begin to laugh. 'This is madness. No, I don't accept. Don't try to make out I was doing something wrong. He was just a nice guy.'

'Ah, why didn't you tell me? A nice guy? In that case, go ahead. Go down now and have tea with him. I'll call down to the pretty receptionist and have her come up for some tea with me.'

A fire roars into my belly. Fucking bastard. He wants other women. The cheek of it. I stare at him open-mouthed with shock while he simply looks at me with a smug expression. I exhale the breath I am holding. Fuck him.

'All right, I will,' I snarl, and stride towards the door. A hand shoots out and catches my wrist. I am slammed into his body. His face is inches away from mine and his eyes are dangerously stormy. We glare at each other.

'Are you trying to drive me crazy?' he growls.

'No.'

'I don't want any man near you, let alone to touch you. God, I can't even bear it when I see them looking at you. You're mine.'

'He wasn't trying to bed me.'

He closes his eyes in exasperation. 'You don't understand men. Whenever one approaches you he has already thought of bedding you.'

'So you think the receptionist is pretty.'

'Maybe.'

'What?' I gasp.

He laughs. 'I was teasing you. There is no one else but you, Lana. You've got me so I can't even think straight.' His eyes move hungrily over my face. 'I crave your mouth, your skin, your hair. Every morning I wake up ravenous for you, then I pace around during the day starving for you, and at night just after I've had you I start to crave your hot, sweet body all over again. Do you really believe any other woman could nourish me? The last thing on my mind is having sex with another woman.'

Inside I melt. 'But you think she is pretty?'

'Not really. Sorab is better looking.'

'But you must have noticed her to mention it.'

He groans. 'Oh for fuck's sake, Lana, I just said the first thing that came into my mind.'

'I just want you to know that I don't appreciate being dragged through hotel lobbies like some recalcitrant child.'

He runs his knuckle tenderly down my cheek. 'Then don't flirt with strange men in silly hats.'

'For the last time, I wasn't flirting.'

In response he cups my buttocks.

'I've really missed you today,' I say a little breathlessly.

'I bet you say that to all the boys,' he says, as his mouth moves down to crush mine with such passion that my feet lift off the ground.

Six

I am given a choice between the four-starred Le Bernadin with its formal dress code and its prestigious three Michelin stars or a red sauce joint in Greenwich Village called Carbone, where, Blake tells me, excess is de rigueur and the diner must abandon any hope of moderation. After staying inside the hotel all day, of course, I choose Carbone. They book thirty days out, but, of course, Laura, who seems forever on the job, swings us a table.

'Doesn't that girl ever sleep?' I ask.

'I never thought to ask,' Blake says, shrugging into his jacket.

I look at him standing there in a charcoal suit and a black, turtle neck sweater and—gorgeousness overload—my stomach does a little flip-flop.

Carbone is packed, lively and loud. Designed to look like the stage set of an old-fashioned Mafia movie, it carries that instinct for entertainment throughout. From the floor pattern to their choice of music—songs my grandmother used to listen to: Sinatra, the rat pack—and strutting, jovial waiters dressed in shiny Liberace style maroon tuxedos. They show us to our table in the VIP section: a rear room made to look like the kind of place where powerful Godfathers might have met—red and black tiled floors, brick walls and no windows.

Deeply fragrant shellfish reduction stock wafts up from the next table as we sit. My eyes are drawn to four flushed men tucking into their food. On other tables the waiters seem to be character actors who have perfected the art of the flashy, bossy restaurant captain. I watch them, with cocky smarminess, lean in conspiratorially, improvise dialog, and kiss the tips of their fingers, as they make wildly exaggerated promises of excellence to sell their wares and smile approvingly when their recommendations are taken.

We are handed menus that are at least three feet long.

Blake orders the veal parm and I am ruthlessly cajoled into having the lobster fra diavolo (the best you'll taste in your lifetime). A four hundred dollar bottle of Barollo is opened with flourish, the cork sniffed appreciatively, and offered to Blake to try. He arches his eyebrow at me. My glass is filled. We clink glasses.

'To us,' Blake says.

'To us,' I echo. The wine is big and rich and very strong.

'What was your day like then?' I ask.

'Grim. I spent all day with people I'd rather not ever see, and then I come back to the hotel and catch you flirting with some hick in a cowboy hat.'

'I wasn't flirting.'

His eyebrows shoot up. 'So, what did you do, besides flirting with strange men?'

'I wasn't flirting!' I say forcefully.

He smiles. 'I love it when you are fierce.'

'Well, I don't like it when you are. You are downright scary.'

'Then don't piss me off.'

I sigh. 'I went downstairs because I couldn't read. I was worried about you.'

A waiter comes with appropriate cutlery for us.

'I wouldn't like you to get bored while I am at work. Is there anything you'd like to do with your time?'

'I want to set up a charity to help children,' I say, quite timidly.

'Really? What sort of charity?'

I lean forward eagerly. 'I haven't decided yet, but I do know that I want to make a huge difference.' I take a sip of wine. 'If you were me, what would you do? What is the most significant thing I can do for the children of the world?'

'If it is the children of the poorest countries, then I'd give them the most precious commodity in the world—water,' he suggests quietly.

'Water?'

'Yes, clean fresh water from tap spigots. Currently two million children die every year from drinking unsafe water, but those figures are about to go through the roof.'

'Why?'

'There is a global water crisis and water is being privatized.'

That surprises me. I know so little. I had much to learn before I could set up my charity. We are still deep in discussion about the mechanics of starting a trust fund when the food arrives. I lean back and finally understand what Billie meant when she said the food portions in American restaurants are the size of garden sheds.

Blake's veal is shock-and-awe huge and served with a fried shaft of bone, ovals of browned buffalo mozzarella, and bright red, fresh tomato sauce. Mine is a two and a half pound lobster that has been de-shelled, cooked with Calabrian chilies and Cognac, and piled back into the shell. It is polished and glistening and reeking of garlic butter. Bread like Mama used to make arrives.

Blake and I tuck into the delicious food. It *is* the best lobster I have tasted.

For dessert we order zabaglione. It is prepared using the yolks from goose eggs in a round-bottomed copper pot over a flame at the table. Afterwards, I have homemade limoncello and Blake knocks back a fig grappa. By the time we leave the premises I am feeling decidedly tipsy.

'Can't wait to get you into bed,' I mumble into his neck.

He looks down at me indulgently and chuckles. 'I'm so glad you're such a greedy little thing.'

We get back to the hotel and fall into each other's arms.

'You are my dream,' he whispers in my ear. 'You have made me who I am.' Neither of us mentions the father he dispatched into the next world for me, or the funeral that must be attended tomorrow, but it is there, silently watching, its long shadow falling over our entwined bodies.

Stay if you must, but I will never pretend I am not glad a predator like you is gone from this world. And that because you are gone, my son is safe.

That night I wake up to sudden movement beside me. I sit up and in the light from the moon I can make out that Blake is caught in a nightmare and thrashing about in distress.

'I killed him!' he yells.

I shake him awake urgently. His bleary eyes focus on my face, and for a micro-second he looks at me with fear and horror, and then his brain gets into gear, and he recognizes me. With a look of relief he clasps me to his body with such force that my lungs can't expand to take the next breath.

'Hey.'

He loosens his hold. 'Oh, Lana, Lana, Lana,' he sighs.

'Were you dreaming about your father?'

'No.'

A cold hand comes to clutch my heart. No. I close my eyes with anguish. I cannot not love him. But oh God! Oh God! Has he killed someone else? Who is this man that I love?

'Who then?' I ask fearfully.

'I don't know him. He is covered in blood.'

My body sags with relief. It was just a nightmare. How incredibly frightened I had been as I formed those two words, 'Who then'. Tears of relief start running down my face. He feels them against his skin and pulls me away from his body.

He touches them with wonder. 'Why?'

I don't tell him the truth. Because for a moment I thought I was in love with a monster.

'Because I love you,' I say. But that, too, is the truth. I loved him even in that corrosive, soul-destroying moment when I thought he was a monster.

Seven

It is Brian who gives me the exact time the funeral will be shown on TV. I tune the TV to the appropriate channel and settle myself in front of the large flat-screen to wait. The film clip is remarkable for two reasons: its brevity and the fact that it is filmed in church. A suitably sober woman's voice announces that the funeral of an industry leader was held that afternoon.

The camera rests for a moment on the widow and I see Blake's mother properly for the first time. In those few seconds it is obvious to me that Blake is her favorite son. Wearing a matt black coat she stands very close to him and seems almost to lean on him. He appears very tall, broad, and unapproachable. Almost I don't recognize that stern, imposing man!

A little farther away Marcus stands beside his immaculate and totally expressionless wife. They are flanked by their two children. I look for Quinn and I think I recognize him. The family resemblance is strong. He is the one standing a little to the left of Blake. Blake seems very protective of him. Then there is a quick shot of the casket and the news item is over and the Barringtons slip seamlessly into their manufactured obscurity. The entire news clip is another carefully crafted PR exercise from a notoriously secretive family.

I switch off the TV and time seems to stop as I wait for him to return.

I try to read, but cannot arouse any interest in the words before me. I put on some music and try to relax in the bath. But I am too wound up and after a few minutes I get out and dress in a blue blouse and black skirt. I hear him at the door and run out to greet him.

He takes off his long dark coat and stands in his funereal garments. His face is grim. I want to run to him and bury my face in his neck, but he seems unreachable. I stare at him without comprehension. He bewilders me, infuriates, makes me feel weak and vulnerable, and yet he is my hero and the strength that carries me through the day.

'How was it?' I ask instead.

'As expected.' His lips curl into an expression I have not seen before.

'Everything went well, then?'

He nods. 'Let's get drunk together,' he says.

I look into his eyes. He looks furious about something. 'OK.'

He goes to the phone and orders up a bottle of Scotch.

They must have asked which brand.

'Just bring your best,' he says impatiently, and puts the phone back on the hook. I go to hold him and he puts his hand out as if to ward me off. 'Don't touch me,' he says, and I freeze.

He runs his hand through his hair. 'I just need a shower. Meet me in the bedroom,' he says, and turning away goes to the bathroom.

The bottle arrives with two glasses and a bucket of ice while he is in the shower. I tip the man, and taking everything into the bedroom, pour two generous measures into the glasses. I can hear the sound of the shower. At any other time I would have gone into the shower and joined him, but I can see that today he is different. He seems like forbidden territory. I shudder. Something has happened that has affected him deeply. I pace the bedroom. Look at myself in the mirror. I look OK.

He comes out and leans in the doorway in a towel loosely hitched around his lean hips. Wow! Divine. I love this man with wet hair. The blood starts to pound in my eardrums. When will the half-naked sight of him cease to affect me this way?

'You are still dressed,' he notes with raised eyebrows.

I say nothing—simply, slowly, start undressing. First the blouse goes over my head, then the skirt ends up at my feet, the bra gets flung away, and finally the knickers go the way of everything else. The balcony windows are open and the slight breeze scatters goose pimples on my skin. I look at him as he approaches me. God! He's so fucking delectable. I watch the muscles rippling as he loses the towel. He stops inches away and twirls my hair in his fingers. The nearness of him makes me want to lick that pulse beating at the base of his throat. That is the only real conversation we have. That pulse that never lies to me. When it beats, I know he wants me, bad.

'Want ice cubes in your drink?' I ask, huskily.

He smiles and shakes his head. 'The ice cubes are for you.'

I smile back. 'Really?'

'Really,' he drawls, and pulls me towards him until I feel his entire length and his hot, hard shaft presses into my abdomen. His mouth descends. My hands rise up and entwine around his neck and we kiss. We kiss. And we kiss. Both he and I know. This is the magic staircase by which he can climb back from whatever dark place he has been in.

He lifts me off the ground and lays me on the bed. I grab his thighs. He looks at me, surprised. I lift myself off the bed and take his beautiful cock in my mouth. He inhales sharply. I straighten my head so he can have a full view of my lips curled tightly around his thick meat. When I look up I meet his eyes. The intensity of his gaze hits me in the bones. I suck so hard my cheeks hollow in, and experience heady power when I see him surrender to pleasure, to me. I swirl my tongue around his shaft confidently.

'Open your legs,' he growls.

Obediently, I spread my legs and show him what he wants to see, but I do not stop sucking and pulling hard at his meat. He eyes my open sex avidly. His face contorts. His body buckles, and he spurts inside my mouth. Even when his eyes have turned languorous, I don't take my mouth away. I hold the semi-hard cock in my mouth and I gaze up at him. He gathers himself, touches my face tenderly, and pulls out of my mouth.

Deliberately, I lick my lips.

He grins wickedly, and turns away. My eyes follow him as he prowls around, buck naked, over to the bottle of whiskey. Tipping it over the ice bucket he starts pouring it out. I rise up on my elbow.

'What're you doing?'

He looks at me over his raised arm. 'Fixing myself a drink,' he says, and continues wasting the whiskey until there is less than a quarter of the bottle left. He drops half a fistful of ice cubes into my glass and brings the bottle and the glass into the bed. He walks towards my body on his knees and holds out my glass. I take a sip—the alcohol is strong, but goes down smooth. I watch him swig straight from the bottle, his head thrown back, his throat strong and powerfully masculine, his skin glowing like polished bronze. What a sight he is. His manhood erect, his thighs rippling and powerful, his shoulders broad.

Always in moments like this he reminds of a Greek god.

He swings the bottle down to hip level, wipes his mouth with the back of his hand, and catches my eyes. His are hooded, dark and full of desire. There is something in him that is different. He looks into my eyes. I feel myself burn under his gaze. A fluttering in my belly. I am nervous. Why? But I am also turned on. Unbelievably excited by this new him.

'Now what?'

He breaks eye contact and looks at the bottle. Very deliberately, he removes the metal ring broken off from the bottle cap and puts it on the bedside table.

He lies on his elbow beside me. The bottle touches my cheek. It is cold. I turn and look into his eyes. What is in them thrills me.

'Do you know that far, far more erotic than a cock inside you is to have an ordinary household object put into you? My excited, scandalized eyes swivel to the bottle and back to him. What I see in his eyes electrifies me.

'Yeah?'

He smiles slowly. 'Yeah.'

I nod and he swipes the pad of his thumb along my bottom lip. Suddenly he is on my mouth, rough, rough…The bottle goes away from my cheek. I part my thighs and gasp into his mouth when he inserts it into me. Fuck me! Cold and hard and erotic. Very, very erotic. I gape at him.

He lifts his head and watches me as he puts his hand under my buttocks and lifts me off the bed so I feel the liquid gurgling into me. I want to cover my mouth. 'Oh!'

'Yes, "Oh",' he murmurs, but his breathing is ragged, his eyes liquid and locked on mine. I am riveted by the fiercely masculine flare in his eyes. The light of ownership. He knows that there is nothing he cannot do to me.

When the bottle is empty he tosses it away.

'What does it feel like?'

'It's sexy.' My voice is a hoarse whisper.

He laughs wickedly. 'All illicit trespasses are.'

Gloriously naked, he reaches for a handful of ice cubes. He runs them over the heated flesh of my sex and inserts them one by one into me, while I squirm helplessly. Suddenly, I feel shy and close my eyes.

'Open your eyes,' he orders.

I snap them open and he trains his stare on me.

'This is my cunt,' he states, his features harsh with lust.

I swallow and nod. My hands fist the bed covering.

'I love watching you face when you are like this: helpless, open, bare, mine.'

He possesses me with his eyes while he continues to stuff me full of ice cubes. 'I want you everyway I can.' Then he kneels between my legs and begins to drink from my pussy.

'The process is a slow sensual assault. Lick, lick, suck, lick, lick, suck, suck as the cold liquid dribbles out of me. I arch my back.

'Yes, right there…Yes.'

The sensations are so foreign, the numbing effect of the cubes, his searing tongue, sometimes teeth, the sloshing of the alcohol. It is tireless. It is decadent. It has turned me boneless with searing need. I am so caught up in the intense sensations I hardly recognize the high-pitched animal sounds coming out of my mouth.

'We're going to take it one level higher.' He lays down beside me. 'Clench your muscles and come sit on my mouth.'

Very carefully I sit up and clenching hard I move over to his face and position myself over his mouth. Having to clench my muscles while he is slowly drinking the dribble is strangely unnerving, and filthy, but exquisite. As if there are no barriers between us. He wants everything I've got. Even my juices. Suddenly he swoops upwards and catching my sex in a hard suction pulls me down on top of him. He grinds my sex over his mouth.

I tense so all the liquid does not gush out, but it is impossible to keep control of my body—it starts contracting and spiraling out of control. I come in a gush. I look down and he is greedily gobbling all the liquids that are pouring out of me. I lift my sex away from his mouth and look at him: smeared with alcohol and all my juices. Then he pulls me back down and licks me clean.

'My Lana,' he says, his eyes glowing possessively.

Eight

I return to England inspired by Carbone and decide to cook a feast of senses for Blake. He is given strict instructions to come home early. Two hours ago I fried some rabbit, pancetta, onions, garlic, sage in a pan and tipped a bottle of Sangiovese into it. Once the mixture was simmering I added rosemary, thyme, some sticks of cinnamon, and cloves.

Now the hare has started to collapse into the sauce, which has become as sticky as runny honey and will nicely coat the handmade rigatoni that Francesca brought in today. I plan to serve this rich, pungent dish with a whole artichoke, slathered in warm olive oil and lemon juice and sprinkled with chopped mint.

In the oven I have a fresh peach tart to be served with Italian gelato.

I glance over at Sorab. He is rubbing his eyes. We were down in the park all afternoon and he looks as if he could do with a nap, but I don't allow him to sleep. This way he will sleep the night through. I hear Blake at the door.

'Daddy's home,' I announce rapturously, and, scooping Sorab off the floor, I run out to the front door to meet him.

'Hey,' he says, pulling a large smile into his face.

Sorab begins to wriggle and lifts his arms in his father's direction. Blake takes him from me and lifting him high into the air blows raspberries on his belly, while Sorab laughs, squirms, and kicks.

He turns his head to look at me and sniffs the air. 'What's that?'

'That,' I grin, 'is your dinner.'

'It smells amazing.'

Holding Sorab to the side of his body he bends and kisses me, bathing my body in a languorous, sensuous glow. There is delicious food waiting in the kitchen, my man is home, my son is in his arms: there is nothing more in this world I could possibly ask for.

Blake reaches for my hand and suddenly stills, his eyes narrowing. 'What's this?' he asks softly, touching the plaster on my finger.

'It's nothing. I nicked my finger while I was cutting some vegetables.'

He frowns and envelops my hand in his. 'I don't want you cooking anymore. I'll get Laura to sort a chef out for you tomorrow.'

'No,' I say immediately. 'I don't want a chef. I enjoyed cooking for us today. I don't want a nanny either. I just want it to be the three of us.'

He looks at me, his jaw is tight.

'Just for a while, Blake. Please.'

'OK. For a while. We are moving to One Hyde Park Place next week anyway.'

'What?'

'It's much better there. You will have access to the Mandarin Oriental's chef.'

'Can't we just stay here for a little while longer? Everything has happened so fast and I'm still so confused about so much. This is like my home now. I feel comfortable here, and Billie's just around the corner.'

He puts an arm around my waist. 'If it makes you happy to stay here then we will stay here for a while longer. But we will have to move eventually.'

'Thank you.' I smile up at him. 'I've got a surprise for you.'

'Yeah?'

I give him the box. 'Give me that child.'

He hands over Sorab to me, opens the box, and looks up at me quizzically. 'Slippers?'

'Yeah. It's comfy. For around the home.'

'Like a grandfather?'

I laugh happily. 'You couldn't look like a grandfather if you tried. Now try them on.' Sorab takes the box and bites the corner while he takes off his shoes and puts on the slippers.

'Well?'

'Like walking on air.'

'Excellent.'

He gazes into my eyes—his are dark and moist. 'Do you know I have never worn slippers?

'Never?'

'Never. You've totally changed my life, Lana.'

'I'm not finished,' I say and pass him the next package.

He opens it. 'Sweats?'

'Hmmnnnn…'

I stand and watch him strip off his office wear and get into the dark blue sweats.

'What do you think?'

'Edible,' I say, and I really mean it. Low-slung pants on slim sexy hips. A little bit of skin shows and I reach out and touch it.

Instantly, he looks deep into my eyes, his expression changing.

'I've got other plans for you tonight,' I tell him and retract my hand. 'Here,' I say and hand the baby over to him.

He takes Sorab and goes off to the living room. I return to the kitchen. Food will be ready in twenty minutes. By the time I put the stretched bread lightly brushed with tomato sauce into the oven, Sorab is sound asleep on his father's body. While Blake puts him down for the night, I turn down the lights in the dining room, and stand back to admire the glow of the candles on the white table linen heavy with all kinds of foods.

Tart giardiniera in oil, olives, cured meats from the deli, salads, ribbons of fried dough dusted with powdered sugar and an intricate terrine of fruits layered with alcohol-soaked sponge. And of course, a very special bottle of red that I have opened and allowed to breathe.

The first piece I slip into his mouth. The expression of rapture and astonishment is gratifying.

'It is how I imagine the food in the paintings of Caravaggio to be—real, hearty, Roman—a bird roasted in a wood oven, ' he says.

'Really?' At that moment I make up my mind to learn about art and music, to become, culturally, his equal. He will never have cause to be ashamed of me in front of his peers.

The rest of the meal becomes a dreamy evening that will forever echo in my heart. Everything was perfect. I watch Blake eat, as a mother watches her child eat. Protectively, proudly.

And he eats without inhibition or his usual control and care—cutting his food into dozens of pieces, which he then carefully picks at as if they are something dangerous. He eats with genuine pleasure, sucking the sauce off his fingers, reveling in every new flavor.

Finally, among the crumbs of our feast, Blake dips a lemon cookie into the dessert wine and brings it, still dripping golden drops, to my lips. I quickly swoop down and bite. The sweet raisin-like taste explodes on my taste buds, as a drop escapes from the side of my mouth. Before I can bring my napkin to my lips he leans in and licks the corner of my mouth. As if he is a wolf or some animal that uses its tongue to wash the body of its mate.

He carries on licking diligently until every last lingering trace is gone and still he licks until he happens upon the two tiny drops on my neck. I stare at him. So close to me, still so foreign and yet, my whole life. This is the man I had not intended to love. And now I cannot imagine my life without him.

He raises his eyes to me. 'I couldn't understand the concept of eating food off a naked woman before. Now I can.' He slips his hand along the inside of my thigh. 'The grace of the human figure, the delicacy of its form is the perfect plate. I'd love to fill your body with all manner of food and slowly lick it off.' His fingers reach the apex of my thighs. I part my legs willingly. '*Soufflé aux fruits de la passion* on your nipples, *sabayon* sauce on your belly, caramel on your pubic bone and *bananas en papilote* between your legs.' One long finger enters me.

I blush as if he has not done far more outrageous things to me. Perhaps the thought of lying on a table and being a platter for food that will be consumed off my body is incredibly erotic. And the thought of Blake slowly licking and sucking actually makes me wet.

The finger retreats. I inhale.

He puts the finger in his mouth. I exhale.

I pour out two glasses of sambuca, place three coffee beans on their surfaces and set them alight. Over the blue flames I catch Blake's eyes. In this light they are so dark they are almost black. The intensity of his gaze makes me catch my breath. I forget about the burning drinks, until he lowers his face without breaking eye contact and blows out the flames.

He dips his finger in the sambuca and smears it on my lips, and lifting me off the chair carries me to the bedroom to be ravished.

'The sambuca…'

'I've had enough.'

'The dishes,' I whisper into his neck.

'Tomorrow.'

'The candles…'

'Later.'

When I wake up again, it is because of a cry or a moan. I turn my head and he is not in bed. I roll out of bed and go into Sorab's room. Blake is holding him and softly crooning him back to sleep. Our eyes meet over our baby's head. His are soft, softer than I have seen them.

I wish I could capture the moment forever.

He brings one forefinger to his lips. So I don't say anything. Simply memorize that magical moment. When a man's beautiful soul is unearthed by his son. When we are all connected. He, Sorab and I.

Nine

'Tonight you get to meet my brother. We are having dinner together.'

I look at Blake, surprised. 'Quinn?'

'No, Marcus actually.' He watches me carefully.

I bite my lip. The memory of his brother's cold, blue eyes is seared into my memory forever. 'I have met him. At the hospital, when you were in a coma.'

'He told me. But briefly, right?'

'Yes, incredibly brief.'

'Didn't go too well, huh?'

'Nope. He didn't want me in the picture.'

His lips tighten. 'You *are* in the picture now. He'd better get used to it.'

'Maybe you should go on your own this time. I'm sure I'll get to meet him on other occasions.'

He puts his finger under my chin. 'You are coming tonight.'

I send Sorab over to Billie's early and I bathe and start getting ready hours before Blake is due to return. I try on a dozen outfits, but nothing looks good to my critical eye. I look at the clock. Blake will be home soon. Black. Black always works. I hunt for something black. I find a simple black dress with a sweetheart neckline and zip myself into it.

I look at myself in the mirror unhappily. I look pale. The solution might lie with red lipstick. I apply some and blot my lips. I still don't look or feel right. There is a ball of apprehension in the pit of my stomach. It feels as if I am about to enter an exam hall unprepared. I'll stick like glue to Blake and that way I know I will be safe. My thoughts are interrupted by Blake's appearance at the bedroom door.

'Oh!' I whirl around startled. 'I didn't hear you come in.'

He grins. 'I wanted to surprise you.'

I clutch my chest dramatically. 'You succeeded. I nearly jumped out of my skin.'

He is carrying a bag that he drops on the bed on his way towards me. When he reaches me he holds me by my elbows. 'You look very, very…very… very beautiful, but that is not what you are wearing today.'

'No?'

He shakes his head slowly as his hands turn me around. For a moment I feel his finger on my bare skin, then the zip starts its downward journey. He turns me back around and gently pulls at the sleeves of the dress. It slips down my body. He winks at me.

'Love the underwear, by the way.'

'Thank you,' I reply primly.

He goes back to the bed and upends the bag he has brought with him on to the bed. A shoebox and something else drop out. The something else is soft and covered in tissue. He shakes it loose of its wrapping and my mouth parts. The dress is stunningly beautiful. Above the waist it is entirely blue appliqué lace design with a V-neck. Below the waist it is a sleek electric blue taffeta figure-hugging skirt. He holds it up.

'Fleur?'

'Of course. What'd you think?'

'Beautiful.'

He helps me get into it and touches my skin through the lace. Then he walks away and opens the shoebox. He brings it to me and, kneeling at my feet, grasps each in turn and fastens the delicate straps around my ankles. I grip his shoulders. When I am securely fastened in my new shoes he stands, and looking at me smiles with satisfaction.

He takes me to the mirror, turns me around so I can see my own reflection. Then he fastens around my throat a necklace glowing with deeply blue stones.

'Wow!'

'Sapphires,' he says. 'To match your eyes.'

I touch them wonderingly.

He reaches for a tissue and gently, as if I was made from the most fragile glass wipes off the red lipstick. My lips part to allow him access. He drops the tissue on the vanity top and picks up lip gloss. Nude. Carefully he dabs it on the insides of my lips.

When he turns me back to face the mirror, I understand what he has done. I meet his gaze with grateful eyes.

'Thank you, for selling yourself to me,' he says with a soft smile.

'Thank you for buying me.'

'I think we should live happily ever after, don't you?'

'Most definitely.'

I look at the blaze of his eyes, the belief shining in them and my heart feels as if it would burst with happiness. And for a moment I even forget the ordeal of sitting down to dinner with Marcus.

'Where are we going?' I ask nervously.

'Your favorite restaurant. The Waterside Inn.'

I smile, remembering the red carpets, the tranquil view of the river, a kindly civilized ambience, unobtrusively attentive waiters, and milk-fed lambs roasted and expertly carved into leaves of flesh at the table. 'Thank you.'

We arrive before Marcus, which is the way Blake planned it, so I would have time to settle myself. Blake parks and comes around to open my door. He helps me out and we stand a moment looking around us. The autumn wind picks up a few brown leaves swirls them in a dance drops them again a little farther down the road.

'Come on,' he says. 'I promise I won't let him eat you.'

'I'm not really scared of him.'

'That's my girl.'

The staff remember us and greet us with genuine warmth, which immediately makes me feel a little more confident. We are shown to a round corner table in the elegant waiting area. I sit back and stare unseeingly at my menu sans prix.

Soon I am accepting the complimentary glass of Michel Roux's champagne. We clink glasses.

'To tonight,' Blake says, and we sip our aperitif. It is perfectly chilled.

'Do you know what you want to eat?'

I shake my head and look again at the menu, but I cannot concentrate on the words. I will have what I had before, it was glorious—salad of crayfish tails and flaked Devon crab with melon and fresh almonds.

Butterflies flutter in my stomach. Canapés appear. I ignore them.

'The smoked eel tempura is nice,' says Blake encouragingly.

I bring it to my mouth. Chew and swallow having tasted nothing.

I shouldn't be so nervous. There is nothing he can do to me and if he disapproves of me so what?

And then Marcus appears.

Ten

Blake stands. I am not sure if I should stand, and eventually I don't. Marcus shakes his brother's hand, but also touches his shoulder in the way that politicians engaging in power games do. Then he turns and nods at me.

'Marcus, I don't believe you have been formally introduced to Lana. Lana, this is my brother, Marcus.'

'Hello,' I say. My voice comes out cold and distant.

But Marcus bends slightly from the waist, tilts his head as if it is a great honor, and allows his good-looking face to curve into a genuine open smile. He offers his hand to me. 'I have to admit I am jealous of my brother. How on earth did he pull off getting a girl as beautiful as you?'

The friendly gestures and words throw me. 'Um...' I close my mouth and take the proffered hand.

His handshake is the right shade of firm. He sits down opposite us, and starts chatting. He is utterly, utterly charming. I find myself staring at him with bewilderment. Could this be the same man I met in the hospital? Was I in such a state of shock that I misread him? I watch him throw his head back and laugh at something Blake has said to him.

The family resemblance is very strong. They are both tall and broad, but his brother lacks the strong sense of purpose that surrounds Blake like a crackling vibrating energy. I can see now why Blake's father decided that it should be Blake who should take over the helm of leadership.

The waitress comes by. Our table is ready.

Marcus stands politely and holds his hand out to help me up. Since he is closest to the door, I have no choice but to put my hand in his. Our eyes meet. His betray nothing but a polite desire to help me up. And yet, there is tension in my body. Before I can extricate my fingers from his, I feel the tug of Blake's hand on my waist.

I look up into his eyes and I realize he was perfectly serious when he said he cannot bear any other man to touch me. Not even his brother, not even in the most innocent social setting. We are shown to our table. I slide into the long seat and Blake slides in after me.

Bread appears to my right. I point to a roll, and it is gently deposited onto my side plate. Our wine glasses are filled with straw-colored wine. Waiters start arriving with our starters. I pick up my fork. Parmesan cream with truffles. There is conversation going on around me, over me. I nod. I smile. I say thank you and I find myself drinking more than normal. Stop, right now, I tell myself.

'Have you been to the opera?' Marcus asks me. His voice is smooth.

I suddenly remember the way I was that night, and flushing bright red with embarrassment and confusion, look to Blake.

'Yes, we went to see L'incoronazione de Poppea in Venice,' Blake cuts in smoothly.

Marcus nods approvingly. 'The only place to experience Monteverdi.' He turns to me. 'Was that your first time?'

'Yes,' I mumble.

'Did you enjoy it?'

The memory makes me blush. I turn my head towards Blake, and my eyes are caught by his. There is hunger in his.

Marcus coughs delicately. I tear my eyes away. 'Yes, very much,' I say huskily.

'Freya, my wife, and I love the opera. We were at the Met for Rossini's La Cenerentola last week.'

Blake glances at me. 'Cinderella,' he says by way of explanation.

I nod gratefully.

'I'm afraid it was a grotesque, painfully anti-musical burlesque, only intermittently redeemed by virtuoso vocalism by the central waif.'

Marcus sips at his Latour.

I bite my lip. Suddenly I feel ignorant, uncultured and inferior. I realize that Blake has been careful never to let me feel less educated than he is. The truth is his world is totally different from mine. I remember Victoria telling me that no matter what I wear or do they will smell me out. In their eyes I will never be good enough. Will I ever be able to wear this mask of apparent reticence and nonchalance that Marcus wears with such ease? Will I ever possess this studied carelessness that hides all that is real about a person? Marcus is still talking. Surreptitiously I sneak a look at Blake. He is buttering his roll and nodding. Will Blake be ashamed of me one day?

'And what about you, Lana?'

Shit. I wasn't listening. 'Um…Please excuse me. I have to go to the…loo.'

The moment I say that word, I actually feel lightheaded. I remember that it was that beast, Rupert Lothian, who taught me it. His sneering words come back to me, 'This lot call it the loo.' I stand up and both men get to their feet. For a moment I look at them confused, and then I realize, of course, it is their way, an exaggerated politeness in the presence of a lady. I nod and walk towards the Ladies.

There is no one in there, and I lean against one of the walls, and close my eyes. Why am I so affected by Marcus? Why have I allowed myself to become such a mess of shattered nerves? Is it because we met in my moment of great fear and confusion that I have allowed him to grow into such a monster in my mind? I go to the basin, wash my hands and look at my own reflection.

'You have nothing to fear from him,' I tell myself. Then I take my mobile out and call Billie.

'How's it going?' she asks.

'Er…I'm not sure.'

'It's a yes or no with reptiles.'

'It's a no.'

'Hmmnnn…Your son is giving trouble.'

'What kind of trouble?'

'He doesn't want to sleep. He thinks he should be allowed to climb through the window, on to the balcony, and probably over it.'

'It's not one of his best ideas.'

'I'll say, but he is surprisingly fast for such a little thing.'

'Tie him up or something. I'll be there soon.'

'Lana. Reptiles are creatures of instinct and repetition. A mammal can out-think them any day.'

'Doesn't feel like it right now.'

'In that case give him a black eye. That always works.'

'Thanks for the advice. I'll be sure to bear it in mind.'

'You're welcome.'

'See you soon.'

'Use all your strength.'

I end the call, reapply lip gloss, and walk back to the table. Again both men stand while I seat myself. A brand new napkin has been put beside my plate. I open it and place it on my lap.

'I was just saying to Blake that both of you should come to Victoria's birthday party.'

My eyes widen. I feel the blood leaving my face.

Blake weaves his fingers through mine. I turn my head towards him.

'Victoria is Marcus's second daughter.'

I turn to face Marcus. He is looking at me innocently, but suddenly I know. He knew I would think he was referring to Blake's ex. He wanted to rattle me. But his revealing action has the opposite effect on me. I feel a little stronger. It was not knowing what I was dealing with that made me so weak. Now I know, it is better.

'When is it?'

Blake's voice is very dry. 'More than three months away.'

So he knows too.

The main course arrives. I thank the waiter and gaze at the Challandais duck, poached quince and chestnut polenta with dismay. There appears to be too much on my plate. How on earth am I going to eat all this when I feel sick to my stomach?

'Bon appétit,' Marcus says and tucks into his escalopes de foie gras.

'Bon appétit,' Blake calls out to me.

'Bon appétit,' I mumble, duck, spice and honey on its way to my mouth.

When the table has been cleared Blake excuses himself, and rises from the table.

'Where are you going?' I ask in a panic.

He winks. 'I'll be back for you, babe.'

I watch him disappear out of sight before bringing my gaze back to Marcus. He is watching me. I smile weakly.

'So,' he says, leaning back in his chair. 'You caught a *very* big fish in your net. What will you do with it now?'

Eleven

'I don't know what you mean, and I resent both your tone and the implication that I have somehow trapped your brother.'

'What would you call it?'

'I *love* your brother.'

'You don't have to pretend with me. I don't care who my brother fucks. It's totally his business if he wants to take every little whore he comes across into his bed.'

'If you are that unconcerned, why do you ask?'

'Just curious,' he says and smiles pompously. At that moment he reminds me of his father, but less dangerous, by far less dangerous. I was afraid of his father, but I am not of him.

My mother's voice is quoting Rumi in my head. *You are searching in the branches for what is only in the roots.* Thank you, Mum. At that moment, I stop feeling inferior. Why should I? He is not more than me. I have done nothing wrong. He is the despicable one. By a quirk of fate he is thousands of times more privileged than 99.99 percent of the population, but that doesn't make him special or give him the right to treat everybody else as if they were beneath him.

'Please forgive me if I refuse to indulge your curiosity.' My voice is deadly calm.

He laughs. His eyes glitter. Malice shines in his face. 'Here's some free advice, sweetheart—Blake *will* tire of you. Start your going away fund right now.'

A waiter comes, removes Blake's used napkin and replaces it with a brand new napkin by carefully sliding it off the plate he had brought it in. He smiles and goes on his way unconcerned with the battle Marcus and I are engaged in.

'Why do you care if I am with Blake or not?'

'I told you I don't.'

He is lying. Of that I am sure. Will I unmask him? 'Ah, but you do.'

He raises his eyebrows, summons an expression of incredulity, but I am not fooled. I have love on my side.

'You're jealous,' I say. 'You're jealous of Blake and you are eaten up with envy because he has found something you don't have. You don't love anyone you'd give everything up for, do you?'

I see a flash of real anger in his eyes. Where is the studied carelessness now? He pretends to laugh, the sound unnatural, ugly. The façade is scratched, the mask slipping. Underneath the water the effortlessly gliding swan is kicking like crazy. He is nothing but a courtier. Trained by his father to put on a performance. Now he is lost to the façade he has put up. He is not to be reviled but pitied.

'Jealous?' he sneers.

I say nothing.

His voice becomes venomous. 'Of Blake?'

I maintain my silence. Keep eye contact.

'Because he has *you*? A two bit whore that he paid to acquire.' His voice is contemptuous.

'Love even in the arms of a two bit whore can be precious.'

'No thanks.'

From the corners of my eyes I see Blake walking towards us. I turn eagerly towards him. He is watching my face carefully.

'Everything all right?' he asks.

'Yes,' I answer, but my expression is stony. At that moment Alain Roux who is doing his customary tour of the dining room stops at our table. I smile stiffly and assure him that everything was wonderful. He nods graciously and moves on. I am ready to go home, but there is still the cheese trolley to endure.

Marcus pronounces the Auvergne cheese flawlessly 'kept', whatever that means.

Blake shrugs non-committally.

'How's your soufflé?' Marcus enquires, suave mask tightly in place.

I look him in the eye. 'Faultless.'

Marcus's smile does not reach his eyes. Mine slide over to Blake and he is smiling into his cheese. I spoon a mouthful of raspberry soufflé into my mouth and know that I have won this round.

Blake orders a box of petits fours.

I look at him questioningly.

'For Billie,' he says and winks at me, and I feel a surge of joy. He is nothing like his brother. This horrible ordeal with Marcus is almost over and it will be just us again.

We say goodbye by Marcus's Bugatti Black Bess. Marcus shakes his brother's hand and touches his shoulder in an attempt to ingratiate himself with Blake. I stand apart and he does not attempt to kiss or touch me. I nod coldly—now you will have to win me over. Hands entwined we watch the lights of his car disappear into the darkness.

'I was proud of you tonight.'

'You left the table on purpose, didn't you?'

'Yes.'

'Why?'

'Because you have to get used to it. Marcus's disapproval is subtle and mild. If you can't hold your own with him, my mother will decimate you.'

'You're scaring me.'

He takes his eyes away from the darkness and focuses them on me. They are full of an emotion I cannot place. Maybe because, even though I love him with every ounce of my being, I don't know him well enough. Maybe because I am a fool in love with a man I cannot understand.

All I know is I love him no matter what.

'I'm preparing you. I wish I could always be by your side to protect you, but I can't. You must learn to fend for yourself. You must realize on your own that they are nothing. You are better than all of them put together.'

I break eye contact and look down at my hands. I am the girl from the council estate. I won tonight, but with great difficulty.

'Be confident, my love. Don't ever ask for their approval or work for it. They will respect you more for it. You will never be one of them, but that's OK. I'd hate it if you were.'

'Are all of them going to be hateful to me, then?'

'They won't dare say anything while I am around, but you'll have to learn to handle the odd catty remark in my absence.'

'Right.'

'Marcus looked like a whipped dog when I came back to the table.'

'He did?'

He grins wolfishly. 'Absolutely.'

I smile but I am thinking of the woman in black who stood next to Blake at the funeral. I know he is her favorite son and she will hate me with a passion. 'When am I meeting your mother?'

He laughs. 'We'll avoid that torture for as long as possible.'

'She's going to hate me, isn't she?'

'Yes. But as the two of you will hardly ever meet that shouldn't bother you at all.'

I sigh loudly. 'They all want you to be with Victoria.'

'That's never going to happen and it's time they got used to it.'

I thrust the box of petits fours into Billie's stomach and she opens it immediately. Blake goes on into Sorab's room, and I stand talking to her as she eats the sweets and looks at me with shrewd eyes.

'Anything to tell me?' she whispers as soon as Blake is out of earshot.

'Tell you tomorrow.'

She nods. 'Mmmmm…These are delicious.'

I reach out and brush a crumb from the corner of her lips. 'God, Billie, how I love you.'

'You should go out to dinner more often with Marcus,' she says.

And for the first time that night I laugh.

Twelve

I look down at my sleeping son and savor the delicious pleasure of his warm weight in my lap. I stroke his downy head. So exposed, so vulnerable. I feel Blake's eyes on me and look up at him. He is looking at both of us with an expression that I can only describe as fierce pride and possession. I feel cocooned in that savage light. As long as he is around we will both be safe.

Blake settles Sorab in his cot while I get out of my dress. I hang it up carefully and start removing my make-up. I don't take off my new jewelry. Blake loves to have me wearing nothing but the jewelry he has put on my body. I brush my hair and teeth, wrap myself in a fluffy bathrobe—it is deliciously warm from the radiator—and go out into the bedroom. He is unbuttoning his shirt. He pulls the ends out of his trousers.

'Come here,' he says.

I go up to him.

'Have I told you how beautiful you looked tonight?'

I nod.

'Have I told you how proud I was of you tonight?'

I nod.

'Hmmnnn…I am in danger of being boring.'

'I love boring men.'

One end of his lips curve.

'Whoa…High alert…Edible sexy ahead,' I whisper.

'Serve warm, eat whole,' he says as his hands move to the belt on my robe. He undoes it deftly and slowly leans into the gaping material to plant a kiss on my right nipple. My heart starts crashing against my chest. His large hands disappear inside the folds of the material and slide sensuously down the sides of my body. They come to a stop at my hips. He squeezes.

'Amazing how I never tire of looking at your body,' he murmurs into the side of my neck, while his fingers caress my throat and the blue stones encircling it.

The robe drops off, my head drops back. A trail of kisses follows. A small sound escapes my throat. Amazing how my body quivers like jelly as soon as he touches me. His hands grasp my wrists and pull them upwards until they are held high above my head.

He holds my wrists in a potent grasp with one hand and looks down at me, while his other hand roams my body freely, possessively. As if I am a slave in an auction that he is considering buying. I look up into his eyes. They are bold and dominant. I let my lips part.

'My Jezebel,' he says huskily, and takes my lower lip between his teeth. He holds the plump flesh between his teeth and pulls so I am forced to move with his head. I stand on tiptoe, skin burning all over, and wet between the legs. He lets go of my lip and moving his dark head away from me, gazes down at my body, arched and stretched out in front of him. There is a look of great satisfaction on his face.

He turns me around. 'Hands on the bed.'

I open my legs, bend over, and put my palms on the bed, shoulder width apart, waist dipped down, ass high in the air. I know what he is doing. He is making me wait.

Anticipation.

I twist my head and watch him unhurriedly shrug out of his shirt, very deliberately pull the belt out of his trouser loops, release the button at the top of the zip, pull down the zip. Hook his fingers inside his underpants. Pull down. He stands behind me. Hot, hard, ready. I watch his glorious body eagerly.

'Who do you belong to?' he purrs.

'You.' My voice is hoarse.

'Which parts belong to me?'

'All.'

'All?'

'All.'

He kneels behind me, his face inches from my sex.

'I can smell your arousal,' he says.

I shut my eyes. I am so open, so exposed. Seconds drip by. I wait. I know it's all a game. Patience and anticipation. My skin prickles. I feel his hot breath fan my wet flesh. The shock of his silky tongue swirling between the swollen folds makes my head jerk back. Instinctively, my hips tilt upwards, in a begging posture. I need him inside me. Now.

'Please, Blake. Please. Enter me.'

'Is this mine?' he asks, and bites my sex.

'Arggg…'

'I'm sorry,' he says pleasantly. 'I couldn't make that out.' He bites me again.

'Yes,' I cry out.

'To do with as I please?'

'Yes, yes.'

His breath fans the flushed, sensitized skin. With his thumbs, he spreads apart the folds and inserts his tongue. I gasp and writhe. He pulls my thighs farther apart, clamps his mouth on my clit and sucks.

'Oh God!'

Just as the delicious waves are starting to take hold, he takes his mouth away. Torture, pure torture. He stands. Is there to be no filling, stretching, or ramming? I am raging with need. To have him deep inside me. To be possessed by him. Frustrated and full of longing I look at him. Silently, he is gazing down at my open, greedy pussy.

'Stay,' he says, and leaving my body, gets on the bed in front of me. I gaze at his erection. My mouth is open, my breathing erratic. He is a fine specimen of a man. I have the strong urge to lick the meatus, take him in my mouth, and suck him so hard he groans helplessly.

But he has an even better idea.

'Come and sit on my cock,' he commands.

The order rolls over my flesh. I don't need a second invitation. I crawl to him and impale myself on the hard shaft. The pleasure. Oh! the pleasure.

'Sit like a frog.'

I reposition myself, opening my knees wide, pulling my feet close to his thighs and laying them flat on the bed. Then I place my palms on his body and straighten my own body. The penetration is too deep. With a small cry I push my palms down and fractionally lift myself off his body, but he shakes his head slowly.

'Mine to do with as I please.'

Biting my lip I relax my arms and let my body take the whole shaft, gasping at the sudden pain. For a while he makes me endure it, the sensation of being too full, the exquisite pain of having him too deep inside me.

'Your pussy feels so fucking good I could stay inside you all night.'

We stare at each other. My eyes must be full of wonder. His blaze with the excitement of dominating me, seeing me in that crouched position, my thighs wide open, his cock buried so deep inside my body I can barely bear it. I whimper, and he takes pity on me.

'Lean forward,' he growls softly.

Immediately I obey, and the pain goes away. All that remains is the pure pleasure of being stretched and filled to the brim. He pushes my breasts inwards and pulling me towards him sucks hard at my nipple, first one then the other. I start to move against his shaft and we groan in unison. My clit rubs against his pubic bone. Back and forth. Back and forth, as far as his greedily sucking mouth will allow me to retreat to. Rubbing. Rubbing. Delicious friction. Our bodies become wet and slippery. It is beautiful.

He waits for me to come before he allows himself to erupt inside me. I collapse on him and lay my cheek upon his chest. I can hear the fast, dull thudding of his heart, and feel his strong shaft still jerking inside me. I lift my head. His eyes are closed, his face is calm.

'Are you sleepy?' I ask.

'No.'

I use the ends of my hair to tickle his chin. 'What's your favorite word?'

He opens his eyes. 'Egg.'

'What?'

'I just like the sound of it.'

'You're one strange man.'

He chuckles. 'What's yours?'

'Lollipop.'

'I'd like to change my word.'

'To what?'

'Lana.'

I laugh. 'That, Mr. Barrington, is the corniest thing you have ever said to me.'

'No, really. Every time I say it, or hear it on someone else's lips, it actually gives me a thrill.'

I feel lazy and relaxed on top of him. 'We know so little about each other, don't we?'

'I know everything I need to know about you. Everything else I'll find out along the way.'

'What is it you think you know about me?'

'Well, for starters I know you're brave.'

I frown. 'Brave? I'm not brave.'

'You're one of the bravest people I know.'

'How am I brave?'

'You left me. That's brave.'

'If you knew how frightened and confused I was when I left.'

'That's the definition of bravery, Lana. Doing something even though you are terrified of the consequences. And I am really proud of the way you handled my brother today, too.'

'You are?' I squeak, immeasurably pleased with the compliment.

'When I was in the toilet I was so nervous about leaving you with him I was gripping the edges of the sink to keep from running back into the restaurant. But I knew I had to let you handle it, and I'm glad now that I did. If you can handle him you can handle all the rest in time.'

'I hope you're right.'

'And if I'm not we'll work it out together.'

Thirteen

Victoria Montgomery

If I had a flower for every time I thought of you…
I could walk through my garden forever,
—Alfred Tennyson

This morning he calls me and tells me he is coming to see me. He sounds puzzlingly distant, but still, I sense that he is desperate to see me again. Finally. I never once—well, maybe once or twice—doubted that he would tire of that thieving bitch. I've always known—he will come back.

I look at the clock. He'll be here in less than an hour! Feeling almost dizzy with excitement and triumph, I slip into white underwear. The silk slides deliciously against my fevered skin. Blake loves a woman in white. The slut knew that, too. Her underwear drawers were full of white bits and pieces. My lips tighten of their own accord. I won't think of her now. Why should I? I've won.

I, too, can drive him crazy with need. I, too, can slowly strip and crawl on the floor towards him. I will unzip his trousers and take his thick manhood, throbbing with power and strength, deep into my throat. I will swallow what he gives me. He is *my* man. I will be Mrs. Blake Law Barrington. I will walk into restaurants and parties and people will see that I am the power behind the throne.

I look at myself in the long mirror and don't just feel reassured and satisfied, but highly pleased with the image that looks back. If there is a woman more desirable than me then I am yet to meet her. I am a class act all the way. That woman—I cannot even bear to say her name—is cheap. Even the best designer clothes cannot hide that fact. It lurks in her eyes, her big lips, her silly butter wouldn't melt in my mouth expression.

I dress simply in a mint green dress, its hem faultlessly grazing the tops of my knees. I encircle my throat with two rows of creamy pearls. Nothing elaborate. It wouldn't be appropriate to display my triumph. Some decorum and subtlety is called for. And yet this dress knows how to ride up my thighs when I sit down. Maybe…He will slide his hand up the inside of my thigh and, moving aside my knickers, insert his strong fingers into me, one, two, maybe even three…Forcing them deeper and deeper, working them furiously, until I gasp. Until I come, drenching his hand.

I imagine him pushing my dress up so it bunches around my waist. He will roughly tear away my knickers, open my long, slender legs wide, and while I arch my spine with uncontrollable lust, he will eat me out like a wild beast. And I will hold him by the hair until…I climax again.

'You taste so much better than her,' he will say to me.

My legs are trembling and my knickers are wet. I push a finger into my own wet hole, and pulling it out put it into my mouth. This is me. That is what he will taste. Then a thought: You don't have much time. I snap out of my fantasy. I must be the picture of calm loyalty.

Quickly, I move to my dressing table.

Nearly black mascara, smoky brown eyeshadow and luscious berry lipstick. I press my lips together, and let the color pigments spread. Nice. Very nice. I'll just be soft and innocent. That always works. I dab perfume—potent and specially created for me—behind my ears, on the insides of my wrists and then a strip on the insides of my thighs. I do not change out of my wet knickers. I actually relish the thought of sitting next to him, wet. Maybe he will smell me.

For an instant I consider changing into something more revealing.

The soft peal of the doorbell stops me cold for a second. Too late. Mint green will have to do. I lay my palm on my stomach. I am as nervous as I was on our first date. What a night that was. We dined at Nobu and ended up at a party. How happy I was then. Everywhere we went people looked at us with envy. We were the golden couple.

I take a deep, steadying breath and walk to the door. My footfalls are light and noiseless on the thick carpet. With each step I become calmer, more clear in my purpose. I open the door smiling softly, knowing I am looking my best, and my face is radiant with the pure love I have for him.

'Hello Victoria,' he says politely.

His eyes. His eyes. So flat and cold. He has changed. He has changed. The rush from heaven to hell is dizzying. I am overwhelmed with grief as one is after a death. I take Blake's hand and, bending one knee in a gesture of respect reserved only for the highest ranking leaders, kiss it.

'Don't,' he grates harshly, yanking his hand away. 'I am not my father.'

Confused and slightly unsteady, I rise. How different he is.

'Please come in.' I let the door yawn wider and he steps through. I can do this. He stands awkwardly in my hallway. I turn away from him and close the door. My heart is breaking. Has that fucking bitch poisoned him against me?

'Let's have some tea,' I say, turning to face him. My eyes are schooled, innocent, seemingly totally unaware of what he has been doing with the *slut.*

He seems about to say something, changes his mind, and nods. I had raised my victory flag too early. I have not won yet. He does not want to be here. He does not want me. I keep my expression neutral, friendly. We go into the living room where a sumptuous tea is waiting. As we enter the living room, I see Maria, my housekeeper, slip out of the front door.

I indicate the divan and we sit next to each other. Tia, my solid chocolate Persian, poses on her chair across from us. My eyes graze the thigh next to mine. Under the fine wool it is sculptured with hard muscles. I have seen the photographs. I grasp the teapot and pour tea into two cups. I know exactly how he likes his—black, two sugars.

'Milk?' I ask.

'Black.'

'Sugar?'

'Two please.'

He watches me as I drop two sugar cubes into his tea. I hold it out to him. I am dying to touch the shapely, masculine fingers, but I don't. He takes the saucer by its lip, far away from my fingers. I raise my eyes towards him and take a small sip of my tea—milk, no sugar.

'I'm sorry about your father. He was a good man.' I smile sadly at him. I don't have to pretend sorrow. The death of his father is a great, great blow to me. He was an ally, a very powerful ally. A friend I could trust with my back. One who shared the same goal. But he is gone now.

'Thank you.' His voice is far away.

'And now you are the head of the Barrington fortune.'

He frowns. It makes him look commanding.

I reach for a gold-rimmed plate of fruitcake. Since he was a boy he never could resist fruitcake. I had these specially ordered from my father's chef. 'Would you like a slice?'

'Thank you.'

I watch him bite into it. He is perfect. From the bold, hard slash of his mouth to the taut cheekbones to his naturally bronze coloring, to the dark hair, he is perfect. He is my heart. He is mine. The thought is fiercely possessive and feels right. I must have him or I will die.

I reach under the white muslin for a scone. It is still warm. I butter it, spread a thin layer of jam, bring it to my mouth, and realize I will be sick if it passes my lips. But he is watching me with the narrowed eyes of a predator. Narrowed and assessing. What is he thinking? I have photos of him when he is with that ridiculous woman, when his eyes are caressing and infinitely tender. I take a small bite, chew until I can no longer bear it in my mouth, and swallow. A mouthful of tea makes it go down.

'Look, I might as well come clean right away. I've fallen in love with Lana,' he announces abruptly.

Fourteen

I think my eyes widen. From the moment I met his cold, dead eyes at the front door I had been expecting such a declaration, but my reaction was involuntary. Simply couldn't help it. Hearing the harshness of his words. No 'Sorry I wasted your fucking time. Sorry I led you on a merry dance all these years. Sorry I irreparably shattered your heart into a thousand sharp shards.' Nothing. Just that arrow right into my heart. A sick fury rises inside me. The fury of being denied, deprived. When I was two I didn't throw myself on the ground in a tantrum, I used to run to the servants and kick and punch them hard. Until the fury was appeased and abated. I cannot show him that rage. I lower my eyes quickly.

'I'm really sorry,' he says.

His voice is gentle, but when I look up at him, his eyes are watchful, utterly, utterly unrepentant and full of the realization of how foolish the idea of marrying me was. How could he ever have thought he could marry me and play house?

'She doesn't understand our ways. She won't have the stomach to do the *necessary* things.'

A veil comes over his eyes. 'I don't want her to do any of those things. I want to keep her out of all that. We will be a normal family.'

'But you have taken the vow.'

'The only vow I have taken is silence. And I won't break that.'

'From the path thou shall not stray.'

'I already have.'

I frown. 'You'd give up ultimate power for her?'

He smiles sadly. 'Oh, Victoria. How little you know me. I was not even going to ask you to do those things. I don't want the power. I detest what we are doing. I went along because I didn't know any better. Let the others fight it out for the ultimate power. The only reason I remain is because leaving is not an option.'

I reach out a hand and touch his sleeve and…He recoils. Imperceptibly, but it is there. An inhuman claw inside my chest squeezes tighter and tighter until I feel I almost cannot breathe at all. So this also is love, I reflect with wonder. No one can imagine just how poisonous is the hate in my heart for that beastly woman who stole my man.

Lana fucking Bloom.

She had no right. I rock with helpless pain.

Instantly, he reaches for my hand. It is satiny soft, but icy and quite lifeless.

'Are you all right?' His voice seems muffled, as if he is talking to me while I am under water.

I nod. I must gather myself. I can still turn this around. I take a deep breath, stop rocking, and, dry-eyed, turn to look at him.

'Are you sure you're all right?' he repeats.

I fix a bright smile on my lips. 'Of course.'

'You deserve to find someone who will love you. We didn't love each other. We were marrying for all the wrong reasons. I know that now,' he says with breathtaking masculine selfishness.

Yes, you found your slut and now you just want to push me away. I recall again how I had decided to offer myself to him when he called me this morning. To show him how good we'd be together.

I nod. 'You are right. This is probably for the best. We would probably have ended up in the divorce courts.' I smile again. Conciliatory.

He reciprocates with a smile of his own. He thinks it is all over. Just like that he can wash his hands of me.

'You have a son?'

Twin lights blossom in his eyes. If he takes out his wallet and shows me a picture of their blasted baby, I swear, I will scream, but he doesn't.

'He's the joy of my life,' he says simply.

In those few words I see a world I can never have. In my head a voice is sneering, 'Resentment is like drinking poison and waiting for the other person to die.' Of their own accord my delicate fingers start drumming dangerously on the glass-topped coffee table. I see his eyes shift to my hand. I jerk it away and clasp it in my other hand. I need to do something quickly. He is fixing to leave. I swallow hard at the lump in my throat and stare at the glass surface. How insidiously smooth and unyielding it is. My vision takes in the edge of the plate with the uneaten scone, the butter knife...It is sheer madness, I could even put my eye out, but in a split second I make my decision.

I let my body pitch forward as if my bones have suddenly melted. The smooth hard glass, the knife's gleaming blade, and sharp edge of the table rise up to meet my face. Anybody else would have halted their fall, saved themselves, given in to the instinct to protect themselves. I didn't.

And what a good thing that I was brave.

I risked gouging out my eye and won. Just inches away from the pointed end of the knife, hard hands catch me by the arms. I am bodily lifted and held close to his body, the scent of him assailing my senses. God, I love this man so much. I keep my eyes closed, my body limp and floppy. My dress has ridden up my thighs.

'Victoria,' Blake calls urgently, but I allow my neck to droop over his arms, so my throat is bared to him and he can savor the vulnerability of my lifeless limbs in his arms. Let him feel masculine and strong and protective. The position is awkward and he stands lifting me up with him. It is unexpectedly and deliciously romantic, and I feel like one of those women on the jacket covers of the voluptuous romances my mother reads.

I wish he could hold me like this forever, but he lays me back on the divan. However, he is so gentle about it that I suddenly realize he must love me. He doesn't know it, but it is I who am the one he truly loves. He must just use her for sex. It is me that he loves. Always me. He pulls my dress down over my thighs. What a gentleman. He could have taken advantage of me. Peeked at my sex. Or even had sex with my inert body.

That is a great fantasy of mine.

That I would lie on a table as if in a swoon and a total stranger, someone dark and dangerous, someone like Blake, would come and roughly thrust my thighs open, and fuck my plump little sex mercilessly, painfully. I would feel everything, but I would be unable to make a single sound of protest as his enormous organ would split me remorselessly.

But as the man realizes how hungry and wet I am for him, he understands that I crave the thorough use of my body. Then he becomes sublimely cruel. My own silence deafens me. I weep silently as he does terrible things to me. Until I am hardly human. Afterwards, he will leave even before I wake up.

Sometimes I would even fantasize that a group of men come, all colors and scents, to use my body while I am lying there. None of them would use condoms. They would use every orifice. They would speak of me as if I was nothing but a piece of meat.

Blake is sliding his hands away from under the backs of my knees and my neck and I sense him standing. Seconds later my head is lifted and a cushion placed under it. I hear him striding towards the bathroom. He returns with a cold face towel that he lays on my forehead. I moan softly and allow my eyelids to flutter slightly. He calls my name. I open my eyes and allow them to roll a little.

'What happened?' I ask weakly.

'You fainted.'

I attempt to rise to my elbows, then pretend as if the effort is making me dizzy. My head sways unsteadily.

'Take it easy. Lie back down.'

I let myself fall back with a sigh. I look up at him. He is frowning.

'Does this happen often?' he asks.

I shake my head. 'I'll be fine in a minute.'

'Can I get you anything?'

'I feel cold.'

He looks around and, seeing nothing with which to cover me, takes off his jacket and lays it on my upper body. The warmth of his body lingers and I just want to close my eyes and savor it. Oh, why, oh why did she come and steal him away from me? Everything was going fine until she came into the picture. He loves me really. We are not strangers. We have grown up together.

'I'm sorry,' he says softly.

I know he is. It is that filthy bitch who has him all tied up with sex. I should have slept with him, I would have him now. My heart is full of bitter regret that I never slept with him.

'It's not your fault,' I whisper. Tears begin to flow from my eyes.

He kneels beside me.

'Do you know what I regret the most?'

'No.'

'I regret that we never made love, even once. Can we? Just once. For old times sake?'

My tears dry as suddenly as they began. I look up at him through damp lashes. He is staring at me without revealing any emotion, but my heart and my eyes are full of hot, hungry craving for him. My whole being is on fire for him. Right then all I want is to feel his burning lips on my lips, face, throat, breasts, between my legs…until I am driven out of my mind. I snake my tongue out, run it along my lower lip.

'Just this once.' My voice is husky and thick, my eyes half-hooded.

He is still staring at me sans expression, so I bend my head so my hair parts and exposes the defenseless white curve that is the nape of my neck. For a moment Blake makes neither move nor response, until unexpectedly, in the downcast line of my vision, I see his leather shoes quietly turn away from me. And start to head towards the door. He is leaving. He is actually going.

The bastard!

For a precious few seconds I lie shocked, silent and paralyzed, the blood running cold in my veins. Even my brain refuses to think. It never, never occurred to me that he could simply walk away from me. What now?

Then I stand and call him.

He doesn't stop.

My stomach lurches. 'You can't leave me.'

He stops and turns around to face me. His laughter rings hollow, rasping and devoid of humor. 'You see something you want, you just reach out and take it, don't you?'

'You're a fine one to talk,' I retort. Shit I shouldn't have said that. I stare at him in a panic. It has all gone so wrong.

'You're so fucking spoilt.' His words do not match his eyes, though. They are weary, the eyes of a man who has had enough. He shakes his head and starts walking away from me. He is already at the door. His hand is reaching for the handle. And suddenly I know. I know exactly how to stop him in his tracks. And I know how to make it convincing, too. I take a rush of air into my lungs.

'I know what it tastes like. I've taken part,' I cry out. My voice is like a bell in the silent room.

His hand freezes. He turns slowly. 'What?'

Fifteen

His expression is one of great shock. My father is not a lowly member to offer his daughter in such a way. There is a seed of distrust in his eyes, and yet there is compassion and softness. She has changed him. I have never seen this look in his eyes.

'I was just a child. I never made a sound. I never saw their faces. They took turns. I can never forget,' I whisper. I am a convincing actress.

He strides over to me and puts his arms around me. 'I'm sorry, Victoria. So sorry. I didn't know. He should have protected you.'

'It doesn't matter now. I just wanted you to know that I've suffered too.'

'I didn't plan it this way,' he says softly. 'It just happened. I fell in love with her.'

I look up at him with great, big eyes. 'I'm not blaming you for falling in love with another woman. I'm not even angry with you or her. But I am hurting. Real bad. It's simple for you. "Let's be friends," you say, but it's not so easy for me. I love you. I always have and I always will. It's inside me, day and night eating at me relentlessly. My heart is bleeding, Blake. I can't eat. I can't sleep. I know you didn't ask for my heart, but I gave it, anyway.' I smile bitterly. 'You'd be shocked if you knew how much I hurt. I feel as if I am going mad.'

He looks into my eyes, saddened, incredibly so. 'Oh, Victoria.'

'The heart was meant to be broken,' I say, quoting Oscar Wilde. I know he will recognize and smile.

He half smiles. 'I didn't know it was like that for you. I don't know what I thought. These arrangements,' he opens his palms out helplessly, 'they are not meant to be like this.' He stops for a moment. 'I didn't think because I didn't care for you, for me, or anyone else for that matter. I was a brute.'

'Welcome to my world,' I say.

I can see that he pities me.

'I have to go,' he mutters.

'Look after my heart. You hold it in your hand.'

He kisses the top of my head and then he is gone, shutting the door quietly behind him.

'I prayed for you,' I whisper at the closed door.

How long I stood staring at the door, utterly devastated and uncomprehending, my dreams and hopes scattered around me, I don't know. Perhaps I thought he might still return. Ring the bell and come in, tell me it has all been a dreadful mistake. I even waited past the obligatory one hundred and eighty seconds while my mind replayed the humiliation of my total rejection. I only really come to when I feel silky fur rubbing against my bare legs. I look down. Tia purrs gently.

I bend down and pick up her warm, soft body. I press her pliant silkiness against my chest and look into her beautiful face. She stares at me with her one blue and one copper eye, blinks and tries to snuggle up between my breasts. Even the cat has found contentment in its life.

Without warning that intense hot bubble of poison that is always lying in wait in the very depths of my bowels shoots sickeningly into my head. It explodes in a shower of red-hot sparks right between my eyes. As if hit by lightning I react. I lose it. Go ape-shit crazy. With a wild cry of fury and with all the viciousness of a female cobra on a nest of unhatched eggs, I hurl the unsuspecting cat against the wall. She crashes into the wall in a screaming confusion of distended nails and flying fur. The animal rights itself, curses, spits and hisses at me before fleeing in a chocolate streak of confused terror and pain.

My curled nails bite deeply into my own flesh, but I feel no pain, only the need to destroy. I turn and look at myself in the mirrored wall. My face is flushed and blazing with color, my eyes are savage, my mouth is open and breathing hard as if I have been running, and my breasts are heaving.

Something sick swirls in my stomach. My heart begins to race. I hear a rattling in my head and my mouth fills with the taste of metal. I feel the tremble begin in my fingers. It's happening. At first slight, so slight it is like the shaking of an alcoholic in the morning before his first drink. But it becomes stronger, more insistent. I let it. It is a fine feeling. The way it sweeps into my body, takes over and becomes a roaring ball of pure energy.

The room in front of me swirls slightly. Objects come into focus, lose their edges and come back into being. My trembling body begins to shake violently. Suddenly, I am sucked into a vortex of energy and I feel myself flying across the room. I grab a bespoke dining chair as if it weighed nothing more than a matchstick, raise it high over my head, and running to the mirrored wall slam it against the surface. The sound of exploding glass is loud, satisfying. Again. And again. The chair breaks. I see myself in the broken mirror. Galvanized, I am indeed a terrible vision, flying hair, bared teeth.

I destroy everything!

Eventually when I fall down in an exhausted heap on the floor, the room is in total shambles. The expensive brocade curtains lie in shreds, every breakable thing accuses me in shattered silence and my beautiful nails are torn and bleeding. My eyes travel over the destruction I have wreaked, but I find no remorse in my heart. I am filled only with defiance.

As a matter of fact, I feel much better now. It's been refreshing and deeply cleansing to damage so indiscriminately. Tomorrow, I will go shopping. And shopping always gives me a fantastic boost. I will get something nice for Tia (I shouldn't have flung her against the wall) and something stunningly expensive and beautiful for me, for when Blake comes back to me. This is just a minor setback. Obviously, he will tire of her.

I stand. A sharp pain tears through my knee. I look down.

A huge bruise is coming up. The hem of my dress is torn too. I limp over to the bathroom and stand in front of the mirror. I gaze at myself. Moisture-filled luminous eyes in a pale face. I realize anew that I really am extraordinarily beautiful. I pout at my own reflection. Transfixed by my own beauty I form words, just to watch my berry lips in movement. Quite of their own volition they say, 'I'll get him back. Of course I will.'

Sixteen

Lana Bloom

I have spent most of the day on the phone with lawyers and advisors discussing the best way for me to set up and run my charity. Now I am in the kitchen making a simple dinner while Sorab is napping inside his playpen. When Blake comes home I don't rush out to the front door because the asparagus will be ready in less than a minute and I don't want to overcook it.

'We're in the kitchen,' I call out, keeping my voice fairly soft in order not to wake Sorab.

I hear Blake close the front door. He appears in the doorway, leans against it and simply looks at me.

'What is it?'

He just shakes his head and continues gazing at me.

'Blake?'

To my horror his eyes fill with tears.

I put down the colander of asparagus and run to him.

I put my fingers on his damp lashes. 'Oh, my darling, what's wrong?'

He catches my fingers in his hand and presses them against his lips. 'Nothing. I am just drinking in the sight of you.'

His lips turn into a soft kiss on my fingertips. He sweeps his hand along my jaw line.

'That's a good thing, right?' I joke.

'I love you, Lana. I never stop thinking of you. Never. The only thing I am afraid of in this life is losing you. You know I'd risk everything for you, don't you?'

Warmth starts spreading throughout my body. 'I am right here, Blake. Where I belong, where I'll always be.'

'I went to see Victoria today.'

'Oh.'

'I told her I'm in love with you.'

'How did she react?'

'She fell apart. I did not expect it. She was pitiful.'

I move slightly away from him. 'It was not your father who paid me to leave. It was her.'

'I know. When I found out that Sorab was mine, I traced the money through its complicated trusts back to her. I was furious—she had caused me a year of excruciating pain—but confronting her was not a priority. All information is power, and everything I knew, and my opponent thought I did not was my advantage. So I never revealed my hand or acted on the knowledge.

'When I went to see her today I was prepared to coldly dismiss her from our lives, but then she said something which made me pity her. The truth is, I did lead her on. I did renege on my promise to marry her. She has some grounds for her anger and suffering. I never wanted revenge and now I actually pity her. I have everything. She has nothing. I wish her well. One day I hope we will be friends.'

'She didn't seem pitiful to me.'

'She is the spoilt daughter of a very wealthy man and she is used to getting what she wants, but even she has been broken by love. She will no longer trouble us.'

I say nothing.

That evening Sorab falls asleep on top of his father's body in the living room. I follow to watch as Blake tucks Sorab in for the night. First Blake, and then I bend to kiss his smooth cheek as he lies asleep on his side. When I raise my eyes to Blake's he is watching me. In the shadows and soft light of the bedroom he looks proudly proprietorial. We are his family.

He comes around the cot, takes me by the hand, leads me into our bedroom…and makes love to me, as he has never done before. With infinite gentleness as if I am a delicate butterfly whose wings can come off as dust pigments on his fingers, if he does not take the greatest care in the way he handles me. All of it is long, or slow, or deep, and when he climaxes he calls my name as if he is falling off a cliff and I am the last thing he sees. The longing in his voice is a balm to my heart.

I stretch luxuriously and lie on my stomach.

He lets his fingers run up and down my spine. 'I love the feel of your spine, the delicate little bones that make your body. They are like skin-covered teeth, only they are not. As you move they flow under my fingers.'

I chuckle. 'Oh my God! We have unearthed the poet in you.'

'It's love. The loved destroys the thing that loves it.'

I turn around to face him, a frown etched on my brow. 'Are you saying your love for me is destroying you?'

He cups my naked breast possessively. 'The more I love you the more of a stranger I have become to myself. Now I do and say things that I would never have dreamed of doing or saying. I can hardly believe that I lived all these years without you.'

I run my finger down his cheek. 'Sometimes I get so scared. Everything I have ever loved has been taken away from me.' I look down to the duvet cover. My voice trembles like the strings of a harp. I bite back the tears that have so suddenly arrived to spoil what should have been a beautiful moment.

He leans in and kisses the top of my left shoulder. 'My love, my love, if you are still living and I am not, then I will haunt you until your dying day.'

I look up at him with hurt eyes. 'That's not funny, Barrington.'

'I know, my darling heart. It's only funny in the fucked up world I exist in. The real truth is, I want us to be like those ancient couples who have never been apart a day in their lives and when one partner dies the other follows in hours.'

'Me too. I even hate saying goodnight to you. It means I'll lose you again for a few more hours.'

He puts a finger against my temple. 'Sometimes I wake up and watch you sleeping.'

'Oh.'

'Do you know you sometimes smile in your sleep?'

'I do?'

'You always look so defenseless and angelic, like one of those fairy princesses from my childhood days.'

'A fairy princess?' I love the idea.

'Yes, often I wish I could lock you away in an enchanted tower. Nobody could get to you except me.'

'You don't have to look me away in a tower. I'm always here for you.'

'The princess is not locked up because she is bad. The princess is locked up because she is precious beyond words, and everyone wants a piece of her.' His voice changes, becomes serious. 'I have to put you somewhere you can't be hurt.'

'I am at that somewhere. Right here, beside you.'

He frowns. 'But when I am not around—'

'Brian and his pack take over.'

'I'd still prefer to lock you up in an enchanted tower.'

'That doesn't sound quite fair. I get locked up while you go into the world and do all the things that you love to do.'

'I don't love what I do, Lana. I do it because I have to.'

'Why can't you walk away? You have more than we can ever spend.'

'Sometimes we are given the illusion of choice. Give a man dying of thirst in a desert a glass of water and tell him it's his choice. Drink or leave it. Is that really a choice, Lana?'

I say nothing. I remember when my mother was so ill that choice became an illusion.

'I am like that man,' he continues. 'If I drink it will mean danger to you and Sorab. I know too much for them to allow me to walk away. I have responsibilities that I must see through.'

'Responsibilities to carry on destroying the world?'

He smiles sadly and puts his finger on my lips. 'No more. That will happen with or without me.'

'Then why do you have to do it?'

'What happens to the whistleblower, Lana?'

'They get put in prison or they or their loved ones meet with "accidents" or they commit "suicide" and the agenda goes on uninterrupted.'

I frown and move my mouth away from his finger. 'Why—?'

His fingers stop my lips, stop any further conversation. His eyes look so sad I wish I had never started this conversation. I move towards him and hug him hard. He is in pain. Terrible pain, but he cannot tell me. He is the man in the desert with a glass full of cool, life-giving water. I am asking him to drink, but he is resisting because of me and Sorab. I realize then that he has reason for the secrecy he maintains. He believes it is for the greater good. He believes harm will befall me and Sorab. I have to accept it. I decide then to stop pestering him. I will do my own research.

'I'm going to church tomorrow.'

'OK, what time would you like us to go?'

I stare at him, astonished. 'You mean you'll come to church with me?'

He shrugs. 'Sure why not?'

'But what about the brotherhood?'

'The cloak of respectability the brotherhood wears is organized religion.'

And I remember that his father's funeral had been held in a church. 'But if you come with me, wouldn't that be a sham?'

He looks me in the eye. 'No, it wouldn't.'

'I'm going to love you like I'll never be hurt.'

He lays his head on the pillow beside me and looks deep into my eyes. 'Often I look at you and I can't believe my luck,' he whispers.

Two days later I am pushing Sorab on High Street Kensington when time suddenly suspends. The blood stills in my veins. For a moment it is as if I am in a movie frame that suddenly freezes.

Victoria is standing only a few yards away. We stare at each other. Her eyes are translucent with a strange mixture of bewilderment and hatred. She reminds me of a wild animal that is caught in a mangle. It is dangerous because it is so desperate. I know I am safe—Brian is only a shout away—but I still feel the icy claw of fear squeeze at my heart.

She takes a step towards me and my internal organs lurch as if I am in a fast-moving lift that suddenly stops. My mind instantly starts making plans to protect Sorab. A voice in my brain says, 'She wouldn't dare,' but I stand ready.

She begins to walk towards me, her head held straight, but her eyes unblinking and deadly are trained on me, the eyeballs moving to the sides of her eyes as she passes by me. So close to me, almost her shoulder brushing mine. The malice and madness I see in her eyes chill me to the bone. And yet, she has done nothing. I turn around and watch her walk away without once turning back.

I clamp my hand over my mouth, as if to cover the horror of the knowledge that she has fooled Blake. She will be trouble. But how will I convince him otherwise? She has done nothing to me.

That night Blake's lips crash against mine, and afterwards he tells me we are going to Dubai—a romantic weekend. I lose myself in the moment and forget the maniacal hatred in Victoria's eyes…momentarily.

Seventeen

When we arrive at the airport I am surprised to note that we are not getting into Blake's Gulfstream jet, but a Boeing 767. We walk through the doors and I gawp in awed silence. It looks like no plane I've ever been in. Brand new and customized to look like the interior of an apartment it is luxurious and stunningly elegant.

I turn to Blake. 'Do you own this?'

'It's registered to the Bank of Utah.'

'But really it's yours?'

He shrugs. 'Own nothing, control everything.'

Smiling staff come forth with smiles and hot towels.

After take-off I turn to Blake. 'Can I explore?'

'Want me to show you?'

'Nope. Want to take it all in on my own.'

He smiles and reaches for his briefcase. 'Knock yourself out.'

I touch my lips to his. 'I will.'

I take Sorab from Jerry and we start exploring the three floors. It is truly amazing. All the spaces have no hard edges, everything curves and swirls around to meet the next environment. There is a dining table that seats twenty, three guest bedroom suites, lifts, a kitchen, an office, a boardroom, two sumptuous lounges with cream couches, a concert hall, a TV room, a gym and a sauna.

We end up in the master bedroom, which is on two levels. I playfully throw Sorab on the massive white bed and he bounces and squeals with startled laughter. He lifts his hands up to me. I pick him up and throw him back down on the bed. He laughs happily and lifts his hands again.

'One last time,' I say, and fling him on the bed again. He bounces, sits up and crawls towards me. I lay on the bed.

He arrives beside me and climbs on my body. I hold him up in the air, his body horizontal to mine.

'Mummy and Daddy will be christening this bed soon,' I tell him.

He cackles loudly.

'I know. Wouldn't that be nice, huh?'

My mobile rings.

'Where are you?'

'In the master bedroom.'

'Don't move.'

We spend an hour together, playing, just as an ordinary family would. When Sorab nods off, we lay for a while with him between us, just looking into each other's eyes.

'We are so lucky, aren't we?' I whisper.

'I can hardly believe I have both of you.'

I grin. 'Wanna have sex?'

His answering grin is wolfish. 'Obviously.'

'What about His Highness?' I jerk my head in the direction of the sleeping child.

'He can have the bed,' he says, and grabbing my hand he slides me off the round bed. And there on the soft white carpet we have quiet sex. It is unfamiliar and in a funny way taboo, and so incredibly exciting.

When we finish I am giggling breathlessly. 'My knees,' I complain.

'We'll use the bed on the return trip,' Blake promises.

I stare at him in wonder. His hair is falling down his forehead, his eyes are sparkling and he looks so young and carefree.

We are flown by helicopter to the roof of the iconic and awesomely beautiful Burj Al Arab, considered the best of the three seven star hotels in the world. As soon as we step out on to the green felt landing pad, waiters in tails and white gloves stand in a line to greet us with champagne and flowers.

There is no check-in and we are immediately charmed into the royal suite. Inside the opulence is shocking. Its luxury and excess are such that it is almost intimidating. There is a butler outside the door who knows us all by name which I frankly find unnerving! I feel as if I am an impostor. Surely only kings and emperors live with gold and gilt on every surface and leopard skin-covered empire chairs.

The royal suite has red silk walls. The entrance hall leads to a grand staircase that has elaborately patterned and carved gold and black banisters. It has a faux leopard skin runner carpet. Even Jerry raises her eyebrows and goes silent on me. When she disappears into her bedroom with Sorab I turn to Blake.

'Well, what do you think?' he asks.

'It's all rather...heroic.'

He grins. 'I'm glad it was you who said it and not me.'

We laugh. At that moment I am the happiest person on earth.

'Shall we check out the bedroom?'

'Shall we wait until it's dark?'

'Chicken,' he teases and taking my hand pulls me towards the bedroom.

We stand at the doorway.

The room is huge with a brightly patterned carpet, gilded furniture, patterned wallpaper and gilded mirrors. The four-poster bed is massive and set on a purple pedestal, with curtains around it. Over it is a domed canopy with a pleated silk interior. There is the impression of a tent, but also the wild excess of Versace.

We turn to look at each other.

'Heroic,' we blurt out at precisely the same time and laugh.

'How much does it cost?'

'More than a hero's ransom.'

I chuckle. 'Come on, let's check out the bathroom.

There: gold marble walls, cream marble columns, and blue-veined chocolate marble floors, gilded mirrors, polished bronze tiles, gold taps and fittings, and Hermes toiletries.

'Looks like fun times ahead for you and me,' Blake says looking meaningfully at the round Jacuzzi bath.

I grin. 'A midnight bath?'

'Who am I to turn down such a beautiful woman?'

'I've never been in a Jacuzzi.'

'Eyes tell a story. Yours tell me to open your legs and devour you.' His voice is low and throbbing with passion.

I watch the heat come into his eyes, the dark hunger, and my stomach twists with excitement. 'I like the word excess. It has sex inside it,' I whisper.

We use the hotel's Ferrari. It is scarlet and roars like some great beast when Blake guns it. Dubai, it turns out, is littered with speed cameras and Blake makes everyone of them flash.

We eat at At.mosphere, the highest restaurant in the world, one hundred and twenty-three floors away from the ground. The views are breathtaking.

'I fancy getting legless,' I announce.

Blake raises his eyebrows, but does not say anything while I knock the cocktails back.

'You don't mind, do you?' I ask, already tipsy.

'No, not at all. I'm actually rather curious. I've never seen you drunk.'

I giggle like a schoolgirl and look at him from beneath my eyelashes.

'What?' he asks.

'It feels as if I've always known you, perhaps even in other lifetimes.'

'You know what you're like?' His voice is but a whisper.

I lean forward. 'Tell me.'

'You're like a force that swept into my life, cast me into the winds, and set me ablaze. Afterwards you made me rise from the ashes, like a phoenix reborn.'

'Wow! That's deep.' I wave a finger towards the glass walls at the sky. 'And there you are flying in the skies.'

'I like drunk Lana.'

'Ooo…Is it already time for dessert?'

What looks like a chocolate ball arrives. I lift my eyes towards Blake.

'Want to taste?'

He shakes his head. 'Enjoy yourself.'

I tuck in. Delicious.

At the 'floating' staircase, going down, I become suddenly nervous. Blake kneels at my feet and takes my shoes off for me. Holding me tight we go down it. In the high-speed lift I start to feel a bit sick, but outside with cool breezes blowing on the fountain terrace, I recover very quickly and start to look forward to the Jacuzzi.

Blake looks at his watch, 'Come on,' he says and takes me closer to the water's edge. Suddenly music fills the air. I look around surprised. It is Pink and Nat Ruess.

'They're playing our song, Lana.'

I gaze up at him. 'You remembered.'

'How could I forget? The night is branded in my mind forever. You were so, so innocent and so very beautiful.' He puts his hands on either side of my cheeks and turns my face towards the fountains. 'Watch the fountains dance,' he says, and stands so close behind me.

I lean back and stare with amazement. All around me people are taking their phones out to record the stupendous spectacle. Indeed, they are dancing fountains. Soaring, leaning, bending, running like fire upon the surface of the water, all in tempo with the music. It is very beautiful and I am so overcome with joy that tears gather in my eyes and streak down my face.

When the last fountain dies down, he turns me around to face him.

'Why are you crying?'

I sniff loudly. 'These are happy tears. Just ignore me.'

'Until I met you I never wanted a woman's tears, but I want yours. I want your sighs, I want your laughter, I want your joy, your smell, your smile. I want it all.'

Behind me I hear fireworks. I turn my face up to the skies and watch the beautiful display. They are still exploding around us when Blake takes a ring out of his jacket and slips it on my finger.

I gaze down at it. It is the biggest pink diamond I have ever seen. It would have been gaudy if not for the plain setting and the astonishing intensity of its color. The light from the fireworks makes it glitter like a pink fire. It is also a perfect fit. It is too big and beautiful to not be…Is it? Could it really be? I look up at him with shocked eyes. The flare from the fireworks streak across his face.

'Are you asking me to marry you?'

'Nope.'

'Oh.' The wind changes. A fine mist of water from the fountain reaches us, lands on my skin. It is deliciously cool on my flushed skin.

'If you ask you might get a no and I'm not taking no for an answer. I'm telling you: we're getting married.'

For a moment I take in the beautiful, beautiful eyes, that tough, unyielding jaw, the straight mouth, the aristocratic nose, then I fling my arms around his neck and our lips meet in the most beautiful kiss. It is deep and lusty and romantic and just perfect. I forget the fireworks, the people, the fountain.

All I know is when he first kissed me a lifetime ago, he didn't kiss my lips, he kissed my soul.

Hey Beautiful,

Thank you! You've kept me company this far into Blake and Lana's journey, and it will be my greatest pleasure to have you around until the series is complete.

The next part, Seduce Me, is told through the point of view of Lana's bridesmaid, Julie Sugar. It will be the conclusion of the Lana and Blake saga, but it is also the story of Julie's search for true love.

See you between the sheets of Seduce Me…

xx Georgia

https://www.facebook.com/georgia.lecarre
https://twitter.com/georgiaLeCarre
http://www.goodreads.com/GeorgiaLeCarre

Bonus Material

BLAKE LAW BARRINGTON POV

Forty 2 Days

Exposed

The Billionaire Banker Series

GEORGIA LE CARRE

Pov

Forty 2 Days

When Blake Met Lana At the Bank

One

For a whole fucking year I hear nothing.

She flies out of Heathrow with her mother, lands in Tehran and then... The trail goes stone cold. That still shocks me. The ease with which a woman can enter Iran, don a drab, loose-fitting garment, and simply disappear, become totally invisible. Without the powerful tentacles of a central bank in that country I have no way of tracking her financially either. The only connection left was the Swiss bank account, but that registered no activity, until recently, when the account was emptied and closed on the same day.

Then there was nothing left of her, but memories and hurt. Hurt like I had never imagined possible.

Sometimes, especially in the beginning when I didn't yet hate her, I used to imagine her veiled and in the desert. She always wanted to go there. My dreams were romantic then. Telescoped without reality or reason we traveled in slow motion upon shifting sands, untroubled by the blazing sun, sharing a camel, only one goatskin water bag between us. In my dreams everything was perfect: the rocking of the camel, perfect. Her, perfect. Us, perfect.

And then I would wake up and feel like shit.

In the day I throw myself into work. At night I trawl the city's night scene looking for the same thing anyone who crawls into the underbelly of cities finds—moments of forgetfulness between the legs of strangers. But nothing would fill the void or the terrible longing for her.

I wanted us on one camel.

In my recurring fantasy, she comes to my office, talks her away around Laura, and opens my door. I am too shocked to stand. She comes towards me hips swaying, a slut. Dressed as I had found her that first night we met, she comes around the desk, swipes all my papers to the floor and sits on the table facing me. With one shoe she pushes my chair a little away. Then she lifts her legs, knees together, the way a girl who has been to finishing school is supposed to get out of a car, and pushes her butt deeper into the desk. I look at her. Her gaze is greedy, the way I know her eyes can be. She leans back so that both the palms of her hands are on the desk behind her, and spreads her legs wide open. My eyes slip down. There it is. Open: running with sweet juices.

'Get your mouth on it,' her red lips command. 'I've been dying for a good suck.'

But it is absolutely true what the philosophers say: love and hate are just two ends of the same string. You love someone, they lie to you, and you love them less; then they cheat on you, and you love them even less, and you keep going down that string until you hate them. So I traveled down that string.

I hate that woman, that is as obvious as hell to me, but it is also as clear as day that I cannot let her go. She cheated me. Kicked me when I was down. Brought me to my knees. No one has ever done that. Ever. If I do not punish her…Betrayal then, forever. I will know myself to be a weak man pretending to be strong. I must have my pound of flesh.

Then three days ago a little light on my computer screen flashed. For a moment my mind went blank. Then hot blood began to pulse again in my veins and my cheek muscles moved, my lips curved. I was smiling again.

'Gotcha.'

I hear footsteps approaching in the corridor and my heart begins to race. The excitement of seeing her again is so uncontrollably strong that it startles me. But I hate her guts. Immensely. This is purely about revenge. This is about me getting what I am owed. I lay my palms flat on the desk. I want to be cold and controlled. I don't want the bitch to have the satisfaction of knowing that she has affected me at all. The footsteps pause outside the door. I take a deep breath. She is nothing, I tell myself. She just wanted to count my money.

My face becomes an unfeeling mask.

I cease my wild thoughts.

A brief knock, and the door opens.

And… All the ugly words that had kept me sane—whore, slut, gold-digger, bitch—become empty balloons that are floating away. I cannot keep a single one. She may be a whore, a slut and a gold-digger, but she is mine. My slut, my bitch, my gold-digger.

Fuck, already I am itching to see her naked. I want to strip off that ugly suit she's wearing, pop her on the table and fuck her until she screams. That's the second part of the fantasy.

She walked in with a smile—big, false, irritating. That hurt. Obviously, she has not suffered as I have. Fortunately for her, the smile doesn't last long. Dies on contact with my person. Her face drains of color and her mouth hangs open. That's more like it, darling. Papa's here to get back what he is owed. You forgot—nobody cheats Papa. While she is doing a better than average impression of a goldfish, I study her. How thin she has become. Starving-African-children thin. Nobody should be that thin.

The employee who showed her in closes the door. Time to take control.

'Hello, Lana,' I say, remaining seated behind the desk. My voice comes out… Good. Encouraged,

I add more words. 'Have a seat,' I invite. That, too, I am pleased to note, comes out smooth.

But she does not move. She keeps doing the goldfish thing, but doesn't find her voice. I see her swallow and try again.

'What are you doing here?' It is barely a hoarse whisper.

'Processing your loan application.'

She frowns. 'What?'

'I'm here to process your loan application,' I repeat with deliberate patience. I am enjoying this head fuck. The element of surprise has completely worked in my favor.

She shakes her head. 'You don't work here. You don't process tiny little loans.'

'I'm here to process yours.'

'Why?' Some thought crosses her mind and she is suddenly galvanized into action. 'So you can turn me down? Don't bother. I'll show myself out,' she cries hotly and begins to turn.

I am on my feet instantly, the chair wheeling away behind me. 'Lana, wait.'

She hesitates, looks up at me blankly.

'I am the one in the entire banking industry most likely to extend you this loan.'

She continues to stare at me.

'Please,' I continue, more carefully this time, 'take a seat.'

Dazed she looks at the two chairs facing me, but she does not move. 'How did you know I would be here today?

I tell her about the nifty little software that flags her name and date of birth if it comes up in the banking system.

She frowns, but says nothing.

I need to engage with her. The shock has dazed her. 'Is all the money in the Swiss account gone?'

She nods distractedly. 'But why are you here?'

'Same reason as before.'

'For sex.'

I sort of lose my head then. 'Sex?' I hiss, my jaw clenching tight. 'God, you have no idea, have you?' I go around the table and advance towards her. Honestly, at that moment I want to throttle her. How easily she had said that word, diminished all my intolerable pain and my insatiable longing into one meaningless action. She carries on staring at me, almost fearfully. I stop a foot in front of her, electricity crackling between us. I take one more step and we are inches apart and suddenly I smell her. I breathe in the scent. *What the…?*

Baby powder!

Sick, but it fires up my imagination the way the most expensive perfume cannot. Like a snake, lust is uncoiling in the pit of my belly, spitting its venom into my veins. I want her so bad I ache. Quickly, I lower my eyelids, but it is as if she has already seen the potency of my desire for her. For the first time since she came into the room, color tinges her skin.

She reaches out a trembling hand toward me.

My reaction is instant and beyond my control. 'Don't,' I rasp, stiffening. I cannot let her have the upper hand. This has to be all my way. And there is no highway for this little bird.

Shocked by the violence of my reaction, she retracts her hand. I see the realization in her eyes. Now she knows she has damaged me. Her face crumples as if she gives a flying fuck. What an actress.

'Please,' she whispers.

She put a lot emotion into that word and I am shocked at how much I want to believe that it is not an act. My pathetic neediness annoys me. I bend my head toward her face. Her eyes are riveted on my lips. What is she remembering? The taste of me?

'Dishonest little Lana,' I murmur, so close to her neck that if I put my tongue out I'd lick that tender skin. I run my hand down the smoothness of her neck—skin like pure silk. I let my fingers wrap around it—so slender, so breakable. I hear her draw in a sharp breath. Languidly I slip my hand into the collar of her cheap blouse.

She begins to tremble. I pay no attention. Instead I watch my fingers slip a button out of its hole and then another. I spread apart the joined material so that her throat, chest, and the lacy tops of her bra are exposed. The desire to rip her clothes is so strong I have to physically fight it. I frown. Yes, she is very beautiful, but I have had other very beautiful women—why does this woman alone have such an effect on me? Even knowing what I know about her doesn't change a thing. Not having total control over my own impulses makes me feel vulnerable and defenseless. It is like falling backwards into nothing.

I hate the sensation. I can never let her see my weakness. I turn coldly furious. The breaths that escape her lips are suddenly shallow and quick. I smile possessively. So nothing has changed on that front.

'You were, by far, more when you squeezed into that little orange dress and your fuck me shoes, and went looking for money,' I taunt. 'Look at you now; you're flapping around inside a man's jacket. Two hundred thousand and you don't even buy yourself a nice suit.'

I tut. 'And this…' I raise my hand to her hair. 'This ugly bun. What were you thinking of?' I ask softly, as I pluck the pins out of her hair and drop them on the ground. I return her hair to its silk curtain. Beautiful. I reach back, pull a tissue out of its box and start wiping away her lipstick, a horrid plum. I am unhurried—let her stew from the outside in.

I toss the stained tissue on the ground. 'That's better.'

She stares at me helplessly, and guess what? It turns me on to have her at my mercy.

'Lick your lips,' I order.

'What?' She looks horrified by the cold command, and yet electrified by the sexual heat that my order obviously arouses. Like a beautifully tuned guitar, the tension in her body matches mine. I feel the same desire rippling through her.

We have played this game before. We both know where it leads.

My jaw hardens. 'You heard me.'

The tip of her small, pink tongue protrudes and I eye its sweet journey avidly. 'That's more like it. That's the mercenary bitch I know,' I say, thrusting a rough hand into her hair. It is exactly as I remember it. Soft and silky. A year of waiting. Bitch! I tug and pull her head back. She gasps with shock, but her eyes are wide, unafraid, and innocent. Fuck you, Lana. You're no innocent. We had a deal and you cheated me. And that fucking Dear John letter? You didn't even have the decency to wait until I got out of hospital. I could have been dead for all she cared. I expect better from a two bit whore. But the thing that hurt the most: she didn't care.

Now I will have my revenge. Another part of my brain is sneering—you're fighting a losing battle here, dude.

The thought powers me to kiss her. This kiss means nothing to me. It is only a way of gauging her reaction. I will not allow myself to get sucked into it. I descend on her roughly, painfully, violently, purposely bruising her soft lips, my mouth so savage that she utters a strangled, soundless cry. That sound wakes up an uncivilized beast. I make room for it. The intense desire to hurt and have my revenge is greater than me. Let her understand that I am not the same man that I was then. Before she betrayed me.

I taste the fury in my kiss: blood!

Really, Blake? But I cannot stop. Cannot control my emotions. Cannot resist her. Cannot live without her. I don't allow myself to feel.

A moan escapes her. And it affects me—in a way I could never have guessed. It almost makes me forget my carefully laid plans. It almost makes me take her on the floor of this drab office. The effect this woman has on me is incredible. I feel raw and starved. No matter what she does or what she is, I want her. All I want is to be buried deep inside her, but I am not a Barrington for nothing. Years of iron control come to my rescue. One of us is going to get hurt this time, and it will not be me.

Her hands reach up to push me away, but her palms meet the solidity of my chest, and as if with minds of their own, they push aside the lapels of my jacket, and her fingers splay open on my shirt. Oh, I know that sign. Pure submission. She's mine. I can do anything with her now. But I want more, more than just sexual surrender. I've got a plan. And I'm sticking to it.

I change the kiss, gentle it. Instantly her body scents victory and tries to burrow closer to me, but I keep my grip on her hair, relentless and tinged with hurting force. I cannot let her get nearer. I am in dangerous territory. One wrong move and I will fall into her honey trap again. She tries pushing her hips toward my crotch. Can't have that. That would give me away.

I end the kiss nonchalantly, as if I have just participated in a meaningless encounter, or a polite social interaction. With the same feigned lack of emotion I put her away and casually prop myself against the desk. I fold my arms across my chest, and watch her with great satisfaction. This is my territory. Here I am boss. This time, Lana honey…

She stands before me aroused, breasts heaving and hands clenched at her sides as she tries to regain some measure of composure.

I smile. Round one—me.

Silently she takes two steps forward, reaches a hand out and puts a finger on my throat. I freeze. I can feel her skin on my frantically beating pulse. And just like that we are connected. We never break eye contact. Fuck her.

Round two—is not over yet.

'Is it sex when I want to see you come apart?' I ask bitterly.

Her face crumples. This woman deserves an Oscar. She takes her finger away from my throat. 'What do you want, Blake?'

'I want you to finish your contract.'

She drops her face into her hands. 'I can't,' she whispers.

'Why not? Because you took the money and ran while I lay in a hospital bed?'

She takes a deep breath, but does not look up. Guilty as charged.

'I was cut up to start with,' I say as coldly as I can. I don't want to give her any more power than she already holds.

She looks up. Butter wouldn't melt in that sweet O. 'You were cut up?'

'Funny thing that, but yes.'

'I thought it was just a sex thing for you,' she murmurs.

'If you wanted money why didn't you ask me?' My voice is harsh.

'I…' She shakes her head.

'You made a serious miscalculation, didn't you, Lana, my love? The honey pot is here.' I pat the middle of my chest.

She simply gazes at my hand.

'But not to worry,' I say sarcastically. 'All is not lost. There's money in the pot.'

How predictable. Her gaze lifts up to my mouth.

'You did me a favor.' I try to sound detached, but my voice comes out bitter and pained. 'You opened my eyes. I see you now for what you were… Are. I was blinded by you. I made the classic mistake. I fell in love with an illusion of purity.'

She carries on looking at me blankly.

'If I had not bought you that night you would have gone with anyone, wouldn't you? You are not admirable. You are despicable.'

'So why do you want me to finish the contract?' she asks breathily.

'I am like the drug addict who knows his drug is poison. He despises it, but he cannot help himself. So that we are totally clear—I *detest* myself. I am ashamed of my need for you.'

'The… The…people who paid me—'

'They can do nothing to you. My family—'

She interrupts. 'What about Victoria?'

And suddenly I feel very angry. What the fuck has Victoria to do with this? This is between me and her. Besides, I am fond of Victoria and hide a measure of guilt for the pain I have caused her. Her shock when I tried to break off our engagement surprised me. I had imagined that she was marrying me for the same reasons I was—consolidation, security, and continuity—but in fact she is in love with me. If anything, the extent of her possessive passion worried me a little. A marriage of convenience only works when both parties exhibit similar detachment. I don't want to think of it now, but the truth is that I do not want Victoria. At that moment I realize that I can never marry Victoria. But for now I will deal with the most pressing problem I have: I cannot think of being with anyone other than the witch standing in front of me.

Angrily I forbid her to ever again drag Victoria into our arrangement. A flash goes off in her eyes. It's gone in a second, but even lidded it reeks of jealousy! I seize the opportunity to manipulate her by exaggerating Victoria's loyalty. I rub it in that Victoria stood by me through my worst period while she swanned off to Iran. 'One day,' I tell her, 'I will wake up and this sickness will be gone. Until then… You owe me forty-two days, Lana.'

She closes her eyes and hangs her head.

'Name your price,' I demand curtly.

Her head snaps up. 'No.' Her voice is very strong and sure. 'You don't have to pay me again. I will finish the contract.'

'Good,' I remark casually, but I turn away from her immediately. Cannot let her see how elated I am by her capitulation. I can hardly believe I have won so easily. My mind is doing victory back-flips as I go around the desk, and retake my position behind it.

Two

I slide into the black swivel chair and open the file in front of me. 'So, you're setting up a business?'

She drops into one of the chairs opposite me and tells me that she and Billie are thinking of starting a business. I ask the appropriate questions but my mind is elsewhere. I am not interested in hearing about her business plans.

'That reminds me, how is your mother?'

To my surprise her face contorts with pain. Seconds pass in acute silence. 'She passed away.'

I lean forward, eyes narrowed, shocked. 'I thought the treatment was working.'

She bites the words out. 'A car. Hit and run.'

'I'm sorry. I'm real sorry to hear that, Lana.' And I am, too, really sorry. She was a good woman. I liked her.

She blinks fast. Oh my God, she is going to burst into tears. She stands. I stand, too. Immediately she puts out a hand to ward me off, and runs to the door. In an instant I don't hate her anymore; all my desire to hurt crumbles to dust and I just want to help her, make it easier, take her in my arms and protect her. I stride toward her and grab her arm. She twists away from me, but my grip is too firm.

'This way. There's a staff restroom,' I say quietly, and quickly opening the door I lead her down the corridor. From the corners of my eyes I can see the tears are streaming down her cheeks. I hold open the toilet door and she rushes in. The door swings closed in my face.

I stand there looking at the door and then I hear her. Wailing for her mother. I lift my hand to push the door open, but I don't. I take a step back. Then I begin to pace. I have never heard anyone cry like that. I come from a family where all our expressions of sorrow are carefully controlled, a dab from a handkerchief to the eye. When my grandfather died, my grandmother did not even stop the journey of her cup to her mouth. Only after she had swallowed her sip of tea did she say, 'Oh dear.' At the funeral not a tear was shed, by anybody.

More than once I go to the door and almost push it open. I want to go in, but I cannot. My feet refuse to move forward. Anyway, it is clear that she does not want me, and that it is unsafe for me. I am already too confused and unhinged by a few minutes in her company. A woman appears in the corridor apparently heading for the toilet. She glances at me and I growl at her. Yeah, that's right, I growl.

She does a hundred and eighty degree right turn and flees. I look at my watch. Five minutes have passed. The wailing has become long sobs. I continue to pace. I jam my fists into the pockets of my trousers. She'll be out soon. Suddenly the sobs stop. I go to the door. The door is cheap and I hear the tap running. I step away instantly and move a few feet away from it. I lean my back against the wall and stare at the ground. For the last year I have been dead inside. Now all kinds of thoughts, desires, and emotions are coming to the fore. They are like those strange, mud-covered creatures that the tide uncovers when it goes back to sea. The door opens. She is standing there, her blouse buttoned to the neck. She won't lift her eyes. She won't meet mine.

'Are you okay?'

She nods.

'Tom will take you home.'

Very slowly her eyes, the eyelashes damp and sticking together, rise up to meet mine. They are like her voice. Level. There is nothing there to hold on to. 'No,' she says. 'Let's get this loan business out of the way.'

If she had slapped me in the face it would have been better.

We go back to the clinical office.

I take up my position behind the desk once more. 'Baby Sorab?' I say and look up from her application form.

And what I see chills my blood. Her face is cold and totally devoid of expression. How could she howl one moment for her mother then sit opposite me with that look. She shrugs carelessly.

'Yes. We thought it was a good name for our business.'

'Why baby clothes?' It seems a curious business for two young girls to get into.

'Billie has always been good with colors. She can put red and pink together and make them look divine. And since Billie had her baby this year we decided to make baby clothes?'

'Billie had a baby?' I frown. I thought she was a lesbian. And then it hits me, of course. It's what they do. Have a baby—the government gives them a flat and an income for the next eighteen years!

'Yeah, a beautiful boy,' she says, and suddenly I have a gut feeling. She's lying about something. She says something else and I reply, but it is all just a charade. One I lose interest in prolonging.

'OK,' I say.

'OK what?'

'OK you got the loan.'

'Just like that?'

'There is one condition.'

She becomes very still.

'You do not get the money for the next forty-two days.'

'Why?'

'Because,' I say softly, 'for the next forty-two days you will exist only for my pleasure. I plan to gorge on your body until I am sick to my stomach.'

'Are you going to house me in some apartment again?'

'Not *some* apartment—the same one as before.'

She sits up straighter. She looks me in the eye. She has some stipulations, too. She wants to bring Billie's baby to the apartment for four nights a week. And she wants Billie and Jack—the guy she thinks of as her brother and I fucking know is in love with her—to be allowed to come to the apartment. I don't like the idea, but I let it go for now. Nothing she has asked for is what I would consider a deal breaker. The baby might be annoying, but I'm cool with Billie. Jack might be another matter but I will handle that with time.

I engineer a bored expression. 'Anything else?'

'No.'

'Fine. Have you plans for tomorrow?'

She shakes her head.

'Good. Keep tomorrow free. Laura will call you to go through the necessary arrangements.'

'OK. If there is nothing else…'

'I'll walk you out.'

Heads turn to watch us. I ignore them all, but Lana seems disturbed by their regard. Again I have that unfamiliar sensation of wanting to protect and shield her. The bank manager catches sight of us and hurries toward me. He has an odd expression on his face, a cross between constipated and stricken, no doubt horribly concerned that I could leave without giving him the chance to flatter me. I lift a finger and he stops abruptly. I pull open the heavy door and we go into the late summer air. It is wet and gray, but it is not cold.

In the drizzle we face each other and make small talk. Suddenly the chitchat dries up in my throat and we are eating each other. The blue of her eyes reaches right up into my body and tears at my soul like a hungry hawk. Its power is enormous. In its claws I feel myself losing my grip. A gust of wind lifts my hair and deposits it on my forehead. She puts a hand out to touch it, but I jerk back. I won't be won over so easily.

'This time you won't fool me,' I say harshly.

We stare at each other. She astonished, and me, contemptuously. Her hand drops limply to her side. Suddenly she looks unbearably young and exhausted. She glances down the road at the bus stand.

'I'll see you tomorrow then.' In the bustle of the street her voice is barely audible.

'Tom's here,' I say, as the Bentley pulls up along the curb.

She shakes her head. 'Thanks, but I'll take the bus.'

'Tom will drop you off,' I insist.

'Fuck you,' she snaps suddenly. 'Our contract doesn't start until tomorrow. So today I'll decide my mode of transport.' She swings away from me.

My hand shoots out and grasps her wrist. 'I will pick you up and put you in that car if necessary. You decide.'

'Oh, yeah? And I'll call the police.'

I laugh. 'After everything I've told you about the system—that's your answer?'

She sags. All the fight gone out of her. 'Of course, who will believe me if I claim that a Barrington tried to force me to take a lift?' She resorts to begging. 'Please, Blake.'

This one is non-negotiable. There is no way that she is taking the bus. I know how to stop her in her tracks. 'Very well, Tom will go with you on the bus.'

At that point she stops arguing, simply turns around, opens the car door, gets in, slams it shut, and stares straight ahead.

Tom turns around and says something to her and she answers as the vehicle pulls away.

I stand on the sidewalk looking at the car, willing her to turn and look back. Now, Lana, now. If she turns before the car disappears out of sight it will all be all right. Turn, Lana. Please turn back. Turn back and look at me. As the car turns at the traffic light she twists her neck and looks at me. Her face is white and expressionless. But inside me wild joy surges. I want to punch the air. Never have I experienced such a strong current of emotion in my body.

Then the oddest thing happens.

Perhaps it is the churn of high emotions that I almost never allow myself to indulge in, or perhaps it is the shock of seeing her again, but I am no longer standing on Kilburn High Street with badly dressed strangers shuffling around me.

I am five years old and alone and terrified in a room lit only by a naked light blub. I look down at my hands and they are covered in blood. My shirt, my shorts, my legs, even the floor around me has turned red. The blood is not fresh: my fingers are stuck to the knife. The knife is not mine. The blood is not mine. I rip the knife from my hand and let it clatter on the floor noisily. I pull my eyes away from the glinting blade, and thought I don't want to, I let them travel along the cement floor. Until…

I come upon what I have done.

I did that!

No. It cannot be.

I open my mouth and scream for my Mommy, but no sound will come out. I scream and scream, but no one comes. No one can hear me.

No one.

Pov

Forty 2 Days

When Blake Met Sorab

I paused at the bathroom door, shocked.

She was laughing, I mean really laughing, the way I had never seen her do while with me. The laughter was like a fountain of fresh, sweet water bubbling up from deep inside her being. I stared at her as if I was a man who had been wandering in a desert for days without food or water.

I don't know how long I stood there simply staring. At the sight of water. So near and yet so far away. You're no better than a heroin addict desperate for his next fix, a voice inside my head taunted. But at that moment there was nothing, nothing I wanted more than to take her in my arms and never ever let her go again.

What was it about this woman that made her impossible to resist even when it was patently clear I shouldn't trust her further than I could throw her?

Slowly, as if in a dream, I was drawn to the centre of her attention—to the shrieking, splashing, lustily laughing baby. It was obvious.

She loved that little creature.

Instantly, I was jealous of it, of the love she had for it. The jealousy didn't strike me like a bolt, more like weevils crawling all over me. The feeling disgusted me. I didn't want to be jealous of a fucking baby. I wanted to hate her guts. A small sound came from my throat.

I didn't plan it: it was involuntary.

Her head whirled around, and right before my eyes, quite interesting really, I watched her withdraw, build a wall around herself. And I had to stop myself from laughing in her face. She knew me so little. Did she really think I was going to hit that wall, and just stop? No wall could keep me out. I would scale it, brick by fucking brick. Nothing, no one could keep me out.

Until I said so she was mine. To do with as I pleased.

'Hi,' she fluttered, nervous, very nervous. And so she should be. A secret thrill fizzled in my veins. I wanted to throttle her. Little bitch. How dare she love the kid and not me?

'Who do we have here?' I said softly, going into the room.

I looked into the child's big, blue eyes—solemn, curious, unafraid—and suddenly, that disassociated, unreal feeling I hadn't felt since I was child drifted in. My mind didn't say, 'Who are you?' It said, 'Who am I?' I felt like one of those turtles in Asia that have had their throats slit while still alive and I was bleeding out to make a blood cocktail for some demented human.

Something was wrong with the picture I was looking at. My mind began to race. The baby grinned toothlessly, and in that instant, I understood everything. The slit in my throat healed itself. The incessant feeling of being empty and lost receded.

That was *my son* in my tub. And that was *my* woman standing beside him.

In that same moment of illumination I felt the danger. It was in the room standing beside me, like an invisible shadow. But by the time I turned to look at her, my eyes were neutral, betraying nothing. We looked at each other.

I saw the fear, but I also saw the love in her eyes. How could I have missed it? I felt rage, murderous rage at what had been done to her, to us, but also wild and leaping joy that she loved me. That she was pure. She had acted as a mother. Only as a mother. I wanted to grab her and kiss her.

'Does he cry a lot?' I asked finally, my voice so smooth and normal even I was impressed.

'No. Most nights he will sleep right through,' she assured quickly.

I saw the relief in her face. I marveled at that. She must think me a fool. It would work in my favor.

'Good,' I said with a nod, and as if losing interest, I turned away and went out.

My legs took me to the dining room. I closed the door, leaned back against it, and closed my eyes. When I opened my eyes I knew what I must do. I knew, too that this apartment was no longer safe for my family, but moving them would alert him. The only thing in my favor was stealth. As long as he thought I didn't know I could lay my plans. Otherwise, he would win. He had nothing to lose, and I everything. I picked up the phone and called a business associate. I talked business for twelve minutes. My voice betrayed nothing.

I opened my briefcase. Took some papers out. Looked them over carefully. Made notes on them. Left messages for Laura to action in the morning. But all the time the best and most efficient part of me was coldly, meticulously planning the future. Hours later, I went into the bedroom. I knew he was listening and watching. Let him listen. Let him watch. He would hear and see nothing different. I closed the door softly. She was already in bed, and by the sound of her even breathing, asleep.

Quietly, I stepped through the connecting door that had been left ajar. A sliver of light came in from the door leading into the corridor. I walked up to the cot and stood over him. I was surprised at the rush of pride that coursed through my body at the sight of his sleeping body. I stood in the dark and fought the intense longing to feel the texture of his skin. I clenched my fists.

Soon, soon I would claim him as mine, but not now.

Tomorrow, when it wouldn't appear 'strange' I would touch him. I listened to my body, to the whisper of the purest emotion I had ever experienced. To love without expecting anything in return. With it came the instinct to protect what was mine. They will not do to him what they did me and Marcus. Without another glance at him l left as quietly as I had entered.

I sat next to her and she opened her eyes sleepily. My beauty. I loved her more than life itself. I would kill with my bare hands for her. I bent my head and kissed her. The kiss was gentle and soft. She came awake and opened her mouth. The kiss deepened. That raw hunger between us throbbed into life.

So: he wanted to watch me with my woman. Let him. Watch while you can, Daddy. I know what you are capable of, but you don't know what I am capable of. I slid my hand down her silky body and tugged at the rim of her knickers. I laid my fingers flat between her legs. Dampness seeped out from under the material.

'You are so wet,' I whispered, and inserted a finger into her.

She tensed.

Immediately I stilled. 'What's the matter?'

'Nothing,' she mumbled. I put my hand out and flicked on the light switch. She blinked and squinted.

I lifted her gown up and turned her over. What I saw cut me to shreds. I wanted to cry. I did that to her!

Pov

The Billionaire Banker

When Blake Saw Rupert Mauling Lana At The Party

The brute had her pinned against a wall, his big body completely hiding her from my view. Must have only been minutes, but it was like a lifetime watching that broad back and thick neck. I had to fight the instinct to go over. Break them up. But I am a strategist, a man who knows when to pounce, how to exploit an opportunity. Not yet. Soon. Lose a battle to win the war. So I clenched my teeth and waited.

A woman came and wrapped herself around me. She laid her perfectly manicured red fingernails on the lapels of my jacket and smiled slyly. I glanced down at her and shuddered. I hate it when women I don't fancy throw themselves at me. At that precise moment Lothian moved his thick body away and I saw Lana. Flattened against the wall, her face white, mascara streaking down her face, and her lips already beginning to swell.

Our eyes met.

Fuck me, I looked into her shocked, defenseless eyes, and I did not feel lust! I did not want to take and use and discard as I had done with all the others. The only thing I registered in my body was the unfamiliar need to protect. Not myself but her. That same sensation I had experienced once a long time ago as a young boy, when I had come across an injured baby bird that had fallen out of its nest. I had scooped it in my cupped hands and warmed it inside my jacket. Taking it home I had made a nest for it and fed it warmed, sweet tea. After it died that evening, I had never again experienced that sensation. Until now.

Stunned by my own reaction I watched as she ran out of the room in her ridiculous shoes. And the dirty looks she got. You should have seen them. You'd have thought she stank of *their* bullshit. I despised my kind then.

In the corridor I saw her lurch unsteadily towards the powder room.

Less than a minute later I removed the red fingernails from my person, made my excuses and went to wait for her in the corridor. What the fuck was I doing? But the rational, thinking Blake had gone numb. And another part, a secret part of me, that I never let out, that I refused to even acknowledge, had come out and taken over. I crossed my arms and lounged against the wall.

When she came out, I almost did not recognize her. Underneath the layer of badly applied make-up she had the face of a schoolgirl. Hell, she had better not be under-aged. That would be all my plans down the toilet. I straightened and waited for her to come up to me. She was no longer crying. Her head was held high and those indescribably turquoise eyes were proud and flashing, and she would have walked right past me, too, if I had not raised a detaining finger.

An Interview With

Blake Law Barrington

Q: What were you thinking or feeling when you approached Rupert Lothian's table where Lana was seated?

A: **Probably confidence. The plan was simple, guaranteed to succeed: When dealing with a psychopath always appeal to the narcissist in them. It doesn't work with sociopaths; they are a different species all together, but it never fails to fell the psychopath. Invite one to a party of his superiors and he will drop whatever plans he has to pander to his need to feel important.**

Obviously, once I got him and the girl at the party I would play it by ear. There has not been a woman yet that I wanted that I have not had, so I was pretty certain I was going to bed that girl.

However, what I heard as I walked to the table made me smile. It wasn't just going to easy. It was the proverbial candy from a baby scenario.

Q: Why were you so determined to bid for Lana?
A: **I told myself it was just sex, but I should have known even then. Who was I kidding? Just sex? With her? That would *never* be enough. Some part of me must have recognised that this girl *was* the siren, the temptress that my father had warned me about. The one specially chosen to bring me to my knees. But at that moment I was the moth flying helplessly towards the flame. I guess, I just wanted her light, more than I wanted anything else…**

Q: What went through your mind during that first kiss with Lana?
A: **Did you just ask me what went through my mind during that first kiss?**

Q: Yes. Some readers expressed an interest in your thoughts?
A: **Chuckles…Thoughts? My mind was blank. I'd never kissed any girl who made me respond the way her lips and body did. I had to struggle to stay normal.**

Q: Can you share with us your true feelings when you had sex for the first time?
A: **She'd pissed me off at the restaurant so I was determined not to go out of my way to be nice. I would simply treat her as one did a whore. I'd paid for her and we had an agreement and that was that. She'd said she didn't want it sweet and flowery, so**

I'd give it to her straight. But then I found out she was virgin and you know the rest...

Q: Do you remember your first impression of Lana's best friend, Billie?
A: **I'd never actually met anyone like her, a woman with spider tattoos on her neck! Obviously, I've seen pictures of women like that, but I'd never met one in person. I was rather shocked though, by how level-headed she was...and her loyalty to Lana surprised and impressed me. She's unique.**

Q: And what about how you felt when you were introduced to Jack?
A: **Straight off I knew that he was in love with Lana and I remember that I didn't like it, but I also knew Lana held him in high esteem so I said nothing. Left it alone and waited to see what would develop.**

Q: Could you describe for my readers what you felt when Lana arrived at Madame Yula?
A: **The first time: pure excitement. Couldn't wait to undress her. And when she came wearing that electric blue blouse and those leather trousers, I experienced in my body the powerful sensation of ownership. That was the moment she became mine. And the more I tried to fight the feeling the more deeply I wanted her.**
That night I wanted brand her, with my lips, my body, my dick. I wanted to come inside her.

Q: And the second time?
A: **Totally different. I was furious with her and I wanted my revenge, and yet even I knew it was more than that. Much more. As soon as she walked through the door, everyone else ceased to exist, I felt that invisible pull, and I all I wanted to do was grab her by the hair, drag her back to the apartment fuck her so hard walking was no longer an option.**

Q: What did you really feel the moment you discovered Lana was a virgin?
A: **Shock. I was shocked. I'd never been with a virgin. And when she cried…I was confused.**

Q: Confused?
A: **Yeah. I was overwhelmed by a strong totally foreign urge to hold and comfort her. And those kinds of emotions I didn't want or need. This was meant to be sex thing. Three months, maybe four, tops six. So wanting to hold on to someone you've paid money to use: warning bells were clanging in my head.**

Q: What was going through your head when you met Lana's mother?
A: **She was sweet and well educated and she obviously loved her daughter very much. I liked her and I was very sorry when I heard she died. Something brave about her. Lana has that same quality. I rate it very highly in a person.**

Q: At what point did you realize your feelings had changed towards Lana?
A: **It happened almost immediately, but I was slow to recognize it, or more likely, I didn't want to recognize it.**

Q; The first morning, waking up together, what did you feel?
A: **The morning-after scene is always a bore, but seduced by the smell of her hair and the feel of her skin—he has the most amazing skin, like a baby soft and silky—I stayed.**

Q: What went through your head when Lana first declared her love to you?
A: **If someone takes money to leave you while you are lying unconsciousness in some hospital and afterwards never bothers to contact you again, what would you think if they then claimed to love you. What would you think? Exactly. I thought she was a fucking liar and I hated her guts, but still I wanted her.**

Q: Which emotion was stronger, anger or lust, when you met Lana again at the bank?
A: **To start with anger, somewhere in the middle of the encounter, lust. And then when she cried over her mother's death, tenderness, and then it was back to fury. And as she rose to leave, pure triumph. I got her...where I wanted her.**

Q: How did you deal with having to choose Lana over his father?
A: **Sometimes I have nightmares. In it I am in the plane with my father. He is in his thirties. His hair without grey and he is slim and tall. He is calmly eating chateaubriand with béarnaise sauce and chips.**
"You betrayed me," he says, wiping his mouth on a napkin. "The same fate awaits you."
And a hole appears in the side of the plane and he is sucked out. His expression is one of indescribable terror. "Your son will do to you what you have done to me."
And I wake up in a cold sweat.

Printed in Great Britain
by Amazon